Also by Abir Mukherjee

A Rising Man
A Necessary Evil
Smoke and Ashes
Death in the East

The Shadows of Men

A Novel

ABIR MUKHERJEE

PEGASUS CRIME

NEW YORK LONDON

THE SHADOWS OF MEN

Pegasus Crime is an imprint of
Pegasus Books, Ltd.
148 West 37th Street, 13th Floor
New York, NY 10018

ISBN: 978-1-64313-744-5

10 9 8 7 6 5 4 3 2 1

Printed in the United States of America
Distributed by Simon & Schuster
www.pegasusbooks.com

For Elora,
the best Mukherjee

"Even if the whole of India, ranged on one side, were to declare that Hindu-Muslim unity is impossible, I will declare that it is perfectly possible."

Mahatma Gandhi

The Shadows of Men

ONE

Surendranath Banerjee

Men, I believe, are defined by the shadows they cast.

Most, despite force of numbers and efforts, leave little trace. Like ants toiling under the noonday sun, their shadows are picayune and ephemeral. Others, like the trees of the forest canopy, cast a pall far greater, their penumbra eclipsing and influencing all who fall beneath. But there are others still, a deadly few, who pass through invisible, yet leave everything altered in their wake. In a world marked by the shadows of men, it is those who have no shadow who are the most dangerous of all.

I should say, this is not Sam's story. It is mine.

In truth, I would much rather *he* told you, but he cannot, at least not everything, because he was not there. Of course that is unlikely to stop him sharing his two annas' worth, with you, or with anyone else who might care to ask, but that is Sam for you, and that is why you require to hear *my* side of the tale, so that you may understand what actually transpired and why I did what I did.

It is a burden I take up with reticence. Sam, naturally, would insist I *grab the bull by the proverbials and just get on with it, Suren.* But then he is always happiest when rushing in where angels fear to tread, generally with his eyes closed and usually head first.

Yet precipitous as it may be, there is little to keep me from such a course of action. It is not as though I currently have any more pressing engagements, and while I may no longer be sitting in a prison cell, my present movements are still curtailed to the few yards either side of this cabin and by the fear that I might be recognised.

I spend the days coming to terms with the consequences of my deeds. Sam believes I only did what needed to be done, and indeed the notion of my guilt baffles him. How could it not? He may be the most congenial of Englishman, but he is still just an Englishman and could never understand a concept such as *izzat*, or the shame I have brought down upon my family. His life, like that of all his kinsmen in India, progresses with an unhindered serenity, as untroubled and uncomprehending of such things as the elephant is by the barking of pariah dogs and oblivious to the Indian point of view. Even the lowest of them glides along with the air of those born to rule – not their *own* country, but ours.

But I procrastinate when I should be recounting to you the story of my fall. The first thing to make clear is that I am not innocent. Still I am not guilty of all of which I am accused. Nevertheless, there are most certainly some actions which, in hindsight, I have come to regret.

And yet if faced with the same circumstances, I cannot see what I would do differently. Sometimes a man must open his eyes and realise the truth about himself and the masters he serves. And sometimes he must sacrifice himself for the greater good.

It began with a summons. A flimsy yellow chitty, waved in my face by Shambu, a rat-faced peon from the top floor: a lackey who considers himself superior to his fellow lackeys in the building on account of his being personal dogsbody for the *burra* sahibs upstairs. If absolute power corrupts absolutely, then Shambu was proof that even a minor dose can prove corrosive.

I should have known, the instant I saw his crooked, betel-stained grin, that like the gathering of the storm clouds on the southern horizon, the Fates were aligning against me. He shambled up to my desk, handed me the note and pointed to the ceiling with one bent finger and both bloodshot eyes.

'*Borro shaheb-er theke chitee.*'

Quickly I unfolded the slip, then held my breath: an immediate summons to the top floor. Lord Taggart, Commissioner of Police, requested my presence. It was not the first time I had been ordered to His Lordship's office. Over the five years preceding, I had attended his inner sanctum on a dozen occasions or more, but always at the request of Sam or another British officer, always the dutiful subaltern, on hand to provide illumination in the face of their ignorance of native matters, or a lightning rod to deflect criticism.

This time, however, the missive had been addressed to me and me alone. I placed the chitty carefully within the pages of my notebook and took a breath. The commissioner wished to see *me*. Did he wish me to lead a case? No Indian detective had ever headed up an inquiry before; not in Calcutta at any rate. Such an honour would be worthy of even my father's begrudging respect.

I dismissed the peon and, after stopping by the mirror in the lavatory to straighten my uniform and run a comb through my habitually unruly hair, made my way towards the stairs, my heart hammering within my breast. Minutes later, I was being led by Lord Taggart's secretary through the doors of his office.

His Lordship looked up, gave me a cursory glance as if to make sure I was indeed the correct Indian, then returned to his scrutiny of the papers on his desk.

'Sergeant Banerjee. Sit.'

I did as ordered, and for half a minute more, he continued poring over his documents while I contented myself with staring at the row of brightly coloured ribbons on his spotless white tunic. Sam, who had worked for Lord Taggart during the war, had on several alcohol-infused occasions regaled me with tales of his missions for the commissioner. Once or twice, when his mood was particularly effervescent, he would even deign to say something nice about the man, but as I say, it was only once or twice.

Lord Taggart eventually looked up. I recall the light falling through the French windows and reflecting off the discs of his spectacles so that, for a moment, his eyes were hidden and he, with his pale skin and blanched tunic, appeared almost ghostlike. Little did I realise, as he began to speak, that my life was about to be torn apart, his words the fateful first domino in the chain of events which would see me accused of a host of crimes as long as a python's tail.

'Tell me, Sergeant, what do you know about Farid Gulmohamed …?'

TWO

Sam Wyndham

The first *I* knew about it was a constable knocking on my door with an electric torch in one hand and an enveloped chit in the other. It was gone midnight, but the chap had hardly woken me, seeing as I'd only just made it home myself. The evening had been long, hot and frustrating and I'd spent most of it in a squalid, pestilential corner of North Calcutta where the air stank of sewage and the families, when they had a room, lived six or seven to it, sleeping on rattan mats and subsisting off little more than rice and dal.

I'd gone there to meet a man called Uddam Singh, Uddam the Lion, which sounded impressive until you realised that a full tenth of the people in the country seemed to be called Singh. Uddam, from the dirt poor province of Bihar, had come penniless to Calcutta, and through nothing more than hard work and a penchant for slitting throats, had risen to become the kingpin of an underworld gang that controlled almost half the city's trade in narcotics, prostitution and a few other illicit activities besides.

We'd met, aptly enough, in a street called Gola-katta Gullee, Cut-throat Alley, a foul-smelling passage of flophouses and hovels, where indolent dogs roamed in packs and itinerant cows grazed on the bounty of an open rubbish tip.

We were there to discuss the fate of Singh's second son, Vinay. His elder boy, Abhay, had been murdered a fortnight earlier, and

Suren and I had been called to the south of the city where we found him propped up in a lane near Kidderpore docks with the business end of a six-inch blade embedded in his oesophagus.

It was merely the latest in a series of rather unpleasant murders – all victims of, or, depending on your point of view, erstwhile participants in, a rather nasty territorial dispute which had broken out between two of the native gangs that vied for control of some of the city's less wholesome business activities.

Normally we'd have left them to it, though Vice Division would keep an eye on things, of course. No one wanted the British or, God forbid, the foreign press picking up on such matters, but given our own stretched resources, we'd have been happy enough for the thugs to keep on merrily killing each other. The problem this time, however, was that the gangs in question hailed not just from different neighbourhoods, but also from different faiths, and we'd learned the hard way that where religion was involved, the deaths of a few *goondahs* could soon explode into the general mass slaughter of Hindu and Muslim.

The murder of Singh's son seemed like an escalation. There's honour among thugs, a gentleman's agreement if you will, that close family of the kingpins on all sides were untouchable. Abhay's murder might have been a terrible mistake, but my gut told me otherwise. There was no reason for him to be down in South Calcutta, so far from his father's turf in the north. It felt to me like a set-up, and his father, it seemed, felt similarly. And now he was out for revenge.

And that's where Suren and I came into the picture, or at least *I* did, because Suren had failed to show up. Normally I'd have carried on regardless and given the sergeant a talking-to later, but on this occasion, his presence was vital, seeing as he'd been the one who'd had the bright idea of arresting Vinay Singh in the first place.

Indeed, the whole plan had been Suren's idea. He'd come up with it in an attempt to placate Lord Taggart who seemed rather put out by the warfare breaking out across his city.

'What the hell's behind the violence?' he'd barked across the no man's land of his desk, and of course Suren and I had no idea whatsoever. Maybe it *was* just a simple turf war; maybe it was the pending municipal elections; or maybe, like everyone else in 1923, the gangs had just gone a little mad. Whatever the cause, Taggart wanted it stopped, post-haste.

It was a week later, as we stood admiring the corpse of another dead sap, this time a Muslim hoodlum with one ear missing and his neck sliced clean, that Suren had had his brainwave.

'We should bring in that fool, Vinay Singh.'

It took me a while to place the particular fool in question.

'You know, Uddam Singh's younger boy.'

The son was a chip off the old block, both in terms of his bullet-headed build and his proclivity for carving second smiles into people's faces. What he lacked, though, was his father's innate instinct for survival – which some called dumb luck – but which I put down to a form of primeval intelligence.

'You think he's involved?'

'That's not the point,' said Suren. 'The important thing is there's nothing to say he isn't.'

I wondered what had happened to the idealistic young idiot I'd taken under my wing almost five years earlier.

'You want to stitch him up? Maybe we should get you a transfer to Vice? Or better still, Scotland Yard.'

He shook his head.

'I'm not saying we charge him, we just *threaten* to. Rather, we threaten his *father* that we're going to charge him.'

I began to see what he was driving at.

'You want to arrest Vinay Singh and then tell his old man we're going to ship his backside off to the Andamans, unless Singh pater calls a halt to this war with the Muslims?'

He grinned. 'Why not?'

Why not? I could have told him that it was unethical to arrest an innocent man in order to put pressure on his family. I could have told him that no fair court in the land would convict him without evidence. And I could have told him that casting aside his principles to go down this road just once would make it harder to resist in the future. But of course I didn't tell him any of that because there was no point. The truth was that the system of justice we administered in this country wasn't particularly concerned with ethics, or with the innocence of a man if he were brown and his accusers were white, and as for the mortgaging of Suren's immortal soul, well, I could hardly counsel against that, seeing as the deeds to mine had been sold, or at the very least mislaid, long ago.

'Why not indeed,' I said.

And that is what we proceeded to do. Suren arrested the bastard soon after, dragging him screaming from his bed and his woman, and out into the streets with enough brouhaha to ensure his old man would know about it by the time young Vinay had managed to get his trousers on. And then we'd waited, a good twenty-four hours, leaving Vinay to sweat in a cell and his father to stew, wondering what we were doing to his boy.

We'd finally contacted him, sent him a message through one of the young street lads he used to ferry drugs, and set up the meeting in Gola-katta Gullee. Suren and I would explain to Singh the elder that the best way to end this rather unfortunate situation would be for him to draw a line under his little war with the Muslims, and then we might see our way clear to letting his son out of the clink with his looks and his teeth intact.

It was all going swimmingly until Suren failed to show.

'Where the hell is he, this Banerjee fucker?'

Uddam Singh, his face pockmarked like a pineapple and prickled with sweat, picked at his teeth with a wooden splinter. He wasn't the sort to appreciate delays, even when caused by members of the Imperial Police Force, though that was possibly because he had a fair number of them on his payroll.

'He'll be here,' I'd said, but after twenty minutes, that assurance had started to ring hollow.

Singh had registered his disapproval with a nod of his head which had summoned a couple of thugs who pinned me to a wall while he took a blade to my throat.

'You are playing games with me, Wyndham sahib? You think I won't kill a *gora* officer?'

I'd felt steel caress my jugular, and while I could have done with a shave, Singh's record hardly marked him out as the most diligent of barbers.

'You do and you'll never see your son alive again.'

The old man had relented, which was decent of him, and pulled the blade back half an inch. That was the thing about Indians. Their children were their weakness. All of them, even the homicidal crime bosses it seemed, doted on their offspring like mother hens fussing over their chicks. Rumour had it that fathers even went as far as to embrace their offspring, which, from a British point of view, was frankly rather alarming.

'Two hours,' Singh had said. 'Get him here, or there will be trouble.'

I'd straightened my shirt, cursed Suren under my breath and set off to look for him.

An hour of searching from Lal Bazar to Cosipore threw up precious little, and in the end I'd headed back to the digs we shared in Premchand Boral Street, in the hope that the boy had either returned home or at least left me a note there. Alas, he'd done neither and I found myself pouring a whisky and walking out onto the balcony in the hope that a drink might provide, if not inspiration, then at least some insight. Sadly neither was forthcoming, so I cursed Suren, then I cursed Uddam Singh, and finally, I cursed Mr Gandhi.

That might have sounded harsh, but the way I figured it, the Mahatma had a lot to answer for. This vision of India, peace-loving and tolerant, which he'd sold and which millions had bought into, had in the space of months, turned to dust, hatred and communal bloodshed.

In the gentlemen's clubs, cricket grounds and other bastions of British power, men crowed that he'd lost his nerve. Others opined that the natives were always bound to fail in the face of British resolve. What was certain was that after a year of his general strike and the supreme sacrifice from his followers, the Mahatma, in a puff of holy smoke, had called the whole thing off and disappeared back to his ashram to feed his goats. He claimed it was in penance at the deaths of some twenty-odd policemen at the hands of a pro-independence mob in some flyblown village somewhere in the United Provinces, but to many it felt like a surrender. The Mahatma went on a fast for his part in stirring passions that had led to such violence, and the viceroy and the men at Government House applauded his decision, waited a few weeks, then promptly arrested him on charges of sedition and packed him off to prison for a nice six-year stretch.

Since then, and without Gandhi to hold things together, the independence movement had collapsed into a morass of infighting and mutual recrimination. It hadn't been helped by the calling of elections – not national elections – we weren't that stupid – but elections to municipal councils – elections which were now only weeks away.

The prospect of those elections had split the Congress Party and begun to reopen the wounds which Indians had always inflicted upon themselves. The pressures which had simmered beneath the surface: the tensions between Hindus and Muslims; between upper and lower castes; between landowners and peasants – all now bubbled to the fore, and we of course were quick to exploit them. After all, you didn't look a gift horse in the mouth. Not if you were British.

The press began to paint the Congress as the party of the Hindus, and Muslims began deserting it in droves. Then came the religious riots, in towns and cities up and down the country. We, for our part, gave it a name: *communalism*, which was a nice, polite term for the indiscriminate butchery of people who happened to worship a different god.

As for Calcutta, if there was trouble to be had, you could bet your last rupee that the city's denizens would be among the first to get involved, taking up arms even against neighbours whom they'd lived beside for generations. The violence between the Hindu and Muslim gangs felt like a precursor to something bigger, and unless we put Uddam Singh back in his box, things could soon spiral.

And so it was that I was standing on the balcony, nursing a whisky sometime after midnight, when the constable cycled up, came to my door and passed me a note informing me that Suren had been arrested on a charge of murder.

THREE

Sam Wyndham

The suburb of Budge Budge was about as picturesque as a frontline trench, and for a policeman, almost as dangerous. Not for the first time was I grateful for a fast car, a diligent driver and the cover of darkness. As the Wolseley sped past derelict mills and hollowed-out wharves, I wondered just what it was Suren thought he was doing, hanging around in a place like this, and, rather more importantly, why he'd felt the need to get himself arrested for killing someone.

The police station was a beleaguered-looking redoubt, the shutters over its barred windows scorched and pitted, and the wood of its doors cladded and stiffened with iron. The car pulled up and I got out to the sound of glass cracking in the dirt beneath my boot. The street seemed deserted save for a grizzled pie-dog who sat in front of the station, gnawing on the shin bone of some beast that probably didn't need it any more, and who growled defensively as I passed.

The doors were shut fast, which made sense. There was probably little point in reinforcing the damn things if you then left them wide open, and anyway, this didn't look like the sort of neighbourhood where the locals made a habit of popping in to the station to hand in a lost wallet.

I rapped on them with the side of my fist, then called out in English, having found long ago that in India the judicious deployment of the English language often helped speed up people and processes that would otherwise take far longer.

Sure enough, the cover over a spyhole shot back like a rifle bolt and I was appraised by a yellowing eyeball. I looked over to my driver, Shiva. Not being overly keen on him waiting alone outside like a sitting duck, I called for him to join me, but he shook his head. I should have expected that. He loved that car as much as his own family. It was only as the bolts slid back and I crossed the threshold into the fortress-like thana that I realised there may have been another reason for his reticence. If the worst did happen and we were suddenly attacked by a mob, having the car meant he'd at least have a decent chance of escape. As for me, I'd be stuck in the station with the constables, ready to be roasted like chickens.

The copper who opened the door attempted a salute that petered out halfway to his head, his expression somewhere between wary and world-weary. I knew how he felt. It was late and I was too tired for pleasantries so I got to the point.

'Where is he?'

The constable gestured with a nod. 'Please follow me, sir.'

There wasn't much to the place: just a room where a few more constables slouched indolently against bare walls; a small office with its door ajar; and a corridor leading to the cells. If there was electricity, someone had cut the supply, because the place was illuminated solely by the flickering light of a hurricane lamp and the air smelled of kerosene and piss.

Suren, dressed in a soot-smeared and bloodstained shirt, sat on a bench behind the iron bars of a cement cell. His face bore the scars that went with what was known in the trade as a *rigorous arrest*: a burst lip and one eye swollen shut. The other, though, seemed surprised to see me.

I rattled the bars of his cell and yelled at a constable who sat warming a desk a foot away. 'Open this bloody door!'

The man rose quickly, hurried over and, in a metallic flurry, pulled out a ring of keys.

'What the hell, Suren?' I said.

The sergeant staggered to his feet.

'It's not what —'

I cut him off with a gesture, waited for the constable to unlock the door, then ordered him and his colleague to wait outside with the other officers. Once they'd gone, I directed Suren to retake his seat.

'What happened to your face?'

He raised a hand to a purple cheek.

'A slight disagreement with the constables who detained me.'

'Lucky it was only *slight*,' I said. 'Any more serious and they might have killed you. What did you do?'

Suren sat down but remained resolutely mute on the matter. I ran a hand through my hair. 'They're saying you killed a man, then set fire to his house.'

He looked up and stared at me with his good eye.

'I didn't kill him.'

The denial was wholehearted but it was still only half a disavowal.

'And the building? You didn't try to torch that?'

Suren paused.

'No ... I mean yes, I *may* have set it alight, but not to ...' His voice tailed off into a sigh. 'It is most difficult to explain.'

'Well, you better find a way,' I said. 'You're up on charges of murder, arson and resisting arrest. More than enough to see your neck in a noose.'

Suren shook his head.

'They can't hang me,' he said with a degree of certainty which the circumstances hardly seemed to warrant.

'They most certainly can,' I said. 'Now tell me what happened so I can sort this out.'

A bead of sweat trickled down from his temple. He shook his head again.

'I cannot, but it is imperative that I to speak to Lord Taggart. You must get a message to him.'

'Why?'

'Because the dead man in that building … it was Prashant Mukherjee.'

The name hit me like a kick from a mule. Mukherjee was a prize ass. The sort of pompous, pontificating high-caste Hindu that made me understand just why so many lower-caste Bengalis had converted to other religions. But to a certain sort of Hindu, mainly the upper-caste, down-on-his-luck variety that blamed all their problems on foreign invaders and Muslim usurpers, Mukherjee was a folk hero. The soft-spoken Hindu high priest who provided the intellectual veneer to justify all manner of thuggery from his hardline co-religionists in the Shiva Sabha.

'Bloody hell, Suren,' I said. 'Of all the people whose murders you could have got yourself mixed up in, you chose Prashant Mukherjee?'

'It was hardly a choice,' he said.

'What am I supposed to do now? I told Uddam Singh that I'd find you and that we'd meet him in half an hour's time to discuss his boy. We stand him up and he'll put a price on your head.'

'Uddam Singh will have to wait,' he said. 'The priority is speaking to Lord Taggart. Without him, I am dead already.'

FOUR

Surendranath Banerjee

What did I know about Farid Gulmohamed?

It was a most peculiar question for the commissioner to ask. I was just a simple Calcutta policeman and a Hindu at that. Gulmohamed, by contrast, was a Bombay financier and a prominent politician – a leading light in the Union of Islam, known for his eloquence and his finely tailored suits. My knowledge of him was distilled from what little I read in the papers and tinged with the usual undercurrent of low-level suspicion about our Mohammedan brothers that most Hindus had inculcated into us from the time we could walk. I told Taggart the former, remained silent about the latter, and received a grunt in acknowledgement.

'He's here. In Calcutta. Arrived last night on the Imperial Mail. A business meeting, apparently, but this close to the elections, I want to make sure that's all he's here for. That's where you come in.'

He paused, then inhaled in a manner not dissimilar to the roadside astrologers on Camac Street on the verge of delivering momentous news. I muttered the name of Maa Durga and braced myself.

'I want you to tail him. Report on his movements: who he meets, when and where.'

My initial elation at being entrusted with a mission was disheartingly short-lived as a thousand questions clouded my thoughts.

How was I supposed to tail Gulmohamed? I had little experience of such subterfuge. How exactly was I to achieve what he expected of me? And where was Sam? Why hadn't the commissioner seen fit to invite him?

How was I to explain to Lord Taggart that, while we all might look the same to him, a Hindu following Gulmohamed into the Muslim parts of town would stick out as much as he would at a meeting of the Women's Institute? In the end, I tempered my questions and muted my concerns, and was thoroughly rebuffed by Lord Taggart with no more than a wave of the hand.

'I'm not asking you to follow him into a mosque and pray to Mecca. If the situation arises, just wait discreetly at a distance outside.'

It seemed churlish to point out that, depending on the mosque, and the neighbourhood in which it was situated, a discreet distance might constitute several miles. In hindsight, I should have done so. It might have saved him a bit of trouble and me a death sentence. But hindsight is as perfect as it is pointless. What matters is kismet and the will of the gods.

I did, however, have one final question. *Why me?*

It seemed to catch him on the chin.

'You're a senior officer, aren't you?'

I had never been regarded as such by a British officer before, and my pay packet also suggested otherwise.

'I am not trained in surveillance, sir.'

He sat back and shook his head.

'A good point, Sergeant. Except there *aren't* any native officers trained in surveillance; not available to me at any rate. I daresay that the intelligence-wallahs of Section H might have someone, but I'm not in the habit of asking favours of the military.'

'How long will Mr Gulmohamed be in town?'

'Two days. You'll need a man to cover the nightshift, make sure he doesn't slip out from his lodgings after dark. I'll let you handle the logistics.'

And with that it was settled. After detailing what he knew of Gulmohamed's plans for accommodation, Taggart dismissed me with a nod towards the door.

I rose from my seat, saluted even though I was hatless, and as I headed for the exit, Taggart called out, halting me in my tracks. 'And, Banerjee. No need to inform Captain Wyndham of any of this.'

FIVE

Sam Wyndham

I was less than thrilled at Suren's reticence in confiding in me, and at the prospect of acting as messenger boy between him and Lord Taggart, and I told him as much. But he can be an obstinate arse when he chooses, and he tends to choose the most inopportune of moments. Yet it was 2 a.m., he'd been beaten black and blue, and I was too tired to argue.

It was a ridiculous hour to wake Lord Taggart, which made me all the more unwilling to do so, but I needed Suren out of this hole of a jail cell so that I could get him to Uddam Singh, even if we were a few hours late.

Then there was the reaction to Mukherjee's death to consider. There would be trouble when word got out. Especially if people thought he'd been murdered by the police. If they discovered that the suspect was being held in the local thana, there was a good chance they'd burn the place to the ground before the morning. All in all, it was ample cause to rob the commissioner of his sleep.

And so I summoned the constable to let me out and lock Suren back in his cell. I headed for the exit, but not before leaving the officer with a few words of advice.

'The man in that cell. You know who he is?'

The constable shook his head. 'No, sahib.'

'That,' I said, 'is Detective Sergeant Surendranath Banerjee. Lal Bazar big shot.'

The man's eyes widened like saucers.

'Detective?'

'That's right, and a personal friend of Lord Taggart.'

The constable's mouth fell open.

'Laat sahib?'

'The very same. Now, between you and me, Detective Banerjee is going to be released first thing in the morning and I'm guessing he's going to be rather annoyed at the beating you and your friends gave him earlier. If you value your jobs, you might want to make sure the rest of his stay here is as pleasant as a night at the Grand Hotel. Understood?'

I left him quaking and smiled to myself. I've found that there's nothing quite like putting the fear of God in others to make you feel better about your own tawdry situation.

Outside, Shiva stood leaning against the bonnet of the Wolseley, sucking on a bidi and metronomically tapping the end of his lathi on the dirt.

'*Shob theek aché?*' I asked.

He spat on the ground and stowed the lathi on the running board.

'All quiet, sahib.'

The drive to Taggart's residence passed in a blur. The streets were quiet and I was so engrossed in my own thoughts that not even the potholes of Budge Budge could distract me. Soon we were in White Town, an altogether different part of the city, where the vistas were grand and the roads level. But even here, in this bastion of Britishness, the other India made its presence felt. Shiva pulled up at the checkpoint – a sandbag and razor-wire redoubt – that marked the entrance to Taggart's street.

A stone-faced Sikh officer, rifle at the ready, scrutinised the minutiae of my warrant card with a mixture of suspicion and diligence, before eventually deigning to wave us through.

Halfway up the road, past a red postbox and a machine-gun nest discreetly hidden behind a hedgerow, lay Taggart's driveway, barred by the sort of security that might grace Buckingham Palace or the Bank of England. This time there were questions to complement the inspection of our documentation, delivered in a firm but genteel Home Counties accent by a young English officer.

'What business have you with the commissioner, sir? ... Are you aware of the hour, sir? ... Is the commissioner expecting you?'

I restricted my answers to the vague and the monosyllabic, and eventually the young man reached for a telephone to speak to what I assumed was a higher authority within Taggart's bungalow. The response was swift, however, and the young man granted us access to the inner sanctum with a nod and stiff salute.

Shiva parked up under the portico and I got out to the sound of the cicadas clicking in the trees. A uniformed bearer showed me up the steps and into the chequerboard hallway where I was met by Taggart's batman, a heavyset Ulsterman named Villiers, with the physique of a bull and a face like an East End knife fight. It looked like he'd pulled his shirt and trousers on in a hurry. Still, I appreciated the effort.

'Captain Wyndham. Rather late for a social call, isn't it?'

'Not for me, Villiers,' I said. 'Have you woken the boss?'

The batman scowled. Like many an Ulsterman, he was a stickler for protocol and not overly keen on me taking His Lordship's name in vain. 'Lord Taggart's been informed of your arrival. He'll be down presently. In the meantime, he's asked that you wait for him in his study.'

Lord Taggart's study was much like Lord Taggart's office at Lal Bazar: tobacco-scented, and unnecessarily large. I made myself comfortable on one of the several chesterfields that dotted the room like islands in an ocean of parquet and tried to compose my thoughts. Before I'd had a chance to compose much of anything, however, the door opened and in walked His Lordship wrapped in a dressing gown and with his face as grey as his hair.

I stood to attention.

'Sit, Wyndham,' he said, as he walked over, 'and tell me what's so bloody urgent that you felt the need to force poor Villiers to get dressed in the middle of the night.'

'It's Banerjee, sir. He's been arrested on a charge of murder.'

'What?'

'It gets worse. The victim was Prashant Mukherjee.'

Taggart stood transfixed, his face unwilling to accept what his ears were hearing, as though he were still wrapped up in bed and that all this was just some ill-starred dream.

'Why the hell would he do that?'

'He claims he didn't, but the local coppers arrested him trying to set fire to Mukherjee's house. And he doesn't deny that part.'

The commissioner made for the drinks cabinet and poured himself a large measure of something from a decanter.

'We need to keep a lid on this. If word spreads that Mukherjee's been murdered, there'll be hell to pay.'

If word spreads ... in my mind, there was precious little chance of it doing anything else. Calcutta might have been a city of a million people, but when it came to gossip, it seemed little different to a village, with scandal spreading like a virus. And like any virus, it would exact a toll. A price to be paid in fire and blood.

Taggart rubbed a hand across his face. For someone with the might of the Imperial Police Force at his fingertips he seemed remarkably jittery. Not that I blamed him. With that authority came a terrible weight of responsibility.

The damn elections were only weeks away and the city was a powder keg. You could feel it: a nervous, pent-up, explosive energy, carried on the air and infused into the oppressive heat as though the end of days were approaching. With the collapse of Gandhi's protest movement, the natives of Calcutta had fallen into a slough of despondency. Confusion had given way to grief, and then grief to anger. And Bengalis were good at anger, especially of the political sort. No one did it quite like them, which was a surprise, given their lack of physical stature. For a short people, they could be surprisingly violent – like the Scots, but with less bulk. And while they weren't averse to the physical stuff, the sort with fists and teeth and boots, where they truly excelled was in the sort that required ingenuity and malice aforethought – or, failing that, kerosene and a box of matches. Indeed, for a people who prided themselves on their love of the arts, Bengalis were surprisingly quick to start burning things whenever matters didn't go their way. And the targets of their incendiary retribution were suitably catholic and comprehensive: from buildings and tram cars to other Bengalis ... especially other Bengalis if they were of a different religion.

'What the devil possessed him?'

'He wouldn't tell me, sir. Said he would only speak to you and that only you would be able to sort it out. I rather got the impression, sir, that he felt he was acting on your orders.'

I felt the chill of his stare.

'You think *I* ordered him to kill Mukherjee?'

'No, sir. As I say, the sergeant denies he killed anybody. But he's adamant that he'll only talk to you.'

Taggart took a long, pensive sip from his glass, then made for the chair behind his desk. He sat down, pulled pen and paper towards him and began to scribble a note, signing off with a flourish.

'Here,' he said, passing me the letter. 'Get him out and get him back here as soon as you can.'

SIX

Surendranath Banerjee

I had returned to my desk in a daze, ignoring the calls and curious glances of my peers, and contemplated the commissioner's orders. To tail Gulmohamed, I would first require to find him. The commissioner may have known the train upon which he had arrived, but not where he was planning to lodge, where he was going, or whom he had come to meet.

'A tip-off from a colleague in Bombay,' he had stated, but that information was over twelve hours old. Gulmohamed could be anywhere by now. Yet in a foreign city, people tended to gravitate to the familiar. He was a senior figure in the Union of Islam, the Mohammedan political party, and with the elections less than a fortnight off, it seemed more than likely that his business here should be of a political rather than financial nature. It stood to reason that the Union's Calcutta cadres would know of his presence here. Their offices on Chowringhee seemed a sensible place to start.

I would of course require a change of attire. Leaving Lal Bazar, I hailed a loitering rickshaw-wallah and headed for the lodgings in Premchand Boral Street which I shared with Sam. My sudden arrival home at this odd hour came as a shock to Sandesh, our manservant, whom I discovered sprawled on the sofa, blissfully napping. However, I soon put the fear of God into the shiftless rogue and within minutes he was rushing around the flat in a whirlwind of domestic industry.

Clothes maketh man as the British say, and different clothes make different men, and while Sandesh brought me a cup of cha, I opted, not for the kurta and dhoti of the high-caste Hindu, but for the more egalitarian shirt-pant worn by all castes and creeds, and also some of the British.

With attire changed and tea consumed, I picked up the dirty cloth satchel that Sandesh used when out buying groceries and returned once more to the street and found the same rickshaw-wallah, squatting on his haunches beside his chariot, his lungi, dirt-smeared and hitched up to his calves, ruminating over a wad of paan leaves.

'*Jaaben?*' I asked him.

'*Kothai?*'

'Esplanade.'

He nodded in non-committal fashion and quoted the fare.

'*Char taka.*'

Sam would have paid him the four rupees. I knew better and beat him down to two.

The eastern side of Chowringhee was a maelstrom of bodies, the shop-lined footpath jammed with office-wallahs and hawkers, while the other side, the one bordering the great expanse of the Maidan, unshaded and open to the full force of an angry sun, was almost empty. Ahead, the myriad copper-green domes of the Tipu Sultan Mosque loomed above brilliant-white walls, gleaming like a mirage from the tales of Scheherazade.

The Union's offices were situated next door, in a shabby, crumbling edifice made to look even shabbier by its proximity to the great mosque. Above the entrance hung a lopsided banner with the words ALL INDIA UNION OF ISLAM stitched in large white capitals and, above it, Arabic script which I presumed intimated the same thing.

I alighted to the sound of the muezzin's call, onto a pavement clogged with bearded Mohammedans. Carving a path between them, I crossed the threshold into an unlit entrance hall. Almost immediately the noise of the street seemed to dissipate, though not the echo of the muezzin. The walls were stained yellow from the rub of bodies, the floor spattered red with the dried juice of betel nut and the air hung heavy with the dust of centuries. At the far end was a desk, and behind it, a gaunt, bespectacled man with a topi on his head and a book in his hands. He looked up, the genesis of a smile quickly forming on his lips. I was on the cusp of launching into a line of questioning when I remembered that I was undercover. At the last moment I changed tack, dispensing with the authority of a policeman and substituting the humility of an appellant.

'Please, *dada*,' I said, then asked him, in my best vernacular, where I might find Mr Gulmohamed.

His smile vanished, its place taken by a look of cold suspicion.

'What business is it of yours?' he spat in the sibilant tones redolent of East Bengal.

Far from acting as deterrent, his response merely served to confirm that he knew Gulmohamed was in town.

'Who are you, anyway?' he said, his voice now carrying the edge of a threat. 'Why do you want to know about Gulmohamed?' He leaned forward. 'Don't make me call my friends to beat it out of you.'

I raised my palms in supplication and thought fast.

'*Na, na, dada*, it's nothing like that.' I smiled apologetically. 'I'm the manservant of Kazi Nazrul, the poet.'

Kazi Nazrul Islam was probably the most famous Muslim in Calcutta, at least since his poem, *Bidrohi – The Rebel –* had been published the previous year. It was a veiled attack on the British; too veiled, as it turned out, to have attracted the censor's pen until it was already too late, and had set the city, and all of Bengal, Hindu and Muslim, alight.

His face brightened like the surface of the Ganges after a passing shower.

'Nazrul,' he whispered in awe.

'My master,' I said in Bangla, 'has been informed of Mr Gulmohamed's presence in the city. He is most keen to meet him.' From my pocket, I pulled the chit from Taggart summoning me to his office and waved it at him. 'See. Here is the invitation to my master's house.'

It was a calculated gamble. My interlocutor did not look the sort to read English, and, as I'd hoped, the mere sight of the foreign script proved to be all the evidence he required of my bòna fides. His reply, when it came, was far more amenable.

'Gulmohamed sahib isn't here. He's in Metiabruz.'

'Metiabruz?'

A shiver passed down my spine. I had never before set foot in Metiabruz. Why would I? Few self-respecting Hindus had call to. It was a Muslim district after all, on the far-flung southern fringes of the city, past the docks at Khiddirpur, which the British mispronounced as Kidderpore, and hemmed in between a bend in the Hooghly and the suburb of Garden Reach. In all honesty, *district* was likely too respectable a term for it. The place was, they said, little better than a bustee, a slum where outsiders didn't venture after dark, or, for that matter, during the day.

He scribbled an address on a slip of paper, and I thanked him before turning and heading back towards the entrance.

'Wait!' he called from behind me.

I turned to see his hands pressed together in supplication. 'Please tell Nazrul-*kabi* that Mr Rehman at the Union is a great admirer and that I would very much be honoured to meet him.'

I nodded, basking in the glow of my imaginary master's reputation, then continued, out into the noonday heat.

Metiabruz. How was I to reach there? Trams were out of the
question. I doubted they even ran that far. As for the horse-drawn
omnibuses, given the recent tensions, they too were unlikely to be
operating. Metiabruz had the reputation as a place where the locals
would not hesitate to vent their anger by setting on fire a bus or
two. As a means of protest, it was as useless as self-immolation and,
I feared, only served to increase their isolation.

Requisitioning a car would have been the most practical means,
but I would hardly be able to slip unnoticed into a place like that
while seated in the rear of such a vehicle. Indeed, short of arriving
on the back of an elephant, I could think of no more conspicuous a
mode of entry.

It would have to be a train. But as to whether Metiabruz had a
station, or even just a halt – those places where the trains stopped
and the masses simply jumped down onto the dirt – I had no clue.
There was, I knew, a line down to Khiddirpur, and I decided that
was close enough. I could always hail a tonga or bicycle rickshaw
from there.

A tram, bursting with people and heading northwards, approached
and I grabbed a passing handhold, leapt onto the footplate and held
on for dear life until the damn thing began to empty and I managed
to push my way inside for the rest of the way to Sealdah.

The station there was packed. I fought my way in, bought a
ticket from the booth and a *kamala lebu* from a station hawker, then
fell into a malodorous river of bodies which carried me towards a
platform and on to the Khiddirpur local. The doors on the local
trains were never closed – if it was necessary to wait for them to be
shut before leaving a station, the trains would never move – and I
stayed close to them, just to avail myself of any passing breeze when
the train finally began its journey. The platform guard blew his

whistle. I clutched one of the steel handholds and steadied myself as the locomotive shuddered into life.

It had been a long time since I had last travelled third class, mainly for the simple reason that they were the natural habitat of the Calcutta pickpocket, and even though I was wedged firmly between other passengers, I knew enough to keep one hand over the pocket of my trousers that contained my wallet and police identification.

The white suburbs passed by gently: Park Circus, Lake Gardens, Tollygunge. At each, the train lightened – the first- and second-class carriages at least. The third class though remained resolutely full, and it was only once the vistas changed – whitewashed walls giving way to the ramshackle of mud brick and corrugated sheeting – that my situation improved. Even so, it was a relief to finally alight the train and stand on the dusty platform at Khiddirpur.

I had passed the journey wrestling with the challenge of locating Gulmohamed without alerting him to my presence, and by the time I exited the station, I had concocted a rudimentary plan of sorts. From a roadside kiosk, I purchased several sheets of cheap foolscap and an envelope. The paper I left blank, merely folding and stuffing it inside the envelope. On the face, I wrote Gulmohamed's name, then licked the gum and sealed the flap.

From there I hailed a tonga to take me onwards, towards Metiabruz, through streets tinged with faded, almost forgotten regal splendour. The legacy of Wajid Ali Shah, the last of the great kings of Awadh. The British had overthrown him, then offered him what they considered fair terms: his entire kingdom in exchange for a pension and a plot of land by the Hooghly. He ended up here, in exile, in a house by the river. They say he missed his capital of Lucknow. So much so that he purchased all the surrounding land and invited many of his former Muslim subjects – artisans, tailors, kathak dancers and chefs – to come and settle and create a little

Lucknow here in colonial Calcutta. He would die here and his pal-
aces would be torn down, Metiabruz would become a slum and the
Muslims he brought from Lucknow would descend into penury,
but Calcutta hadn't completely turned its back on the king and his
legacy. We took his recipe for biriyani and made it ours.

The dirt road closed in, narrowing to little more than a lane a
cart's width, and was clogged with men and beasts. The casual
observer might think it no different to the bustees further north:
the same pie-dogs lazed in the shade; the same street fowl pecked
at the rubbish heaps beside open drains; but a closer inspection
would reveal that the cows and itinerant hogs that grazed on the
streets of the lower-class Hindu neighbourhoods were notable by
their absence.

The tonga wallowed its way through a mud-filled depression at
the foot of a grand Mogul arch. Eventually, the road opened out
once more and soon the scent of the river drifted over on the breeze.
I breathed it in, experiencing that flutter of the divine that I always
felt when I inhaled it. That scent, earthy, intoxicating, had perme-
ated my whole life, punctuating its key moments. The life of a
Brahmin was tied to it. This holy river: watering not just the soil of
Bengal, but the soul of its people too. Its bounty fed us, nourished
us. Our religious rituals, from birth to death, were linked to its
waters that sprang a thousand miles away in the Himalaya and
flowed to the sea, *our* sea, the Bay of Bengal, carrying with it our
votive offerings, our dreams and our prayers. How ironic, then,
that sailing against the flow of our sacred river, should come the
British. That they should make landing here, at this bend in the
river, and that together we would build Calcutta. They would tell
you that *they* built it, but we knew better. They might write the history books, but we passed our history down too, in song and in
poetry and in word of mouth, and we knew. We knew that this city
was as much ours as theirs. And if we shared the city, we shared the

river too. Their boats brought the world to Bengal, and took us to the world. When my father decreed I was to be educated in England, it was from here, at Khiddirpur, that I sailed, bidding farewell to Bengal from the bow of a British ship.

My father had prepared me. 'It is hard,' he had said, 'to explain the sorrow a Hindu feels when wrenched from this land. It is impossible to explain, even to a Bengali not of our faith. For what do the Muslims or the Christians know of our holy river? They do not seek it out in pilgrimage. Their holy places are not here, in the sacred soil of Bengal but in some far-off, desert land. Our gods were here, not in Mecca, or Jerusalem or Rome.'

Over time I had come to see the truth in his words. The British, in their hymns, imagined Jesus had walked the hills of their green and pleasant land. Well, our gods *had* walked our land and continued to do so. They were of us and we of them. Their spirit infused our trees and rivers and even our dust.

We were estranged now, my father and I, on account of my position with the Imperial Police. And while that pained me, I could see no alternative other than my capitulation to his views. But a man must live by his own conscience, not his father's.

My thoughts evaporated as the tonga crashed through yet another pothole. To one side, a high wall loomed, the foot of which had been commandeered as the backbone for a number of flimsy bamboo shacks. The horse slowed, and to the base hoot of a steamer on the Hooghly, turned the carriage between the pillars of a large Islamic arch cut into the brick. A moment later we had left the slum and entered another world. Where there had been shacks, the road was now lined with palms, beyond which lay the gardens of a number of amply proportioned mansions the measure of any in White Town or Shyambazar. Ahead, a flower garden bisected by a gravel path meandered to a final mansion, beyond which flowed the languid Hooghly.

The driver brought the tonga to a halt at the edge of the garden and I alighted. A stillness descended, the silence punctuated only by the heavy breathing of the horse and the sound of crows calling from the nearby trees.

'Which one?' I asked, pressing a few coins into his palm.

The driver gestured with a nod. '*Oi-thō. Borro-tā.*'

The biggest one.

I set off across the gravel towards the mansion. A measure of a breeze, anaemic but nonetheless welcome, whispered in from the river and tempered the broiling heat. Stone steps led to a pair of carved teak doors set amidst a pillared veranda.

The strains of a santoor accompanied by the rhythmic beat of tablas floated over. The metallic notes, at first ponderous, increased in tempo as I approached. Two figures were seated cross-legged on the veranda; one, a man in a pristine white sherwani, eyes closed, head almost upon his breast, was nodding in time with the beats of his tablas. Yet it was the other who drew my gaze, a woman so beautiful I almost fell over. The light glinted off the green silk of her sari and dust motes danced in the air around her long, almost auburn hair. She, though, was in thrall to her santoor, the metal prongs in her pale hands flashing across the face of the instrument and giving life to a flurry of notes. Once more the tempo of the tabla quickened. Once more the woman kept time, her hands all but a blur, her notes falling like monsoon rain.

The santoor. They say you can practise it for thirty years and still be only a novice. The music, or maybe the girl, stopped me in my tracks. I stared at her, almost hypnotised, as she played on, the tempo rising and falling like waves on the sea, oblivious to me, and the tabla player, lost in the ecstasy of her own creation.

What more could I say about her? What words could express the feelings in my breast at that moment? And yet even as I felt the elation, I cautioned myself. Regardless of the girl's beauty, or her skill with the santoor, regardless of her family's wealth or station, she was a Muslim. If she were Hindu and I were not estranged from my kin, I might think of mentioning her to my father, in the hope of an introduction or a petition from one family to another. But there could be no thought of any such thing here, because wealth, education, physical attraction and anything we might have in common, all were dashed on the rocks of religious difference. This girl and I might inhabit the same city, but our worlds were separate, and by necessity would always be so.

Finally, like the passing of a shower, the notes slowed and died, releasing me from my trance.

I couldn't help myself. 'That was beautiful,' I stammered. It was not the sort of comment a servant had any business making.

The tabla player opened his eyes. The woman looked up in surprise. Noticing me for the first time, she quickly adjusted the *anchal* of her sari so that it covered the top of her head.

'What do you want?' asked the man, making to rise from behind his drums.

I tore my gaze from the woman and, for the second time that day, raised my hand, offered my *aadabs* and smiled in the ingratiating manner expected of a servant. I was about to deliver once more my cover of having been tasked by the poet Nazrul with delivering a dinner invitation for Mr Gulmohamed, but at the last moment I thought better of it. These two were clearly accomplished artists. They may be musicians, but art was art, and there was a chance they would already know the poet. Indeed, given my luck, they were probably firm friends. So I altered my story.

I pulled the envelope with the blank letter inside from my pocket and held it out.

'I'm from the Union of Islam.'

SEVEN

Sam Wyndham

Leaving Lord Taggart, I returned to Shiva and the car, and once more made the trek to Budge Budge, this time to retrieve Suren and then make the same trip in reverse. I was beginning to feel a little like the ball in a game of long-distance ping-pong.

It was still pitch-dark, and save for the stray chink of light escaping a crack in one of the shuttered windows, the squat grey bulk of the thana remained shrouded like a widow at a funeral.

I got out the car and headed for the entrance. This time I didn't ask Shiva to come. Instead I left him with a command.

'*Keep the engine running.*'

I knocked on the door and was admitted with an alacrity that had been sorely absent during my previous visit. I sought out the same constable who'd shown me round last time and handed him the chit from the commissioner. He read it slowly, thoroughly digesting each word. I decided to speed him on, pointing out the signature at the bottom.

'Lord Taggart himself,' I said, and was met with a look of trepidation. 'I told you your prisoner was a *burra babu*.'

He led me through to the cells at a clip, maybe in the hope that efficiency at this late stage might yet save his bacon. His apologies began even as he fumbled the key into the lock. The door swung open and he all but prostrated himself at his prisoner's feet. For his part,

35

Suren was, I felt, rather ungracious, ignoring the man as he exited the cell.

'You all right?' I asked.

He shook his head. 'I could do with a cup of tea.'

'Cha, sahib?' asked the constable hopefully.

'No time,' I said.

Instead I lit Suren a cigarette and led him out of the building as the first hues of pink coloured the sky to the east.

'Feeling more talkative?' We were sitting in the back of the car as, around us, the waking city sped by. Suren finished the smoke, flicking the butt out of the window.

'Do you think the commissioner might offer us breakfast?'

I stared at him. 'You *do* know how much trouble you're in?'

'I haven't eaten in twenty hours.'

'I doubt the commissioner's going to be waiting for you with bacon and eggs.'

His face fell. 'No, I suppose not.'

He had, I realised, avoided answering my question. Indeed, so far he'd told me precious little of what he'd actually done. Soon we'd be back in Alipore and there was no guarantee the commissioner would take me into his office or his confidence when he debriefed Suren. If I were to get the truth out of him, I needed to confront Suren now. On a whim, I leaned forward and ordered Shiva to pull over at a pavement eatery, just a rough bench beside a glowing brazier, in the hope that filling the hole in Suren's stomach might induce him to spill the beans.

He took a bite out of a *shinghara*, a triangle of fried pastry, this one filled with spiced mutton and peas: like a Cornish pasty but with a Bengali kick.

'So?' I said to him, taking a dirty rupee from my pocket and handing it to the crone who ran the place. 'I've bought you breakfast. In your religion, that means you're morally obligated to tell me what happened last night.'

He looked at me, a half-hearted smile on his lips.

'Are you sure that's Hinduism?'

'Absolutely,' I said. 'It's in the *Gita* I believe. Towards the back somewhere.'

Suren took another, more contemplative bite of his *shingara*, and I decided to try a different tack.

'I never told you about Ypres, did I?'

Suren stopped chewing.

'It was 1918,' I said. 'The Russians had given up a few months before. Signed some God-awful treaty with the Germans that meant a million-odd battle-hardened Huns that had previously faced east were suddenly sat on trains en route for the Western Front. The top brass were scared witless. As you know, I used to work for Taggart back then too – he was a colonel at the time, high up in military intelligence.

'He called me into his office one day. Told me the situation was grave. Said we'd had reports the Boche were building up their forces opposite our sector. Fed me some rot about king and country and all that. *"Accurate, on-the-ground information. That's what we need, Sam."* He asked me to volunteer to accompany a platoon into no man's land. A raid on a Boche trench. *"Capture one or two of their men – officers if possible – and whatever plans and documents you can find. You speak a bit of German, don't you?"'*

I paused to extract a cigarette from a crumpled packet of Capstans, lifted it to a dry mouth, fumbled for a match and lit it with a hand still trembling at the memory.

'Going out into no man's land under cover of darkness was bad enough, but a raid on a German trench was a suicide mission. We both knew it. I suppose that's why he stressed the need to volunteer.'

As I exhaled a protective cloud of blue-grey smoke, Suren placed the remnants of his pasty on a dried-leaf plate, and for the first time since his arrest, seemed to give me his full attention.

'And did you? Volunteer?'

'Yes. As Taggart knew I would. The worst of it was that my German wasn't even that good, just schoolbook stuff and the odd phrase picked up from those leaflets they dropped on our trenches telling us how our women were all sleeping with the men left back at home. I'd be as likely to pick up their trench commander's laundry list as I would any documents of merit, but that didn't seem to matter.'

'What happened?'

'Long story short: I was sent to join a party of infantrymen specially trained for such raids. Officer in charge was a captain by the name of Graves, which wasn't exactly a propitious omen. I was told to join them behind the lines for a few days' training: infiltration, exfiltration, hand-to-hand combat. All the dark arts intended to give you a fighting chance, assuming you first make it past the Maxim gun.

'Then, too soon, we were given our orders. As darkness fell, we slipped out of the trench, climbed up onto the parapet and slithered over the other side as quickly as possible. I half expected the Boche guns to open fire there and then, but they didn't. Almost silently, Graves gave the order to advance. We rose from the slime and followed him blindly between the maze of razor wire like rats in the sewers. Ten yards, twenty, thirty, and then we were out, into the churned-up hell of mud and corpses that made up the distance between our line and theirs. We crawled forward on our bellies till we found a shell hole as close to the German lines as practical. I can't tell you the relief I felt as I fell into that hole. The thing was no more than a shallow crater only yards from the enemy, but at that moment it felt like it offered the sanctuary of a church. Our task was to wait for a Boche patrol, ambush it and use them as cover for our raid.

'For a few hours, there was this surreal calm. The whole world seemed reduced to the confines of that hole. Beyond it, only a black and barren void. It must have been around midnight that it all started. We heard the creak of a coil being unrolled. Some unfortunate saps had been sent out from the Boche lines to repair their barbed wire. I felt an electricity pass through me. We listened, trying to locate the position of the repair crew, then Graves gave some of his men the signal. They slithered out of the hole and into the darkness, crawling towards the German lines.

'I heard the rustle as they moved forward, then the muffled, strangled violence. Things were going to plan but then one of the Hun managed a cry and a shot rang out.'

I stopped and took a pull on my cigarette. Suren, though, was eager for the rest of the tale.

'What happened?'

'Well, that was it. Within seconds the German line came to life and all hell broke loose. The lead began flying all over the shop. I kept my head down and prayed. I heard the screams of Graves's men, cut down on their retreat to our shell hole. The Boche repair party must have been wiped out too. Soon there were only three of us left in that hole.'

I took a long, bitter drag on the cigarette, then passed it to Suren.

'Eventually the shooting died down. One of Graves's men was groaning, still alive out in no man's land. I stuck my head over the crater lip. He was about ten yards away. I signalled to Graves, told him I could reach the man. "You stay here," he said. "'We'll get him."

'He and the other soldier crawled out of the hole. It took time, but they made it as far as the wounded man. They even managed to pull him back a few inches, but I think that's what the Boche were waiting for. They used that poor wounded bastard as bait, waited till they'd flushed some more of us out, then let loose again.

'None of them made it back. I waited in that hole for two hours before finally crawling home to our lines.'

I felt the unwelcome prickle of sweat, on my neck and my back, and in my fist the empty cigarette packet crushed to a ball. I looked up. Suren was staring at the dirt.

'The point is,' I said, 'Taggart knew he was probably sending me to my death, but he did it, because it suited his purpose.'

Suren shook his head. 'You think Lord Taggart sent me to do his dirty work?'

'Whatever he sent you to do is not my business,' I said, but take it from one who knows, you'd be wise not to rely on the commissioner's support if he thinks you've become a liability. Just remember who your real friends are.'

EIGHT

Surendranath Banerjee

'He's not here.'

The tabla player continued to eye me with suspicion and I cursed my luck.

'That is indeed a pity,' I mumbled. 'My boss, Rehman-sahib at the Union, was most insistent. He said it was imperative that Mr Gulmohamed receive this letter most urgently.'

'He should be back this evening.' This time it was the woman who spoke. While the tabla player seemed barely to acknowledge my presence, she looked at me with what felt like benevolence. 'I'm his niece,' she said. 'You may give the letter to me. I'll make sure he gets it.'

Her companion returned to his instrument and began idly beating a slow rhythm that echoed the thumping of my heart. I found myself holding my breath.

'I'm sorry, memsahib,' I said, remembering to exhale. 'Rehman-sahib was most specific. He told me I must hand it to Mr Gulmohamed personally. If I return without passing on the letter, he will ... well, you know what these *burra babus* are like ...'

The woman smiled in sympathy.

'Maybe you might tell me where he has gone?' I continued. 'I could try to find him.'

'You have a pencil?'

I reached into my bag, found the stub of Sandesh's pencil and passed it to her.

'And the envelope?' she asked.

'Excuse me?'

She looked at me as though I were a simpleton.

'I need to write the address somewhere.'

'Of course.' I grinned, and handed her the envelope, cursing myself for my lack of thought. If there was a silver lining, however, it was also the same lack of thought that one expected of a servant.

Turning the envelope to an odd angle, she began writing in the crooked manner of the left-handed. I too was left-handed, or at least I had been as a child, until my mother, convinced it was a mark of malevolence, beat it out of me. These days I used my right. Indeed I was surprised that this woman, so obviously of high standing, would not have undergone a similar process of exorcism.

'There,' she said, returning the envelope. On the reverse, in neat Bengali script, was an address in Budge Budge of all places, a restaurant called Lotus Hotel. Budge Budge was another ramshackle riverside township even further to the south and west of the city. Again, it was the sort of locale one didn't venture into without good reason. And I'd never had one. Not till now.

I pressed my palms together, thanked her profusely, and realised I had absolutely no idea of how to get to Budge Budge.

'One more thing,' I said. 'If I may ask. Do you know how I might get there?'

The tabla player gave a dismissive laugh. The woman, however, was again more amenable.

'There's a bus every few hours. It stops at the *more* outside the arch. But the buses aren't that reliable. The quickest way might be to take a ferry from the ghat along the river.

'Thank you, memsahib,' I said. I offered *aadabs* once more and turned to leave as behind me the tabla player increased his tempo.

I walked back down the path as the first notes from the santoor were struck and I found myself wishing I could have stayed longer, hidden myself away and simply listened to her play all day.

From the river I caught the ferry to Budge Budge, a dilapidated, antiquated thing, belching smoke and overloaded with passengers. It wallowed its way south with its engine complaining loudly. The boat never strayed far from the bank, thank the gods. I had never learned to swim, which is to say that no one had ever taught me, but this is not uncommon among Bengalis, which I have always found perplexing. For a people whose diet consists largely of fish, we are surprisingly fearful of all but the shallowest of water.

Budge Budge arrived thirty minutes later and not a moment too soon. Our ferry appeared to be taking on a troubling level of water, the bilge mixing with oil and soot and forming a most noxious effluent that pitched and rolled around our feet. I was one of the first to alight, and even the usually heart-stopping shuffle along half-rotten wooden planks from the boat to the jetty above the river and mud, seemed less precarious than usual.

Once back upon land, I removed my sandals, dried my feet with the cloth satchel, and took stock. The riverfront was dotted with tumbledown fishing huts and the occasional whitewashed temple between the hollowed-out carcasses of long abandoned wharves.

At the roadside stood a rickshaw stand and a tea stall congested with the usual assembly of the gainfully under-employed. I cleared my throat, and made my way over. We Bengalis are drawn to a tea stall like Englishmen to a club. It had been at least six hours since my last cup and I had the devil's own thirst to slake. I bought a *bhar*, took a sip and ambled over to a group of rickshaw-wallahs who were reposed on the ground nearby, playing cards. One, probably the next in line for a fare, looked up. He was a grizzled old *dadū*, with silvery stubble and sleeveless vest.

'Lotus Hotel,' I said.

The man nodded. *'Ak tākā.'*

One rupee seemed excessive. From the look on his face, I sensed that he wasn't about to haggle, not in the company of his comrades. Rickshaw-wallahs are curious fellows. Individually, they would happily strike a deal, but when there are two or more together, they display the ruthless determination of the most militant of unions.

'Chalo,' I said. 'Let's go.'

The Lotus Hotel was a hotel only in the Indian sense, which is to say it wasn't a hotel at all but a restaurant, though in this case, even the latter term seemed like pretence. It was a single-storey structure, squatting on a dusty street with an open sewer in front and resting between a bicycle repair shop and a Chinese laundry. Opposite sat a *pūkūr* of stagnant green water, its surface strangled with the usual bustee flotsam and the occasional lotus flower. The exterior was crudely fashioned from orange bricks and bare cement, with holes for where the windows and door should have been. Along the top, the hotel's name had been painted in shabby blue letters which dripped across the metal casing of a roll-down shutter.

I wondered what on earth would bring a Bombay politician to this dive of a place in a part of town which most right-thinking people did not even consider to be part of Calcutta.

There was one way to find out.

Gulmohamed did not know me. In my present garb, and in these surroundings, I looked no more conspicuous than a tree in a forest. Even if he did see me enter, I doubted he'd remember my face a minute later. I stepped over the slab above the open sewer, through the jaws of the entrance and into the gloom beyond.

The interior was bigger than I had expected, yet no more remarkable than the exterior. Two dozen square tables, packed tightly together, most occupied by groups of young men, smoking bidis and deep in *adda* over cups of tea. Around them, a gaggle of waiters waded to and from the kitchen through the fog of cigarette smoke.

I took a seat at one of the few empty tables – this one along the back wall, picked up a discarded, day-old copy of *Ananda Bazar* and pretended to scan its pages. I spotted Gulmohamed almost immediately. He was significantly older and better dressed than most of the clientele. Across from him sat another man: younger, shaven-headed and fair-skinned, but not fair enough to be an Englishman, and built, as Sam might say, like a brick latrine. He was dressed in a white shirt the cut of which suggested it was expensive. Before I could examine them further, however, a waiter approached to take my order.

'*Cha,*' I said.

He left with a nod and I returned to my perusal of the two men. Gulmohamed was speaking, as much with his hands as his mouth, and from my vantage point, appeared unsettled. His companion though seemed to be taking it calmly: nodding, listening, and finally raising a smile and a placatory hand.

I doubted this was their first meeting. In my experience, politicians rarely became heated with a brand-new acquaintance. What's more, from their attire, I doubted either man would be the type to consider the Lotus Hotel an appropriate venue for a first meeting, not if they intended to make a good impression.

The fair-skinned gentleman leaned conspiratorially across the table, just as the waiter returned with my tea. Waving him away, I returned my attention to Gulmohamed's friend. He had taken out a pen and was sketching something on a paper napkin. It seemed to placate Gulmohamed, though his expression suggested that full agreement had yet to be reached.

The two continued to negotiate, while I sipped my tea. Fifteen minutes later, the shaven-headed gentleman rose to his feet. He held out a hand and Gulmohamed half rose to shake it, then dropped back onto his chair as the other placed a few rupees on the table and made for the exit.

Gulmohamed watched him leave, and for some moments, simply sat there. Finally he reached into the breast pocket of his suit, pulled out a silver cigarette case and flipped it open.

He selected a cigarette, gold-filtered and foreign, tapped it gently on the table, and, with a flick of his thumb, lit it with a flash of flame from a matching lighter. He smoked it slowly, as though it were an aide to his contemplation. Only once, as he returned it to the table, did I see his hand shake.

Finally, he checked his watch. Taking one last pull, he then pushed the golden stub firmly into the flimsy tin ashtray on the table and rose. Within seconds he was striding out of the door as I called for the waiter, threw a few coins on the table and set off after him.

Gulmohamed was already twenty yards down the street, passing a bent-backed workman pulling a cart laden with jute sacks. From his pocket, he extracted a piece of paper: the note, I assumed, that the well-dressed Eurasian had written. He stopped to consult it, crossed over the road and turned into the shaded entrance to a narrow, puddle-filled *gullee*.

Taking care to maintain an appropriate distance, I too crossed over, pausing at the mouth of the *gullee* to make sure he didn't double back. I stared into the darkness of the lane but saw nothing. Gulmohamed had disappeared, enveloped by its shadows.

NINE

Sam Wyndham

With the coming of the dawn, the crows began calling and the checkpoints had disappeared from Taggart's road. There had been a time when they'd been a permanent, twenty-four-hour fixture, but the other residents had complained and now, like some nocturnal beast, they and the officers who manned them, only came out during hours of darkness.

The guard at the entrance to his driveway, however, was still very much in place; a stony-faced sentry armed with scowl and a Number 1 Lee—Enfield rifle. Taggart must have told him to expect us as the car was waved through with only the most cursory of inspections.

Shiva brought the Wolseley to a halt halfway up the gravel path as the route further was blocked by a dog warming itself in the morning sun. Normally he'd have blown his horn or shouted, or, as a last resort, got out of the car and kicked the damn thing out of the way, but this was the commissioner's dog, and so outranked all three of us in the car.

Suren and I got out and walked the rest of the way to the front door, where Taggart's batman, Villiers, met us and led us through to the study. His Lordship was already waiting, dressed this time in a starched white uniform and staring out of the window at a lawn as verdant and flat as a bowling green.

He turned, and in that instant, I saw the burdens of office etched into the lines around his eyes.

'What happened?'

The question was aimed at Suren.

'It's difficult to explain, sir.'

'Well, you had better try, Sergeant.'

Suren swallowed hard. 'I did as you ordered, sir. I tracked down Gulmohamed to a hotel in Budge Budge.'

'Budge Budge?' said Taggart, as though it might as well have been the moon.

'Yes, sir. He met a man there. A well-dressed type. Eurasian, or maybe Anglo-Indian. I couldn't see what they were discussing, but Gulmohamed seemed agitated. He waited for the other man to depart before setting off himself.'

He took a breath before continuing.

'I followed at a distance. It was not easy. Budge Budge is just a knot of narrow lanes and winding alleys. He appeared to be searching for a particular address. I lost him at the mouth of a *gullee*, but then heard a noise – a gate closing. I tracked the sound to the entrance to a compound. The gate was unlocked and appeared unattended. I waited a few minutes and then thought I might enter to see what Gulmohamed was up to. As I passed through, however, I was attacked from behind.'

His hand went to the back of his head. 'I blacked out. When I came to, there was no sign of Gulmohamed. I steadied myself, then made my way out into the alley, but that was deserted.'

Taggart raised a sceptical eyebrow. 'Gulmohamed attacked you while you were supposed to be covertly following him?'

Suren reddened. 'It would seem so, sir. I determined to go back to the compound, and inspect the house on the chance that Gulmohamed was still there. I circumnavigated the building. From outside it appeared deserted; all windows shuttered. It was when I checked the front door that my suspicions became heightened. It was open. I listened for voices but heard nothing. At that point I made the decision to enter. If challenged, I would say that I had been attacked and needed assistance. There were, however, no signs of life. I was about to leave when I spotted an open door towards the rear of the house. Through the gap it looked as though someone was lying prostrate on the floor. From the attire I could tell it was a man. He wasn't moving, so I entered the room to see if he was all right.'

Suren shook his head.

'I turned him over. There was bruising on his neck and his head fell forward. I suspected the vertebrae had most likely been snapped clean. I felt for breath or a pulse but found none. Only at that juncture did I recognise the dead man. Prashant Mukherjee ... Well, you can imagine my shock at finding the *pundit* lying there, still warm. There was no rigor. I could only surmise that Gulmohamed had just killed him. He had gone there with that express purpose, and when he realised I was following him, he knocked me out, then murdered Mukherjee. I realised what would happen if word got out that Mukherjee had been murdered. And if people discovered that the killer was a Muslim, especially that it was Gulmohamed, the carnage across the city would be unthinkable.'

He paused and swallowed hard.

'That is when I decided ...'

'What?' asked Taggart.

'To burn the evidence. In the heat of the moment, I could think of no better option, especially given the alternative of a religious riot. I hoped to make it look like an accident, as though Mukherjee had fallen asleep and dropped a lit cigarette onto the sofa, which had then gone up in flames and killed him. That would allow me to report back to you, without the whole country going up in flames. I moved Mukherjee's body onto the sofa, put one of my cigarettes in his hand, then set fire to the whole pyre. Alas, it took several attempts to set the sofa alight and by the time a fire had started, someone must have reported something, as the local police turned up in force and arrested me, most vigorously.'

Taggart took a sharp breath. 'That's quite an accusation.'

'But you didn't actually *see* Gulmohamed enter the house?' I asked.

'I don't recall exactly. The whole matter is still rather foggy.'

Suren's account raised as many questions as it answered. What was Mukherjee doing there? Was it his house or had he been lured there? If he did live there, where was his family? Where were the servants? What was a Hindu ideologue, respected by goodness knows how many zealots, doing living in a hole of a place like Budge Budge? And all of that was before we even got to the fact that Suren couldn't remember actually having seen Gulmohamed enter the house, let alone kill Mukherjee.

But before I could ask any more questions, Taggart took over.

TEN

Sam Wyndham

Taggart walked over to his desk, dropped into his chair and pinched the bridge of his nose.

'Bloody hell.'

The sentiment was hard to fault.

He removed his spectacles, rubbed ponderously at his chin and turned to Suren.

'So a respected, nationally prominent Muslim comes a thousand miles across the country, murders a Hindu, all under *your* nose, and your reaction is to burn the place down and then get yourself arrested by the local constables who, I might add, are hardly known for their alacrity? Have you taken leave of your senses?'

The sensible response would be to stay mum, look remorseful, maybe focus on a patch of carpet and wait for the commissioner's tirade to blow itself out. I fully expected Suren to adopt it, but *Suren* and the concept of *'sensible'* didn't seem to be much on speaking terms these days. Instead he raised his head and asked for permission to speak.

'Speak?' said Taggart. 'Of course! Please! Enlighten us as to what the devil possessed you?'

'It seemed a judicious course of action, sir ... given the circumstances. I hoped to forestall further violence ... afford us the opportunity to apprehend Gulmohamed while averting a riot. I simply hadn't expected the local constables to arrive.'

The hangman's grimace on Taggart's face suggested he was less convinced, and though I still harboured a sea of doubts, it seemed an appropriate moment for me to come to Suren's defence.

'I have to agree with the sergeant, sir,' I said. 'He might just have bought us some time to figure a way out of this mess.'

The commissioner turned his ire on me.

'Thank you, Mahatma bloody Wyndham. You think you're pouring oil on troubled waters?'

In truth my words were doing just that. There came a diminution in the volume of the commissioner's invective, and then a gradual, reluctant acceptance that, having been dealt a rather bad hand, the sergeant, other than finding himself up on charges of murder and arson, might just have played it rather well. And the key to extricating him from those was to find and question Gulmohamed.

'Well?' said Taggart finally. 'What are you waiting for? Get out there and find the man. Don't arrest him. Detain him on some grounds and make sure you bring him straight to me at Lal Bazar.'

'Yes, sir,' I said, and turned for the door. Suren made to follow.

'Not you, Banerjee,' roared Taggart. 'You're coming with me.'

Suren blinked.

'To Lal Bazar?'

'Not a chance. You may recall you're under arrest. I can't change that for now, but I can make it house arrest.'

The sergeant's jaw fell open. 'So the charges against me still stand?'

'For now. We'll discuss this further on the way to your lodgings.'

It appeared the sergeant was about to protest, but then thought better of it.

'Yes, sir.'

Taggart took a sheaf of papers from his desk and stuffed them into a leather briefcase that looked like it had fought in the war. He summoned a native bearer, who, with a nod, picked up the valise and fell into step behind us as we walked back out to the veranda.

The commissioner's exit seemed to have caught his aide, Villiers, by surprise. The man dashed for the telephone to summon Taggart's chauffeur, then, noticing that our car was still parked in the drive, raced down the steps beyond the front door to remonstrate with Shiva who'd escaped the vehicle for the shade of a nearby peepul tree. Words were exchanged, or rather shouted by Villiers in Shiva's direction. The driver ran to crank up the engine as Taggart's car appeared at the entrance to the driveway.

'Wyndham,' said Taggart, 'once you've brought in Gulmohamed, I want you to go to Mukherjee's house. Speak to his family and the Hindu hotheads he surrounded himself with. Convey our sympathies. Tell them we've the matter in hand. Above all, don't give them any indication that this might have been a religious killing ... or, for that matter, a murder by a serving police officer.'

'What exactly should I tell them?' I asked.

'Tell them we've detained a suspect for questioning and that we'll make an announcement shortly.'

'I'm not sure that'll placate them, sir.'

'Then think of something that will.'

Taggart turned to Suren.

'With me, Sergeant. No point dawdling.'

The two of them headed down the steps and into the sun as I waited for Shiva to start the car. Finally the engine burst into life. Shiva removed the crank and threw it into the footwell, then opened the rear door for me. At the mouth of the driveway, Taggart's chauffeur was doing likewise for the commissioner. But as I walked down the steps, all hell broke loose. As if from nowhere, I heard the sound of a car screeching to a halt. I looked over to see the stony-faced sentry rush forwards, raising his rifle as he went. But he was too slow. A shot rang out and the man crumpled like an empty coat. Taggart reached for his revolver but he too never made it. The world seemed to slow. Something was thrown from the car. A small, dull metallic sphere not much larger than a cricket ball. I watched it arc through the air and knew immediately what it was: a crude, home-made bomb. The type favoured as much by Bengali terrorists as Irish ones and which was as likely to blow up its thrower as it was its intended target. But this time there was no such luck. It landed a few feet from Taggart and exploded. A flash of white light, a noise like a thunderclap and suddenly the scene was shrouded in smoke. Bombs like that generally had a pitifully small blast radius, but even so, with nothing between it and the commissioner, it would be more than enough to kill him. Amid the smoke I searched for Suren.

More shots rang out. Four times in quick succession. Instinct kicked in. I dropped to the ground and reached for my Webley. Rising to a crouch, I peered along the street. The smoke was clearing. The glass in the windows of Taggart's car had been shattered and crystalline fragments lay strewn on the concrete. Taggart was on the ground, with Suren dragging him towards the relative protection of the car's armour-plated door. I got up and sprinted over to them as the bullets continued to fly, this time, I thought, from several positions. Maybe some of Taggart's protection detail had got their act together and were now returning fire.

In the shadow of the vehicle, Suren seemed to be cradling the commissioner's head. Then I saw his uniform: a horrific red blossom spreading over the white tunic. I dived in beside them.

'How is he?'

Suren shook his head. 'God knows.'

Taggart's face was blood-smeared and ashen. Suren's shirt was torn and bloody, but with whose blood was unclear.

'And you?' I asked.

'Just a scratch.'

Together we positioned the commissioner so that he was sitting slouched against the wheels of the car. I turned towards the house and shouted to Villiers who had taken cover behind a palm in an earthen pot.

'Call a doctor, damn you!'

Suren leaned over Taggart's prone body and reached for the commissioner's holster.

'What the hell are you doing?' I asked.

'I need a gun,' he said.

He grabbed Taggart's revolver, then sprinted out into the street, past the motionless body of the sentry who'd waved us in earlier. There came a screech of tyres and the growl of an engine accelerating. Suren let off a shot, then began to give chase. Around him, other officers continued to fire.

Suddenly Villiers was beside me.

'Ambulance is on its way.'

'Look after him,' I said, then got up and followed Suren into the street.

In the distance, the car roared off and turned a corner, its tyres howling in protest. Suren was a good two hundred yards behind it. He slowed to a stop, then doubled over, catching his breath. Above the shouts of policemen, the sound of sirens wailed somewhere in the air. I caught up with him.

He continued to breathe heavily, his forehead bristling with sweat. His hands, still holding Taggart's pistol, were smeared with dirt and blood.

'Did you get a look at them?' I asked.

He shook his head.

'The registration plate?'

'Missing. How's the commissioner?'

'Villiers is with him. An ambulance is on its way.'

He stared helplessly in the direction of the fleeing car.

'Come on,' I said. 'We should get back.'

That's when he pointed the gun at my chest.

ELEVEN

Surendranath Banerjee

I had not intended to.

It was simply one of those *heat of the moment* things. In hindsight, pointing a pistol at a senior officer was not the most judicious course of action, especially given the murder charge already levelled against me. More so given that Sam was my closest friend. He was sure to take my aiming a revolver at him personally. At the time, though, I was hard pressed think of a better alternative.

Lord Taggart, the only man who could prove I had been in Budge Budge on police orders and not because I was hell-bent on murdering a Hindu scholar, had just been attacked at the gates to his own house, and to my, albeit untrained, eye, the chances of him surviving looked slim. That left me, and by extension Sam, in a difficult position. I was under house arrest, and, if Lord Taggart failed to survive, I might quickly find myself swapping those lodgings for a jail cell and then, quite possibly, the hangman's noose. My hopes of redemption rested squarely on the apprehension of Gulmohamed, and while Sam was an able officer – the best it had been my pleasure to work for – he still found it easier dealing with his own kind than with Indians. The differences between Hindu and Muslim, or Bengali and Gujarati, or Aryan or Dravidian were lost on him, and now was not an opportune time to further his education.

If my future depended on finding Gulmohamed, then the likelihood of his capture would be greatly increased if I were able to take part in the search. I, after all, already knew where he was staying, and had some knowledge of whom he'd met. Explaining all that to Sam would take time and put him in a tricky position. I'd no doubt that he'd put friendship before duty, but it would be wrong to place him in such a predicament. Therefore it seemed expedient, not to mention more efficient, to simply stick a gun in his face and explain matters more thoroughly at a later, more appropriate juncture.

Sam stared at it, then at me, his face registering a mixture of disbelief and weariness – as though I were a child throwing a tantrum.

'What the bloody hell are you doing now?'

'I need to find Gulmohamed,' I said.

Behind him a police ambulance sped up the street, its siren wailing like the conch shells of the priests at Kalighat, and pulled to a halt near the gates to the commissioner's bungalow.

'You should see to Taggart,' I said, shouting above the siren. 'If he dies, then so do I.'

Sam hesitated.

'You're not going to shoot me, Suren.'

That much was true.

'Please,' I implored. 'Don't try to follow me.'

And to his credit, he didn't.

I turned and ran. First along the road that Taggart's attackers had taken, then, to avoid the throng of police and vehicles approaching from all points, through the back lanes used by the native cooks, cleaners and servants to traverse to their employers' abodes. For once I was grateful of the obsession that so many of Calcutta's

British residents had of keeping their Indian servants out of sight and out of mind.

The sun rose higher and I ran, perspiration coursing down my back and with my heart hammering against the frame of my chest till I felt I must collapse. I stopped and rested against the high wall of a bungalow, hoping for at least a few minutes' respite before an overweening durwan approached and told me to '*hatao!*' It was then that I heard it: the metallic rattling, the electric spark, the chiming of the brass bell, of the tram car that would be my salvation.

Summoning my last reserves, I stood once more and ran. I made it to the main road in time to see the northbound tram, full to the gunnels, pull away from a halt. Shouting, I waved my hands in the air and implored the conductor to wait. Lord Ganesh, remover of obstacles, must have taken pity on me, for the tram slowed, then stopped. The conductor stepped out and waved me inside like a schoolmaster chiding a late-running pupil at the school gates.

'*Tara-tari! Gari derri hoch-ché!*'

TWELVE

Sam Wyndham

He wouldn't have done it.

Pointing a gun is one thing. Pulling the trigger, that's something else entirely. Yes he'd shot a man before, but that man had deserved it. I, on the other hand, had given him a place to stay when he had nowhere else to go, and while the standard of the accommodation was debatable, I doubted it merited a bullet in the chest.

Still, with Lord Taggart lying yards away and bleeding to death, and with his attackers making their getaway, this didn't seem like the right time to debate things rationally with the sergeant. And Suren had a point. Given the gravity of the charges against him, house arrest could quickly give way to incarceration in the Central Jail to await a trial; and with Taggart out of the picture, there was no one to corroborate his story: of being ordered to Budge Budge, tailing a VIP from Bombay who'd murdered Mukherjee, while *he* had just set fire to the place. It just sounded ridiculous, so I let him go, and watched for a moment as he ran.

Medical orderlies, khaki-clad and with the demeanour of funeral attendants were already seeing to Taggart. Close by, Villiers looked on like a courtier beside a fallen king. Men were cordoning off the street and the air reverberated to the growl of lorries as yet more police reinforcements descended.

I rushed back, hoping Taggart might still be conscious, but was halted at a distance by a blond officer with a white coat over his uniform. I might have pushed past him had it not been for the large sentry behind him with a bayonet attached to his rifle.

'I need to speak to the commissioner.'

The officer seemed nonplussed.

'And who are you, exactly?'

'Wyndham,' I said. 'CID.'

The man made an instant assessment which I must have failed. 'He's in no state to speak to anyone.'

'It doesn't matter. He's barely conscious.'

I turned to find Villiers, ashen-faced and bloody. The man seemed to have shrunk, hardly filling his blood-smeared uniform. I fished out my last cigarette, and offered it to him.

'How is he?'

Villiers shook his head. 'Not good. The docs won't comment till they get him to a hospital.' He exhaled deeply, the cigarette offering absolution.

The orderlies were raising Taggart onto a stretcher as a military staff car negotiated the *cordon sanitaire* and stopped a few feet from the ambulance. Behind it, two army trucks pulled up and began disgorging a phalanx of troops. The driver stepped out smartly and opened the rear door. Brown boots, polished to a shine, touched the ground, and an officer in a uniform bearing the pips of a major stepped out. The man was well built, with the thoughtful expression of an academic and the cold eyes of a fanatic. In a different time, he might have been a crusader or a warrior monk, but in this era his insignia told me he was an officer of the Intelligence Corps.

'Who's this?' asked Villiers.

I didn't recognise the man, but I'd had dealings with the organisation he represented, and suddenly I wished I'd kept that last cigarette for myself.

'Section H,' I said. 'Military intelligence.'

The major strode over with the certainty of a hero from a Kipling poem. He examined both Villiers and me, and didn't seem impressed by what he saw.

'Who's in charge here?'

'That would be me, sir. Inspector Villiers,' stammered the batman.

'Well, Inspector Villiers,' said the major, 'the military will take it from here. Tell your men to stand down.'

Villiers looked like a man reprieved from the gallows.

'On whose orders?' I asked.

The major seemed to be expecting the enquiry.

'You must be Wyndham,' he said matter-of-factly. 'You're the other reason I'm here.'

That came as a surprise.

'You have me at a loss, Major,' I said. 'And you didn't answer my question. On whose authority are you assuming control? This is the scene of a crime. The Imperial Police have jurisdiction.'

The officer scrutinised me closely.

'My name's Boyle, and I'm here on the orders of high command at Fort William. As for jurisdiction, you see those men lying dead there?' He pointed at two shroud-covered corpses that had been part of Taggart's guard detail. 'Those men were military. That makes this a military matter.'

He turned to Villiers.

'Now, Inspector, if you'd be so kind ...'

Villiers didn't need to be told again. A curt nod and he was practically running back to the police cordon to order his men to stand down. That left me facing Major Boyle alone.

'Where's Dawson?' I asked.

'Excuse me?'

'Colonel Dawson,' I said. 'I'd have thought a matter like this would deserve the attention of a colonel rather than a major.'

'That's none of your concern. Instead, maybe you could tell me what *you're* doing here?'

'I had a meeting with the commissioner.'

The major eyed me with a hint of suspicion.

'At his residence rather than the office?'

'It was a matter of some urgency.'

'What, exactly?'

There was no point in lying to him. He'd only need to question Villiers to know that I'd come here with Suren. Omitting his name wouldn't be doing the sergeant any favours, and I had the distinct impression that the major might already be aware of more than he was letting on. Yet no good ever came from telling Section H the whole truth, so I tried to appear helpful without saying too much or, hopefully, anything of value.

'I and another officer were investigating some native distur-bance out in Budge Budge.'

The major parroted my words. *'A native disturbance out in Budge Budge?* Seems a trivial matter for the commissioner to be interested in, especially so early in the morning?'

'I can't comment on the commissioner's priorities.'

'No, I daresay you can't. And this other officer. Who would that be?'

'A detective sergeant,' I said. 'Name of Banerjee.'

Boyle's lips pursed, sourly.

'There was a Sergeant Banerjee arrested in Budge Budge last night on suspicion of murder. Wouldn't happen to be the same man, would it?'

I wasn't surprised that Section H already knew of Suren's arrest. They had informers everywhere, not least among the police force. Their job was to maintain the stability of the Raj and, as such, they took a particular interest in political crimes that might impact that stability. Mukherjee's murder, with its potential to set the whole of Bengal alight, certainly qualified.

'That's correct,' I said. 'Taggart ordered his release from custody and asked me to bring him here.'

'You have those orders in writing?'

'Not any more. I handed them to the officers at Budge Budge.'

'And where is he now, your friend, Banerjee?'

That was a good question.

'He went chasing after the attackers.'

Boyle raised an eyebrow.

'You let him go wandering off? Need I remind you that he was under arrest?'

'The sergeant was doing his duty.'

'And now he's rather conveniently disappeared. Unarmed?'

'What?'

'The sergeant,' said Boyle. 'I take it he was unarmed. He was under arrest, after all.'

'It's possible he could have taken a weapon from one of the dead or wounded sentries. I was too far away to see.'

The major stared. 'You weren't with him?'

'I was leaving when the attack took place. Taggart ordered me back to Budge Budge. He was going to proceed with the sergeant.'

'You were leaving when the attack took place ... and yet you don't seem to have suffered a scratch?'

'I happened to be a distance from the blast,' I said. 'My driver had parked the car up the drive, near the entrance to the house. The commissioner's car was further down, closer to the street.'

'So if your car hadn't been in the driveway, the chances are the commissioner's car would have parked there, too far away to be reached by a bomb lobbed from the street?'

My head began to spin.

'I don't know what you're driving at, but —'

'What I'm driving at, Captain is that you brought a man suspected of murdering a senior member of the Hindu movement to

Lord Taggart's house, and shortly thereafter, there's an *unprecedented* attack on the commissioner himself?'

'It was hardly unprecedented,' I protested. 'There've been at least three attempts on Taggart's life while he's been commissioner. He even keeps one of the unexploded bombs on his desk as a paperweight.'

'Four attempts, actually,' said the major, 'but this is the first one to have succeeded in harming him. That in my book makes it pretty damn unprecedented. Odd that it should happen when he's in the company of a native officer who's just murdered a senior Hindu radical and has now disappeared.'

'Banerjee's got nothing to do with this attack,' I said. 'He owes his career to the commissioner. He'd never harm him.'

Boyle gave a snort of derision. 'Indians are a law unto themselves. Just how well *do* you actually know your colleague? The son of a leading lawyer opposed to British rule; the scion of a rather influential, anti-British family. The apple doesn't fall far from the tree. Maybe he's been secretly harbouring those same views all along and has decided that now is the time to strike. Maybe he's trying to trigger a revolution? He commits a murder which could see the Hindus up in arms. When they find out a policeman's responsible, they'll take to the streets and burn every police station from Calcutta to Karachi. Can you think of a better moment to try to assassinate the chief of police of Bengal?'

I couldn't believe any of it.

'That's ridiculous. Suren didn't kill Mukherjee.'

'Really? He told you that, did he? Then who did kill him?'

I realised I was close to telling Boyle everything. Maybe that's what he'd been angling for all along.

'We don't know. He was already dead when Banerjee found him.'

Boyle shook his head. He leaned in and pressed a finger to my chest.

'Well, here's some advice for you, Wyndham. Find your sergeant, and do it fast. Because if you don't, we will. And if he's responsible for the deaths of these soldiers, some of my colleagues might be keen to settle the score.'

THIRTEEN

Surendranath Banerjee

I alighted at Alipore station. It was not an easy decision. My throat rasped, my belly was empty, and every fibre of my body cried out in fatigue and begged to stay where I was, wedged into a corner of the tram, ignored and anonymous. Weariness dulled my reasoning. As the tram had trundled along, I'd imagined jumping off and disappearing into the masses, then making my way to Howrah and catching a train to Bombay or Delhi.

It was ridiculous of course. There was no refuge to be had in Bombay or Delhi or anywhere else. Any hope of salvation lay in apprehending Gulmohamed and proving that he, and not I, had killed Mukherjee. To have any chance of that I had to get back to the mansion in Metiabruz where he'd been staying. If I could arrest him there, before he managed to leave town, I might just have a chance of saving myself from the gallows.

I stumbled off the tram, shambled into Alipore station and bought a ticket back to Khiddirpur. The platform was quiet, almost genteel and most unlike the station platforms of North Calcutta, which swarmed at all hours with travellers, hawkers, fortune tellers, bootblacks and vagrants. Indeed, other than a few suited and booted Anglo-Indians, the only other persons on the platform were two uniformed men of the railway police, lounging on a bench smoking bidis with their rifles at their feet. Sweat pricked my back.

I told myself there was nothing to fear. While knowledge of my flight would by now have reached Lal Bazar, there was little chance that word of it would have yet reached these two fine gentlemen, and from their languorous repose, it was clear that they were not on the lookout for an escaped fugitive. Nevertheless, I decided to give them a wide berth and turned and walked to the opposite end of the platform. There I sat on a bench under the shade of a neem tree and kept my back to them.

My thoughts turned to Sam and immediately my temples flushed hot. I should not have pointed that pistol at him. He had shown me kindness and loyalty and I had repaid him in the worst possible coin. He would, no doubt, be facing some difficult questions regarding my flight and I wondered what he might say. Would he tell his interlocutors that I had threatened him with a revolver? I expected he'd probably seek to gloss over that most inconvenient fact as it did not reflect particularly positively upon either of us.

The train, when it arrived, was half empty. On another occasion I may have thanked the gods for such an auspicious event, but today I'd have much preferred the camouflage of a crowd, the thicker the better. Nevertheless I boarded a desolate carriage and did my damnedest to disappear, feigning sleep in the shadows of a corner seat.

A conductor in a threadbare coat bearing the insignia of the Eastern Railways appeared just as the train pulled in to the station.

'Fi-nal stop, Khiddirpur. All change please. All change. Khiddirpur!'

I alighted alongside the paltry few remaining passengers and positioned myself as best I could towards the middle of the group and climbed the stairs to the bridge from the platform to the station exit. Ahead, the group began to concertina and I noticed a guard stationed at foot of the descending staircase carefully checking tickets. Of itself, that did not pose difficulty. I had a valid ticket after all. More troubling though was the sight of another officer of the railway police standing directly behind him with a rifle slung over one shoulder and looking far more alert than his two colleagues back in Alipore. I tried to remain calm. Ticket inspections, especially in the rougher parts of town, were sometimes carried out under the auspices of armed support, mainly because only the threat of a bullet between the ears was enough to make some Calcuttans buy a ticket. But those checks tended to be at rush hour, when the number of fines levied, and the number of bribes paid to avoid those fines, would be much higher. The timing seemed curious.

I cursed myself for my stupidity. I could have simply walked to the other end of the platform, then crossed the tracks on foot like a commoner and disappeared into Khiddirpur. Instead I had reverted to my conditioning. I'd used the footbridge like the *bhadralok* idiot I was. If I was to avoid capture, I would need to forget gentlemanly ways and think like a fugitive. I stopped and turned, hoping to double-back towards the platforms, but several more constables had now stationed themselves at the far end, presumably waiting for anyone trying to do just that. Like a guard dog, one of them looked over, aroused by my sudden about-face. I had to think fast. Quickly I peered at the ground, as though I'd dropped my ticket, then bent down and pretended to pick it up. By now I had all but fallen out of the pack of travellers trying to negotiate their way past the ticket inspector. I hastened to join them, hoping to force my way into the centre of the pitifully small group.

The inspector did not seem particularly interested in checking the tickets held out for him, but the look on the face of the armed guard beside him told a different story. He was alert, scrutinising every face. Was it possible that my colleagues were already hunting for me? I kept my head down, controlled my breathing and shuffled forward. The barrier inched closer until I was level with the ticket inspector. I thrust my ticket at him and walked past as calmly as I could.

'Stop!' came a shout from behind me. My entrails froze. I reached into my pocket for the revolver and began to turn. Just then a man hurtled past me, almost knocking me to the ground.

'Stop!' shouted the inspector once more.

Beside him, the guard raised his rifle. But the inspector put a hand on his arm. '*Chèré-dow!*' he cried. 'Let him go! He's a drunken fool. Not worth a bullet.'

I preferred not to wait to see the guard's response. Instead I walked briskly from the station and hailed a tonga to take me back to the mansion in Metiabruz.

FOURTEEN

Sam Wyndham

I trailed Taggart's ambulance to the hospital. As for his condition, the doctors wouldn't say much more than that for now he was alive. I felt the best thing to do was to carry out the orders he'd given me before the attack, namely to find Gulmohamed and bring him in for questioning, and then to speak to Mukherjee's family. Before I had the chance, however, I was accosted by a constable bearing a note recalling me to headquarters.

I made my way back to Lal Bazar, stopping off at a kiosk en route to pick up a copy of the *Statesman* and a new Bengali-language paper, the *Ananda Bazar Patrika*. The latter had launched a few months earlier and was already agitating for Indian independence. The translation of its contents would have to wait till I reached Lal Bazar, but the *Statesman* I scanned right there at the kerbside. There was no mention yet of the attack on the commissioner – it had happened too late for the morning editions – but that wasn't what I was looking for. I scoured the headlines and bylines. There was nothing on the front page, or the next two, for that matter. But there, on page 4, I found it.

Blaze in Budge Budge kills prominent Hindu scholar

There was no mention of murder or the arrest of a serving officer. I breathed a tentative sigh of relief tempered by the knowledge that this was merely the British account of things. What mattered was the Bengali view, and specifically the Hindu view, reflected in their native papers, and something told me the news there wouldn't be found as far back as page 4.

In the end I didn't need to wait for the translation. The scene at Lal Bazar was enough to confirm my fears. Officers wore the grim expressions of men expecting bloodshed, and constables rushed in all directions like wasps departing a hive. The armoury was doing a brisk trade. A line had formed, men waiting for rifles like the faithful outside the temple at Dakshineshwar waiting to be blessed. A steady stream of olive-green trucks trundled into the central courtyard, filling the place with their bass growls and diesel fumes, waiting to be engorged with men before speeding off to the killing zones that were euphemistically called 'flashpoints' across the city.

I made my way to the situation room, a large office on the first floor staffed by a dozen men and with its walls and tables covered in maps of the city and its environs. In emergencies, it was here that reports from all over town arrived, by radio or by messenger, and from which a picture was built of what was happening. Judging by the frenzy, the situation was fluid.

Arrows on a large map marked the movements of a crowd, gathering in the northern suburbs and heading south. Every few minutes, an update would arrive and was marked on the map. A tidal wave, passing along Cossipore ... then Upper Circular Road ... to Harrison Road and Bow Bazar ... washing up against the station at Sealdah ... stopped by police at Dharmatola and funnelled along Lower Circular Road ... At the same time, arrows from the south, from Kidderpore and Kalighat, heading north. All making for the Maidan.

It's difficult to describe a Calcutta riot to one who hasn't witnessed it first hand. I've seen riots in London, big men looting and pillaging down the Mile End Road like the last of the Vikings, but those chaps have nothing on the little folk of this city. It starts, as most riots do, as a protest – a march, a *hartal*, a sit-in – but then something happens. Some invisible force grabs hold and it escalates, intensifying from grievance to raw anger to collective madness like a bush fire whipped into an inferno by unseen winds, and the shadow of death descends as surely as the coming of the night.

There is, I believe, something in the Bengali psyche which is predisposed towards self-destruction. How else can one explain the actions of a people capable of reaching the highest pinnacles of art and poetry and philosophy and yet so quick to fall back into barbarity and the butchering of their own in the name of religion?

There was a summons waiting for me on my desk. The deputy commissioner – a man named Halifax – wanted to see me *urgently*.

Today was the sort of day when everything ended with that particular suffix, but Halifax was the type of man who had to stress the point for fear that otherwise the whole summons would be ignored. He wasn't a bad officer, or a bad man, for that matter. Mild and inoffensive, I'd no doubt that he was a capable administrator; but as a leader, he was like a glass of milk: palatable but you'd prefer something stronger.

His office was on the same floor as Taggart's, but there the similarities ended. The commissioner's office was the size of a small banqueting hall and furnished in the fashion of a French aristocrat. Halifax's room, by contrast, felt closer to classical Sparta than *fin-de-siècle* France. It was small, only slightly larger than the anteroom used by Taggart's secretary, and stocked with little more than a desk, a few chairs, a filing cabinet and a large map of the city, parts of which I imagined might soon be burning to the ground.

Today he could have been forgiven for wanting a bit more space. I knocked and entered a room packed with uniforms and reeking of sweat and tobacco smoke. Four sets of eyes turned to greet me and a space cleared in front of Halifax's desk. The deputy commissioner was seated behind it, looking like a man being forced to partake in a game of Russian roulette.

'Wyndham,' he said. 'Thank God.'

It made a pleasant change from how Lord Taggart usually greeted me.

'Gentlemen,' he said to the assembled officers, 'this is Captain Wyndham. He was with the commissioner when the attack took place.'

One of them, a moustachioed chap in a khaki uniform, addressed me.

'How is he?'

The colour of his uniform and the quantity of silver on his epaulettes marked him out as a senior officer from somewhere outside the city's boundaries. The rest of them, Halifax included, stared expectantly as though I were the prophet Isaiah come to issue a proclamation.

'Alive,' I said.

'Is he going to pull through?'

'The doctors couldn't say.'

Then suddenly the dam broke and I was swamped by a deluge of questions, all of which were highly relevant and none of which I felt like answering.

Halifax looked queasy. 'What happened exactly?'

I told him what I'd told Boyle from Section H: that I'd been too far away to see what had transpired. I knew a car had driven up and bombs had been thrown. Once more, I hoped to leave Banerjee's name out of it, and once more that hope proved forlorn.

'We should move on to the other matter,' said Halifax. He looked up at one of the officers. 'Superintendent Travers?'

The officer cleared his throat.

'As you are aware,' he said, 'the Hindu theologian, Prashant Mukherjee, was murdered yesterday at a house in Budge Budge. Local officers received a report of suspicious persons in the vicinity of the premises. On arrival at the scene, my men apprehended a suspect committing an act of arson. The officers put out the blaze and arrested the individual. The fire had been restricted to two rooms on the ground floor. In one of those rooms were found Mukherjee's charred remains. The body was burned but still iden-tifiable. The arrested individual was taken to Budge Budge thana where he identified himself as Detective Sergeant Surendranath Banerjee, a serving officer here at Lal Bazar.'

The deputy commissioner looked at me.

'I take it he means your chap, Surrender-not.'

I nodded.

'Further to the arrest,' continued Travers, 'we understand that the suspect was subsequently released into the custody of Captain Wyndham upon the orders of Lord Taggart.'

'And where is he now?' asked Halifax.

'At present, sir,' I said, 'his whereabouts are unknown.'

Taggart's deputy blinked.

'What?'

'He was last seen pursuing Lord Taggart's attackers.'

'God's teeth, Wyndham,' said Halifax. 'You mean he's absconded?'

I felt the oppressive stares of the officers upon me. My pulse quickened and abruptly I became aware of the whirr of the ceiling fan, its blades hurtling along their circular course above my head. My throat felt dry.

'It's more complicated than that.'

'Really,' said Halifax. 'Please, enlighten us.'

'Banerjee was in Budge Budge on Lord Taggart's orders. He was attacked outside a building, and when he came to, he stumbled inside in search of assistance. He hadn't a clue whose house it was.

When he wandered in, he found Mukherjee there, already dead. Of course he realised what that meant. News of Mukherjee's murder might spark off a riot, and, he, in what I must say was a foolhardy act of misplaced selflessness, decided that the best course of action was to burn the place down, making it look like Mukherjee had fallen asleep while smoking and died accidentally.'

Travers gave a snort. 'And he expected you to believe that?'

'Lord Taggart believed it,' I said. 'He charged me with apprehending the real killer.'

'And who would that be?'

I'd managed to keep that particular detail from the Section H operative Boyle earlier. I wasn't keen on imparting it to these men either. I looked to Halifax for guidance. The deputy commissioner seemed surprised that I should even need it.

'For God's sake, man, tell him!'

'A Muslim politician by the name of Farid Gulmohamed.'

Halifax stared, transfixed. Travers laughed in disbelief.

'The Union of Islam chap from Bombay?'

'That's correct,' I said. 'Lord Taggart had tasked Banerjee with keeping tabs on him. He followed him to the house in Budge Budge.'

'Is he even *in* Calcutta?' asked Halifax.

'Yes, sir,' I said. 'He arrived two nights ago.'

'It's preposterous,' protested Halifax. 'Why would Gulmohamed come a thousand miles across the country to murder a man like Mukherjee?'

'Lord Taggart raised a similar concern,' I said.

'Wait,' said Travers. 'That may not be as far-fetched as it sounds. Gulmohamed is a Muslim politician. Mukherjee was a Hindu one. The two were natural enemies.'

It sounded as though the man was taking my side. It took me a moment to get over the surprise.

Halifax shook his head. 'That's hardly proof of anything. By that token, every Union of Islam supporter and politician in Calcutta could have killed Mukherjee instead and saved Gulmohamed the train fare.'

Travers raised a placatory hand. 'I'm not saying I believe Wyndham's story, merely that the concept isn't as far-fetched as it might initially seem.'

'It's not *my* story,' I said, 'and it makes more sense than the alternative, that a police officer of five years' loyal service is somehow responsible. Consider it: Banerjee is a Hindu. What possible motive could he have to murder Mukherjee, a co-religionist and man he'd probably never even met before?'

'And the attack on Taggart?' asked Travers. 'It was just a coincidence then that your man Banerjee disappears along with the attackers?'

'Believe me,' I said, 'there's no way the sergeant could have been aware of it. He spent last night languishing in a prison cell. He had no idea that Taggart would ask me to bring him to his house rather than Lal Bazar.'

'In my eyes he's still a suspect,' said Travers. 'Maybe he and you were followed from Budge Budge to Taggart's house by his accomplices? Maybe the bomb attack wasn't an assassination attempt but a bid to free Banerjee? Maybe Taggart's presence was, for them, a fortuitous extra?'

'If they were there to rescue Banerjee,' I said, 'then why didn't they take him with them? The truth is, they drove up, threw their bombs, fired their guns, and then drove off. Banerjee tried to stop them, not accompany them.'

Travers gave a thin smile. 'And yet, Captain, he's now nowhere to be found.'

'Travers is right,' said Halifax. 'Our priorities are to find Banerjee and keep a lid on this Mukherjee situation. The family has requested the body back *tout de suite* – a request I've granted. There are already reports of rioting in Cossipore. Any insinuation that this was a religious murder needs to be nipped in the bud and it has to be done now.'

'If I may,' said Travers. 'Section H are already conducting the investigation into the attack on Lord Taggart. As the issue of Mukherjee's murder and the absconding of Sergeant Banerjee seem linked to it, would it not make sense for them to take charge of both of these matters?'

I made to protest but the deputy commissioner cut me short.

'Be quiet, Wyndham. You're to have no further involvement in any of this. You're too close to the whole bloody mess anyway.' He turned to Travers. 'The Mukherjee situation I'll try to pass to Section H. As for Banerjee ... for now it's better if we conduct the hunt for one of our own.'

FIFTEEN

Surendranath Banerjee

The shutters were falling on the shopfronts.

Across Metiabruz, fear infused the air as word spread that trouble was coming. In the Hindu heartlands to the north, smoke, soot-black and charred, was already rising, ominous as an approaching storm.

This road, when I had passed along it the previous day, had been vibrant with the colours of the bazaar: the reds and emerald greens of the vegetable market, the silver of the fish and the entreaties of the stallholders. Now the market was dead, the stalls reduced to skeletons of bamboo and canvas, shorn of produce or patrons.

I wondered if the people here knew what had occurred. How did they know to batten down the hatches? Was it sixth sense or perhaps collective memory? Did smoke rising in the north necessarily portend to violence heading south? I wondered how many of them even knew who Mukherjee was, and why his death should trigger a saffron-clad cataclysm. Or did they consider it just another act of God, as inexplicable as a flood or a plague of locusts?

I ordered the tonga-wallah to halt so that I might purchase a newspaper – a Bangla paper – the only kind on sale here, from an old man who was hurriedly locking up the box, no more than a few feet high and wide in which he sat, cross-legged, for twelve hours a day. He seemed bemused that anyone should seek to buy a newspaper when the news itself was would soon fall upon us.

The front page carried news of Mukherjee's demise and declared the circumstances 'suspicious'. The language was inflammatory – quite literally, in that it noted the fire at the house he was found in. There was scant mention of suspects, but the claim of arson, perpetrated by those opposed to the man's views, was clear. And while blame was apportioned obliquely rather than squarely, it left its readership in no doubt that the finger of accusation was pointed at the door of the Muslims. I felt nauseous, as though I'd been kicked in the stomach. My attempt to mask the killing – an act committed in desperation and a heartfelt desire to avoid a bloodbath – had not just failed, but was now being co-opted into the very narrative of hatred which I had sought to derail.

I should have known better. People always fit the facts to suit their own agenda. My actions had done nothing to prevent communal violence, merely changed the perceived means of murder from a strangulation to arson. And for that I had put my own head in a noose.

I returned to the tonga and once more continued the journey down the road, through the Islamic arch, to the mansions by the Hooghly where I had met the woman playing the santoor and where Gulmohamed was supposed to be staying. Once more I walked up the gravel path. This time there was no music. Indeed there was no sound of any kind. Even the birds in the trees had fallen silent.

I walked up the steps, past stone balustrades intricately carved into geometric patterns which cast a latticework of shadows on the ground. The veranda was empty, its rattan chairs and table abandoned like the deck of a ghost ship. The solid double door was shut fast, barred from the inside. I tugged at the bell-pull and waited.

The air broiled and minutes passed; enough time for me to take stock of my pitiable situation. I had attempted to save lives, to avert a calamity, and because of that, I was now a fugitive, on the run from my colleagues and a hangman's noose. I remembered my thoughts from the previous time I had stood here. I had stared at Gulmohamed's niece and cautioned myself against any romantic flights of fancy. Well, that would not be necessary now, or ever again. My life as I had known it was finished. My career was over, and with it had gone any hopes of a suitable marriage and all the other trappings, large and petty, which marked out the position and progress of the *bhadralok* through life. There was no way back. Salvation, if there was any to be had, lay in moving forward, and following matters to their bitter conclusion.

From above came the metallic creak of an unoiled hinge and the thump of a wooden shutter striking the wall.

'*Ké?*' The voice was female.

I stepped back off the veranda in order to make myself visible. A maid looked out from between the bars of a first-floor window.

'*Kee chow?*' she asked angrily.

I sensed fear in her voice; apprehension masked with aggression. As a policeman my instinct was to take advantage of that fear, threaten her with the direst of consequences if she failed to comply with my instructions. But that was not possible now. I could not tell her I was a policeman, indeed I could not be sure that I still was one, and I feared that threats might only make matters worse. The circumstances dictated delicacy.

'*Didi,*' I said, '*ami Gulmohamed sahiber sandhān kōrchee. Bapār-ta khoobi dorkāree.*' I told her I was looking for Gulmohamed, impressed upon her the urgency.

She turned from the window and exchanged whispered words with someone veiled by the shadows.

'*Darao,*' she said, returning to the window. *Wait there.*

I did as she commanded, walked back to the door and waited. From inside came the scrape of a beam being lifted and a chain being loosened.

The door opened and before me stood not the maidservant but the woman who'd earlier mesmerised me with her playing of the santoor, Gulmohamed's niece.

'So,' she said, 'Mr Union of Islam. You've returned.'

'That's correct, memsahib.'

'What happened to your face?'

Instinctively I reached for the bruises.

'I had some trouble with the *dadas* of a certain *pārā*.'

'You were attacked?'

'We had a disagreement,' I conceded. 'Please, it is imperative that I speak with your uncle. He is here?'

She looked at me the way another woman might examine a new sari in a textile shop, as though assessing whether I was worth more of her time and attention. '*Imperative*? Well, in that case you'd better come in.'

I smiled gratefully, removed the cap from my head and followed her inside.

The house was decorated, if not like a Mogul's palace, then at least like his hunting lodge. On the walls, portraits of bejewelled princes jockeyed for position with sepia-hued photographs of moon-faced maharanis with the eyes of temptresses.

She led me through to the drawing room with Mogul miniatures on the mantel and a tired-looking tiger-skin on the floor. In the centre were two fading, brocaded sofas. I had hoped to find Gulmohamed seated there but the room was empty. The woman directed me to one of the sofas while she took a seat on the other. I did as directed, avoiding standing on the skin of the poor tiger, whose head still remained attached, jaws open in a final, silent snarl.

She pressed a brass button in the wall beside her. The door opened and I turned as the maid entered, head bowed.

'Tea?' asked the woman.

Was it normal in Muslim circles to offer tea to a lowly messenger?

I declined. 'I simply need to speak to your uncle.'

'Of course,' she said with a nod, but there was something in the manner of it, something which felt disturbing. She turned to the maid. '*Jao.*'

The servant left silently, closing the door behind her.

'Will Mr Gulmohamed be long?'

She smiled. 'I'm sorry,' she said. 'I didn't ask your name.'

'My name?' I stammered. I hadn't thought to give myself a name. 'Asif,' I mumbled. It was the first one to pop into my head. 'Asif Khan.'

'You are from Calcutta?'

'No, memsahib. From Dhaka.'

She leaned forward. 'Really? I have family in Dhaka. Perhaps we are neighbours?'

A family of her wealth and standing would never live in the same neighbourhood as the family of the poor boy I was claiming to be. She was toying with me. I just didn't know why.

I smiled like a fool and shook my head. '*Nā, memsahib.* I don't think so.'

'Where in Dhaka does your family live?' she continued.

'Why do you ask?'

It was her turn to smile. 'I want to know in which school in Dhaka you learned an English word like *imperative.*'

I cursed myself for my stupidity. The word *imperative* would not feature in a poor boy's lexicon. For that matter, neither would the word *lexicon*.

'Why don't you tell me who you *really* are.'

I thought it over for a moment and decided I had precious little to lose by telling her the truth. She would find out soon enough anyway given I was here to arrest her uncle.

'I'm from the police,' I said.

Her eyes opened wide. 'A spy?'

'A detective.'

'You don't look very much like a detective.'

'It has been a difficult few days.'

'That much is clear,' she said, gesturing to my blackened eye. 'And you have identification?'

I reached into my pocket and realised that my papers were still sitting in the safe in Budge Budge thana.

'Not upon me,' I said. 'I have been working undercover. I must speak to your uncle *now*. Or people across this city are going to die.'

A shadow fell across her face; an errant cloud venturing before the sun.

'You're trying to frighten me?'

I shook my head. 'I wish that were so, but it's not. Now, miss, if you would rather not be arrested, please tell me what I need to know. Where is your uncle?'

'I don't know.'

I was not sure whether to believe her.

'Please tell me the truth. North Calcutta is already burning and unless I can find your uncle, things may get a lot worse.'

'He's not here,' she said. 'He left almost an hour ago.'

'Where was he going?'

She shrugged. 'Back to Bombay.'

Sam would have cautioned me against trusting her. He would have reminded me that I had a propensity for accepting the word of a woman without scrutiny. He would say it without irony too, forgetting the many, many occasions where he had believed a woman more on the strength of her perfume than of her statement. But Sam was not here and I did not believe that this woman was lying. I opted to trust my instinct, and in any case, I had very little option. What was the alternative? Was I to single-handedly search the whole house? All it required was one telephone call to the local thana to check my credentials and the game would be up. The black truth was that the authorities were hunting for me, not Gulmo-hamed, and my time was running out.

'Is he leaving from Howrah station?'

She looked at me as though I was being obtuse. 'Unless he's decided to take the scenic route and go by steamer, how else would he get there?'

I doubted very much that Gulmohamed would be taking the scenic route.

'And before you ask,' she continued, 'the fastest route from here to Howrah would be by boat, and no, I don't know the times of the ferry. Now, I take it there is nothing else you wish to ask?'

'A few last things,' I said. 'May I know your name, miss?'

'Ayisha,' she said with a smile.

'Well, Miss Ayisha, you couldn't, by any chance, lend me twenty rupees?'

She could not help but laugh.

'The disguise of a poor peon has certain drawbacks,' I said, 'one of which is a limit to the amount of cash I am able to carry. I didn't envisage chasing your uncle twice to Metiabruz and back.'

It was a lie, of course. I had started out yesterday with my wallet brimming with silver. Most of it though, as well as the wallet, was now in the pockets of the arresting officers at Budge Budge.

She rose, walked over to a sideboard and opened a drawer, before returning with two crisp ten-rupee notes. She held them out, but then thought better of it.

'Before I give you these, don't you think I deserve to know your real name too? I mean, how can I be sure I'll get my money back?'

'Believe me, I shall make sure you get it back,' I said. 'And my name is Surendranath Banerjee.'

'Surendranath Banerjee,' she said, trying it out. 'Now that *is* the name of a man who'd know a word like *imperative*.'

SIXTEEN

Sam Wyndham

It didn't matter what Halifax or any of the other top brass thought. I knew Suren was innocent. The question was how I could prove it. Halifax had barred me from the investigation and insisted I focus on the other cases on my desk, but that wasn't going to happen. For one thing, those consisted of a forgery case and the murder of an accountant in South Calcutta where the perpetrator was clearly the wife, because, well, who doesn't marry an accountant and end up regretting it?

Even at the best of times, I'd have had no great inclination to follow up either. Now, with Suren facing the gallows, I wasn't about to waste my time looking for a petty criminal churning out bent five-bob notes in Howrah or locking up a forty-year-old Catholic woman who'd given the best years of her life to a bean-counter and decided quite reasonably that she'd had enough of it.

I returned to my office, picked up my jacket, revolver and, most importantly, my cigarettes, and headed out into the afternoon heat. I made my way across the courtyard to the garages in search of a car. An oil-stained engineer sat on a stool outside, smoking. He saw me approach and shook his head.

'Can't help ya, guvnor,' he said, dropping the fag end and crushing it under his boot. 'All vehicles've already been requisitioned. 'Alifax's orders.'

'You've got nothing?' I asked. 'Not even a motorcycle?'

'You got a chit?'

'What?'

'You're supposed to 'ave a signed requisition chit before we release any vehicles. Normally we let it slide, but 'Alifax wants it enforced. No chit, no motorbike.'

'Make an exception,' I said. 'It's a life-and-death situation.'

'*Life'n death*? It's always life'n death wi' you chaps, innit? Well, today the whole *city's* havin' a life'n death situation in case you ain't noticed.'

I tried one last, reasonable roll of the dice.

'Maybe one of your men could drop me where I need to go.'

The engineer smirked, and I saw satisfaction in his eyes: the revenge of the forgotten man getting one over on his superiors.

'We ain't runnin' a taxi service, mate.'

I gave up and walked out of the courtyard into the deserted streets beyond. Even the ever-eager rickshaw-wallahs were missing. This wasn't just the post-noon siesta that saw natives and Englishmen alike forsake the streets and the sun for the fan-induced cool of the interior. This was something different, something more dangerous. The air seemed to burn, charged with the electric threat of violence.

I headed east along Bow Bazar, towards a distant roar, like waves smashing against a cliff. From the reports, the ring of steel protecting the central district was only a few blocks away, somewhere close to the Upper Circular Road.

I walked past shuttered shopfronts and smiling advertising hoardings that felt like they'd fallen from a different city. Signs of the tumult ahead, though, were soon apparent, be it the growing crescendo of a crowd or the oil-tinged, throat-rasping smoke that hung in the air.

I reached as far as the intersection with Amherst Street. On the far side, the route was blocked by a ragged line of white and a couple of burning tram cars. The constables, armed with lathis and little else, looked on nervously as a large body of men, several thousand strong, headed past them, chanting slogans, brandishing makeshift weapons and crude banners bearing words daubed in black and red.

A constable with the insignia of the traffic police on his shoulder and armed with only a bamboo shield and lathi ran over. He seemed relieved to see me, as though I might be the cavalry.

'Who's in charge?' I said.

His brow creased in consternation.

'No one, sir.'

'What are your orders?'

'To prevent looting and to guide the crowd along Circular Road.'

I looked over at the burning tram cars and the motley collection of a dozen men holding the line. Their usual job was to direct traffic and here they were facing a religious mob. They were doing their best to avoid the gaze of the crowd, which felt like some huge beast wending its way south. If it had a change of heart, it could wipe out this paltry detachment in minutes.

From windows and balconies above, people looked on. Religious disturbances were hardly something new. They tended to break out every year on some pretext or another: Muslims rioting because some Hindus played loud music too close to a mosque; Hindus because of rumours that Muslims had slaughtered a cow somewhere or carried out a procession in the wrong part of town. But this seemed to be on a different scale. The crowds seemed bigger, more organised.

The main body took a good ten minutes to pass, and then came the idiots and hotheads, and that's when the trouble started.

A hail of missiles pummelled the police line, and not for the first time I cursed the ease with which bricks were to be found lying around Calcutta. A few of the younger constables were itching to join battle, but their older colleagues would tell them that was foolhardy, given the proximity of the main body of the protest. All it would take would be the incendiary spark of policemen beating up a few miscreants for the whole mass of thousands to turn round and fall on us like a storm.

'Sir?' asked the constable, as though I had any more idea of how to deal with a rioting mob than he did.

I looked around. To one side a number of carts and bicycle wagons – the type used to transport goods around the city – lay abandoned outside boarded-up shops.

'Pull those carts over,' I said. 'Tell your men to set up a secondary perimeter. Block the road and take what shelter you can behind it. If any of those rock-throwing bastards try to get past, we'll deal with them individually.'

'Yes, sir,' he said, as a dozen feet away, a glass bottle dropped from the sky and exploded into flames.

I dived for cover. 'Go!' I shouted and the constable sprinted off to organise his colleagues. The hail of projectiles grew heavier. Picking myself up, I reached for my Webley and ran for the middle of the street.

A revolver in the face has a way of focusing the mind and immediately the deluge lightened. The thugs took a few steps back; a few moments to consider their options and their futures. The respite would only be temporary. Young *goondahs* were like wolves confronting fire. You could scare them for a while, but they'd regroup and be back. I just hoped I'd bought enough time for the constables to establish their makeshift barricade.

The rioters began to hurl their bricks again, but from further back and from behind the acrid black smoke billowing from the abandoned tram cars. The constables, displaying admirable grace under fire, wheeled the carts into position and I hopped behind the hastily assembled fortification as another volley of petrol bombs descended.

I ventured a glance over the parapet. Our retreat seemed to have emboldened them and the numbers on the other side were growing. I hoped these new arrivals were just stragglers from the main crowd, rather than more thugs looking for violence, but such people have a way of sniffing out trouble, and before long, the mob in front of us had swelled to what seemed like fifty or sixty youths wielding blades and makeshift weapons.

The constable who had become my de facto second in command looked nervously towards me. By now he must have realised that I was less the cavalry and more General Custer. None of them were trained for this sort of thing. Indeed some of them looked like they hadn't trained for anything at all in years.

The mob was becoming more brazen, sensing their own strength and our weakness, inching forward, every minute getting closer to the barricade. The wind shifted, blowing the smoke from the blazing tram cars no longer at our attackers but down the road.

I thought fast. Our sorry band was in danger of being overrun and this wasn't the ditch I intended to die in. I turned to the constable.

'On my command, get your men ready to fall back.'

His face flushed in relief. He nodded and passed the word along.

'Now!' I shouted. I drew my pistol, clambered up onto one of the carts and fired a shot, making sure to aim a few inches above head height.

Those in the front line ducked or lay flat on the ground. The others retreated, taking shelter in doorways. I loosed off another shot then looked round. Behind me, the traffic-wallahs had scarpered. They seemed to have taken my command to fall back as a general invitation to run for their lives, and I couldn't really blame

them. It seemed high time I too got out of there, and as if to empha-
sise the point, a brick came out of nowhere and struck me on the
shoulder. I lost my footing and crashed onto the cart. A roar went
up from the mob and several of the youths ran forward.

I clambered to my feet, but it was too late. Men were climbing
onto the barricade. Retreat was still possible, but only if I shot
someone, and I didn't want to have to do that. But the matter was
taken out of my hands. A thug in a black shirt and a handkerchief
tied over his mouth jumped up and came at me with a makeshift
machete – the large curved blade of a *boti*, the Bengali fish-gutting
knife, nailed to a wooden handle. He swung at me, hacking the air
as I swerved to avoid it. I gambled, bent low and took my boot to
his knee. The man cried out and I pushed him back over the barricade. There wasn't time for any further heroics. I jumped down,
hoping to follow my erstwhile troops back along Bow Bazar and
ran, making for the mouth of a *gullee* and praying that the youths
would be too busy looking to loot the shops on the main road to
bother following me.

I sprinted to the corner and down the darkened lane, splashing
through waste water and mud. It was only when I reached Harrison
Road that I saw the carnage. Burnt-out buildings, and bodies,
hacked to pieces and left for the crows in the middle of the street.
There was nothing to be done. No one to help. The dead were dead
and the living had fled, leaving the streets to the dogs.

I uttered a string of curses: against Indians both Hindu and
Muslim, against my own kind for stirring up the passions between
the two, and against Calcutta, for just existing. At that moment I
hated the benighted city and its people more than I had ever hated
the Boche during the war. I hated what it was and what its people
did to one another. And, I realised, I hated it all because this damn
city had become my home. Halifax had ordered me to steer clear of
the Mukherjee case, and I was hardly about to do that. Not when

Suren's fate was at stake, and certainly not when the whole city seemed intent on tearing itself apart.

In a daze, I headed for home. There was a chance, albeit a small one, that Suren would have gone there. With the police now charged with his capture, it might be a foolhardy move, but there'd been a window of a few hours, between his flight from Taggart's house and the authorities getting their act together, for him to have gone there and maybe left a note, telling me what he was up to.

Premchand Boral Street was thankfully untouched by the violence, probably because it wasn't much of a target. It was a road of misfits, of low-rent boarding houses and mid-rent brothels and university dormitories. And that had probably saved it too. Not even Calcutta students are keen on burning down their own part of town.

It was the domain of idling academics by day and lonely middle-aged men after dark, and a strange choice for lodgings, especially if you valued your sleep, but it was also the sort of place where nobody interfered in your business, and that was worth more to me than quiet nights and whitewashed walls.

I climbed the stairs with the doleful tread of the weary. I'd have been only too happy to simply retreat to my room, fall into my bed and sleep for ten hours straight. And maybe when I awoke this whole nightmare would have passed. But I knew that wasn't going to happen. The only way to get through this was to find Suren and arrest the man who'd really killed Mukherjee.

I made it to the first-floor landing and froze. The front door was ajar. Silently I reached for my Webley, inching forward, past the door and into the darkened hallway. The place was still as a tomb, but I sensed trouble. Light was streaming in from the sitting room and I slowly made my way through. The place looked like it had been struck by a typhoon. Books and chairs lay strewn and broken on the floor. There was no sign of Suren or our manservant, Sandesh. I dashed through and checked the other rooms. In each the scene was similar, uprooted furniture and overturned belongings.

I was in Suren's bedroom when I heard the creak of a door behind me. I swung round and found myself pointing the revolver straight at Sandesh. He sported a burst lip and the beginnings of a black eye.

I breathed out in relief and lowered the gun.

'Sam *babu*, you are alive!'

I hadn't expected quite such a fervent reaction. Maybe he was concussed.

'Are you OK?'

He gave a slight bow of the head. '*Hā*, sahib.'

'Who did this?' I asked. 'The police?'

The question seemed to shock him. That was understandable. He knew both I and Suren were policemen. Why then would the police raid our flat and beat him up?

'No, sahib. *Goondahs* came. Looking for Suren babu. I tell them he is not coming home yesterday. They not believing.'

I muttered a curse. That sounded like Uddam Singh's men. In all that had happened, the gangster had hardly been at the forefront of my concerns. And yet, with Hindu mobs on the rampage and the city in flames, there was no doubt that Singh's men were involved, or at least taking full advantage.

'Sahib,' Sandesh continued, 'Suren *babu* is all right?'

'I hope so,' I said.

I walked back to the sitting room with Sandesh two paces behind, and surveyed the damage. On second inspection it seemed the devastation had been meant as a threat. I ran a hand through my hair. I needed to sort out this matter with Singh before someone, probably me, ended up dead.

'Sahib.'

I turned to find Sandesh brandishing a bottle.

'I saved the whisky.'

I left Sandesh and headed back out to the street. I had a lot to do, from speaking to Mukherjee's widow to finding Suren. I added Uddam Singh to the list and another man, a young politician I'd met several years earlier and threatened to arrest. Now I hoped he might be able to do me a favour.

But to do any of that I first needed transport. I couldn't get a police vehicle, not without a chit from Halifax, and of my few friends, only a couple owned cars. Explaining to them that I wanted to borrow their vehicle for a jaunt around town in the midst of a riot might prove tricky. Fortunately, there was one person whom I thought might see their way clear to lending me a car. It would take a lot of persuasion though, and possibly some flowers too.

SEVENTEEN

Sam Wyndham

It was a smart block. The type you might find in St John's Wood or Knightsbridge and where the residences inside were called apartments by their owners rather than flats. It was situated on a leafy lane just off Park Street, glinting so bright in the afternoon sun that it might have been painted the week before. I climbed the steps to the columned entrance and introduced myself to a concierge who, short of a visiting maharajah, was possibly the finest dressed Indian in the city.

'Captain Wyndham to see Miss Grant.'

The man looked up from behind a large desk and a pair of thick spectacles and eyed me warily.

I didn't blame him. I'd been up for over thirty-six hours straight, and hadn't had a shave or change of clothes in that time. Still, I did have a bunch of flowers. Ne'er-do-wells didn't often turn up with a bouquet when they're out casing a joint.

'Memsahib is expecting you?' he asked.

I gave him a smile.

'Absolutely.'

He picked up the telephone receiver from the desk in front of him and dialled. 'One moment, sir.'

I waited, strumming my fingers on his desk while he waited for a connection to Annie's apartment. There came a click from the receiver and the concierge sat straighter. From the sudden change in his posture I guessed Annie herself had answered.

'A Captain Wyndham here to see you, Miss Grant.'

I held my breath.

The concierge replaced the receiver and looked up.

'Please follow me.'

It was only one flight of stairs but the concierge insisted we take the lift, and who was I to argue with a man with so much gold braid on his uniform?

He opened the grate and I followed him into an elevator car bedecked in walnut. Pulling the cage closed, he pressed a polished brass button and the contraption jerked to life. Annie hadn't been here long. Having found the suburbs too dull, she'd moved back to the city just over six months earlier and I'd only visited her here once before, though *visited* was probably not the right word. I'd been invited essentially for a dressing-down. A chap she'd been out with by the name of Hobbs, had been stopped outside the Great Eastern by a copper for being drunk and disorderly. He tried to deal with the issue in the time-honoured fashion by giving the chap a little *donation* to go away and was promptly arrested on a charge of attempting to bribe an officer of the Crown and thrown in a cell for twenty-four hours. Somehow, Annie had got it into her head that the whole thing had been my doing. Granted I *had* bought him several drinks earlier that evening, and agreed, it was a freak occurrence that Suren should be the police officer passing when the drunken fool had stumbled out of the hotel, and yes, as a detective sergeant, cautioning drunkards was outside of his usual purview – but as I pointed out to Miss Grant, Suren was a dedicated officer, ready to uphold the law wherever and in whatever capacity the situation called for, and to accuse either him or me of some form of vendetta was both ludicrous and insulting.

Annie was waiting at the door to her apartment. She didn't seem exactly thrilled to see me, but she'd told the concierge to bring me up so how furious could she really be?

'Sam Wyndham, as I live and breathe. To what do I owe the pleasure?'

I held out the flowers, and she stared at them as though I were presenting her with my laundry. I remembered another man who'd once bought her flowers. He'd been a prince and had sent her two bouquets a day. He was murdered soon afterwards. There was probably a lesson in there somewhere.

'Flowers?' she said suspiciously. 'What do you want?'

I considered giving her some flannel, something about contrition and an apology for past sins, but she deserved better than that.

'I need to borrow your car.'

'Just like that? You turn up here for the first time in months and it's not to say sorry for what you did to poor Reggie Hobbs but to ask for my car? That's brazen, even by your standards.'

'You're right,' I said, palms raised in surrender, 'and this is hardly the sort of conversation I wish to be having, but there's no time for a proper explanation. You know what's going on out there. What's more, Suren's disappeared and he's mixed up in it all.'

Annie sighed. 'It's never straightforward with you, is it, Sam?'

She had a point.

I puffed out my cheeks. 'Where's the fun in straightforward?'

She went into one of the rooms, leaving me standing in the hallway, before returning, holding up a set of keys.

'Here you go,' she said, throwing them over. I caught them and was about to say something, then thought better of it. Annie, however, read the expression on my face.

'Don't tell me you want my chauffeur too?'

'Would you mind?'

She shook her head, then reached for the telephone on the side-board. I waited as she put the call in to the concierge.

'Ram, tell my driver to be ready. Captain Wyndham will be borrowing him and the car.

She replaced the receiver. 'Anything else?'

I felt her tone to be needlessly sarcastic.

'Just one last thing. Are you seeing anyone at the moment?'

She stared at me. 'Why? Do you want to know who else to throw in jail?'

'I just thought I might take you to dinner sometime.'

She shook her head in that exasperated manner of hers.

'Get out, Sam. Go and do whatever it is you need to do. And when you find Suren, tell him I'll be having words with him.'

EIGHTEEN

Surendranath Banerjee

The ferries were running late, most likely due to whatever was occurring further upriver. By the time one arrived the sky was already ochre, presaging the onset of dusk, and as the boat sailed north, the few passengers on board fell into an unnatural silence as the dark pall of smoke hanging over the northern suburbs came closer.

'*Gālō*,' tutted a man close by. '*Purō shohōr ta gālō*,' – and at that point I found it difficult to dispute his sentiment that the whole city was finished.

On the left bank, the lights of Howrah began to emerge, blinking solemnly. The smoke was heavier here, the air tinged with the scent of burning. Then, as the boat rounded a bend in the river, out of the haze appeared the great bulk of the station, steady like a rock in the midst of a sea of lorry lights. It was then that I began to appreciate the true horror of what was happening.

Our ferry might have been all but empty, but those arriving from upriver sat low in the water, weighed down by a mass of bodies and possessions. At the ghat-side the boats queued, waiting to disgorge their passengers and behind them, on the east bank, Calcutta burned.

I worried for my family in Shyambazar, and consoled myself with the thought that communal violence, like most violence, tended to be carried out upon the poor, and that the better off, regardless of religion, generally came through the whole episode more or less unscathed.

The ferry eventually reached the quayside, tying up beside another which had docked at the jetty, and we passengers had to jump from one boat to the next in order to reach the gangplanks over the slick black mud of the riverbank.

No one was checking tickets at the landing. The few men of the ferry company were overwhelmed by the sheer number of souls, carrying everything from blankets to livestock, fighting to reach the station. Instead the booths stood empty and the turnstiles clattered round unmanned. I joined the lines of the destitute, streaming through the gates and made for the station.

The station approaches too were a maelstrom, as the waves of bodies pressed to gain entry against a cordon of sepoys, while other detachments, ferried in from the outlying areas, waited for army lorries to take them to their assignments across the city. At certain points the cordon blossomed, the single ring of troops expanded into groups of men checking the papers of those seeking to enter. At these points, rudimentary lines were forming and a semblance of order beginning to take shape.

I looked on from my vantage point, wondering what the criteria for entry would be. Maybe they were allowing entry only to those already holding a ticket. Maybe it was a system based upon destination, with access granted only to trains leaving within the hour. Whatever it was, I realised that as a nationally renowned politician, Gulmohamed was more than likely to be able to talk his way inside, whereas I, a fugitive from my own colleagues, would doubtless find it more difficult. For all I knew, Gulmohamed may already have arrived and made his way past the cordon and into the station. Nevertheless, I still had to try to find him before he boarded the Bombay train.

I joined the ranks of those queuing at what seemed the shortest line. Ahead, some two hundred souls stood snaking down to the riverbank. The queue moved in the manner of a newborn foal, every so often shuffling a few uncertain steps forward before stuttering to a halt once more. The act of queuing, at least in a line of my own countrymen, had become somewhat foreign to me. In the native districts of Calcutta, a policeman generally would not have to. Yesterday, I might simply have waltzed to the front, brandished my papers, made up some story and passed through without a second thought. But that was yesterday and it was staggering to comprehend just how precipitously I'd fallen since then.

Yet I had to do something. At the rate this line was moving, Gulmohamed would be in Bombay before I reached the front of it. I required a speedier method of ingress. It was then that I had my flash of inspiration.

Leaving my place in the line, I ran for the front of the station, to the area that usually functioned as the taxi rank but had now been commandeered by the military for use as a loading point, where soldiers arriving on the troop trains boarded the lorries for dispatch across the city. Here the cordon was thinner, irregular and porous on account of the fact that behind it were whole battalions of troops. No unauthorised civilians had much hope of entering the station past them. But not *all* civilians were unauthorised.

To one side stood the men I was looking for, their thin, red-shirted bodies huddled close in conversation. Grim-faced, they smoked their bidis and disapprovingly surveyed the scene.

At first the exodus from the city must have seemed to them a godsend. With such numbers making for the station, some with all their worldly possessions on their backs, it should have been a time for these men, the porters of Howrah station, to make hay. They could charge double, treble or ten times the usual rate to transport goods into the station and someone would still pay it. But then the army had arrived and restricted access. Now the men stood around listlessly, smoking and waiting when they should have been making a small fortune.

I ambled over, watched warily by several of them. Men are curious creatures. Some are essentially unknowable, while others have their souls written on their faces. I selected the one with the kindest expression – an older fellow in a grimy red turban and with stiff silver bristles on his chin.

'*Dada*,' I said in Bengali, 'I need your help.'

I explained to him that my wife and child had arrived shortly before the army had closed access and were waiting inside the station. I'd had to tend to my ailing mother, and had been delayed in reaching here and was now stuck on the wrong side of the cordon. From my pocket I took ten rupees from the twenty that Gulmohamed's niece, Ayisha, had lent me. I held out the note and asked to swap clothes.

Five minutes later, I was dressed in his sweat-coarsened red shirt and turban, and with my eyes down I headed for a gap in the military cordon.

NINETEEN

Sam Wyndham

You had to hand it to Annie. Her taste in cars was better than her taste in men. This one was a red Lancia, fitted with the sort of springs that made it glide along like a feather bed.

My initial stop was at Lal Bazar to locate a couple of addresses. The first was that of Prashant Mukherjee where I hoped I could find his widow. That wasn't difficult. It was an address in Ballygunge, not Budge Budge, and it was recorded in the FIR – the First Information Report – effectively the charge sheet against Suren.

The other was for Subhash Bose. Bose was a young acolyte of the Congress leader, C. R. Das, whom I'd first met during the Prince of Wales's visit to Calcutta in the winter of '21, when Suren and I were on the hunt for a serial killer. Like Suren, Bose was a Cambridge graduate and, by all accounts, just as full of himself. Indeed, the government had hoped he'd join the Civil Service and work for us, but instead he'd sat the exams, come pretty much top and then immediately resigned his position and joined the independence movement. He was a clever man and a capable one, which made him a target of vilification for the editors and readers of the *Statesman* and the *Englishman*, a hero to Indians, and a general pain in the backside for the police.

He lived, I recalled, somewhere along the Elgin Road, and again, finding his address was hardly difficult. He'd been placed under police surveillance several times in the last few years and his house was even marked on the maps in certain offices at police headquarters.

I decided on finding Bose first. Elgin Road was in South Calcutta, en route to Ballygunge, so it made logistical sense. What's more, and with due respect to the widow Mukherjee, I felt Bose would be of more use in stemming the violence, which, as I'd seen for myself, was now threatening to spiral.

I directed Annie's chauffeur to head south, past the detachments of troops deployed in the *cordon sanitaire* around the centre of town and the white suburbs. The hope was to contain the violence to the north of the city, with the river acting as a natural breakwater to the west and the salt lakes providing the same role to the east. It was fine in theory, but communal riots weren't a tide that could be stemmed by ditches or rings of steel. They were more like bushfires that broke out in several places simultaneously and randomly. Just because you limited one riot to North Calcutta didn't mean another one wouldn't break out in the south or across the river in Howrah. The authorities knew that of course, but there was a limit to the number of men available for deployment, and in a case of finite resources, the first priorities were always the white parts of town.

Bose's house was a curious affair. It didn't seem particularly grand from the roadside, at least not by the standards of South Calcutta, just a three-storey edifice, built all the way to the pavement with a gate offering access to a driveway along one side. It was only once you took that turn and entered the drive that you realised the house was almost a city block long, with a low, colonnaded veranda and upper floors burnished with intricately carved, green-painted balconies.

The driver pulled to a halt under the portico and I stepped out and made for the steps to the front door. The veranda fizzed with an energy borne of adversity, as earnest-looking men in white shirts and dhotis rushed in and out carrying, I assumed, situation reports from across town, much in the same way our police runners were bringing updates to the top brass at headquarters.

Outside the door stood a young lad with the smooth cheeks of an adolescent and the bored countenance of a university student.

'Can I help you?' he asked.

'I'm looking for Subhash Bose,' I said. 'My name's Wyndham and I'm from the police.'

The boy's face turned sour.

'Don't worry,' I said, 'I'm not here to arrest him. I'm here because I need his help.'

He smiled in surprise. 'The police want Subhash-da's help? He will find that most amusing. Come.' He turned and gestured for me to follow.

The hallway beyond had been turned into a waiting room, with a row of chairs lined up against either wall, most occupied by young men, some engaged in heated conversation and others simply sitting there, reading papers or pamphlets or smoking.

My guide walked up to a chap who sat behind a desk at the end of the room and said something in rapid-fire Bengali which I presumed was an introduction of sorts. The other stared at me as though assessing my credentials, and I stared straight back. Was he a secretary? He certainly looked like one: small, bookish, bespectacled, and probably with a Napoleon complex to boot.

He turned back to the boy who'd brought me in. There was another brief conversation in Bengali and then the secretary gestured with a nod towards the chairs.

The boy looked at me somewhat red-faced. 'He says please take a seat with the others.'

I didn't have time for that. But if a twenty-year career as a policeman had imbued me with anything, it was a robust and finely honed technique of intimidating people.

Moving my guide out of the way, I stood above the little secretary, leaned over and placed my hands on the desk in front of him.

'If you don't get Bose out here now, I'll have you arrested on a charge of obstruction.'

The man looked at me impassively.

'You think I am afraid to go to prison?' He held out his wrists, inviting the handcuffs. 'I have been to jail three times already.'

Before I could respond, the door behind him opened and out stepped Bose.

'*Arré*, Raja. Enough of the bravado. If this nice officer arrests you, it'll play havoc with my schedule, and today of all days I can't afford to lose you.'

He turned to me with a curious smile. 'We've met before, haven't we? Have I at some point already had the pleasure of being arrested by you?'

'I'm afraid not,' I said. 'And the pleasure would have been all mine. But you're right, we have met: a few years ago around the time of the Prince of Wales's visit. You were helping C. R. Das bring the city to a standstill.'

His face brightened with the spark of recognition. 'Of course! You're Suren *babu*'s friend. Wyndham, is it?'

'That's right.'

'And how is old Suren? It's been an age since I saw him.'

'He's fine,' I said.

'He's not here with you?'

'He had other business to attend to.'

Bose patted my arm as though we were old friends. 'You British devils are working him too hard.'

I always found it difficult to know how to deal with these Gandhi-inspired independence-wallahs. They'd stand onstage and claim the British were little better than vampires, sucking the life blood of India, and we would respond with mass incarcerations and the cracking of a skull now and then. But away from the glare of the world, they were often the most pleasant of chaps, inviting you in for tea before you arrested them, and who, if it weren't for the colour of their skin and the fundamental objection they had with the way we ran their country, you wouldn't be surprised to find taking a drink or playing a round at your golf club. In a country where so many millions were illiterate, there was something extremely educated about the way these people operated a campaign of insurrection.

'Please,' he continued. 'Come into my office.'

I followed him into a spartan room, its walls washed pale green, furnished with a small desk, a few chairs and in one corner an old sofa leaking its stuffing. He took a seat on one of the wooden chairs and directed me to the sofa.

'Now, how can I help you, Captain?'

'The riots,' I said. 'They're getting worse. I was told you might be able to help stop them.'

Bose shook his head.

'And who might be telling you that?'

'Let's just say I've heard some people comment that you're the future of this country.'

He seemed to appreciate the compliment.

'Most flattering,' he said, 'but the future of this country is freedom.'

I'd heard this speech before and didn't care to hear it again.

'And how are you going to achieve that freedom with the Hindus and Muslims at each other's throats?'

Bose conceded the issue with a nod.

'A good point. If we are to achieve freedom, there needs to be unity of all Indians regardless of caste or creed. I believe those who appeal to religion in the name of politics, or set the followers of one religion against another are committing an act of desecration. I shall have no part of it.'

'So you'll call for an end to the violence?'

Bose squeezed the fingers of one hand in the palm of the other and sighed.

'What would you have me do – write an editorial in a newspaper? The riots are happening right now. People are burning newspapers, not reading them. I can appeal for calm, but for that, I'd need to hold rallies. Will your people allow that?'

That was a good question. Under normal circumstances, the chances of a man like Bose getting a permit for a mass rally were slim to nothing, and while these were hardly normal circumstances, the violence was still restricted to the native areas. Unless and until the blood and the flames were actually lapping at the gates of White Town, I doubted whether the government would deem it in their interests to change the policy. What's more, with Taggart lying gravely injured, the victim of anti-British terrorists, no one in the military would sanction a separatist like Bose holding a rally on the Maidan. He sensed my hesitation.

'No, I thought not. I'm afraid your superiors don't consider this to be anything other than an issue of law and order. Allowing me to hold a rally calling for a cessation of violence will appear to the world as though they've lost control of the situation. I will, of course, call for an end to this calamitous state of affairs at every opportunity, but if you'll pardon the irony, I'm very much preaching to the converted. Those attending a Congress Party meeting are, in very large measure, already convinced of the need for unity between the religions. If you want to stop this madness, you will need to convince those who stand to gain most from the violence to disavow it.'

'I'm on my way down to Ballygunge to speak to Mukherjee's widow,' I said.

Bose shook his head.

'I'm afraid that is likely to achieve very little. I doubt she'll even talk to you. She is in mourning after all, and if she is of the same mindset as her late husband, she is likely to be a very orthodox Brahmin. Even if she isn't, the chances are, the people around her, the Shiva Sabha types, will make sure she doesn't rock the boat.'

'I still have to try.'

He considered the point.

'Mukherjee's body – it has been released to the family?'

I nodded. 'They carried out the swiftest of post-mortems and returned it this morning. The family threatened to kick up a stink if it took any longer.'

'In that case, save yourself some time. It's dusk,' he said. 'Mrs Mukherjee won't be in Ballygunge. Most likely, she'll be in Kalighat, at the cremation grounds.'

I left Bose, feeling worse than when I'd arrived. He might have felt disgusted by the violence that was tearing the city apart but there seemed little that he could practically do about it. What's more, he was probably right about Mukherjee's widow.

I took his advice about where to find her though, and headed for Kalighat, a native neighbourhood to the south. Despite the straight road, it took a while to get there, mainly on account of the hundreds of men heading the other way towards the Maidan and central Calcutta. Here, at least, there didn't seem to have been any trouble, possibly because the military had been deployed in force. On every street corner, wary men in khaki uniforms and tin helmets stood with rifles to hand.

Nestling on the banks of the Tolly Canal, the temple to the goddess Kali and its burning grounds were not what I'd been expecting. When people talked of the temple to Kali, my thoughts naturally turned to the huge complex at Dakhineshwar on the banks of the river, north of the city. There, thousands of people clamoured night and day, offering their prayers and sacrificial offerings to the goddess, amid the clanging of bells and a fog of incense. This place, by contrast, was a much simpler affair, and quieter too, at least by Hindu standards. The bells still chimed and incense still burned, but the atmosphere was sombre, as befitted a place where the dead went for their eternal souls to be freed to return to the spiritual realm where they'd prepare for reincarnation in a new form.

The entrance was down a narrow alleyway clogged with men dressed in funereal white, as well as one wearing a different white – that of the Calcutta police force. I made my way over to the constable.

He must have thought I'd taken a wrong turning. 'Can I help you, sir?'

I flashed my warrant card.

'I'm looking for Prashant Mukherjee's widow, Mrs. Kamala Mukherjee.'

'She is at the burning ghat, sir. Offering prayers.'

The way he said it sounded like I had no business going there, and while I respected her loss, there were larger matters to consider.

'Take me there,' I ordered.

The constable led the way down an ash-strewn path hidden in the darkness between shallow islands of hurricane lamplight, emerging close to the canal where, in the half-light, a circle of grieving souls stood gathered around the dying embers of a funeral pyre. At the centre, a grey-haired woman clad in a white sari held her hands together in *pranam* while a priest offered final prayers for the departed.

I waited there, oblivious to the glances of the assembled guests until the mantras had been chanted and the crowd began to disperse. The woman, her arm held by a much younger man, began to walk slowly towards me. In her hand she held a clay dish, packed with what looked like mud.

'Mrs Mukherjee,' I called.

The woman looked over. Despite the grey hair, her face seemed curiously unlined. Her eyes too betrayed no sign of tears.

'May I speak to you?'

Beside her, the young man bridled.

'Who are you?'

That should have been evident from the constable standing behind me, but I showed him my warrant card anyway.

'My name is Wyndham. I'm a detective at Lal Bazar.'

It seemed to cut little ice with him.

'And you think this is a good time to be questioning a woman, minutes after her husband's cremation?'

'And you are?'

'Priyo Mukherjee. Her son.'

'I appreciate it's untimely,' I said, 'but you'll be aware that the situation beyond these walls is worsening. A better time may not present itself. If I can have a few moments to speak to your mother, it might save a lot of lives.'

The boy made to remonstrate but his mother held him back.

'Mr Wyndham,' she said, 'please, if you think it may help, ask your questions.'

I thanked her with a nod. 'I need to know what your husband was doing in Budge Budge.'

The woman glanced at her son.

'I'm afraid I don't know for certain,' she said, 'he wasn't in the habit of sharing his plans, but I believe it was a meeting of sorts. He hadn't been down there in a long while. Not since he stopped lecturing. Still, he was looking forward to it. It was the most animated he had been in months.'

'And you, Priyo?' I asked. 'Do you have any idea of what your father was doing down there?'

The boy stared at me. 'Maybe you should be the one answering the questions, Mr Detective? First the police tell us that my father died in a fire, but then we receive his body and his neck is broken.'

From his pocket he pulled out a flimsy sheet of paper and thrust it at me. It was a flyer of some sort with large Bengali letters printed in black and white.

'Are the Shiva Sabha correct? Was he murdered by the Muslims?'

'Honestly,' I said, 'I don't know what happened to your father. But I am trying to find out. The task is made a hundred times harder by these riots. Until they stop, our investigation is hamstrung.'

The son shook his head with the impatience of youth. 'So you are not going to do anything?'

'That's not what I'm saying.'

'What *are* you saying, Mr Wyndham?' asked Mrs Mukherjee.

'I was hoping you, or your son, might make a statement calling for calm.'

The woman gave a thin smile.

'I very much doubt anything we say will stop the killing. Only the leader of the Shiva Sabha could do that, and it is unlikely Dr Nagpaul would wish to do so.'

She looked across at a chap standing not far away, surrounded by a coterie of men. I thought I heard a hint of something in her voice.

'You don't approve of the man?'

'I don't approve of the way he treated my husband, or how he twisted my husband's words.'

'*Maa*, please,' said the boy, taking her arm and trying to steer her away.

'*Chhaaro!*' she said, yanking her arm free. She turned to me. 'My husband was not the man they painted him to be. He was no politician, and he was no hero of Hindutva. He was merely a scholar. A man who loved his religion and studied it closely. It was others who twisted his work. And now he is dead because of them, and they lionise him.'

The man whom she'd glanced at earlier, the one at the centre of the group, looked over, as though alert to the widow's words. I realised I recognised him from somewhere, a picture in the papers, probably. Kamala Mukherjee adjusted the *anchal* of her sari covering the top of her head. 'I can't tell you anything else, Mr Wyndham,' she said, 'not now and certainly not here. But I suggest you have a word with Dr Nagpaul over there. He made his name on the back of my husband's work. And how did he repay him? When my husband questioned his views, he cut him out.'

'Out?'

'Ostracised him. Put a stop to his teaching, cancelled his stipend from the Sabha. And now he has the gall to come here and shed sham tears at my husband's funeral.

'*Maa,*' said the boy again. This time he seemed almost nervous '*Maa,* we should go. Now.'

I decided to heed Kamala Mukherjee's words.

While her son guided her to the exit, I moved to head off the man she'd singled out, Dr Nagpaul, head of the Shiva Sabha, the Hindu-first party. He stood amid a circle of four other men and watched the widow Mukherjee and her son leave.

'Dr Nagpaul,' I called.

He looked over, as though he'd already anticipated I'd want to speak to him.

He was fortyish, dressed, like the others, head to toe in white – dhoti, kurta and an embroidered cream-coloured shawl draped over one shoulder. Every inch the patrician Bengali Brahmin. His face was soft, moustachioed and bespectacled – hardly what one expected of a man famous for his speeches rousing the baser passions among his followers. But then he wouldn't be the first person with clean hands and a PhD who made a career out of exhorting others to violence.

'Dr Nagpaul,' I said again, as the circle around him parted, 'may I have a word?'

The man bowed graciously.

'And you are?'

'Captain Wyndham. Lal Bazar CID.'

He gave a half-hearted smile. 'I'm afraid I really am pushed for time, Captain. I'm due to address a gathering on the Maidan in forty minutes and my car is waiting.'

I marvelled at the speed of it all. Bengalis weren't exactly known for their organisational alacrity, but they could move pretty quickly when they wanted to. Mukherjee hadn't been dead much more than twenty-four hours and here was Nagpaul off to rouse the rabble in the centre of town.

'It'll only take a few minutes,' I said. 'I'm sure you appreciate the urgency of the situation. We can talk on the way to your car.'

It wasn't something he could object to, and I fell into step beside him, with his entourage bringing up the rear.

'Your speech at the Maidan. Might I enquire as to the content?' I asked.

He glanced over. 'My dear Captain, surely you are not thinking of censoring what I plan to say?'

The truth was I had the power to do just that, or, if I so deemed, have him arrested. At least I did in theory. In reality, the decision to arrest an Indian for the content of his speech was taken at a pay grade far higher than mine, and by a man in the khaki uniform of the military or the pinstripe suit of the India Office.

'Not at all,' I said. 'But you'll be conscious of the volatile nature of things out there. I'm sure you wouldn't wish to say anything which might further inflame the situation.'

'Rest assured, Captain, I will merely be offering my eulogy to Prashant Mukherjee, a martyr to the cause and a true Indian patriot.'

'A martyr?' I asked.

'But of course.' He smiled. 'How else would you describe him?'

'I don't know,' I said. 'I never met the man. But his wife didn't seem to think he deserved that particular title.'

Nagpaul ignored the reference to Mukherjee's widow. 'He died for his religion, at the hands of the Muslims.'

'As far as I'm aware, there's no proof he was murdered by Muslims.'

Nagpaul gave a snort. 'Who else would kill him?'

'That's what I'm trying to find out,' I said, 'but in the meantime, it would be irresponsible to go throwing around unsubstantiated rumours.'

'And if they were substantiated, Captain? Would your vaunted chief commissioner tell us?'

It was my turn to ignore the comment.

'I shall tell the truth, Captain Wyndham, about what a great man Mukherjee was and what a loss he will be to our cause.'

'You knew him well, then?'

'Extremely. For many years I studied at his feet.'

'And when was the last time you saw him?'

'I cannot exactly recall.'

'Was it in the last few days? Or weeks? Or longer still?'

'I'm afraid I don't see the relevance of your question.'

'I only ask as I'm trying to build a picture of his recent mental state. His widow informed me he'd been rather depressed of late and I wondered if you might corroborate that.'

Nagpaul shrugged. 'It was a period of time ago, and I don't think I'm qualified to offer an opinion on his state of mind.'

'Mukherjee's widow stated that you hadn't seen her husband for several months.'

'I've been extremely busy, what with the elections —'

'It's just that Mrs Mukherjee believed you'd had a falling-out.'

'A mere disagreement among comrades,' he said. 'Nothing serious.'

'Do you know what Mukherjee was doing in Budge Budge yesterday?'

'Why would I? As we've established, I hadn't seen him in a while.'

We had reached the gates of the burning grounds. Nagpaul's chauffeur was already opening the rear door of his car for him.

'I'm afraid we must leave it there,' said Nagpaul. 'I do hope you quickly arrest whoever is responsible. The Hindus of this country will be watching you.'

'And I hope,' I said, 'that you'll heed my advice about the content of your speech at the Maidan. Any rumours or false accusations and I'll be down on you like a ton of bricks. Because this particular policeman will be watching you.'

TWENTY

Surendranath Banerjee

The guards barely noticed me. It is strange how a red shirt and turban can make one invisible. To most people in Calcutta, station porters, like rickshaw-wallahs, are all but ephemeral, not really persons at all but creatures to be summoned when a strong back is required and dismissed just as quickly when the labour is complete.

And so it was that I passed through a ring of armed soldiers intent on questioning every soul entering the station without receiving so much as a glance.

Joining the trickle of those granted access, I ascended the great steps of the portico.

'Hey!' an English voice called out behind me. 'Hey, you! Wait!'

I kept on walking.

'Hey, you! Porter-wallah! I'm talking to you.'

I stopped and turned slowly. A red-faced Englishman in a flannel suit was hurrying towards me, scraping a scuffed and bulging valise on the ground behind him.

'Are you deaf?'

'No, sahib,' I said.

'I've been calling after you for about five minutes!'

Five minutes earlier I was behind a low wall, changing my clothes and tying a turban, but the English have a tendency to exaggerate, at least in front of Indians. He was standing before me now, inches from my face, sweating and trying to catch his breath. I feigned ignorance.

'Five minutes,' he repeated, poking the watch on his wrist with a fat finger. The watch looked cheap. So did the man. A salesman, I guessed, judging by the state of his suitcase.

'Now take this,' he said, pointing to it, 'and bring it to platform 3. *Three*,' he repeated, this time holding up three fingers and all but shouting the word at me as though I was maybe in another room. '*Theen*,' he said in Bengali. '*Theen*. Three. Understand?'

He was clearly a scholar.

'*Ak tākā*,' I said, then, to show him that I too was well versed in many languages, added, 'One rupee.'

'A rupee? It's five annas at the worst of times!'

That might have been true. I personally had never paid more than three, but I needed the money, especially if I was to pay back Miss Ayisha.

I shook my head. 'No, sahib. *This* is worst of times. Price is one rupee.'

He blustered and threatened to report me: first to the station authorities, then the police and finally the army.

'One rupee,' I repeated before he elevated his complaint to the viceroy. He fell silent, looked for another porter, then truculently accepted my price.

'*Chalo*,' he said.

'Money first,' I said and held out my hand.

'Daylight robbery,' he puffed, passing me the note. I took the money and his case and made for the station concourse, all the while noting that when an Indian overcharges an Englishman, it is termed fraud, but when an Englishman overcharges an Indian, it's called capitalism.

Despite the cordon outside, the station concourse seemed no less tumultuous than normal, with civilians, troops and luggage competing for space with jute-covered goods and the baskets of produce brought into the city by farmers each day. The noise was deafening, with military shouts adding to the usual cacophony of steam engines, confused travellers and a tannoy system incomprehensible in either English or Bengali. Finding anyone within this bedlam without physically stumbling into them would be close to impossible. Still, I had to try.

I hoped that platform 3, towards which my new salesman friend had ordered me, might be hosting the train for Bombay. That, however, would have entailed a significant degree of divine assistance, and after the last two days, it was crystal clear that in the matter of trailing Gulmohamed, the gods had well and truly washed their hands of me. Instead, the train was for Patna and the salesman, having shown his ticket to the guard at the platform entrance, proceeded to head for a second-class compartment at the far end of the train which looked to be about half a mile away.

My legs began to buckle under the weight of the suitcase and I wondered just what it was that the man sold.

Bricks possibly.

I declined to indulge him any further and stopped at the platform entrance.

'What do you think you're doing?' he asked.

'This is platform 3,' I said. 'Here is your case.'

I deposited the valise, which is to say I dropped it, and turned tail before the fellow could hurl any further invective or request a refund. I stared up at the huge board upon which the departures were displayed. Assuming all went to schedule, the Bombay Mail would leave from platform 1 at eight o'clock.

Automatically I went to consult my wristwatch only to remember that it, like my money, was somewhere back in Budge Budge. A moment later, I saw him: a flash of silver hair and a grey Savile Row suit, he was making his way through the scrum on the concourse, other travellers parting to make a path for him as though he were Moses and they were the Red Sea. As quickly as he'd appeared, he vanished once more from sight, hidden by the crowd, with only his suitcase visible atop the turban of a porter trailing dutifully along in his wake.

I began to push my own way through the crowd to intercept him. It was not easy. I had to stop him before he reached the guard at the platform entrance, and judging by the speed at which his suitcase was moving, he was already halfway there. I, by contrast, was having to fight every step of the way, weaving through a sudden stampede of passengers heading for the all-stops Bandel local on platform 2. Still, I kept going, contriving a path through the melee so as to intercept him just shy of the platform.

I got there mere moments before the approaching suitcase, and then I saw him, properly this time, and stopped in my tracks. On either side of him walked a police officer, one British, the other Indian. My first thought was that maybe they'd arrested him already, but that made little sense. He wasn't in handcuffs and he was being escorted to his train rather than a cell at Lal Bazar.

Sweat trickled down my back. Gulmohamed was now inches away, heading straight for me. I considered my options and quickly realised that I had none. I could not arrest him, not in light of the men accompanying him.

Gulmohamed brushed past and one of his minders, the Indian, attempted to walk straight through me.

'*Hatao!*' he roared, following with a push that, were it not for the mass of bodies around me, would have sent me sprawling.

I looked on as Gulmohamed waved his ticket at the platform guard and sailed past accompanied by his entourage and his porter, still carrying his suitcase atop his turban. Gulmohamed walked past third and second class, stopping at the entrance to a first-class sleeper compartment and turning to his associates. The coolie lowered his valise and placed it inside the carriage door as Gulmo-hamed reached into his pocket for a coin and tossed it to him.

My only hope now was if the two officers, having delivered him to the station, would now set off back whence they came, affording me the opportunity to somehow give the platform guard the slip and board the train. Unfortunately neither of the gentlemen seemed in any hurry to leave.

I looked up at the station clock. There were only minutes before the train was scheduled to depart. After what felt an eternity, the two officers finally began to walk back towards the concourse. It was now or never. I scanned the vicinity till I found what I was looking for – a suitcase, not exactly unattended, but the gentleman to whom it belonged was engrossed in the company of a young woman and had his back to it. With my heart pounding, I walked over and picked up the case as naturally as I could, then kept walking. I braced myself, but neither the man nor his companion had noticed.

I muttered my thanks to Maa Kali and, with the suitcase now on my head, made for platform 1. Gulmohamed's minders had now reached the concourse, but to my horror, instead of continuing towards the exit, they stopped and turned. Perhaps they were under orders to remain until the train physically departed. It seemed I had no alternative. With my life at stake, I had to continue with my plan.

I walked past them, taking care not to pass too close, and hur-ried towards the ticket inspector, who eyed me with the type of disregard with which one does a *para* dog.

'*Shaheb aashché*,' I said, pointing vaguely behind me to indicate that my sahib was coming.

'*Jao*,' he said, waving me through.

And with that, I was on the platform. Affording myself a smile of relief, I hastened towards Gulmohamed's carriage with new-found optimism. At least until a whistle blew. For a moment I thought it was the guard blowing for departure, but it continued, a long, piercing, shriek of a whistle. Then came the shouts.

'Stop! Thief!'

I turned to see the Englishman whose case I'd appropriated bounding down the platform. The guard was running too, still blowing his damned whistle. Worse, the two officers, alerted to the incident, were also beginning to make towards me. I dropped the case and ran, not an easy task in a turban and a pair of torn sandals. I had thirty yards on the pack but the gap was quickly closing. I looked back. The Englishman had stopped beside his case. The guard too had given up the chase, but the two officers were a different matter. They flew down the platform like hounds after a hare. Someone in a third-class compartment shouted at me. 'Thief!'

Another whistle sounded, this time from the engine. The train began to move. I kept running, past some second-class carriages, past the buffet car.

The train accelerated, its carriages beginning to match my stride. Soon they'd be overtaking me. The sound of the officers' boots rang out behind me. There was nothing for it. I waited till I was level with a carriage entrance, reached for the hand rail and leapt. One of my sandals came loose, falling between the train and the platform, and was crushed beneath the wheels of the train.

I paused for breath, my heart pounding against the confines of my chest, and turned to look behind me. The officers were following my lead, jumping onto the train two carriages further down.

There was no time to think. Kicking off the remaining sandal, I pushed on, through the swing door and into the carriage. It turned out to be a second-class sleeper car, with the bunks running along one side and a corridor filled with travellers arranging their luggage on the other. I hurried forward in the knowledge that, should a guard come along it from the opposite direction, I would be trapped.

I pushed my way through, past protesting passengers. Outside the window, the platform slipped away. I made it to the end just as my pursuers entered the carriage behind me. The English officer saw me, shouted something and went for his revolver. I didn't waste time waiting for him to aim the damn thing, instead I plunged through the door and into the gap between carriages. On either side, the steel of a dozen railway tracks shimmered in the moonlight as the train picked up speed. The next carriage was the first-class buffet car, and I rushed through it, sending crockery smashing to the floor and ignoring the shrieks of several English ladies settling down to supper.

I reached the first of the sleeper cars. There, at the end of the corridor, stood Gulmohamed, smoking a cigarette. Any relief I experienced evaporated almost immediately however, for before I could progress towards him, the guard for the first-class compartments, a man the size of a small bungalow, entered the carriage behind him, took one look at me and decided that today was the day that the gods had decided he might wield his fists in the service of the Eastern Railway Company. He strode forward, readying himself to wring my neck. Gulmohamed got out of his way, ducking into his cabin with the dispatch of a rabbit into a burrow.

There was nowhere to go. I was out of time and, I feared, out of options. I reached for my gun, the one I'd picked up outside Lord Taggart's residence, grabbed it from my trouser pocket and pointed it at the advancing conductor. He stopped dead and raised his hands, and I urged him to lie down in the corridor, then stepped past him as, behind me, the officers entered the carriage.

'You there!' shouted the Englishman. 'Stop!'

Gulmohamed was only feet away. I was so close. I tried the door of his cabin, but he'd locked it. I thought about shooting the lock and diving into his cabin, but there was no time.

The Englishman raised his revolver and fired, the bullet missing me by inches before puncturing a hole in the carriage wall behind. I ran and dived through the door at the end of the compartment and into the space between the carriages. The train had picked up speed and was now travelling at pace. I heard the door smash open. It was foolhardy, but I had no choice.

I jumped.

TWENTY-ONE

Sam Wyndham

I ordered Annie's chauffeur to drive north towards Cossipore. It was late now, but the usual veil of darkness that draped the city was tonight hemmed by the amber glow of fires on the horizon. He didn't seem particularly keen to take me that far, either on account of his own safety or possibly that of the car's. I assured him that nothing untoward would happen, but I sensed he didn't quite believe me. Still, paid employment is hard to come by in India, and the man did as he was told. It is sometimes easier taking a risk on your life than it is on your livelihood.

My destination once more, was, Gola-katta Gullee, in the midst of territory controlled by Uddam Singh. I told the driver to drop me on the corner then return in an hour's time and wait for a maximum of thirty minutes. If I still hadn't shown up, he was to drive to the nearest thana and report me missing, possibly detained at the pleasure of Uddam Singh.

Singh ran his operations from the back room of a shebeen halfway down the lane. It was a lousy place, even for Cossipore, constructed from worm-weathered boards, metal sheeting and rusted chicken wire, but then its patrons hardly went there for the decor.

I seemed to surprise the thug at the front door, which was odd given I'd been here less than twenty-four hours earlier.

'I need to see your boss,' I said.

The man crossed his arms.

'You have appointment?'

'Absolutely,' I said, pulling out my Webley. 'It's right here.'

I ordered him to turn round and stuck the barrel in his back. 'Now, what say we go and see Mr Singh?'

The man led the way, shouldering open a door whose hinges screamed in protest. The interior was lit by a half-dozen hurricane lamps and reeked of kerosene.

A few of Singh's men turned in our direction. Several even rose from their seats till I waved them back with the Webley. The man took me to the door to the back room. I thanked him, stored my revolver, then knocked and entered.

Immediately, I felt my arms grabbed by two sets of iron hands and twisted behind my back. I was pushed forward and a moment later the wind was knocked from my lungs and my face was forced onto the wood of a tabletop.

I heard Singh utter a command, '*Chéré-dao*,' and I felt the hands loosen. With a little difficulty, I stood up and straightened my shirt.

'Captain Wyndham,' said Singh. 'They told me you were dead.' His face suggested he wasn't best pleased by the evidence to the contrary. I wondered why he'd thought that. And then it hit me. Could Singh have been behind the attack at Taggart's house? When Suren and I had failed to show at the time I'd promised, had he taken it personally and ordered a hit on the both of us? He probably had informers in Budge Budge. Had they tailed us to Taggart's house? Had they meant to kill me and Suren and merely hit the commissioner by accident? For years, planned attacks on Taggart had failed, and in the end, was it an attempted attack on me that had done for him? In other circumstances I might even have laughed. But now was not the time.

'I don't know what to tell you,' I said.

'Why are you here?' he asked. 'Is it too much to hope that you've brought me the head of your colleague, Banerjee?'

'I'm afraid so,' I said, 'but I *have* come with an offer.'

Singh raised an eyebrow. 'Tell me.'

'I want you to call off your thugs stoking up trouble against the Muslims. And in return, I'll get your son out of jail.'

Singh gave a harsh laugh. 'You expect me to trust you?'

'You have my word,' I said, 'and an Englishman's word is his bond.' That was rubbish, of course, but by some act of colonial black magic, we'd managed to convince the natives it was true. 'It might take a few days, but I'll get him out. And in the meantime, given what's going on in the city right now, a cell at Lal Bazar is probably the safest place for him.'

The gang lord considered it for a moment.

'This violence in the streets,' he said. 'You think it is my doing?'

'Isn't it?'

'People are fed up with the Muslims. They are taking matters into their own hands.'

'The attacks need to stop. The deal depends on it.'

Singh rubbed at the stubble of his beard. 'I can guarantee nothing, but if you give me your word you will free Vinay, I will tell my men to stop. But there is one more thing ...'

'Name it.'

'I want you to find the man who killed Abhay, my firstborn. I want your word you will find him and bring me his head.'

I couldn't agree to any of that, not in good conscience at any rate. I'd no idea who'd killed his boy, and even if I did, I'd arrest him and see that he faced trial in a court. Yet I needed to stop the violence. How many lives would otherwise be lost?

'You have my word,' I said.

TWENTY-TWO

Surendranath Banerjee

It is, I have learned, easy to misjudge the momentum of things in the dark. The train did not seem to be travelling at any great velocity, but contact with the ground soon disabused me of that particular notion. I landed badly and at speed, promptly lost my footing and tumbled head first down a gravel bank until a fortuitously placed peepul tree broke my momentum.

Pain, the likes of which I have seldom experienced, even at the hands of the Budge Budge constabulary, convulsed through me. My instinct was to lie there, but if the two officers had followed me off the train, there was a risk that I might just die there. I had to start moving. An electric jolt shot through my arms as I hauled myself up. I looked towards the bank and peered into the darkness. For a long moment I saw nothing. Then in the distance, as my eyes adjusted, the hulking outline of the Bombay Mail became clearer, the lights of its compartments visible several hundred yards down the track. I breathed a sigh of relief, which died in my throat and turned to horror as it dawned on me that the damn thing was not moving. My stomach turned over. The third-class passengers were getting restless. I could see several, silhouetted against the light and peering through the window bars, wondering what was going on.

The sound of muffled voices carried over on the air. Shouts. I reached for my revolver and a cold dread descended as I realised it was no longer in my pocket. I'd lost it, somewhere between the jump from the train and my final resting place at the foot of the tree. There was no time to look for it. I had to move, to get away as quickly as possible. I had no shoes, no notion of where I was, or in which direction I should run, but I decided it did not matter, as long as it was away from my pursuers.

Setting off silently through the screen of trees, I limped away from the tracks and the dim lights of the shacks and godowns of what I presumed were the outskirts of Howrah.

Behind me my pursuers were fanning out. I thanked the goddess. In the dark, I was but a needle in a haystack and the further I moved from the train, the greater the area they would have to search. I kept running till my lungs burned and my feet bled and then collapsed among the foliage. For a full minute I could hear nothing over the sound of my own laboured breathing and pounding heart. Then, as the blood settled and my wits returned, I concentrated, trying to catch any noise on the wind. I waited and whispered pleas to Maa Durga and Maa Kali with a degree of fervour which my prayers seldom entailed. The sound of voices began to recede, and minutes later came the agitated whistle of the train. I dropped my head to the ground in relief and remained there for some time. I decided that lying low was still the safest option. Simply because the train was leaving did not mean that my pursuers were aboard it. They might still be out here, waiting for me. Most of all though, I simply hadn't the energy to move.

I cannot say how long I lay there, but a crescent moon was overhead by the time I reopened my eyes. It took a moment to remember where I was and what had transpired, and then I wished I had not woken at all. I rose unsteadily and tried to ascertain my bearings.

The muscles of my legs were stiff, and the flesh of the soles of my feet, cut ragged. In the distance, a few lights flickered, and I made for them, driven by the logic that where there were lamps there were houses, and where there were houses there were generally roads.

Sure enough the light came from hurricane lamps hanging from a series of shacks beside a lotus-covered *pūkūr* and a dirt road. The question was whether to turn left or right. It was not that I was unsure as to which direction led back to Calcutta – that was obvious from the glow of flames upon the horizon. The question was more fundamental: *What was I to do now?* Gulmohamed was gone, and I was a fugitive. Returning to Calcutta entailed the risk of capture by my colleagues, a trial and a hangman's noose. But where else was I to go? If I had any chance of survival, it was in proving that Gulmohamed, and not I, had killed Mukherjee, and to do that, I realised, I needed Sam. So with resignation I started walking, east, back towards the city – my city; the city of my birth, my youth, my life; the city now aflame; each of its burning districts like wounds upon my soul.

TWENTY-THREE

Sam Wyndham

To the north, the horizon glowed red. A false dawn born of the embers of the violence. It was late by the time I got back to Premchand Boral Street and dismissed the driver. The street was quieter than usual, the brisk trade of gentlemen that usually kept the brothels busy had dried to nothing, and the girls, dressed in diaphanous saris, lazed on verandas and balconies while their touts did their best to drum up whatever passing trade they could. They knew better than to proposition me, of course, not if they valued their liberty. But on a night as barren as this, I felt that one or two were sorely tempted to ask me anyway.

I made the long walk up the stairs to the flat, hoping against hope that I might find Suren there waiting for me. The flat, however, was in darkness. I closed the door, switched on the light and called out for our manservant, Sandesh, who appeared on the third time of asking, bleary-eyed and dishevelled.

'Has Suren come home?' I asked.

He looked around as though the answer was to be found somewhere in the hallway. 'No, sahib,' he said with remarkable conviction for a man who'd probably been asleep under the dining table for the last few hours. Sandesh had his own bed and his own quarters, but nevertheless preferred to sleep under the table in the dining room. It was an idiosyncrasy which Suren and I ignored, mainly on account of him being half decent at keeping the place clean and exemplary at keeping the drinks cabinet well stocked. Such men were hard to come by and especially at such a reasonable weekly wage.

'Whisky, sahib?'

It was a calculated distraction but I wasn't about to turn it down.

'Have we any left in the bottle?'

He grinned. 'Enough for a razor blade.'

Just enough whisky for the thinnest of measures. He had taken the expression to heart, as he did any English idiom which made no literal sense.

I walked through to the sitting room and out onto the balcony. Leaning against the parapet, I lit a cigarette and looked out into the night. Suren was out there somewhere. I just hoped that whatever trouble he was getting himself into, it wouldn't be more than I could get him out of.

Behind me, Sandesh coughed gently.

'Razor blade, sahib,' he said, passing me the whisky. 'Also, one *chitee* is coming for you.'

He held out a white envelope. I downed the whisky, swapped the glass for the envelope and ripped open the seal. Inside was a single sheaf of paper.

Chang's, Tirretta Bazar. You know the place. Midnight tonight. Make sure you're not followed.

I staggered back and all but fell into one of the cane chairs. Was this someone's idea of a joke? If so, I wasn't laughing. I checked the back of the letter, then the envelope, for any clue as to who might have sent it, but both were blank.

'Who brought this?'

Sandesh looked sheepish. 'Don't know, sahib. Some persons is leaving it beneath the front door. I am finding it there only.'

I read the note again. *You know the place.*

I did know the place, but I doubted many other people did, certainly not Suren, whom I'd hoped the note might be from. It was the first opium den I ever visited. I'd stumbled across it within a fortnight of my arrival in the city. That had been almost five years ago and I hadn't been back there much since. I found myself suddenly perspiring.

'Sandesh,' I said. 'Crack open another bottle of whisky. And make it a double.'

TWENTY-FOUR

Surendranath Banerjee

Howrah is not a particularly pleasant place. Not by day and certainly not by night. It is comprised of factories, tanneries, godowns and the occasional dwelling, and is populated in part by the sort of cut-throats who in previous eras might have made jolly fine pirates. If there existed a silver lining, it was that, given my state of dress, no dacoit with any degree of self-respect would think to try and rob me. Indeed in that regard, Howrah was probably safer for me than anywhere in Calcutta proper.

Yet I had to keep going. I had to make contact with Sam. With Gulmohamed gone, I now had nowhere else to turn. The question was how? Our lodgings in Premchand Boral Street would be under surveillance, and no doubt my parents' residence in Shyambazar too. But my first concern was how to cross the Hooghly back into the city.

The simplest means would be to traverse the bridge near the station. It also had the advantage of being free, which in my current impecunious circumstances was a most definite attraction. But it was also extremely risky. The bridge was one of the most strategic points in the whole city. With the chaos in North Calcutta, the military would have it heavily guarded, restricting access and checking the papers of anyone trying to cross. Even if I were not immediately recognised as a fugitive, the chances of them allowing a shoeless itinerant, which is what most I resembled, to cross into the city in the middle of the night seemed low. As for the passenger ferries, they would have stopped sailing by the time I reached the water's edge.

That left the small boats, the *naukas*, operated by men who ate and slept on their wooden vessels. Unrestricted by timetables, they could sail at any time of day or night, for an appropriate fee of course, and they had the advantage of being able to berth almost anywhere along the other riverbank, though it might involve wading up to your knees in mud. I would never normally consider hiring one of these contraptions, but tonight, even the thought of making it through the slime of the opposite bank was as nothing compared to my need to reach safety.

I walked south. Away from the bridge to a quieter, more secluded spot where a few such boats rocked gently at the end of a jetty. Reaching into my pocket, I pulled out the one-rupee note I'd charged the Englishman back at the station. It was a lot to pay for crossing the river, but I hoped a rupee would buy not only passage but a lack of questions also.

I chose the *nauka* that bobbed furthest from the centre and made my way gingerly down a riverbank treacherous with mud and detritus. A shaft of light speared through a hole in the sacking that acted as both door and screen to the tiny covered compartment at the stern.

I stood close by and shouted. '*Oh dada! Jaben?*'

From inside came the clanging of metal vessels. A hand lifted the sackcloth and a face, gaunt and bristled, peered out.

'*Kothai?*' he said. *Where?*

The Armenian ghat was the nearest landing on the opposite bank but that seemed rather too close to the bridge for my comfort. A more propitious spot would be somewhere further downriver, ideally near the Outram *ghat*, but that was quite a distance and I didn't want to chance my luck. Between Armenian and Outram was the ghat at Fairlie Place. It would have to do.

'*Oi-tho*,' I said, '*Fairlie ghat.*'

He pondered it for a moment. '*Fairlie? Athho ratheer-é?*' As though shocked that anyone would seek to go there at this time of night.

I sensed the beginning of a negotiation and headed it off with a flourish of the one-rupee note. '*Ak tākā.*'

It brought the matter to a prompt conclusion.

'*Cholō*,' he said with a nod, then came out onto the deck and held out a hand to help steady my embarkation.

The boatman returned to the stern, levered all of his meagre body weight onto the oversized oar that jutted from the rear, and pushed off from the bank. Ahead lay a half-hour journey across the ink-black river. I had never crossed so late at night before, nor in a vessel so close to the waterline, and it soon became apparent that traversing the Hooghly in such a craft was far more dangerous than taking a ferry, especially in the dead of night. The lip of the boat was mere inches from the water, and indeed I could have reached over and touched the surface had I been so inclined. Furthermore we had no navigation lights, were all but invisible save for a hurricane lamp at the bow, and dodging sea-going cargo ships in one of the busiest shipping lanes in the world. One slip of the oar or miscalculation of the current and a freighter might crack our hull like an egg, sailing over us without even noticing.

But the man knew the waters and guided his vessel expertly between the wakes of towering steel hulls and eventually the concrete jetty of Fairlie ghat loomed out of the darkness. I scoured the bank for signs of activity, for a police or military presence, but it appeared splendidly deserted.

The boat-wallah steered his *nauka* towards it, angling the boat so that it arrived at the platform with the gentlest of kisses. I thanked him, paid him his rupee and jumped off.

The night air was still, with only the faintest hint of charred smoke carried on the riverine breeze. From here it was hard to believe that the city was in chaos, and that a few miles away, shops and houses and people were burning.

The issue was where to go now. I had to speak to Sam, but going back to our digs in Premchand Boral Street was out of the question. Yet there was one way to get hold of him, one place I could meet him without the police, secret or otherwise, finding out. I just needed to reach it without being arrested.

I kept my head down and set off for Rawdon Street.

TWENTY-FIVE

Sam Wyndham

I took the girls at the brothel downstairs rather by surprise.

'Is this a raid, Captain sahib?' The young woman who opened the door smiled. 'Or are you here for pleasure?'

I knew her as Pia, but that wasn't her name. She was a pretty girl, probably not much older than seventeen, though you'd be hard pressed to tell from her rather forward manner, and was originally from the hill country up near Nepal. I knew all this because I'd shared the occasional smoke with her on the veranda in front of our building when she was between shifts, so to speak.

'You know better than that, Pia,' I said.

'Then why? You want to speak to Singh-auntie?'

The place was overseen by an affable woman whose husband, Mr Singh, had brought her to Calcutta as a young bride, all the way from her native village near Amritsar in the Punjab. After two months of marriage, he'd promptly fled town, escaping, depending on who you believed, creditors, or the police, or possibly his new wife. A lesser woman might have returned to her village, but that would have entailed a degree of shame which Mrs Singh was unwilling to bear. The facts remain uncertain, but the lady in question had kept his name yet sold his possessions, and her honour, in order to survive. Over time she went from being a working girl to a madam, and indeed a quite successful businesswoman, but at heart,

139

she saw herself as a protector of the young girls who found themselves abandoned in the city or sold into prostitution by families who, one assumed, had fallen into debt.

'No,' I said. 'I just need to use the door to the back courtyard.'

The girl stared up at me. 'Why you want to go in yard so late?'

'I'm looking for Suren *babu*,' I said. 'He hasn't come home.'

'You think he is in the courtyard?'

I didn't answer.

She shook her head. 'For two grown mens you are both always acting like children. *Chalo*,' she said and led the way.

The walk to Tiretti Bazar took about forty-five minutes: longer than it should have, but I took the scenic route, sticking to the alleyways, avoiding the military patrols and doubling back on myself to ensure I wasn't being followed. And all the while I recalled the times I'd walked this route before in the dead of night. Unpleasant, haunting memories: part opium-addled hallucination; part nightmare reality. But that was the past. I'd been clean for a year now, and while it hadn't been easy, I knew the alternative to be far worse.

The place I was seeking was an opium den housed in the basement of a nondescript dwelling. The place was hardly a secret. Opium was not strictly illegal – not for Calcutta's Chinese population at any rate – but it didn't pay to advertise your presence. The police still raided opium dens, ostensibly in search of fugitives or contraband or whatever else was deemed offensive, but actually to remind our friends from the east that this was British territory and that they shouldn't get too comfortable.

I rapped on the steel door and waited for the spyhole to open, feeling a nervousness I hadn't experienced for years. To my shock, rather than the grate sliding open, there came the metallic rasp of a door bolt being pulled back and a moment later I was face-to-face with a thin Chinese man dressed in black and who didn't ask any of the usual questions.

Instead, he beckoned me in as though I were, if not quite a friend, then at least as someone he'd known and tolerated for a decent length of time. I followed him down a flight of stairs to a room that seemed more claustrophobic and less inviting than when I'd been here as an addict. The earthy-sweet scent of opium smoke infused the air and I felt the sweat break out on my neck.

By sparse candlelight, I made out the usual haul of soporific men lying on mats on the floor, each in his own personal nirvana. The man led me past them towards a door at the far end.

'Let me guess,' I said. 'The VIP room?'

He ignored the comment and instead knocked on the door. Something in the air had changed, I struggled to identify it. It was the smell. The scent of opium smoke was less strong here, and it merged with something else. Was it tobacco? Not cigarette tobacco, but something else, and a rather unusual blend, smoked by only one person I knew.

From behind the door came footsteps and the turning of a handle, but before it opened, I knew who'd be standing there.

TWENTY-SIX

Surendranath Banerjee

I knew Miss Grant's block by sight, not due to any curiosity on my part, but because Sam had, on more than one occasion, pointed it out to me. Yet knowing the location of a building and gaining entry were very different things.

I disliked this section of town: not because of the architecture, which was most handsome, or the location, which was convenient for all of central Calcutta, but because of the type of persons who resided here and also because of the type of people they employed.

While Englishmen with wives gravitated southwards to suburbs like Alipore and Tollygunge, the area around Park Street was the preserve of the well-heeled British bachelor, whose wealth acted as insulation from even the few hardships which lesser Englishmen suffered here and amplified their sense of superiority over Indians. Somehow that arrogance became instilled into the very Indians who worked for them and who were most directly on the receiving end of their scorn, from personal secretaries to chauffeurs and, unfortunately for me, the concierges who sat in the lobbies of their mansion blocks.

Under other circumstances, access might have proved inconvenient but not impossible. After enduring the caretaker's appraising glance, I would have just explained who I was, who I worked for and who I had come to see. Tonight, of course, such things were rather more complicated. I was shoeless, covered in dirt and dressed in the tattered red shirt of a station coolie. In light of that, any claims I might make of being a police detective were likely to fall on deaf ears.

If I was to reach Miss Grant's apartment, I would require to employ a more circumspect approach. At this time of night, the regular concierge would most likely be safely abed, his duties deputised to the durwan, the nightwatchman. Even in this most affluent part of town, such men were paid a pittance and the calling tended not to attract the most alert nor enterprising of souls. That at least was something in my favour. What's more, a good durwan would spend much of his time patrolling the perimeter of the premises. Indeed night-time Calcutta reverberated to the sound of thirty thousand such men tapping their bamboo lathis as they went about their beat, informing any would-be miscreants that their building was not to trifled with.

I waited in the shadows, hoping that the man might appear and commence his rounds, but this particular durwan seemed more than happy to remain at his desk. I had no choice but to take matters into my own hands. I scoured the lane behind the street till I came across what I was looking for: a large mound of sand and bricks. It was one of the peculiarities of Calcutta that our climate – a pestilential mix of monsoon and baking heat – tended to dissolve buildings faster than a spoonful of sugar in a cup of hot tea. As a result, one was never far from a pile of materials needed for running repairs: bricks and sand, and supplemented in the poorer quarters with wood, and sacking and corrugated sheeting. I grabbed a brick and returned to Miss Grant's block. There, not wishing to cause a scene if it might be avoided, I afforded the durwan a final few minutes to come out and commence his round. When he failed to appear, I proceeded to the side of the building and launched my missile at a ground-floor window. The glass fractured with a satisfying crack which I hoped was loud enough for the durwan to hear. I ran back to my shrouded vantage point and waited. On higher floors, electric lights were switched on and windows came to life. Then, finally, the durwan raced out of the door, lathi in hand and whistle flying around his neck on its chain.

Once he'd passed around to the side of the building, I sprinted up the steps and into the lobby. There I quickly located Miss Grant's name etched onto the brass disc of the postbox for apartment 21. Before I could do much else, a voice rang out.

'Who the bloody hell are you?!'

I turned to see an Englishman in a maroon silk dressing gown staring across the foyer at me.

'Where's Dennis?' he asked.

I assumed he meant the durwan though I doubted the chap's name was actually Dennis.

'Outside, sahib,' I said in that ingratiating tone which the Britishers prefer us to employ. It seemed to mollify him somewhat.

'And what are you doing here, coolie?'

I thought quickly. 'Picking up luggages for taking to Howrah station, sahib.'

The gentleman appeared to approve of my answer.

'Didn't know you chaps provided that sort of service.'

I grinned at him and pressed my palms together. 'Excuse me please, sahib. I must go and retrieve the luggages.'

With that, I took my leave and all but ran for the secondary stairwell used by servants and workmen.

I was out of breath by the time I located Miss Grant's door on the third floor. Perspiring heavily, I knocked loudly and continuously until it finally opened.

Before me stood Miss Grant's maid, whom I'd met once or twice at her mistress's previous abode. She appeared as though roused from sleep, but my appearance helped to jolt her awake. She tried closing the door in my face, but I managed to place my foot in the gap.

'Please, Anju,' I said as the pain shot up my leg. 'It's me, Suren *babu*, Captain Wyndham's friend. I need to speak to Miss Grant urgently.'

TWENTY-SEVEN

Sam Wyndham

'Wyndham,' he said. 'Good of you to come.'

Before me stood Colonel Dawson, spymaster of the army's intelligence department, Section H.

'I could hardly resist such a cryptic invitation,' I said. 'Interesting choice of venue.'

Dawson smiled. 'I thought you might appreciate that. I expect this place holds fond memories for you.'

He turned, and with the assistance of his cane, hobbled back to a table and chairs in the centre of the claustrophobic room. 'Please,' he said, pointing to a chair.

'What's this about?' I asked.

He waited till I was seated before answering.

'Your chum, Banerjee. I understand he's landed himself in some rather hot water.'

That Dawson knew of Suren's predicament was hardly surprising. The man had informers everywhere, including a few at police headquarters.

'You know where he is?'

'Not as such,' said Dawson, 'but I suspect he might be mixed up in something bigger. Something involving imperial security.'

That last phrase made me sit up.

'What exactly?'

He extracted his pipe and tobacco pouch, and began preparing his smoke.

'That I don't know.'

'Isn't it your job to know?'

He fixed me with a stare.

'That's why we're here. We've intercepted certain … communications, around a visit by that Union of Islam chap, Gulmohamed, to the city.'

'Suren was tailing Gulmohamed on Taggart's orders,' I said. 'He thinks Gulmohamed's involved in Mukherjee's murder. If you stop him leaving town, bring him in for a bit of questioning, we can get to the bottom of this.'

The spymaster shifted in his seat.

'I'm afraid that's not going to be possible.'

'Why?'

'He's too high-profile, the situation is too volatile, especially this close to the elections. We bring him in now and before you know it, the Muslims will be up in arms. And if he *is* involved in some conspiracy around Mukherjee's murder, arresting him now, without knowing the facts, might cause any co-conspirators to go to ground. We need to consider the bigger picture.'

'I'm all for considering the bigger picture,' I said, 'but not when my colleague's life is at risk.'

Dawson took a puff of his pipe.

'There are other factors at play here, Wyndham. Gulmohamed has certain critically placed friends in Bombay.'

'*Critically* placed? As opposed to highly placed?'

Dawson smiled graciously.

Highly placed would have meant friends in the political administration. *Critically* placed suggested something slightly different.

The military? But the top brass was headquartered in Delhi, not Bombay. Why would Dawson be wary of arresting a friend of some generals based in Bombay? And them I realised.

'Are you saying Gulmohamed's an agent of the Section?'

Dawson took out his pipe and grimaced. 'I always did say you were perceptive. But no, he's not an agent. At least not to my knowledge. But I *do* know that my colleagues in Bombay have some special interest in the man. It's possible they may have got wind of some plot he's involved in.'

I felt he was holding something back.

'Then why didn't they stop it? And why didn't they tell you about it?'

The spymaster leaned forward.

'Spheres of influence, Wyndham. I'm Head of Section here in Calcutta. It might have escaped your notice, but the big decisions in this country aren't made here any more.'

'It would seem only common courtesy they'd inform you,' I said.

Dawson coughed. 'Bombay station has some young Turks running it these days and they're not overly keen to share what they're up to with Calcutta.'

He was being remarkably open with me. I might have applauded this amenability if I didn't suspect it hid an ulterior motive.

'Why are you telling me all this?'

His expression hardened. 'Because it might be quite nice for me to know what my colleagues in Bombay are up to. I don't take kindly to being kept in the dark, especially when it comes to attacks on my patch. The regular channels appear closed to me, and I felt you and I might have a common interest. If you want to save Banerjee from the gallows, you'll need to figure out what Gulmohamed and his friends are up to. It's the only way you'll get him out of it.'

And there it was. The reason for my summons. Dawson's colleagues from out of town were involved in something in Bengal and had frozen him out. He was a proud man and no doubt saw it as an insult. He wanted to find out what was going on and I was to be his instrument. But involving me was dangerous. He must have known that were I to figure out what was going on, I'd hardly keep it to myself. Indeed, if it was necessary to save Suren, I'd do my damnedest to upset whatever plans the Section had set in motion. And then it struck me. Dawson didn't just want to know what was going on, he wanted me to stop it, wanted me to blow the whole thing out of the water, simply to put his colleagues in Bombay in their place. Hell hath no fury like a spymaster scorned.

'What do you expect me to do?' I said. 'I don't even know where Suren is.'

Dawson smiled. 'Sergeant Banerjee was last seen several hours ago jumping off the Bombay Mail outside Howrah. He seems to have been after Gulmohamed, but before he could reach him he was spotted by two policemen. He evaded capture by leaping from the train. Resourceful little bugger, isn't he?'

I nodded. 'And a pain in the backside.'

'My guess,' Dawson continued, 'is he'll make his way back to Calcutta and try to contact you. When he does, telephone me on this number.' He pulled out a scrap of paper with the digits of a South Calcutta telephone number. 'Memorise it, then destroy it. Any questions?'

'Just one,' I said. 'Of all the opium dens in the city, why did you choose this one?'

'It *was* your first, wasn't it?'

'It was,' I said, 'but you didn't even know I existed then.'

'I knew all about you before you even stepped off the boat at Kidderpore docks. It was my job. I knew about your little problem from the very start. I probably knew you'd end up an opium fiend before you realised it yourself.'

I tried in vain to control my expression.

'Don't look so shocked, Wyndham. In your heart of hearts, you must have figured that out.'

'If you knew about my problem,' I said, 'why did you never tell Taggart? You could have ended my career whenever you chose to.'

Dawson sighed. 'You can be an irritating arse at times, Wyndham, self-righteous to the point of nausea. But you're a tenacious bastard with a knack for getting to the bottom of things. Did it ever occur to you that I might *want* you being precisely those things here in Calcutta?'

'So I'm a useful bastard?'

The spymaster gave a bitter laugh. 'Let's just hope you can sort out this business and save your friend Banerjee's hide. He's done wonders for your career.'

TWENTY-EIGHT

Surendranath Banerjee

'What the hell happened to you?'

Miss Grant stared at me as though I were an apparition.

'You look like you've been run over by a bus.'

Such a fate might have been preferable to what I had actually been through.

I stood at her doorway, waiting to be invited in.

'You *do* know Sam's looking for you?'

'May I enter?' I asked.

Miss Grant emerged from her initial shock.

'Of course. What am I thinking? Come in, you poor chap.'

She led me to the sitting room and to a sofa and then turned to the maid.

'Anju. Bring brandy.'

I made the pretence of declining but she waved away my objections.

'It's medicinal. Trust me, you'll appreciate a stiff drink. Heaven knows I will too.'

Anju returned with the bottle and glasses on a tray.

I thanked them both and took a sip, then emptied the glass. The liquid burned my throat. It felt satisfying.

Miss Grant took a sip of her own. 'I assume this is somehow all Sam's doing?'

I shook my head. 'Sam is innocent in all this.'

She appeared sceptical.

'But I do need to speak to him,' I continued.

'All in good time. First, tell me what happened to you.'

'It's a complicated story.'

Miss Grant thought for a moment. 'In that case, get yourself cleaned up. Anju will show you to the bathroom. I'll telephone Sam and tell him you're here.'

'No!' I said. 'Please do not mention my name over the telephone. The line may be monitored.'

Miss Grant arched an eyebrow. 'My word, Suren. What have you got mixed up in? Very well, I'll get Sam here on some other pretext, and while we're waiting for him, you can tell me your complicated story.'

Twenty minutes later, with a towel wrapped around my flanks, my feet raw but washed, and wearing one of Miss Grant's dressing gowns, I stepped sheepishly back into the sitting room. I caught sight of my reflection in a mirror on the mantel: my disfigured face, bruised and mottled; the cuts upon my chest and shoulders from the fall from the train; and now this. How had things reached such an impasse? My face burned with embarrassment. Despite everything that had happened to me in the previous forty-eight hours, entering a lady's sitting room dressed in nothing but a towel and one of her robes felt like the most shameful of acts. Miss Grant, to her credit, made no mention of my enforced attire, though I sensed her amusement.

'Sam wasn't at home,' she said. 'Probably out looking for you. I left a message with your manservant telling Sam to call me as soon as he gets back. Now take a seat and tell me your troubles.'

TWENTY-NINE

Sam Wyndham

There's no rest for the wicked. It was almost 2 a.m. by the time I made it back to Premchand Boral Street. Once more there was a message waiting for me, and once more I hoped it was from Suren.

Strangely it turned out to be from Annie. She'd called an hour earlier and wanted me to telephone back, no matter how late it was. I wondered what could be quite so urgent as to vex Her Ladyship at such an hour. Maybe something had waylaid her chauffeur and he hadn't returned after dropping me off earlier in the evening. I was sure the chap was fine. With all that was going on in the city, he'd probably just gone to check up on his loved ones.

Nevertheless I lifted the receiver, gave the operator her telephone number and asked to be put through.

She answered after a single ring.

'Annie,' I said wearily, 'I expect this is about your driver —'

'Do be quiet and listen, Sam,' she said in a tone which seemed harsh for two in the morning. 'I need you to come to the flat. There's been some trouble here.'

'What sort of trouble?'

'So far nothing too bad. A few smashed windows and the like, but I'm nervous. You know this sort of thing's happened before. I'd appreciate it if you were to come over, just to take a look.'

I sighed to myself. I hadn't slept since God knew when, I'd still no idea where that blasted idiot Suren was, and now Annie wanted me to soothe her nerves over a broken window. There had been a time when I'd have leapt to action at her merest word, but those days were past. I was older now, more jaded, and I was tired. Yet I could understand her concern, and she had lent me her car.

'Annie,' I heard myself answer, 'I'll be there as soon as I can.'

'Wonderful,' she said. 'I'll send the chauffeur.'

It was less wonderful than she imagined. I didn't have the energy to explain to her that I suspected our lodgings were being watched by operatives of the security forces.

'Tell him to wait for me outside the Shiva Temple at the College Street end of the road. I'll be there in fifteen minutes.'

I ended the call, and taking the scrap of paper with Dawson's number out of my pocket, I memorised it, then ripped the sheet to small shreds and threw half of the pieces in the bin. The remaining pieces I took out to the balcony, threw them over the railing and watched them scatter on the breeze.

There, out of the corner of my eye, I saw something. A movement in the shadows thrown by the orange glow of ill-spaced street lamps. I peered out, focusing on a patch across the street. It was hard to make out, and I couldn't be sure, but in my bones I felt there was someone there, watching.

I stalked back into the flat and into my bedroom, making a show of turning on the light, then five minutes later, I turned it off and closed the shutters. If someone *was* watching they'd assume I was finally turning in for the night. I gave it five minutes more, then grabbed my revolver, walked back through the darkened flat and out of the door.

If the girls in the brothel were surprised to see me skulk out through their courtyard again, they hid it well beneath a veil of ennui.

'You are busy, tonight, Captain sahib,' said Pia. 'Or are you just plucking up the courage to visit us properly?'

'Any more talk like that,' I said, 'and I'll have the Vice Division arrest you.'

Pia fluttered her eyelids. 'Oh please, Captain sahib. You know Singh-auntie pays the police more in a month than you earn in a year. You will only embarrass yourself.'

The girl was probably right, but I wasn't about to admit it.

'We'll have to finish this conversation later, Pia,' I said. 'Right now I need to go visit a different sort of madam.'

The Lancia was idling on the corner of College Street beside the little conical-domed shrine to the god Shiva. It was only as I opened the door that I registered that at the wheel was not the chauffeur but Annie herself.

'What?' she said, noting my surprise. 'It's the middle of the night, Sam. You think my chauffeur is on call twenty-four hours a day? And don't bother to get in just yet. You need to go back to your digs.'

Her demands were becoming increasingly erratic, but I decided to humour her.

'May I ask why, exactly?'

'Because you need to pick up some clothes for your friend, Suren.'

The sound of the stupid fool's name sent a shock through my synapses.

'You know where he is?'

She looked at me and rolled her eyes.

'He's at my flat of course. Are you *sure* you're a detective?'

'It's late,' I said. 'And why does he need a change of clothes?'

'He swapped his own with a station coolie.'

THIRTY

Sam Wyndham

As reunions went, this one was on the awkward side. Of course I would be relieved to see him, but that didn't really make up for him sticking a gun in my face earlier.

Yet any ill feeling I may have had instantly gave way to mirth when I saw him sitting there in what looked like Annie's bathrobe.

'Impressive disguise,' I said, 'though you could probably benefit from some lipstick and heels.'

He didn't seem to find it amusing.

I held out the bag containing his clothes. 'D'you want these or are you happy with your current attire?'

'You could be a little warmer with your welcome, Sam,' said Annie beside me. 'The poor boy's been through an awful lot.'

'He told you, did he?' I said. 'Did he also tell you that he threatened to shoot me this morning?'

'Oh, grow up, Sam,' she said. 'I doubt there are many people in this town who *haven't* threatened to shoot you at some point or other. I'm just surprised it took Suren this long. I've been tempted to do it myself on several occasions.'

Suren piped up. 'If it is any consolation, I would not actually have done it.'

'Glad to hear it,' I said.

156

'With you dead, I could not afford the rent by myself.'

Before I could think of a riposte, Annie's maid, Anju, entered the room with a pot of coffee. I'd asked for something stronger but Annie had deemed that *inappropriate* for three in the morning.

Suren took the bag and thanked me for the clothes.

'You OK?' I asked.

'I am, as you like to say, still alive.'

'Want to tell me where you've been all day?'

'Chasing Gulmohamed,' he said. 'I tracked him to Howrah but he was in the company of some military officers. I was not able to apprehend him.'

'Word is you jumped off his train,' I said.

He stared at me.

'Did Miss Grant tell you?'

'No. Colonel Dawson did.'

Suren's face fell. 'So Section H *are* looking for me, then. I had a feeling those were Dawson's men on the train.'

I took a sip of black coffee.

'You're right, those men on the train were Section H, but they weren't following Dawson's orders, and they weren't looking for you. Our friend Dawson appears to have rather fallen out with some of his colleagues in the Section.'

'Is that good?'

'It's good for *you*,' I said. 'He seems to want to help to clear your name.'

'Why?'

'Let's call it office politics.'

Suren scratched at an earlobe.

'I do not see how he can help me now that Gulmohamed is on his way back to Bombay.'

'Well, let's find out,' I said. 'He asked me to call him once you showed up.'

'And you trust him?'

I thought back to my conversation with the spymaster. He could have chosen anywhere for our meeting but he'd picked a location he knew would make me ask questions, which he in turn had answered. I saw now that he'd freely given up some of his secrets in order to win my trust. It was possible he was trying to fool me, but I doubted it. The authorities would eventually catch Suren with or without my help, and it really did seem as though Dawson had an issue with his colleagues. My gut said to take him at his word while my head counselled caution.

'We'll play it by ear.'

Suren went to change into something less comfortable and I telephoned the number Dawson had given me.

'It's me,' I said 'I've found him.'

From the other end came a momentary pause before the colonel finally spoke.

'What's his assessment?'

'He's sticking to his tale. Says our man from Bombay is responsible for what happened down in Budge Budge. But seeing as that bird has flown the coop, he's not sure what to do now.'

'I'd have thought,' said the spymaster, 'that the logical step would be to go to Bombay. The gentleman in question shouldn't be too hard to track down once you're there.'

Dawson was right. Tracking down Gulmohamed in Bombay was the obvious course of action, but the obvious option wasn't always the smartest. For a start, there were the logistics of the thing. The next train to Bombay wouldn't leave for another eighteen hours or so, and the journey itself would be close to another thirty-six. Even if the police didn't stop Suren at Howrah, the passage would be fraught with danger. And if we did manage to make it to Bombay, the city was a thousand miles away, a place where

Gulmohamed was a powerful man and where we would have no connections and no allies.

'It's a risk,' I said, 'putting my friend on a train for a day and a half. If Halifax finds out, he'll be a sitting duck.'

There came silence from the other end as Dawson ruminated.

'Let's see what we can do about that,' he said. 'D'you know the ordnance factory at Dum Dum?'

I wondered where this was going. 'Do you plan to shoot us out of a cannon?'

'Get to the factory by 5 a.m. I'll meet you there.'

'Dawson,' I said, 'if this is some ruse of yours to capture my colleague —'

'Don't be obtuse,' he said. 'There are bigger things at stake here than the arrest of your subaltern. Just get to Dum Dum by 5 a.m. The longer you delay, the harder it'll be to get him out of the city.'

THIRTY-ONE

Surendranath Banerjee

I wondered if Sam had taken leave of his senses. Trusting Colonel Dawson seemed as sensible as housetraining a tiger. But Sam's 'gut' had told him otherwise and I had not demurred. I simply hoped his gut knew what it was doing.

Miss Grant offered to drive us to Dum Dum, which was most sporting of her. I sometimes wondered what she made of Captain Wyndham and me. Given the lengths to which Sam went, often with my reluctantly co-opted assistance, to meddle in her personal affairs, she could be forgiven for wishing a pox upon both of us. Yet, instead, she had provided me with refuge in my hour of need and was now acting as our chauffeur to North Calcutta when much of its environs were aflame. Sam had tried to convince her to let us simply take the car, but she had refused, rather forcefully if truth be told, on the grounds that the Lancia had cost a pretty penny and she doubted she might ever see it again if she let us take it. It was indeed a fair point.

There would be checkpoints en route, so I was forced to lie on the floor of the rear of the vehicle, masked by blankets and a picnic hamper, while Sam sat up front next to Miss Grant. If stopped, they would claim to be on a day trip to view the temples at Jessore, some seventy miles away, thus precipitating the early start. That, together with Sam's police ID, should, we hoped, be enough to staunch any further inquiry.

Dum Dum comprised a military cantonment, a railway junction and the ordnance factory famous for one thing: the terrible Dum Dum bullet, which could crack a man's skull as though it were a watermelon and which did such terrible damage to human flesh.

Miss Grant was what Sam referred to as 'an eager driver', and indeed her eagerness to get us there quickly was never in much doubt as she threw the car over potholes at a breakneck, suicidal speed. After twenty minutes of a most bruising ride, I felt the car slow to a stop.

There came a muffled voice: a soldier, I assumed, manning a checkpoint. I heard Sam reply. His tone was nonchalant, as though driving through Calcutta at four in the morning was the most natural of things. It must have worked, for the car was soon moving again and I resumed my joust with the potholes.

The sky was still dark when the car next stopped and Sam pulled the blankets from my head.

'Rise and shine,' he said. 'We've work to do.'

I rose to find we'd stopped in an alley of ramshackle dwellings.

'This isn't the ordnance factory,' I said.

'Very perceptive,' he said. 'The factory's a five-minute walk away. I thought we might scout out the terrain, just to make sure Dawson isn't trying to double-cross us. And you could probably do with stretching your legs.'

'You think of everything,' I said.

Sam turned to Miss Grant. 'You'd better head home. Dawson's going to either blast us to Bombay or arrest us for murder and obstruction. Either way, you'd best be out of it.'

'Right,' she said, 'but telephone me once you've met Dawson ... just to let me know you're OK.'

'Your concern is most touching, Miss Grant,' he said. 'We shall most definitely call you, assuming Dawson hasn't shot us first.'

He set off down the alley and I made to follow, but turned one last time.

'Miss Grant,' I said. 'Thank you.'

She looked at me with what I felt was sincere affection. 'Take good care of yourself, Suren, and of Sam too. I'll see you back in Calcutta.'

I turned to go.

'And, Suren,' she said, calling me from behind. 'In future, I hope you'll think twice before arresting my friends just because Sam tells you to.'

It was not quite five in the morning, yet a fair number of souls were already on the streets. Calcutta is a city that rises early in order to make the most of the cooler hours. The passers-by paid us scant attention, the morning chill ensuring they had enough to be getting on with and no time to waste gawking at strangers.

The munitions factory was ringed by a corps of armed troops. This too was unsurprising given the events of the past twenty-four hours. When people are rioting, it is sensible to protect a warehouse stocked with weapons and ammunition. Sam went ahead to seek out Dawson, while I loitered in the shadows.

He returned several minutes later, in the back seat of a military staff car driven by an Indian chauffeur.

'Dawson sent his car,' he said. 'Get in.'

This time I had no cause to hide on the floor. A military car was unlikely to be stopped. Instead I sat back beside Sam.

'Where are we going?'

'Wait and see,' he said. 'I think I know what Dawson has in mind. And I think you're going to hate it.'

The car sped on, through the waking streets of Dum Dum and out into the mist-laden country beyond. It was only as we passed a sign for the military airfield that the penny dropped. My stomach turned.

'Are we?'

'Yes,' he said. 'I think we are.'

'And you're certain it is not a trap?'

'Oh, quite.'

'That is a shame,' I said.

Dawson was waiting inside a hut close to where several flying contraptions stood looming like vultures.

'Wyndham,' he said, by way of greeting. 'And I see you've brought your friend. Good show. Now listen carefully. For the purposes of this journey and your time in Bombay, you are both employees of the Post Office.'

Sam and I exchanged a glance. Extracting some documents from his pocket, he turned to me.

'Sergeant. Your name is Mr Nihar Dey. You are employed by the Post Office's Calcutta division, travelling to Bombay on postal business. Accommodation has been arranged for you at the Far Bengal Guest House, close to Victoria Terminus. It's Bengali-owned and is the natural home for travelling *babus* who find themselves in Bombay. Is that all clear?'

He handed me the papers and I examined them as a child would a new storybook. Alongside letters of introduction was a small booklet with a royal-blue cover, embossed with the lion and unicorn coat of arms and the words BRITISH INDIAN PASSPORT above it and INDIAN EMPIRE below. In a window at the bottom, the name MR N. DEY had been written in black ink.

'A passport?' I enquired. 'Is it required for Bombay?'

'No,' he said, 'but it was the easiest document to procure at short notice.'

'What Post Office business am I travelling to conduct?'

The colonel sighed in exasperation. 'That's irrelevant. No one is going to ask you, and if they do, make something up.'

He turned his attention to Sam.

'Wyndham, you're staying at Watson's Hotel. If you don't know where it is, ask a taxi driver when you get there.'

'No secret identity for me?'

'Last time I looked,' said Dawson, 'you weren't a fugitive. You can travel under your own name. No one's going to question you, but if they do, remember, you work for the Post Office. Now pay attention. There's a transport leaving in half an hour. It'll call at Cuttack, Nagpore and some other places en route, but it'll get you to Bombay before Gulmohamed's train arrives. Try not to talk to anyone during the flight and make sure you don't leave the plane till it reaches its final destination, not even to stretch your legs. I can't guarantee how long your cover is going to last. Once you have something to report, telephone me on the number I gave you. You do remember it, don't you?'

'Yes,' said Sam before pausing. 'But it wouldn't hurt if you were to write it down again.'

THIRTY-TWO

Sam Wyndham

The spymaster left, and I looked at Suren. One eye was still badly bruised, and his cheek bore the scar of a cut. For an official of the Post Office, he certainly lived a dangerous life. Nevertheless from his expression one would think that all of the trials he'd been through in the last forty-eight hours were as naught compared to what he was about to embark on. I should maybe have offered him some comforting words, but I've never been one for sentiment, and besides I had a telephone call to make.

'Wait here. I'll be back in a minute.'

'Where are you going?'

'To leave a message for Annie,' I said. 'Let her know we're still alive.'

I made for a Nissen hut close by. Inside, an airman in blue over-alls sat snoozing behind a desk, waking with a start as I entered and slammed the door behind me.

'Can I help you?'

'I need to use your telephone,' I said, in the tone that officers learn at prep school and which the lower orders are conditioned not to question. 'Official business.'

'Of course, sir,' said the airman, oblivious to my civvies and lack of identification. The deference which honest hard-working Eng-lishmen paid to those of their countrymen who pronounced their 't's, enunciated their 'aitches' was as predictable as the tides. Not that I was complaining. Having attended the most minor of minor public schools, the right accent had opened more than a few doors and now given me access to a military telephone.

I dialled the operator and asked to be connected to Chowringhee 2657.

Annie's maid answered after what felt like several rings too many.

'Memsahib gone to bed. She is returning home only few minutes ago,' she protested.

'Please fetch her,' I said. 'It's important.'

Annie came on the line half a minute later.

'Sam? Is everything all right?'

'For now. Dawson's arranged passage on an aircraft for Suren and me. We should be in Bombay before the evening.'

'How very pleasant for you both.'

'It's hardly pleasant,' I said. 'Suren's still a fugitive and I have to pretend I'm working for the Post Office.'

'Post Office? Not the police?'

'No.'

'Does that mean you can't arrest Gulmohamed?'

'That would seem to be the case.'

'Any idea what you're going to do?'

'I'll think of something,' I said. 'Maybe I could post him back to Calcutta. Second class.'

'I've some friends in Bombay,' she said. 'Influential people. I could put you in touch.'

A stab of jealousy flashed across my chest. Of course she did. There were bound to be men in Bombay who fawned over her in the same way her admirers in Calcutta did.

'I'm sure Suren and I can handle this without their help,' I said.

It was a stupid thing to say. One should never look a gift horse in the mouth, even if the particular horse was an admirer of Annie's.

'Of course you can,' she said, her voice taking on that exasperated tone I'd become all too familiar with. 'Just like the two of you have handled everything so fantastically so far. But I'm not going to argue with you, Sam. Just let me know when you reach Bombay.'

The plane was one of those huge, lumbering Vickers numbers: two sets of wings hung around a bulbous fuselage and engines the size of small cars. I'd always been keen on aircraft, even through the war years, stuck in a trench as the flyers of the RFC free-wheeled in their kites overhead.

I greeted the captain and crew, which is more than I can say for Suren, who seemed struck dumb by the whole experience. Indeed, getting him onto the plane was like persuading a dog into a bathtub.

'I've never been on an aeroplane before,' he said.

'I can see that.'

'Are they safe?'

'Absolutely,' I said. 'Unless there's a crash. But that's pretty rare these days. Otherwise I expect those fine flying johnnies in the cockpit would be doing a different job.'

'Have you flown before?'

'A few times,' I said, 'during the war. Reconnaissance work over German positions. Compared to that, this'll be a breeze. For starters I don't expect anyone'll be shooting at us. Not until we land at any rate.'

The interior was just a hollowed-out tube with a row of shelf-like seats along both sides, with harnesses to stop passengers from flying across the cabin in the event of turbulence. We seemed to be the only passengers, other than a sackful of military correspondence. The engines started with a roar and the Vickers Vernon began to rumble across the airfield. Suren, his knuckles taut, dug his fingers into the padding that passed for seats, screwed his eyes shut and uttered a prayer, I assumed, to the Hindu god of aircraft.

My stomach lurched as the beast took off. Suren still had his eyes closed but his expression suggested it was now less out of fear and more out of an attempt to keep his breakfast down. It was only once the plane had levelled off that he summoned the courage to open them.

'Are we *up*?' he said, shouting to be heard over the noise of the engines.

I nodded and pointed him to a porthole.

With a bit of goading, I persuaded him to unbuckle his harness and look out of the window. He peered out then turned round and beamed like a schoolboy.

'Everything is so small. So beautiful!'

That much was true. From up here, the country looked ordered and picturesque, a land of green fields and model villages. It was only when you got back down to earth that the truth punched you in the face.

From then on, he was glued to the window almost all the way to Cuttack, strapping himself in at the last minute and closing his eyes for the landing.

As the plane sat on the field, a staff car drew up. I held my breath as an officer stepped out, accompanied by an adjutant with a briefcase. They shook hands and the adjutant handed over the case. The officer made for the plane. He had one of those faces – like the melted wax at the base of a candle.

The door opened and the man, a major, judging by the pips on his shoulders, ducked beneath the low ceiling.

He was surprised to see two men in civvies sitting there, more so as one of them was an Indian with his face swollen like an aubergine. Still, he was polite about it, introducing himself as Major Parker of the Rajputana Rifles. I knew little about the regiment but still more than I did about the Indian postal service, which both Suren and I purported to represent.

Fortunately the major didn't prove to be the talkative type, preferring to spend his time sitting at the opposite end of the cabin, and as the plane took off once more, he buried his nose in a file of documents pulled from his briefcase.

As for Suren, with both his fear and the novelty of the flight beginning to wane, the lad finally fell asleep and I too must have succumbed at some point, because the next thing I knew, the plane was descending and out of the window I saw the turquoise blue of the Arabian Sea.

I nudged him and he awoke with a start.

'Look out there.' I pointed to the azure waters beyond the porthole.

He stifled a yawn. 'Where are we?'

'Just over Bombay.'

THIRTY-THREE

Surendranath Banerjee

I have reached the conclusion that I do not like landings. I am not enamoured of take-offs either, nor of mid-flight turbulence, but landings I find especially troublesome.

Our descent into Bombay was the worst of our several landings that day, with the plane tilting most ferociously and hitting the ground like a walrus landing on the deck of a boat. Sam blamed this on crosswinds blowing in off the Arabian Sea, but he is not a pilot and I could not see how he arrived at this conclusion so comprehensively. I voiced no doubts though, because I have found that it is generally easier to nod and accept the captain's comments as gospel truth than to express any scepticism or reservations on the matter.

And I was hardly in a position to quibble. Sam had kept me out of jail, at least for the present, and, I felt, afforded us a fighting chance of finding Gulmohamed and getting to the truth.

The plane came to a halt close to a row of wooden huts. The engines soon fell silent and it took my ears several minutes to adjust to their absence.

The military officer from Cuttack bade his adieus to Sam. Some Englishmen, especially military types, can be peculiar about consorting with Indians, so not wishing to cause any embarrassment, I got up and looked out of the porthole.

A fuel lorry and a staff car were approaching, the latter I assumed for the major. Otherwise, and to my great relief, there appeared to be little interest in our plane, and I stressed as much to Sam

'What were you expecting?' he asked. 'A brass band? Still,' he ruminated, 'a car and a driver might have been nice. Who knows how far we are from the centre of town. Which reminds me. How much cash do you have on you?'

The question came as a shock.

'I have nothing,' I said.

Sam puffed out his cheeks. 'That's unfortunate. I've only got about thirty rupees in my wallet.'

'At least you *still* have a wallet,' I said. 'Mine is likely lining the pocket of some constable from Budge Budge.'

'That's not the point,' he said. 'How long are we going to survive in Bombay with thirty rupees between us?'

'You didn't bring your chequebook?'

He looked at me as though the question were ridiculous.

'You may recall, Suren, that when I left the flat last night to come and provide you with more to wear than Miss Grant's dressing gown, I didn't think to myself *"I'm going to be in Bombay in a few hours. I better take my chequebook"*.'

'So what do we do?'

'We can worry about that later. For now, let's just get to town.'

Bombay is a curious city. Unlike Delhi or London, or even Calcutta, where the centre of town is located, as one would expect, in the centre, with suburbs radiating out in all directions, Bombay is built on a series of islands, an inverted triangle, with the 'centre' of the metropolis placed firmly at the southern tip. The airfield, it transpired, was situated in a locale known as Juhu, about fifteen miles to the north. We both agreed that requesting a lift from the military would be a foolhardy course of action. Sooner or later, the

Imperial Police or Dawson's colleagues in Section H would deduce that Sam and I were no longer in Calcutta, and join the dots of our escape. At that point, a lift in a military vehicle to the doors of our respective hotels would prove a significant liability. Therefore we had to either find a taxi or walk.

In the end we haggled a taxi-wallah down to an acceptable fare and got in. Out of sheer exhaustion we had not given much thought to devising a strategy to track down Gulmohamed. Indeed it was only as the car lurched forward that we considered the matter.

'Gulmohamed's train won't arrive till the small hours,' said Sam. 'That gives us time to come up with something. I suggest you go to your boarding house and get some rest. It's probably best if you lie low. We can meet five hours from now, tonight at 8 p.m.'

'Where?' I asked. 'It could raise suspicions if I came to your hotel. And even more so, the other way round.'

'We could meet at the station,' he said 'but there might be a lot of police or military activity there, and who knows how long we'll have before our friends back home realise you've flown the coop.'

'Another place then,' I said.

Sam smiled. 'Why not at that arch they're building? The one that's always in the papers and getting retired colonels all hot and bothered about the colossal waste of money. What are they calling it? The India Arch or something.'

'The Gateway of India.'

'That's it. Shouldn't be too difficult to find.'

'Very well,' I said. 'We can meet there.'

The taxi-wallah halted outside a black door in a crumbling wall. Above it, a pristine sign read *Guest House Far Bengal*.

I turned to Sam. It was hard to believe that only fifteen hours ago I had been dressed as a coolie and crossing the Hooghly in the dead of night. Now I was a thousand miles away in central Bombay.

If it hadn't been for him, I might be rotting in a prison cell, awaiting trial for Mukherjee's murder. I was by no means out of the woods, but that didn't mean I wasn't grateful.

'Thank you, Sam,' I said.

He looked genuinely confused. 'For what?'

'For ... everything.'

He is not one for great displays of emotion, or for that matter, any emotion; a fact his expression made clear.

'Get out,' he said, 'and get some rest.'

THIRTY-FOUR

Sam Wyndham

Watson's Hotel was a five-minute drive from Suren's lodgings. It was a handsome structure, a whitewashed, five-storey block with a colonnaded ground level and balconies wrapping the upper floors.

I walked in and crossed an acre of tiled floor to the mahogany counter and gave my name to the morning-suited duty-manager. I signed the guest register and was shown up to the third floor by a shiny-looking bellboy who had no luggage to carry but seemed to expect a tip nonetheless. I was about to fling him out on his ear when a different thought occurred. I opened my wallet and dipped into the meagre funds within, then tipped the lad rather generously given the circumstances. He seemed happy enough, beaming through a set of extremely white teeth and pointing to a button set in a brass plaque on the wall. 'Anything you need, sahib, just ring the bell and ask for Lawrence. I will be at the door, day or night, and in a jiffy.'

I wondered where a Bombay bellboy picked up a name like Lawrence or a word like *jiffy*. The name was probably bestowed upon him by the hotel, and as for *jiffy*, he might have picked it up from some guest, a passing governor-general maybe, or a viceroy in transit.

'I'll remember that,' I said. 'You could start by telling me where I can find a telephone.'

'Downstairs, sahib. At back of main lobby. Several telephone booths are there.'

He saw himself out and I opened the French windows to the balcony and the sounds of the city beyond. The room was as plush as could be expected, given the military were paying. A single bed, a desk, a wardrobe against the wall and even a sink in the corner.

I turned on the tap and washed my face, then headed out and made my way back down to the lobby. There I located the telephone booths and asked the operator to place a trunk call to Calcutta.

Dawson came on the line sooner than I'd expected.

'Hello?'

'It's your friend from the Post Office,' I said. 'We've arrived.'

'Your disappearance has been noticed,' he growled. 'Your colleagues paid a visit to your flat this morning, looking for your chum.' I could hear his teeth clicking against the pipe in his mouth.

'Do they know where —'

'No,' he said, 'at present, they're none the wiser as to your whereabouts. But that might change. You'll need to work quickly.'

That was easy for him to say. Gulmohamed was a powerful politician, on home turf, while I had no jurisdiction here and Suren was a wanted man. We didn't even have the inkling of a plan to apprehend him.

'Anything you can do to help?' I asked.

'Not for the present. Whatever I do now might alert suspicion.'

'There's a problem,' I said. 'We're rather low on funds.'

'How low?'

'About thirty-five rupees between us.'

I heard Dawson sigh and could almost picture his face. 'Christ. You didn't think to take a bit more?'

'You'll forgive me for not having had a chance to pop to the bank before we left,' I said, 'what with doing my job and half the city being on fire.'

'I can't help you,' he said, 'and we should keep this conversation brief. Anything else?'

'How's Taggart?' I asked.

'Still with us. The doctors report his condition as stable, but he's not out of the woods yet, not by a long chalk. Now if that's all, contact me when you've got something to report.'

With that he was gone and for a moment I thought I heard breathing on the line. It might have been the operator, or it might have been someone more sinister. I tried to shake the thought from my mind. Dawson had given me the number I assumed, because he knew it to be secure. He couldn't have been wrong.

I inserted another coin and asked the operator for a second trunk call, this one to Chowringhee 2657. The response was slower this time, but the call was taken eventually.

'Miss Grant's residence.'

'Anju,' I said, 'is Miss Grant there?'

'Memsahib is in her bedroom.' Her tone always seemed to harden once she realised it was me she was speaking to.

'Please call her to the telephone, Anju.'

'Memsahib is sleeping, possibly.'

'Then wake her ... please.'

There was silence on the line as the domestic servant and self-appointed gatekeeper went to fetch her mistress.

Annie eventually came on the line.

'Sam?'

'We're in Bombay.'

'And Suren's OK?'

'He's fine for now.'

'Good,' she said, 'I'm glad to hear it. Take care of him ... and yourself.'

I steeled myself, then launched in to the real reason for my calling her.

'Listen, Annie. I need another favour.'

'Of course you do, Sam.' I couldn't decide whether her tone was one of irritation or just plain exasperation.

'I wouldn't ask if it wasn't important. It's for Suren, if that makes a difference.'

'It doesn't make a difference.' Now I was sure it was irritation. 'Tell me what you need.'

'Money,' I said. 'I've got about thirty-five rupees on me and Suren hasn't got a bean, and we can hardly walk into a bank and request a wire transfer.'

'So what do you want me to do?'

I took a breath and swallowed my pride. Annie was a rich woman, with, it seemed, at least one rich friend in every port; some man who'd jump to attention at the sound of her voice. I didn't particularly like those men, but *needs must* and all that.

'You mentioned your friends in Bombay. Do you think any of them might be persuaded to advance me a small sum on your behalf? You could tell them I'm a friend from Calcutta who's come to Bombay and been robbed en route. I'd pay you back as soon as we get home ... assuming Suren and I aren't under arrest of course ... in which case it might take a bit longer, but I —'

'Sam,' she said, 'stop talking. Telephone me again tomorrow morning at eight. I'll see what I can do.'

THIRTY-FIVE

Surendranath Banerjee

The guest house was indeed as Colonel Dawson had described, a small corner of Calcutta in the heart of Bombay, where a travelling Bengali businessman or administrator could find sanctuary, swap his suit for a dhoti, and settle down to a dinner of *bhāt mach* in the mess hall.

I signed in under my newly adopted name, handing over the pass book of Mr Nihar Dey to a rather uninterested lady behind the counter who gave it a perfunctory scan before sliding it back and returning her nose to her copy of *Prabasi*.

'Pharst floor,' she said, pointing out the stairs with a gesture of the head. 'Breakfast, seven o'clock, *aar* dinner saarvice *chotta thekké aat-ta.*'

'Thank you, *mashi*,' I said and made dutifully for the stairs.

The room was larger than I'd expected and came complete with double bed, steel almirah and a window looking onto the busy road below. I removed my shirt, placed it on the back of a solitary chair, and decided to follow Sam's advice and take a rest.

Sleep though was difficult to come by. Instead, I simply lay back on the bed and took stock.

Forty-eight hours earlier, I had been a respected detective sergeant of the Imperial Police Force. Now I was a fugitive, wanted for murder and also, according to Sam at least, in connection with the bomb attack on Lord Taggart. If those were the items in the debit column, I struggled to find many which might be credits. I still had my freedom, and an opportunity to catch Gulmohamed, but my best chance to stop him had disappeared with a leap from the train outside Howrah.

At some point I must have dozed off, because when I awoke, the skies were dark and I looked out onto a wholly different Bombay.

THIRTY-SIX

Sam Wyndham

Policemen shouldn't take naps. I should have known that. After all, the very phrase *'copper caught napping'*, when it appears in a report to one's superiors, or, God forbid, a newspaper headline is seldom a harbinger of anything save disaster or opprobrium. In this case, the matter would be the worse for being literal.

After my call to Annie, I'd returned to my room and, for want of anything better to do, settled down on the bed for a few minutes' shut-eye, forty winks which turned into a fair few more. I awoke to a throbbing head and the persistent droning of a ship's horn out in the bay.

I sat up too quickly, wincing at white pain and closing my eyes in an attempt to lessen the sense that some insane dhol player was going to town on my temples. My mouth tasted like glue. Slowly, I rose from the mattress and made for the sink. Turning on the tap, I cupped a few handfuls of metallic water to my mouth, wiped my hands on my trousers and walked over to the balcony. From the street below came sound of tyres screeching to a halt. There was nothing particularly unusual in that. If road conditions in Bombay were anything like those in Calcutta, drivers would be required to press the brake pedal as firmly as they did the accelerator, just to avoid the bullock carts and bicycles that would plague their route at every turn. But then came the sound of slammed doors and commands issued in crisp military tones. I edged further out onto the balcony, close to the wall to ensure I was hidden in the shade, but far enough to catch a glimpse of what was taking place below.

In the street, two black cars had stopped outside the entrance and disgorged half a dozen men between them. None wore uniforms, but they didn't need to. I'd seen enough gorillas in suits and fedoras in my time to spot a plain–clothes man a mile off. I watched as several headed for the rear of the building while the other three entered the lobby. There was, I supposed, a chance that they were here on a matter unconnected to Suren and me, but there'd be snow in the streets of Calcutta before I'd take that particular bet.

I checked my watch. It had just gone six. Two hours yet till my rendezvous with Suren. I slipped into my shoes, jerked on my jacket and opened the door. The corridor was clear, but taking the lift or the main stairs was out of the question. I headed instead for the secondary stairwell, the one used by the chambermaids, which I found at the far end of the corridor. Opening the door, I headed in and down, but stopped dead after half a floor. I heard a door below open and slam against a wall, then the ring of boots on stone stairs. I wasn't going to find an exit that way. Turning, I ran silently back up to the third floor and along the corridor to my room. Once inside, I locked the door. Did I have to run? The most they could charge me with was aiding and abetting a fugitive and even that would prove hard to substantiate. But they would take me into custody and, at the very least, question me for the rest of the evening before putting me on the first transport back to Calcutta. And that would leave Suren stranded in Bombay without any possibility of clearing his name. Sooner or later, Section H would track him down and hand him over to the police and then, ultimately, a hangman's noose. Well, I had the answer to my question. Running was the only logical course of action.

I made for the balcony just as someone rapped loudly on my door. Gently closing the French windows behind me, I vaulted over the railing that separated my few square feet of terrace with that squared off for the adjoining room and kept going, vaulting over more railings till I reached a metal stairwell. The choice was straightforward: up to the roof or down to the street. The sight of a fedora-covered head in the alley below made the decision for me. I'd take my chances on the roof, and within seconds I was climbing the stairs, two at a time.

At the top, I stopped to catch my breath. How the hell had they tracked me down so quickly? Had Dawson set us up? But then why send us all the way to Bombay? He could have just arrested us both at the airfield in Dum Dum. Had *he* been compromised? I thought back to the odd noise on the end of the telephone line when I'd called him ... or ... I stopped in my tracks. There was an even darker possibility. Section H didn't just want to arrest Suren, they wanted to eliminate him. Making him disappear would be easier a thousand miles away in Bombay than it would in Calcutta, where he had friends.

Shouts from below roused me back to action. I scanned the surroundings for an escape. To my left lay a sheer five-storey drop to the street. To the right, the gap to the neighbouring building was too great a jump for anyone other than a pole vaulter or a madman. On the far side, however, the gap seemed reasonable, or at least not suicidal.

I sprinted forward, sweat sticking the shirt to my back, not just from the heat and exertion but also from the dawning realisation that I'd miscalculated the relative heights of the buildings. The roof of the adjoining block was a good ten feet lower than the one I was racing across. Even if I made the jump, the landing was likely to snap a limb or two. Discretion, as they say, is the better part of a broken leg, and I pulled to a halt just shy of the roof's edge. Going back was not an option. My pursuers would have gained access to my room by now. It wouldn't take long for them to check the balcony, and that would lead them to the roof. I knew because that's what I would do in their place. Down in the gully below, I made out the figure of another plain-clothes officer. The leap to the next building still looked like my only option, no matter how hard the landing.

I scanned the roof opposite. At one end, set back by a foot or so from the edge, was a concrete water tank. It jutted a few feet higher than its surroundings and if I could make the distance, the jump might be feasible without injury.

Over the noise of the traffic in the street, I thought I made out the sound of boots on metal. My time was slipping away. I steeled myself, broke into a run and leapt for my life, landing on the edge of the water tank and losing my balance. Momentum carried me forward, face first onto the concrete. The wind knocked out of me, I lay there summoning my wits and cursing Suren for getting me into this bloody mess in the first place.

Men were now on the hotel roof behind me. I could hear them. In my current position, sprawled atop the water tank, I would still be invisible to them if they remained at the far end of the roof. If and when they came closer, however, they'd be bound to spot me. I pulled myself together, crawled slowly to the side of the tank and dropped down behind it. As long as my pursuers stayed on the roof of the hotel, the water tank's bulk would hide me from view. If they attempted the leap I'd just made, however, all bets would be off.

I lay there waiting, attuned to any sound, any vibration in the air that suggested the men now on the roof of Watson's Hotel were considering the jump across. They stood at the threshold for what felt an inordinate length of time, but with every passing second my hopes rose. Eventually the voices died away, replaced by the sound of the traffic below and the cawing of crows above.

I decided to give it a good twenty minutes more before moving. I wasn't due to meet Suren till eight, assuming he hadn't already been traced to his guest house and arrested, so there was no need to leave my sanctuary while the men searching for me were still on high alert. Besides, my body still ached from the exertion of the run and the seven-foot drop onto the water tank.

When I did finally haul myself up, the sun had dipped below the horizon leaving only a crimson halo hanging low above the Arabian Sea. I slipped quietly across the roof, then jumped to another building before making my way down a stairwell to the street.

My clothes were caked in cement dust, but in the dark, I presumed no one would notice unless they looked closely, and I didn't plan on standing still long enough for anyone to manage that.

Maybe it was the sea air, but the backstreets of downtown Bombay seemed less fetid than those of Calcutta, which at this time of year were somewhere between a swamp and a steam bath. I took my time, spending half an hour meandering through the streets and skirting the docks between the hotel and the rendez-vous with Suren beside the new arch at Wellington Pier. Even then I was a good twenty minutes early and before long discovered the downside of choosing such a location for a clandestine meet-ing. The Gateway was situated on the waterfront, and though its grand arch was still not complete, that hadn't stopped the place becoming a bit of a tourist attraction. At this hour, the promenade beside it was thick with couples taking the evening air and hawk-ers attempting to sell them all manner of tat, and I was soon accosted, not by a policeman, but by a native with a pencil mous-tache and two pens clipped officiously to the inside of his shirt pocket. He claimed to be a guide and, for a most reasonable price, would show me all the sights of nocturnal Bombay that a gentle-man traveller might wish for.

'Everything from the hanging gardens,' he said with a smile, 'to our city's famous *nauch* girls.'

I told him I wasn't interested, but he merely took that as a challenge to try harder.

'You are staying at Taj Hotel, sahib? Wonderful hotel. Best hotel in whole world,' he said with a pride that suggested he might have had a hand in building it. In the end it took a flash of my warrant card to finally persuade him that I wanted neither a tour of the city's architectural highlights nor its carnal delights but simply to be left in peace. Even then, he gifted me a parting message.

'Remember, sahib, if you change your mind, I shall be round here only. My name is Mahesh. You ask personally for me. Some of these other buggers are rascals! They charge for moon, then take you all low-class places. With Mahesh only, you are sure of tip-top service.'

THIRTY-SEVEN

Surendranath Banerjee

It took several minutes to locate Sam among the crowds on the waterfront, but finally I found him near the arch, lurking, I must say, rather furtively and looking for all the world like a travelling salesman who had mislaid his stock.

'Am I glad to see you,' he said, with a degree of sincerity that left me frankly unnerved.

'I am only a few minutes late,' I said. 'The distance was further from the guest house than I had anticipated.'

'You've come straight from there?'

'Yes,' I said, not quite sure as to the purpose of the question.

'And you were there the whole time since the taxi dropped you off?'

'That's right,' I said. 'Why?'

He let out a breath, then reached into his pockets for his cigarettes. He passed me one, popped another in his own mouth, then lit us both.

'Let's just say I had a visit from some rather large plain-clothes types. Probably some of Dawson's erstwhile colleagues, or possibly Bombay CID.'

I could not help but stare. 'They didn't —'

'No,' he said. 'I gave them the slip.' He took a pull on his cigarette and exhaled a stream of blue smoke. 'I got out just before they reached my room. Had to jump across a couple of rooftops. Damn near broke my neck.'

'How did they know where to find you?'

'I've been wondering that myself,' he said. 'At first I thought Dawson might have been setting us up, getting us out of Calcutta before having us arrested, or possibly killed. But the fact that no one came looking for you suggests it probably wasn't his doing, otherwise they'd have picked us up simultaneously.'

'Then how?' I asked.

'The number Dawson gave me, the one he asked me to memorise, well, I think the line isn't as secure as Dawson thinks it is.'

'They've tapped his phone?'

'It's the only explanation. I telephone him from the hotel, then an hour later, two carloads of men turn up looking for me.'

'So now what?' I asked.

'Well, I'll need a new place to stay for a start. More importantly, if they know we're in Bombay, they might also know why we're here. If so, they'll be keeping an eye on Gulmohamed. I'm beginning to think that accosting him as he gets off the train tonight might be a tad suicidal.'

My stomach turned as my hopes fell. He was correct of course. There was no way we would be able to get to Gulmohamed tonight. And if the authorities knew we were in Bombay, it would be only a matter of time until they found us.

'That's it, then,' I said. 'My goose is well and truly cooked.'

Sam shook his head. 'It means nothing of the sort.' He clapped me on the back. 'Your goose is fine, and remember, there's more than one way to skin a cat.'

THIRTY-EIGHT

Sam Wyndham

Gulmohamed's train was running late. We knew because we'd promised a platform boy two annas to come to the all-night canteen where we'd taken refuge and give us half an hour's warning of its arrival. The boy was one of the countless orphans who lived on the railway lines and knew its comings and goings as intimately as any stationmaster, so we were in good hands.

The delay was hardly surprising. We British might have given India its railways, but someone really should have thrown in a timetable to go with it. Too many trains in the country seemed to depart with only the vaguest notion of when they might actually arrive at their destinations. Indeed, the essential requirement for railway travel in India was not a train ticket but a good book that could see you through the interminable delays.

The wait was inconvenient, all the more so given that there was a limit to just how many cups of tea Suren and I could consume in the interim. Still, it gave us time to if not fine-tune our plan, then to at least paper over some of its more gaping holes.

'And he won't recognise you?' I asked.

Suren shrugged. 'I sincerely hope not. The last time he saw me I was turban-clad and dressed as a coolie. It was merely for half a minute and I believe his attention was focused less on my face and more on the gun in my hand. Not that it matters. This is never going to work.'

He was probably right, but I wasn't about to say so. Even in his darkest hours, a man needs hope, or failing that, a belief in God.

'Trust me, it'll work.'

Suren raised an eyebrow. Behind him, the door opened and the platform boy hurried in, a broad smile on his face.

'*Sahib, train lagabhag aa chukee hai.*'

'How long?'

'Twenty-five minutes.'

I passed the boy his two annas and looked up at the clock on the wall. 3 a.m. and then some. Gulmohamed's train would arrive by half past.

I turned to Suren. 'Let's go.'

I'd spotted the car beforehand. A black Crossley, parked in a side street lock-up that hadn't been locked up particularly securely. There should have been a durwan somewhere watching over it, but he was probably taking a nap in one of the garages close by. With the aid of a rock, Suren and I broke the worm-eaten wood around the hinges of one of the garage doors, thus removing any need to worry about the heavy chain and padlock that fastened it to its partner.

The car inside was covered in a decent coating of dust which in England might have suggested it had been off the road for a month but in India signified a hiatus of anything as short as forty-eight hours.

Taking some rags from the footwell, we got to work wiping it down, then gently wheeled it out of its bed, down the street and round a corner to the nearest main road.

There, Suren took up station behind the wheel while I made for the crank handle at the front. It took several arm-wrenching turns before the bloody thing fired finally to life.

'I am still not confident about this,' he said, as I took the seat next to him.

'You have to do it,' I said. 'It'll look odd if I drive. You only need to manage a minute or two till we're away from the station. I'll take over from there.'

I'd explained to him the rudiments of driving over several cups of canteen tea. Now it was time to put theory into practice.

'Now,' I said, 'just as we practised, foot down ... engage gear ... gently off the clutch and onto the accel—'

The car jerked then spluttered to a halt.

'Right,' I said. 'Let's try it again.'

With ten minutes' practice behind us, and five left to spare before Gulmohamed's train was due to pull in, Suren had sufficiently mastered first gear to a level where, with the assistance of the gods, he could trundle quite a fair distance without stalling.

'Good enough,' I said. 'Let's go.'

I sat in the back while he manoeuvred the car and brought it stuttering to a halt at the station's taxi rank. Ahead of us, two other cars were parked up – real taxis, I presumed – with their drivers dozing in their cabs.

From here, the main entrance to the station was clearly visible. Of course there were other exits, but from what I'd read in the press, Farid Gulmohamed didn't strike me as the sort of man who used side exits. With luck, he'd come out of the station, with or without an armed guard, and get into a car which we'd follow until he reached his home. And while his escort might stay with him tonight, it'd be that much easier to get to him later, once we knew where he lived.

I scanned the steps and the area around the entrance. Save for a couple of sari-clad cleaner-women with their dried-grass brooms and a railwayman having a smoke, the place was devoid of life. If there were any Section H or police operatives in the area, they were either inside the station or remarkably well hidden.

As we sat there, a rotund chap in a white shirt and a Congress cap emerged from a small wooden hut near the front of the rank.

'Taxi marshal,' said Suren.

The man walked to the lead car in the rank, bent over to have a word with the driver, then straightened up and noticed our little Crossley parked at the end. He began to walk over, his expression suggesting he knew we weren't one of his regular cabs and that illicit parking in his rank might constitute a cardinal sin.

He marched over to Suren's window, demanding to see his credentials.

'Permit, *dikhao!*'

While Suren tried to placate the man in what even I could tell was garbled Hindustani, I spotted Gulmohamed exiting the station. From his photographs in the paper, I'd expected him to be taller. Beside him strode a policeman. Not an inspector or even a sergeant, but a regular beat constable.

'Suren,' I said, tapping him on the shoulder, but he was too busy remonstrating with the taxi marshal to notice. We didn't have time for that, so I stuck my head forward and the little man in the Congress cap stepped back in shock.

The sight of a white face had the same effect it always does on a certain type of Indian. He seemed suddenly lost for words, the wind blown out of his sails, and when he did relocate his tongue, his tone was far more measured.

'Tell him we won't be here much longer,' I said to Suren. 'A minute or two at most.'

'What?'

I gestured out of the window with a nod. 'There's our man.'

Gulmohamed had left the constable on the station steps and was even now walking towards the taxi rank.

The taxi marshal too noticed his approach and was straightening up.

'Stop him,' I said to Suren.

He turned in his seat. 'The marshal?'

'Quickly,' I said. 'I've got an idea.'

'*Bhai saahb!*' shouted Suren. '*Ek* minute.'

I took out my warrant card and shoved it at the sergeant.

'Show him that. Tell him you're on police business and that you're going to pick up that fare.'

Suren did as ordered and for an instant it seemed the fat marshal was about to protest. But any such thoughts were quickly staunched as I stepped out of the car with my revolver in my hand. The man got the message, then scuttled off to tell the lead taxi-wallah that he would have to wait a while longer for a customer.

I turned to Suren. 'Pick up Gulmohamed. Ask him where he wants to go, then drive round the corner. I'll be waiting there.'

'What?' he said in shock.

'Just do it.'

With a grinding crunch of gears, Suren set off towards the front of the rank where the marshal waived him forward as though he were landing an aircraft. Gulmohamed reached the rank and began to chat to the man, no doubt negotiating the fare. The lack of police presence puzzled me. If they were letting him go home unaccompanied, it suggested that the men who had pitched up at my hotel earlier were not the same people in charge of Gulmohamed's security, or at least they hadn't been informed that *he* was the reason why Suren and I had come to Bombay. That bolstered my growing belief that Dawson hadn't sold us out, but rather that his phone had been tapped.

I assumed that those who'd tapped Dawson's line were his colleagues in Section H, as the idea that the police could tap his phone without him getting wind of it was laughable. Lal Bazar leaked like a colander and Dawson probably knew as much of what went on in the building as the Commissioner himself. Those responsible for

Gulmohamed's safety, however, would have been police. The authorities in Calcutta would have been alarmed by the Hindu—Muslim rioting and made sure that such a high-profile leader was safely escorted out of the city. Once out of Bengal, he was no longer their problem, and in Bombay, still thankfully free from the violence, the local authorities must have considered the only precaution necessary was for a constable to meet him at the station. There was of course another possibility: that even now Section H did indeed have him under surveillance, and that I'd just failed to spot their agents. If so, Suren and I might be driving straight into a trap. With a sudden dread, I watched Gulmohamed get into the back of Suren's taxi. If this *was* a trap, we'd find out soon enough.

THIRTY-NINE

Surendranath Banerjee

The rear door opened and Gulmohamed stepped in.

'Kemp's Corner,' said the man who had effectively sentenced me to death.

I had tailed him all the way to the house in Budge Budge and brandished a gun at him on the train at Howrah, but thankfully he still displayed no sign of recognition.

'*Jee, saahb,*' I said, and jerked the car forward. Ponderously I guided the vehicle round the corner and came to a halt at the spot where Sam had instructed me. The street appeared deserted.

Gulmohamed looked up.

'Why are you stopping?' he asked, and received his answer in the form of a door opening and a revolver being pushed in his face.

'Good evening, Mr Gulmohamed,' said Sam. 'I'm afraid we're going to be making a slight detour on your way home.'

Sam and I switched places. He took the seat behind the wheel, while I took the gun and stepped into the back next to Gulmohamed.

The politician appeared more confused than scared, possibly because the man who'd first pointed a revolver at him was an Englishman, and Englishmen weren't in the habit of robbing Indians, unless it was on a national scale.

'What the hell is this?'

194

'Please keep quiet,' I said. 'You'll be offered your chance to talk soon enough.'

Recognition dawned on his face.

'I know you! You're that lunatic who boarded the train! But you ... you jumped off!'

'I told you not to talk.'

It was a simple enough instruction and it should have sufficed given I had a revolver in my hand, but the man didn't seem to take the point.

'Where are you taking me?'

That was a good question. I certainly didn't know and I doubted Sam did either. Wherever it was, at least we were getting us there at a fair rate of knots.

'Keep quiet,' I repeated, this time with an air of aggression. A moment later I was thrown on top of our hostage as, with a scream of the tyres, Sam slewed the vehicle hard to the right. Gulmo-hamed snatched at my revolver, but a tad too slowly, and he sensibly decided to adjust his behaviour as I pushed the gun in his ribs. After that he was hardly any trouble.

To the right, art deco buildings flew by, and to our left the Bombay seafront, illuminated by a string of street lamps, stretched out in an arc. The car raced along, then up a twisting, winding hill road.

Sam brought the car to a halt on an unlit road, bordered on one side by sleeping mansion blocks and by railings and overgrown foliage on the other.

'Time to get out,' he said, and I guided our prisoner onto the pavement. Gulmohamed seemed to recognise the locale.

'The Hanging Gardens?' he asked.

'Close enough,' said Sam. 'I like the sound of the place.' His voice had taken on a hint of menace 'Let's hope for your sake we don't need to make it literal. Now we're going to take a little walk.'

The road was deserted, shorn even of stray dogs, and Sam led the way towards some rough ground fenced off by iron railings. The gate was locked and chained shut, which proved less of a hindrance than might have been assumed as the railings beside it were only three feet high. Sam vaulted them and, with the revolver as encouragement, I gestured for Gulmohamed to follow suit. Within minutes we had crossed the coarse ground and were now hidden from view by a screen of trees. I felt the breeze on my face, tinged with the scent of brine.

Sam continued walking, stopping finally at the edge of a sheer drop. The moonlit shimmer of grass was replaced by dead black, and beyond it, the rippling emptiness of the Arabian Sea.

'Far enough,' he said.

The sight of the cliff edge seemed to unnerve Gulmohamed.

'What do you want from me?' His voice was a whisper.

Sam gave me a nod.

'Prashant Mukherjee,' I said. 'What business did you have with him?'

Gulmohamed stared blankly.

'Who?'

I looked at Sam, who simply shrugged.

'Please do not try to play innocent with us,' I said. 'You went to see him at a house in Calcutta, and we know you killed him.'

Gulmohamed shook his head. 'I don't know what you're talking about. I didn't meet anyone by that name and I certainly didn't kill anyone. Who are you anyway?'

'Prashant Mukherjee,' I said. 'The Shiva Sabha theologian. The man whose death sparked all the violence in Calcutta.'

'I don't know anything about —'

Sam had had enough.

'Look,' he said, edging towards Gulmohamed and taking a grip of his tie. He dragged the politician close to the cliff edge, then swept his feet from under him. Gulmohamed landed with his head and shoulders hanging over the precipice, with Sam still holding on to his tie. 'Now you tell my friend here what he wants to know or you'll be getting a much closer view of the rocks down there.'

The sweat on Gulmohamed's face glistened in the moonlight. 'I'm telling you, I've never met anyone called Mukherjee!'

'The house,' I said. 'The place in Budge Budge you visited three days ago. You remember *that* place?'

Gulmohamed said nothing.

Sam lifted him to his feet and, still with a grip of his tie, pushed him to the edge of the drop. That seemed to jog his memory.

'All right!' shouted Gulmohamed. 'I remember it! What of it?'

'Mukherjee was found dead in that house,' I said. 'I followed you there. Your accomplice knocked me out while you murdered Mukherjee.'

'Accomplice? What are you talking about? I didn't murder anyone. That's not what —'

Sam gave him another little nudge.

'Wait!' said Gulmohamed. He was breathing heavily now, panting. 'You have it completely wrong!'

Sam dragged him back from the edge, pushed him in the direction of a nearby rock and urged him rather physically to sit.

'So what *did* happen?'

Gulmohamed caught his breath and swallowed.

'I was in Calcutta at the behest of an acquaintance. A man I'd met here in Bombay. He said there was a gentleman in Calcutta, a potential benefactor he called Yusuf, who wanted to meet me. He claimed the chap was interested in donating a substantial amount to the party.' He took a breath. 'I suggested he meet our people in Calcutta, but I was told the gentleman didn't want anyone in Calcutta knowing about his donation. He would speak only to me. So I agreed to go there to meet him.'

'And?'

'My acquaintance was supposed to take me to meet this Yusuf, but he reneged at the last minute, claiming Yusuf insisted on meeting me alone. I wasn't pleased, but I went, nevertheless. But something felt wrong. A life in politics helps one develop a nose for such things. The suburb where this Yusuf supposedly resided seemed rather common. Not the sort of place one would expect a wealthy man to live. But people can be eccentric, so I kept going. My suspicions grew as I realised also that the area was hardly a Muslim one. There seemed to be saffron flags on every other street corner. Still I continued, all the way to this man's front gate. It was only then that I stopped. On the ground in front of the door was a faded rangoli. The kind that Hindu women draw at puja time. It couldn't have been the home of a Muslim, especially not one willing to donate money to our cause. I checked the address, but it was the correct house. I'd been sent on a wild goose chase.'

'What did you do then?' asked Sam.

'I left. I returned to Metiabruz where I was staying. I tried reaching my contact at his hotel, only to be told he had checked out. And then, the next day, all hell broke loose and I took the first train back to Bombay.'

Gulmohamed dropped his head to his hands. 'Now you're try-ing to pin the murder of some Hindu firebrand on me.'

Sam brandished the gun at him.

'Don't lie to us. You were seen by my colleague here, going into that house. We know you killed him.'

Gulmohamed shook his head. 'I don't know who you are, but I'm telling you the truth. Why would I possibly travel all the way to Calcutta to kill a man I'd never met? And if I wanted him dead, do you think I'd be fool enough to do it myself?'

Sam turned to me, his thoughts evident from the look on his face. Gulmohamed had a point. And the truth was, having been clubbed in the street outside, I never actually saw Gulmohamed enter the building.

'This acquaintance of yours,' I said, 'the one you claim set up the meeting. He has a name?'

'I'd rather not say. He's a man who values his privacy.'

Once more Sam grabbed him by the collar and began to drag him back towards the precipice.

'We're not fooling around here,' he growled, picking up momentum, halting so close to the edge that Gulmohamed's shoes kicked dust off the ledge. 'Now what's his name?'

'Irani!' gasped Gulmohamed. 'Cyrus Irani.'

'Tell me about him.'

'I don't know much. He's a Parsee businessman from Rangoon. Arrived in Bombay some months ago.'

'Describe him,' I said.

'He's a big chap. Shaven-headed. Stands out in a crowd.'

It sounded like the man I had seen him with at the Lotus Hotel the day Mukherjee was murdered.

'Have you spoken to him since?'

'No, I told you, he wasn't at his hotel when I telephoned.'

Sam led him back to the rock and forced him to sit.

'Wait here,' he said, then pulled me to one side. He kept the gun pointed at Gulmohamed. 'What do you think?'

'He has to be lying,' I said.

Sam stood there, his face impassive as he thought it through. 'I'm not so sure.'

'Maybe Dawson is wrong,' I protested, 'and Gulmohamed actually is working for Section H?'

'I doubt it,' said Sam. 'Section H know we're in town. If he was their agent, they'd have sent someone to meet him at the station. We wouldn't have caught a sniff of him.'

'So what now?' I asked.

'I truly don't know,' he said. 'It's not as though we can arrest him. He's got more clout here than we do.'

I did not want to believe it. 'So we just let him go?'

Sam walked back to Gulmohamed.

'How do we find this Irani?' he asked.

Gulmohamed seemed surprised by the question. 'You found me. You can find him.'

'Humour us.'

'Try the Taj Hotel. He has a suite there.'

Sam nodded. 'Well then. You're no doubt tired after your long journey. I suppose we should get you home.'

FORTY

Sam Wyndham

We dropped Gulmohamed at Kemp's Corner. If it was unusual to interrogate a man and then drop him home, it was also a tad embarrassing, as being strangers to the city, we had to rely on his directions. Still, he could console himself with the knowledge that we didn't charge him the cab fare, even though we could have done with the money.

We left him near his front door with a smile and a warning that should he mention this evening's events to anyone, we'd pay him another visit that wouldn't end quite so amicably.

Back in the car, Suren and I headed for the lockdown near the station to return our borrowed vehicle. The sergeant was taciturn. For the best part of three days he'd chased Gulmohamed and now, having caught him, we had no option but to let him go. But this was no time to fester.

'Come on, spit it out.' I said as we drove through deserted, lamp-lit streets.

Suren weighed his response as though each word was a burden.

'All this time I have been sustaining myself on the hope that when we caught Gulmohamed, I would be able to prove my innocence. That appears naive now.'

'Nonsense,' I said. 'Tomorrow, we'll start tracking down this Irani chap.'

Suren looked straight ahead. 'I doubt that will make a difference. If we cannot link Gulmohamed to the case, what chance is there that we will have more luck with some Parsee businessman? He probably has no involvement at all. Parsees are about the most law-abiding people in the whole empire. When was the last time you heard of a Parsee so much as littering let alone committing a murder?'

I couldn't help but laugh.

'How many times have I told you that no one is ever totally innocent, not the Parsees, and not even your sainted Mahatma Gandhi sitting in his prison cell. We'll get to the bottom of this.'

'Even if it kills *me*?'

'Let's hope it doesn't come to that.'

'Very well,' he said, regaining a measure of optimism. 'As you say, first thing tomorrow, we start looking for Cyrus Irani.'

'Second thing,' I corrected him. 'First thing, I need to telephone Miss Grant.'

He gave me a look. 'You have to check in with her every morning? She must be *most* concerned as to your welfare.'

'Hardly,' I said. 'I asked her to sort us out with some cash.'

'Asking a lady for money? This is not proper.'

He was right of course, but we had little option.

'As you might have noticed,' I said, 'I can't go back to my hotel and we're pretty much flat broke. So unless you have a better idea, we're going to need to rely on the charity of Miss Grant.'

'Where *are* you going to sleep tonight?'

That was a good question. Spending the night on the floor of Suren's room at the Far Bengal Guest House was as ludicrous as going back to Watson's. The notion of a sahib spending the night in an establishment patronised by Indians was just the sort of thing to attract undesired attention.

'I'll find somewhere.'

We rolled the car back into the lock-up, past an open-jawed dur-wan who showed no sign that he'd noticed it had ever gone missing in the first place.

The man seemed unsure of how to react. His job was to prevent the theft of items under his care. No one had ever stipulated what to do in the event of stolen property being returned. Raising the alarm now would be like closing the stable door not only after the horse had bolted, but after it had gone for a run, won the Grand National and then returned home safe and well. In the end, he decided to do nothing.

Suren and I parted a few minutes later, he heading to the Far Bengal Guest House and I ... well that remained to be seen.

'You are certain you will be OK?' he asked with the concern of a mother hen.

I was a veteran of the trenches of the Western Front, not to mention a former opium addict. I'd found billets in far more hellish locales than South Bombay and managed a decent night's sleep to boot. 'I'll see you at the Gateway again. Tomorrow morning. Nine sharp.'

I watched him head north and then I set off in the direction of the dockyards.

On a cobbled backstreet, out of sight of the docks yet still close enough for the air to smell of rotting fish and diesel fumes, I found what I was looking for: a row of dilapidated buildings, each with identical worn and cracked brick facades and bearing hand-painted blue-and-white signs above their entrances.

The sign above the smallest, which also happened to be the closest to me, read *Punjabi Seamen's Lodging House*. The one beside it, a little larger yet just as dilapidated, had a similar sign, this one stating it catered to Kharwa sailors. And so it went on, a roll-call of the seafaring communities of India, the Konkanis, the Goanese, a separate lodging for Muslims, regardless of ethnicity, Bengali lascars and Tamils.

Outside them, sailors loitered in groups, smoking, playing poker and *thanee*, drinking bathtub hooch from tin cups and wearing the look of men unused to having time on their hands or money in their pockets.

Finally, and set apart slightly from the others, was the European Seamen's Lodging House. Here a man could get a mattress for the night and a coffee in the morning for little money down and fewer questions asked. It wasn't the Ritz, but by the same token it wasn't a waterlogged trench on the Marne, so I wasn't about to complain.

I walked into an ill-lit reception where a man with a ginger beard and the physique of a bear snored in a chair behind a counter. I leaned over and woke him as gently as possible with a prod of one of his substantial arms.

He let out a snort, opened his eyes slowly, as though the act required a degree of effort bordering on the Herculean, and then passed a burst of wind.

'Yeah?'

'I need a bed,' I said.

The man scrutinised me with the energy of a sloth.

'Ain't seen you in 'ere before. You new?'

'Just got in,' I said. 'First time in town.'

That seemed more information than he cared for, and with the formalities over, he shoved an open ledger and a pen on a greasy string across the counter towards me.

'Fill in yer details,' he said. 'Charge is 'alf a rupee a night.'

I made up a name, and a vessel that I'd sailed in on, added an indecipherable scrawl as a signature and paid for two nights.

The bear took back the ledger without a glance and placed the money in a battered cash box.

'You'll find a bunk in room 3 on the second floor.'

FORTY-ONE

Surendranath Banerjee

For a Bengali, Bombay is, in certain respects, stranger than England. We have spent a hundred and fifty years with the English. Enough time to come to terms with their eccentricities, their starched collars and their strange preference for hounds and horses to human beings. Our Gujarati and Maratha brothers and sisters though, the bulk of the Indian population of this fair city, are a different issue entirely. The fact is, that while unified by religion and a certain distant kinship, a Bengali will never be fully trusting of any Indian who prefers roti to rice, and vegetables to fish. But then, it is hard to blame these non-Bengalis for their choice, given the paltry offerings of the Arabian Sea as compared to the piscine bounty of our Bay of Bengal. Take the favoured local fish: the pomfret. It is flat, ugly-looking, and in terms of taste, not a patch on our own handsome hilsa or noble ruhi. Furthermore, and as a keen cricketer, I felt there was a certain justice in the fact that the pomfret was known here as Bombay *duck*.

So it was indeed a relief to finally return to the Far Bengal Guest House and find the kitchen still open and manned by a bristling, *goondah*-looking fellow in a lungi and a half-sleeve vest who went by the name of Bhontu-dā. He was the sort of chap, who, back in Calcutta I might have given a wide berth – much brawn and very little brain – a rather un-Bengali sort of Bengali, but here, far from home, the mere opportunity to exchange a few words with another soul in our shared mother tongue provided comfort.

'So, *dada*,' he said, ladling a generous helping of *machher-jhōl* onto my plate, 'you have been out late. Enjoying the city?'

The familiar aroma evoked memories of my mother's own cooking, which I had not savoured in far too long.

'I have been working,' I said.

'Working? At this hour? What is your business?'

And immediately I regretted my nostalgia for Bengali conversation.

'What is it you do,' he repeated, 'to be out so late?'

There was nothing for it. In normal circumstances I might have invented something convincing, but now, having been given a cover story, I felt I had little choice but to stick to it. I marvelled at the absurdity, that the truth could be replaced with a lie, but not a lie with another one.

'I work for the Post Office.'

'Hmmm.' He nodded sagely. 'My cousin Bala in Konnagar is also a postman. Like you, he delivers his letters very early. But he gets to sleep all day.'

I made my excuses, carried my plate to a corner table and sat down.

Removing a single green chilli from atop the fish, I tore off a morsel of the now mustard-coloured flesh, and taking some rice, began to eat.

Despite Sam's exhortations to the contrary, I was doubtful we would even get close to Irani, let alone find a way of questioning him about whether he had indeed sent Gulmohamed to the house in Budge Budge, and if so, why? None of it made sense to me, and if I could not explain it, then what hope was there that a judge would fare any better when I put it forward as my defence in a murder trial? As I sat there in the mess hall of a Bombay guest house, slowly savouring the dish of my homeland, the truth crept up on me like a winter fever. I would not be able to prove my innocence. There would be a trial and I would be found guilty, and then I would be hanged.

I was not, I told myself, scared of death. But it was one thing to die in the line of duty, or in the service of a greater cause, quite another to be hanged for a crime, and more so one which I had not committed. *That* would be a futile and shameful death.

I pushed my plate away, reeling at the thought. It felt as though a ton weight had smashed into my stomach. My head swam in a sudden maelstrom as all the hitherto certainties of my life crashed around me and disintegrated to dust. Tears, borne on a tide of self-pity, welled up, and I felt the first treacherous one trickle down my cheek. This emotion was not fitting. What would my father say if he saw me indulging in such shameful despair? I wiped the tear angrily away and pulled myself together. If that were to be my fate, then so be it. I would face it. There were worse things in the world.

FORTY-TWO

Sam Wyndham

I pulled the thin blanket up to my neck in a bid to staunch the shivering. A year ago, such shakes might have been from opium withdrawal, but this morning they were from a good old-fashioned chill in the air. Bombay wasn't cold, but it also wasn't Calcutta, which at times made a steam bath seem frigid, and the dawn here was punctuated by a sea breeze that blocked my sinuses and inflicted an ache in my temples.

I got up to the sound of mynah birds outside and the sawtoothed snores of the sailors within. The room reeked of rough tobacco, stale sweat and the melancholy sense of listlessness that haunts merchant seamen on furlough. They were men shorn of routine and purpose, cast adrift in a foreign land with too much time to ponder on fragmented lives lived fleetingly, on loves lost and chances sacrificed. In some ways, they weren't that different from policemen.

Breakfast was consumed in a shabby mess hall and comprised a cup of coffee and a ship's biscuit that could have been better used lining the hull of the *Titanic*. Still, the coffee was strong and, more importantly, hot, and that came as a blessed relief after thirty seconds spent under the deluge of an ice-cold bucket shower.

The big chap with the ginger beard was still behind the counter as I left the lodgings and walked back towards the main road. The early mornings are the best time in any city in the tropics. The air has yet to broil, the citizens are still too sluggish to cause trouble, and there's a certain translucent quality to the light that imbues everything with a hope-inducing freshness that generally lasts until one's first interaction with another human being. In this case, that first interaction was with Annie's maid, Anju, on the other end of a trunk call made from a post office on Cuffe Parade.

'Madam is asleep.'

'It's eight o'clock in the morning, Anju,' I said. 'Can you wake her? She told me to telephone her at this time.'

'She did not tell me to wake her for telephone.'

'It's rather urgent.'

'Madam is leaving message for you,' she said, like a judge offering a glimmer of hope to a condemned man.

'You might have started with that.'

'*Kee?*'

'Just give me the message.'

'Madam is saying you to contact one Ooravis Colah.' She read out an address on Malabar Hill. 'Madam has made arrangements as you requested. You are expected any time before noon.'

I asked her for the exact spelling and then, for want of anywhere better, wrote down the name and the address on the palm of my hand and breathed a sigh of relief.

'You want anything else?' Anju said baldly.

'Yes, as a matter of fact,' I said. 'I'm afraid I really do need to speak to the memsahib.'

Anju eventually relented and went to call her mistress. There was a click on the line, and then, finally, I heard Annie's voice.

'Sam?'

'I'm sorry to wake you.'

'Didn't Anju give you the details?'

'She did,' I said, hoping to strike a placatory tone, 'and thank you for that. There's just one other thing . . .'

There was silence on the other end of the line.

'You know I wouldn't ask, but it's important.'

When she spoke, her voice held none of the irritation I'd expected.

'I've just picked up the paper. Suren's name is on the front page. They say he's wanted in connection with the attempted assassination of a senior policeman.'

I staggered back in shock.

'What?'

'Surendranath Banerjee, sergeant with the Imperial Police, stationed at Lal Bazar. Wanted in connection with an attack in Alipore. Sam, it's not —'

'No, it's not true. He had nothing to do with that, but if we're going to prove it, I'm going to need to ask another favour of you. I need you to contact a man called Dawson. You need to go and see him personally. Phone his secretary at Fort William. Tell her who you are, that you've a message from a mutual friend, and that you need to meet him urgently. He should be able to work it out. When you meet him, tell him I suspect the secure telephone line he uses has been tapped. Ask him for another number and a time when we can speak. Have you got that?'

'Yes,' she said, then proceeded to repeat the details.

I gave her the spymaster's telephone number at Fort William.

'And, Annie,' I said. 'Thank you.'

Suren was waiting for me at the Gateway, fending off a peanut vendor with a practised scowl.

'You're early,' I said.

Suren rubbed at his chin. 'I couldn't sleep.'

'You didn't have any problems then? No visits from the authorities in the middle of the night?'

'Thankfully, no.'

I considered handing him the newspaper I'd picked up en route, but decided it could wait awhile. It was a Bombay edition of the *Times of India*, but the story was still on the front page:

CALCUTTA BOMB PLOT, SENIOR POLICEMAN INJURED
Manhunt for fugitive thought to be in Bombay

His name was there. Sergeant Surendranath Banerjee. What's more it was spelled correctly. He'd have appreciated that in other circumstances. All that was missing was a police sketch. It was a small mercy, but a significant one. It meant we still had a degree of freedom to move around. All the same, it would be dangerous for him to go back to the guest house.

'If the police suspect you're in Bombay,' I said, 'there's a good chance that sooner or later they'll track you down. And I'd bet a Bengali guest house would be pretty high up on the list of places to search for a Bengali fugitive. It may be best if you move out.'

'And go where?'

'We'll work something out,' I said. 'You had breakfast?'

He shook his head. 'I couldn't face it.'

'A bite to eat, then,' I said. 'We've got a busy day ahead and I can't afford you being cranky.'

He grunted a laugh. 'I'm surprised we can even afford breakfast.'

Twenty minutes later we were seated in the shaded recesses of a sleepy cafe, close to the waterfront.

'There's something you need to see,' I said, as Suren pushed a greasy omelette round his plate. He looked up and read my expression.

'What is it?'

I passed him the paper.

'The good news,' I said as he read, 'is that Taggart is still alive – at least he was at the time of printing. That and the fact that you're travelling under a false identity and there's no picture of you in the paper. If we play it smart, we should be able to outfox them.'

He placed the paper on the table. 'For how long? We have no money, nowhere to stay and no real leads.'

'That's not strictly true,' I said. 'We do have a lead. We have this man Irani to track down. As for money, Annie's come through for us. She's spoken to some chap, a friend of hers called —' I read the ink-smeared name written on my palm – 'Ooravis Colah or some such. He's agreed to stump up a loan for us. Damn decent of her, but if I were a betting man, I'd wager this Colah character is probably a bad egg. Who knows what he'll want from her in return?'

Suren looked up. 'How long have you been in India now?'

I failed to see the point of the question. Still I felt it best to humour him.

'Five years, give or take.'

'Five years?'

'Correct,' I said. 'If you're thinking of throwing me a party, I wouldn't bo—'

'I was *thinking*,' he interjected, 'that in five years you haven't learned to pronounce Indian names or even learn their gender. This *chap* of yours, Ooravis Colah, she's a woman.'

I sat back. 'That's a tad harsh,' I said. 'In five years, I've never met anyone called anything remotely similar.'

'The name *is* unusual,' he granted, 'but it is clearly Parsee. Just like Irani.'

That was interesting.

'Coincidence?'

Suren shrugged. 'There aren't that many Parsees in the world, but most of them are probably in Bombay. What do you know about them?'

'More than the average Englishman, I suppose. But not much more.'

I thought I heard him sigh. 'I shall never understand the British,' he said. 'You wear your ignorance of others almost as a badge of honour.'

'Well, it's important to be good at something,' I said.

'The Parsees,' said Suren, as though embarking on a history lesson, 'came to India centuries ago from Persia, fleeing persecution from the Muslims who'd conquered their homeland. They're followers of a prophet called Zoroaster, whom you British call Zarathustra. Legend has it they were given sanctuary by a king of Gujarat, and they've prospered ever since, at least in terms of wealth if not numbers. They're a tight-knit bunch, but the ones I've met have all been the nicest people.'

'How thrilling,' I said. 'Anything else I should know?'

'Their food's not bad either.'

'Anyway,' I said, 'Miss or Mrs Colah will be waiting for us at her house until noon.'

'What's the address?'

I checked my hand. 'Somewhere in Malabar Hill. I think it's near where we took Gulmohamed for a stroll last night.'

'She's rich, then. Malabar Hill is exclusive. Grade-A Britishers and millionaire Indians only.'

'I'm beginning to warm to her,' I said, flagging down the waiter and ordering another round of tea. 'Maybe we should ask her for a bit more money?'

FORTY-THREE

Surendranath Banerjee

We found a taxi, a real one this time, driven by a bona fide cabbie, near the foot of the Queen's Road and Sam gave him Miss Colah's address.

'I've been thinking,' said Sam, as the cab sped along the water-front. 'This Colah woman, we should ask her if she's met Cyrus Irani. I mean, it stands to reason. He's a Parsee, she's a Parsee; and as you say, they're a tight-knit bunch.'

'It is possible,' I said, 'but how do you propose asking a question like that? We cannot simply turn up on her doorstep, ask for money and then start questioning her. And we will need a cover story to explain who we are and how we managed to wash up in Bombay without money or even a change of clothes.'

'I told Annie to say I was a friend from Calcutta who'd been robbed en route.'

'And me?' I asked. 'What did you tell her to say about me?'

Sam scratched at his earlobe. 'I didn't mention you.'

'You didn't mention me?'

'You're a fugitive, remember? I thought it best to leave you out of it.'

'So what then? Should I just wait outside and hide in the bushes?'

'No … We'll just have to come up with a new story.'

*

The house was at the end of a meandering, sun-dappled driveway that seemed hacked out of the raw jungle. The bungalow itself sat in splendid isolation, pristine and freshly whitewashed and reposing languorously between verdant lawns like a satrap on silk cushions.

Sam paid the cabbie and asked him to wait at the end of the drive.

We set off across the gravel towards a set of doors as dark and wide as a dining table. Above them hung a golden *faravahar*, the symbol of the bearded Parsee god, Ahura Mazda, with his sun disc and pair of outstretched wings. I pointed it out to Sam as he pressed the brass doorbell.

'Any more thoughts on that new plan?' I asked.

'We could always try telling the truth,' he said.

'Is that wise?'

'Probably not.'

The door was opened by a grey-haired manservant dressed in a tie and tailcoat. There is no sight more incongruous, nothing that speaks more to our moral subjugation, than that of an Indian in a morning suit. There is no reason for it, save to salve the sensibilities of our masters.

'Captain Wyndham to see Mrs Colah, and this is my associate, Mr Dey,' said Sam.

The butler seemed unmoved. 'Do you have a card, sir?'

'D'you know, I seem to have left them at my hotel. But we are expected. We're friends of Miss Grant from Calcutta.'

The man appeared to relent, despite his better judgement. I could understand his predicament. I, at least, had shaved. Sam, for his part, looked like a docker.

'This way please, *gentlemen*,' he said, the final word all but an afterthought.

We followed him across a cool white hallway that seemed hewn from the same marble as the Taj Mahal and to a sitting room dominated by two leather chesterfields around a carpet of Persian silk.

The servant seemed almost relieved to have shepherded us to this well-appointed holding cell without us having damaged or stolen anything.

'If you would not mind waiting, I shall inform Miss Colah of your arrival,' he said, and shuffled out, closing the door behind him.

Sam made straight for the sofa, while I gravitated towards the windows and their views over the lawns to the trees beyond.

'Nice place,' said Sam. 'And did you hear the butler? He said *Miss* Colah. An eligible millionairess, Suren. You could do a lot worse.'

'Absolutely,' I said. 'And if you ever get round to convincing Miss Grant to marry you, we could have a double wedding.'

Our conversation was curtailed by the sound of footsteps in the hallway. The door opened and, preceded by a mist of perfume, in walked a rather striking woman.

I could not tell you her age, because I cannot estimate such things, but her skin had the smoothness of youth and the fairness of a European. Her eyes, though, were Indian, almond-shaped and fawn-coloured, and her hair was cut short in the sort of cosmopolitan style that would have raised eyebrows in Calcutta.

Sam has often accused me of losing my head at the sight of any attractive girl, but he was the one who seemed fascinated by her. Maybe it had something to do with the fact that she appeared to be wearing trousers. I'd never met an Indian woman in trousers before, and I doubted Sam had either. Even the British ladies in Calcutta only wore them when they were out riding their fat horses on the Maidan.

She didn't seem to notice me, not at first anyway, but moved towards the sofa where Sam was seated.

'Captain Wyndham?' she said, breaking into a smile. 'Annie has told me so much about you.'

Sam seemed as shocked by that as I was. If Miss Colah already knew who we were, it rather undermined the plausibility of any stories we might tell her about being here on Post Office business.

'She has?' he said. 'All good I hope?'

Miss Colah elegantly sidestepped the question. 'You're not what I expected.' She turned to me as I joined Sam on the sofa. 'And you must be Sergeant Surendranath Banerjee.'

No one with skin that fair had ever pronounced my name properly before, let alone a woman in trousers. I was about to respond when I noticed the newspaper on the table beside her. Was it the *Times*? If so, had she read it? Had she seen the article with my name writ large, a fugitive on the run? I was too stunned to do more than mumble confirmation at her.

'Annie said you were a chap of few words. May I offer you both some refreshment? Some tea or *nimbu pani* maybe? Alas it's a touch early for a proper drink.'

Maybe she hadn't read the article? Most women weren't in the habit of inviting men into their house and offering them light refreshment if they knew one of them was a fugitive. But then most women didn't wear trousers like Ooravis Colah.

Without waiting for a reply, she picked up a glass bell from a side table, rang it softly, then turned back to Sam.

'Annie tells me you're in need of some funds. Something about being robbed on a train. That sounds rather far-fetched.'

'Really?'

She looked at him askance. 'Come now, Captain. Two strapping policemen, robbed of all their worldly possessions on a train. It's laughable.'

'The truth is rather more complicated,' Sam admitted.

The door behind her opened a fraction and in wafted a slip of a maidservant as silently as if she were made of something ephemeral. Like the butler, she was Indian but wore a European maid's uniform, a white-trimmed black cotton dress, black stockings and shoes.

'Tea?' asked Miss Colah.

Sam demurred, then settled for sweet lime juice and I stuttered assent. The maid nodded and slipped from the room as unobtrusively as a whisper.

'You were saying,' continued Miss Colah, 'about the truth being more complicated?'

'It's a long story,' breezed Sam.

She flashed him a smile, the sort of disarming beam that made me wonder why we spent so much time interrogating suspects when a smile from a woman like that was enough to loosen the stubbornest of tongues.

'I'll bet it is.' She leaned over and lifted the newspaper from the side table and fanned herself with it. 'I've no pressing engagements, Captain. And I love a good story. If it makes you feel better, you can consider it interest on the loan Annie requested for you.'

Sam turned to me, wide-eyed, as though I might have some idea of what to say. I simply shrugged back at him. He seemed to grin, then turned back to Miss Colah.

'Maybe Suren should explain. It's more *his* case than mine.'

I did not particularly wish to give Miss Colah the embarrassing chapter and verse, but there seemed little choice but to offer her some version of the truth.

'I take it you've read the article in the paper,' I said.

She smiled. 'I hadn't, not till Annie mentioned it to me over the telephone. She said you were innocent, and that I'd realise the same the minute I clapped eyes on you.'

I wasn't sure whether to be glad or offended.

'It's the truth,' I said. 'I had nothing to do with that attack.'

'And the rest of the story?'

I opted for a redacted summary, enough to give her the pertinent details, but omitting the small matter of my arrest and subsequent flight from justice.

'A few days ago, a man was murdered in Calcutta,' I said. 'A rather prominent personage, and the killing has led to some violence in the city. Our investigations led us to conclude that the culprit may have fled to Bombay, so we flew here via military transport plane.'

'And in your haste, you forgot to bring any money?'

I felt my cheeks burn.

'Sometimes things get forgotten in the heat of the moment,' said Sam. 'And as we're operating undercover, we can't simply walk into a bank and make a withdrawal.'

She raised a ponderous hand, the tips of two manicured fingers touching her lips, then smiled. 'It sounds fascinating! So who is this murderer you're chasing?'

There came the faintest of knocks and the maid entered once more, this time with three tall glasses balanced on a silver tray, which she placed on the table beside her mistress. Miss Colah picked up a glass. Droplets of condensation dappled the exterior, coalescing into rivulets as she lifted it to her mouth.

The maid proffered Sam a glass from the tray and finally offered one to me. I gratefully took a sip of the sweet *nimbu pani*, quenching a thirst I hadn't realised I had.

Miss Colah waited for the maid to leave before repeating her question.

'Well, gentlemen? Who are you after?'

Sam coughed. 'You'll understand, Miss Colah —'

'Please, call me Ooravis.'

'You'll understand, Ooravis, that we're not at liberty to divulge that kind of thing.'

Miss Colah drew her face into the sort of pout only a child or a very rich woman is permitted.

'But you might be able to help us with something,' Sam continued.

'Really?' she said, brightening.

'You're a Parsee, aren't you?'

That brought a smile to Miss Colah's face. 'That's an astute deduction, Captain. Not many Englishmen from outside of Bombay know much about Parsees.'

'It's not *that* astute,' he said matter-of-factly. 'Your name might be unusual, but it's clearly Parsee. And then there's the *faravahar* hanging above your front door.'

They say a little knowledge is a dangerous thing, but when it came to Sam I'd found the opposite to be true. The man had a gift for spinning an ounce of information into a nugget of gold. Indeed I half expected Miss Colah to clap her hands in glee, such was her apparent delight at Sam's knowledge of her people: knowledge that had been fully acquired in the last half an hour, and which was now completely exhausted.

'What do you need to know?' she beamed.

'There's a man whose name has come up in conversation, not a suspect, but simply someone who might be able to help with our inquiries,' he clarified, 'who we understand has recently moved here from Burma and who, like you, is Parsee.'

'Of course,' she said. 'What's his name?'

'Cyrus Irani,' said Sam. 'He's staying at the Taj Hotel. Do you know him?'

Miss Colah reached for her glass and took a sip.

'I know *of* him. Businessman apparently. In shipping or trading or some such. Arrived in town a few months ago. I can't say I've ever met him, though, which is rather strange. The first thing a Parsee from out of town likes to do when arriving in Bombay is to get to know the elders at the Panchyat, maybe show face at the Fire Temple, but as far as I know, Irani's done neither.'

'Maybe he's lapsed in his faith?' I said.

Miss Colah nodded tentatively. 'That's certainly possible. What he *has* been doing, however, is courting some city bigwigs, wining and dining businessmen and politicians.'

'Any idea why?'

'The usual probably. Greasing palms, obtaining permits for this or that. If you want something done in Bombay, you need to have the right official or politician on side.'

'I think,' said Sam, 'we should pay Mr Irani a visit.'

'And do what?' I asked. 'Won't he be suspicious of two random gentlemen from the Post Office?'

'True, but I could pose as a local businessman. I can say I was given his name by some broker, then ask him a few questions. Check out his politics. Maybe get a feel for the man.'

Ooravis Colah laughed. 'Dressed like that? If you'll forgive me, Captain, but in your present state, I doubt they'd let the two of you into the lobby of the Taj. They're more likely to call the police, and given Sergeant Banerjee's current predicament, I wouldn't have thought that advisable.'

Sam scratched the stubble on his jaw. 'What about his office?'

'You'll have the same issue.' She took another sip from her glass, then placed it back on the table. 'There's really only one thing for it. We'll need to go on a shopping trip, get you both some decent clothes, and, I'm guessing from the state of you, a place to stay.'

Sam made to protest, but Miss Colah cut him short.

'There's no use arguing the point, Captain. Your situation seems dire to me. You can't afford to make any more mistakes.'

FORTY-FOUR

Sam Wyndham

Irani's office, according to the concierge at the Taj Hotel, was in a building in Backbay, a fifteen-minute walk away. It was nearly one p.m. by the time we got there though, what with Miss Colah's insistence that I shower and shave and that she then accompany Suren and me to a discreet emporium on Breech Candy to acquire attire less likely to get us thrown out of high-class hotels or arrested for vagrancy. The absurdity of it wasn't lost on Suren. A woman buying him clothes while he was on the run for his life. Still, if it kept him one step ahead of the hangman's noose, he was happy to live with it.

The ever-compelling Miss Colah then insisted, like a force of nature, or a limpet, depending on your point of view, that she accompany us to Irani's bureau under the premise that it took a Parsee to know a Parsee, and that anyway it was her car we were using and, by dint of purchase, her clothes we were wearing.

There came a point where further debate on the matter was moot and I decided to let her have her way. After all, he who fights and runs away, lives to lose another day.

Still, as Miss Colah's car pulled up under the shade of a banyan tree, its garbled roots and limbs making a devastation of the concrete pavement, I ordered both her and Suren to stay with the chauffeur while I went up to interrogate Irani. Suren listened, Miss Colah did not.

The office was on the second floor of a five-storey building, at the arse end of a corridor and reached by a decrepit-looking lift or a stairwell that smelled of stale urine.

Miss Colah and I took the stairs. I wasn't so much concerned by the state of the lift as I was by the health of the consumptive-seeming lift-wallah who sat inside, coughing into a yellowing handkerchief. And besides, I needed the exercise.

The door to Irani's office was a thin sheet of wood with a panel of glass that might have been frosted or just covered in grime. I knocked, rattling the thing to its core, and turned the handle. If the door was flimsy, the woman on the other side of it certainly wasn't. She was short, dark, dressed in a floral print blouse and as sturdy as the desk she sat behind. Around her neck hung a thin golden crucifix on a thinner gold chain.

Her look was more one of surprise than welcome, as though the Irani Trading Company Ltd didn't receive many visitors.

'Can I help you?' she said.

'We're looking for Mr. Irani,' I said.

'I'm afraid he's not in today.'

That was a shame, but not wholly unexpected. Gulmohamed had only arrived back from Calcutta in the small hours. Even if Irani had taken an earlier train, he couldn't have been back long.

'We had an appointment,' Ooravis Colah pouted. 'He told us to meet him here at 1 p.m. Do you know what time he's expected?'

The secretary made a show of checking an oversized appointments diary which appeared devoid of appointments, then scratched at an earlobe. 'I don't believe he is coming in at all today. You are certain your meeting was scheduled for this afternoon?'

'Positive,' Miss Colah said, affecting an air of frustration.

'What about tomorrow?' I asked. 'Will he be back then?'

She turned the page of the diary, more I felt for effect than for any real expectation of finding an answer, then looked up shamefacedly, as though the elusive Mr Irani's absence were some-how her fault. 'I'm afraid I cannot say, at the moment. If you leave me your card, I can try and get a message to him.'

I thanked her and we made to leave, Miss Colah once more making a show of frustration but reassuring the secretary that this was hardly her fault of course.

'You are sure you don't want to leave your card?' she asked.

'It's quite all right,' I said with a shake of the head. 'I'll just take my business elsewhere.'

Suren was leaning against the banyan, smoking a cigarette. Spotting us, he threw away the butt and walked over. For the first time in a week, his face wore that look of baseless optimism that he was so fond of and that reminded me of a puppy yet to acquaint itself with the boots of men and the general capricious-ness of the world. God only knew why. He was still a wanted man, and other than a set of new clothes and the chance of a fresh bed, we had precious little to show for our efforts. Yet his hope sprang eternal.

He held out an open pack of cigarettes. 'Well?'

'He's not there,' I said, taking one. 'It was always a long shot. We spoke to his secretary though.'

Miss Colah proffered her lighter, sparking a flame.

'Did she say when he'll be back?' asked Suren.

'She doesn't know.' I lit my cigarette and took a drag. 'We'll have to try the Taj.'

'And say what? A businessman looking to do a deal would not just walk into the hotel looking for the man.'

Beside him, Ooravis blew a ring of blue smoke into the air. 'There might be another way.'

*

We drove out of the bustle of Backbay and headed once more for the verdant seclusion of Miss Colah's bungalow on Malabar Hill. She showed us to the drawing room, then excused herself.

'I'll need to make a telephone call.'

During the journey, she'd explained her alternative. A gentleman friend of hers, a businessman called Jehangir Panthaki, was, she said, hosting one of his regular parties at the racecourse that evening. It was generally a small, cosmopolitan affair, just a few hundred of Bombay's upper crust, and she felt she could persuade him to invite Irani. The way she described it, for a man looking to do business in Bombay, an invitation to a Panthaki party was virtually a ticket to the top table.

'He won't be able to say no,' she said. 'Everyone will be there, from the governor and politicians, to businessmen, even the odd maharajah or two and a few writers thrown in for good measure. The great and the good like having a few cultured types around. It makes them feel they're patronising the arts.'

'And the writers?' I asked. 'What's in it for them?'

'Oh, that's easy,' she said. 'They come for the free drink.'

She returned from her call with her face wreathed in the broadest of smiles and her hand around a gin and tonic.

'I spoke to Jehangir,' she said. 'He's agreed to send a boy round to Irani's suite at the Taj with an invitation for tonight. I told him it's very important that Irani attends, so the boy is going to wait for an RSVP. I've got *you* an invitation too.'

'What did you tell him, exactly?'

Ooravis let out a laugh. 'Don't worry. I didn't tell him you're a policeman, just that you were a friend of a friend from out of town and you were very keen to meet Mr Irani to discuss some shipping deal.'

'He seems very accommodating, this Mr Panthaki of yours.'

'He's a darling,' she beamed. 'Jehangir is that rarest of creatures: a man with intelligence, a kindness of spirit *and* a bank vault full of money. I may have to marry him one day.'

She turned to Suren.

'I'm afraid I didn't get you an invitation. I hope you don't mind.'

Suren took it graciously. 'Please, think nothing of it. As a wanted man, it's probably best if I cut down on the number of soirees I attend for the moment.'

'You know, Suren,' I said, 'there's an opportunity here.'

He gave me that look of his, the one he employed whenever he feared I was about to make a suggestion which might involve him doing a portion of the heavy lifting.

'What kind of opportunity?'

'If you're not coming to the ball, Cinderella, well, there's nothing stopping you from paying a little clandestine visit to Irani's office.'

Suren seemed nonplussed. 'You want to add breaking and entering to my charge sheet?'

'Would it really make a difference in the grand scheme of things?'

'True,' he said. 'I suppose they can only hang me once.'

'And if you find something linking Irani to Mukherjee's death, they might not hang you at all.'

'Then it's settled,' said Ooravis. 'Captain, you'll accompany me to the Turf Club tonight, after which, Suren, I'll send the car back for you. You can tell the chauffeur to wait while you visit Irani's office.'

'Why are you doing this?' I asked her.

'Doing what?'

'All this. Helping us, giving us money and shelter instead of kicking us out on our ear?'

Ooravis Colah smiled. 'A girl needs something to do, Captain. And you and Sergeant Banerjee are the most unusual couple of strays that have wandered my way in quite a while.'

I left Suren to the tender mercies of Miss Colah and went off to the vestibule to telephone Annie. For once it was she, and not Anju, who answered.

'Annie,' I said, 'it's me.'

'I had a visit from the police, Sam. Looking for Suren.'

I wondered how the police had come to suspect that Annie might have knowledge of Suren's whereabouts. Maybe someone had seen her car idling on Premchand Boral Street the night we fled Calcutta.

'What did you tell them?'

'I told them I hadn't seen him, and that anyway, the papers were saying he was in Bombay. They asked about you too. Said you hadn't turned up for work yesterday, and that you might be assisting a fugitive. I said you were more likely nursing a hangover somewhere.'

'That was good of you,' I said. 'Did you manage to contact Dawson?'

'Eventually. His secretary, Miss Braithwaite, is a bit of a battleaxe but once she realised I was talking about you, she sorted things out quick smart.'

'So you met Dawson?'

'No. I met Miss Braithwaite. Your friend Dawson thought two women meeting for lunch in Park Street would attract less suspicion than him meeting me in person.'

'And?'

'And she gave me a new number for you to call. Fort William 437.'

Once more I wrote the details on my hand.

'Thank you, Annie,' I said, 'and thank you for the introduction to Miss Colah. She's been more than generous in her help.'

'So you managed to charm some cash out of her?'

'I doubt charm had anything to do with it. She just seems happy to help. Where'd she get so much money, by the way?'

'Her father's big in diamonds, and she's the sole heiress. I thought she'd be the right person to go to,' said Annie. 'She's a good woman.'

'As are you,' I said. 'If it weren't for you, Suren would surely be languishing in a prison cell right now, looking forward to a date with the hangman. When this is over, I promise I'll —'

'Don't make promises, Sam. Especially under duress. Just do what you need to do and bring yourself and Suren home safely.'

I cut the connection, then waited before asking the operator for the number which Annie had given me.

Dawson answered on the first ring.

'Wyndham?'

'That's right.'

'Tell me what happened.'

'A few hours after I telephoned you from Watson's, a couple of carloads of your Bombay friends showed up at my hotel. I barely made it out with the shirt on my back.'

'You think my line's tapped?'

'I don't see how else they could have known I was there. I suppose they could have the lines at Watson's tapped, but that's unlikely. They'd have to listen in to a lot of calls on the off chance they'd pick up something useful. The odds are it's your line they've tapped.'

'Where are you now?'

'That doesn't matter,' I said.

'And Banerjee?'

'Safe, for now.'

'Did you get to Gulmohamed?'

'We did. The results were … inconclusive.'

He paused. 'So what do you propose to do now?'

'I need you to do a little digging,' I said. 'Gulmohamed mentioned a man called Cyrus Irani. From Rangoon. Involved in shipping or trading. Suren thinks he saw him with Gulmohamed on the day Mukherjee was murdered. Does the name mean anything to you?'

'Irani . . .' said Dawson, mulling it over. 'Can't say I recall anyone by that name.'

'Can you look into it? Maybe speak to your people in Rangoon. By the size of him, Suren thought he might be ex-army.'

'I'll see what I can do.'

'How long will you need?'

'Burma's a foreign country, technically,' he said. 'It might take a day.'

'I'll call you tonight.'

FORTY-FIVE

Sam Wyndham

In one sense Bombay was similar to Calcutta. Parties started late.

It was almost 10 p.m. before we set off for the racecourse. Ooravis Colah was dressed like she'd just stepped off a film set in a sari of pink silk embroidered in silver, with matching jewellery and a pair of heels that might have given a lesser woman a nosebleed.

As for me, I felt like her pet monkey, dressed in a new suit which she insisted on purchasing. I'd protested that there was nothing wrong with the jacket I'd escaped from Watson's Hotel in, or indeed the trousers I'd purchased earlier in the day. Her response had been nothing but a cold, hard stare which effectively ended any further discussion.

The Western India Turf Club was a good twenty-minute drive from Malabar Hill, and by the time the chauffeur drew up to the line of limousines waiting for entry, there was a distinct chill in the air, not that Miss Colah seemed to notice.

'Come on,' she said, opening her door. 'Let's send the car back for Suren. We can walk from here.'

She set off imperiously, past the green railings, through the gates and towards the strains of a string quartet floating over from the tall pillbox structure of the main stand. Then, suddenly, she stopped, her high heels floundering on the reefs and shoals of a treacherous gravel path.

'Captain Wyndham,' she said. 'If you'd be so kind.'

I took her arm and was rewarded with a gracious nod of the head. The scent of frangipani fragranced the air, and around us, the serried ranks of Bombay's elite processed towards the clubhouse.

Panthaki's party, it turned out, wasn't to be inside the stand, but in the open space that lodged between it and the rails of the race-track, possibly to take advantage of the cooling night air, though probably because there were just too many people in attendance for them to fit comfortably inside. There seemed to be a good few hundred people milling about, men and women, British and Indian, all elegantly, if rather informally attired, at least by Calcutta standards. Between them buzzed a small army of waiters with trays of champagne and hors d'oeuvres. To one side, on row of linen-draped tables, a buffet of silver steam pans and chaffing dishes had been set up and manned by a host of white-jacketed attendants. On the other, and attracting considerably more attention, was a bar that seemed well stocked and ready to cater for those with a thirst for something stronger than Bollinger.

A starched waiter came over and, by way of welcome, proffered a tray of champagne at us. I took a couple of flutes and passed one to Miss Colah. She took a sip, then scanned the gathering like a general scouring a battlefield before the commencement of hostilities. She gestured towards a knot of people, mainly women, who were seemingly enraptured by the utterances of an elegant man who stood in their midst sporting a goatee and a navy-blue suit. Such was their attention that I might have taken him to be an intellectual or at least a writer, had it not been for the fact that his suit looked expensive.

'There's Jehangir,' she said, staring distastefully at the scrum around him. 'Come, let's go and rescue him.'

I followed her as she cut an elegant swathe through the crowd, leaving a host of memsahibs in summer dresses and sari-clad local women in her wake.

'Jay,' she called, landing a kiss on the air either side of his face in a gesture that was neither Indian nor British but might have been appropriated from somewhere on the Continent. 'Let me introduce my dear friend from Calcutta, Captain Wyndham.'

The term *dear* might have been overegging things slightly, seeing as we'd only just met that morning, but in India, where social connections were currency and so many doors only opened if you knew the right people, being considered a good friend of Miss Colah's could do no harm.

Panthaki extended a hand and a smile. 'A pleasure to meet you.'

'The pleasure's mine,' I said. 'Thank you for the invitation, especially at such short notice.'

'Nonsense,' he said, in that *noblesse oblige* manner of the millionaire class. 'Anything for a friend of Ooravis's.'

'Quite right too, Jay,' chimed Miss Colah. 'I've sung your praises to the captain. Told him that you throw the best parties in town.'

Panthaki gave a deprecating shake of the head. 'So what brings you to Bombay?'

'Business,' I said. 'I'm with the Post Office. And please, call me Sam.'

'Well, I hope you'll have an opportunity to enjoy Bombay while you're here. I think you'll find it an agreeable place. Our climate is not as oppressive as yours in Calcutta.'

That seemed to be true in more than just the meteorological sense. There was something different about Bombay, something fresher. It lacked some of the starch of Calcutta. People here seemed to mix a tad more freely. Maybe because it had never been the seat of empire, people's prejudices were less ingrained. Or maybe the normal rules didn't apply to millionaires. After all, cash, as they say, is king.

'I'd like that,' I said, 'but I doubt I'll have time.'

Panthaki placed a gentle hand on my shoulder. 'You must make time. There's no one who knows Bombay better than Ooravis.'

'Miss Colah raised her glass in a toast. 'Absolutely! We should make a trip to Alibagh on the other side of the bay. Jay has a house there. You'll come, won't you, Jay?'

'If you organise it.'

I seemed to have found myself in the middle of some kind of courtship ritual of the rich and glamorous, and while as a student of human psychology it was fascinating to behold, I had other priorities.

I turned to Miss Colah. 'I might head to the bar; see if I can spot Mr Irani.' I raised my glass and saluted our host

'Irani's over there by the buffet,' said Panthaki, 'talking to one of the bank managers from Grindlay's.'

I glanced over at a shaved-headed man of about six foot three with a chest that looked like it might stop a howitzer shell. Suren had said he was big, but that felt like an understatement. Cyrus Irani basically resembled a gorilla in a business suit.

Ooravis sized him up. 'So that's the man you've been looking for? He doesn't look particularly Parsee. I expected someone less thuggish.'

I'd hoped something similar. Questioning Irani in the way we'd done with Gulmohamed was out of the question. Even with Suren, I doubted we'd be able to intimidate a brute that big. What's more, he had the hard, impassive expression of a soldier – a professional, not a conscript; and a killer at that.

I made my excuses and headed for the bar. If I was going to tackle a man the size of Irani, I'd need a stiff drink or two.

Squeezing a way through, I flagged the attention of the barman and ordered a whisky, drank it down and then ordered another.

The first began working its magic, the spirit warming my gut and fortifying my resolve, as I turned and, nursing the second, began walking over towards Irani.

FORTY-SIX

Surendranath Banerjee

It was some time past ten o'clock when I heard the growl of the engine. I stepped out of Miss Colah's bungalow and, dressed not in the attire of a burglar but of a businessman, walked hurriedly to her car. The clothing was a conscious choice. In India, as I suspect might be the case the world over, the best defence against interrogation by a zealous durwan was to adopt an air of entitlement. Wealth is a vaccine that inoculates against many maladies.

I do not know what the chauffeur made of it, being ordered to drive me on such clandestine journeys, but while the man was as professional as ever, keeping his responses to a brief 'yes, sir', the expression on his face reflected in the rear-view mirror suggested that he did not entirely approve of me.

We drove, first down the meandering, canopied lanes of Malabar Hill, and then, at its foot, onto the graceful, lamplit arc of the Queen's Road, which the locals called Marine Drive. Above, the night sky was pierced by a thousand stars, clearer and brighter than they ever appeared over Calcutta with its eternal shroud of industrial smog.

The bay-front was deserted, save for the lungi-clad municipality workers, sweeping detritus from the gutters and emptying the bins so that this most elegant of promenades would once more be pristine in time for the locale's British residents to partake of their morning constitutionals.

Rather than halting a block or so from Irani's office, I ordered the chauffeur to pull into the In and Out driveway and park immediately outside the entrance.

The car, like my suit, looked the part, and to all the world I appeared to be a businessman returning to the office for some late-night emergency. I walked up the steps to the glass door and rang the night bell. Inside the foyer, the nightwatchman rose from his chair behind the front desk and rushed over.

'Hā *saahb*?'

I gave the man short shrift, browbeating him into opening the door with a mixture of choice English words and rudimentary Hindi. Such an action, I am ashamed to say, came naturally to me. Growing up in a household not short on servants and not all of whom spoke Bengali, I was well enough versed in the ways the more boorish of the *bhadralok* classes dealt with the lower orders. I'd like to say that we learned these things from our British masters, but even if that were true, the fact was that in this area at least, we proved ourselves to be model students.

The poor man, suitably cowed, failed even to ask my name as I strode past him and up the stairs. At the first-floor landing, I stopped and waited. Sam had briefed me that Irani's office was on the second floor, but for now I required to hold position right here. I had imparted clear instructions to Miss Colah's chauffeur. It was simply a question of waiting the few minutes before he carried them out and hoping the nightwatchman too played his part. I realised I was shaking, as much from the encounter with him as in anticipation of what was to come. I steadied myself, concentrated on my breathing and reminded myself I had been in worse scrapes, which, though true, made little difference to my heart rate.

The seconds ticked down, each punctuated by the pounding of blood in my ears. Five, four, three, two, one ...

From outside came a horn blast, then another, and finally, a long, constant piercing drone. I steeled myself and crept slowly back down the stairs. At the front desk, the watchman was up from his chair. I willed him to leave his post to investigate, but he simply stood there. I realised I had miscalculated. To most men of his position, an automobile was a fantastical contraption, mechanical yet also magical. To him, the blaring of the horn was like the snorting of a dragon – it grabbed the attention, but was not something you wished to get too close to.

A minute passed. The wailing continued and I was about to give up hope when, finally, he picked up a torch from under his desk and went off to investigate. I waited till he was outside before slipping into the space behind his desk. There, on the wall beside it was the wooden box that held the spare keys to all the offices in the building. Each key was on a hook, in rows sorted by floor and position. I narrowed Irani's key to one of three. Outside, I could hear the nightwatchman remonstrating with the chauffeur. I figured I had thirty seconds at most before my driver would miraculously fix the fault with the hooter. I had no way of knowing which was the correct key, and so instead I swiped all three. Closing the box, I sprinted for the stairs just as the sound of the horn began to ebb.

The ringing continued to echo in my ears even as I ran back up the stairs, not fully subsiding until I was trying each of the keys on Irani's door. As ever it was the final key that did the trick. I heard the click and felt the key turn, and in an instant, I was inside and closing the door behind me.

Taking the torch from my pocket, I flicked the switch and cast its narrow golden beam in an arc, illuminating a desk in front of me. Sam had mentioned the anteroom where Irani's secretary sat, kept company by a visitors' sofa and a row of gunmetal filing cabinets that loomed out of the darkness like battleships.

I started with the drawers of the desk, finding nothing of interest, merely letterheaded stationery and a trashy novel of the sort sold for two annas on street corners and station platforms.

The filing cabinets were unlocked, and with good reason. Two were empty and the third contained half a dozen thin manila files, each with the most rudimentary of paperwork relating to merchant vessels plying the trade routes of the Indian Ocean.

I carried on to the next room, which I assumed was Irani's, and which certainly contained a better standard of furniture: a leather-topped desk, a chair on casters which creaked more than it rotated, and several more filing cabinets. Again they were unlocked and I went through them with the exactitude of a tax inspector, albeit one working illicitly and by torchlight. Once more I found little of value. Just more manila files and marbled box folders filled with nothing more interesting, or incriminating, than a few flimsy bills from the electricity company and the foolscap pages of an office rental agreement at what seemed an eye-watering amount for such a small set of rooms. There were other files of course, papers on ships and vessels, insurance details, registration, tonnage, and other facts as dry as the Thar Desert, but as I read them, a thought gradually dawned. What was interesting was what *was not* there. There were no sales contracts, or bills of lading, or invoices, or correspondence with customers or clients of any sort. For a man running a trading business, Irani did not seem to be trading much of anything. That was a curious omission. As Sherlock Holmes might have said, *it was the dog that didn't bark*, and its silence grabbed my attention.

How did a man maintain an office in South Bombay and a suite at the Taj without any income? It was possible that his operations in Rangoon were so successful that he could afford it, but it begged the question that if things were so good in Burma, why had he not made even the slightest headway in establishing his business here in Bombay?

Something didn't smell right, and by the look of things, I wasn't going to find the answers here in this Potemkin office.

I headed for the door. Locking it behind me, I made for the stairwell, wondering how I was to return the keys to their box without drawing the attention of the nightwatchman. I had expended all my intellectual effort in planning how to steal them and had overlooked the fact that I would also require to replace them. In the end I decided the best thing would be to simply engage the man in conversation and surreptitiously slip the keys onto a corner of his desk. It wasn't much of a plan, but then I was not much of a criminal. Fortunately it turned out that *he* wasn't much of a nightwatchman either. He was slumped, snoring in his chair with his arms folded across his chest.

I reassessed my options. Dropping the keys on the desk was still the safest course of action. Indeed it was the sensible thing to do. But now I could see the cabinet on the wall behind him, temptingly close. If I could return the keys to the box, now that would be a job well done. I held my breath and crept towards him, inching silently through the gap between his chair and the wall behind. I reached over and pulled gently at the wooden door of the cabinet. It yielded with a creak that ought to have been loud enough to wake the dead. Slowly, I extracted the keys from my pocket. Beside me, the durwan's snores stopped abruptly. I froze. The man groaned, a noise not dissimilar to a performing street bear when the owner pulls on the ring through its muzzle. I turned, expecting to see him rising irately to his feet. Instead he lifted a hand to his face, scratched at his chin and began snoring once more.

I wasted no more time, opening the cabinet and replacing all three keys on their hook. A minute later I was out of the front door, thanking Maa Kali, and hailing the chauffeur.

'Miss Colah's residence, sahib?' he asked once I was safely ensconced in the back.

'Yes,' I said, as the car began to move.

He pulled carefully out of the driveway and set course for Malabar Hill.

'One moment,' I said.

I checked my watch. It was approaching eleven.

'On second thoughts, there's somewhere else we might go first.'

FORTY-SEVEN

Sam Wyndham

The laws of perspective seemed to apply differently to Irani. There was no mistaking he was a big man, even from a distance, but rather like a mountain, the closer you got, the more he seemed to loom larger than your eyes had first appreciated.

He was talking to a group of Englishmen, each armed with a drink and a cigar, the shield and sword of these latter-day crusaders in foreign parts. It struck me as odd that with my city burning and the rest of the country on the brink, these brave men of the King's Own Bombay Gin drinkers were carrying on as if it were business as usual. I didn't know whether to applaud the stiff-upper-lip-ness of it all or simply lament the ostrich-headed stupidity. Still, that was a debate for another time. Right now, my priority was to become as one with them.

I attached myself to the fringes of the circle and caught the scraps of a conversation about racehorses.

'Stud farms,' opined a chap in a cravat. 'They'll transform this business, mark my words. The ones coming up outside Poona ... good as anything in the east.'

I didn't know much about horses, but then I'd never found a lack of knowledge an impediment to voicing an opinion on a subject. Besides, every fool knew that in India the best horses, and by extension the best races, were to be found in Calcutta, and I told them as much.

The chap in the cravat sized me up. 'And you are?'

I could have made up a name or claimed affiliation with the Bengal Turf Club or some such rot. That would have been the sensible thing to do, but the truth is I was sick of it all. It felt like time to throw the tiger among the mynah birds.

'Wyndham,' I said. 'I'm a detective from Calcutta.'

The words hit home and the reaction was as it always was. People take notice when you tell them you're a detective. They reappraise you, they stand a little straighter, as though you're suddenly worthier of their attention. Irani, though, didn't flinch. Instead he raised his glass in salute.

'And what brings you to Bombay, Mr Wyndham?'

'A case.'

'What sort of case would that be?'

'The only sort that interests me,' I said. 'Murder.'

I sensed Irani tighten his grip on his drink. In his hand it looked like a child's toy.

'Murder?' exclaimed an older fellow in a regimental tie.

'Correct,' I said. 'Nasty business. A man strangled in his own house.'

Our conversation was attracting attention. Others drifted over to listen as though I were delivering the Sermon on the Mount.

'And you think the killer's here?'

I stared at Irani. 'And you are?'

'Irani,' he said. 'Cyrus Irani.'

'You're a local?'

'I'm from Rangoon.'

'Well, Mr Irani,' I said, 'in answer to your question, I do think the killer is in Bombay. There's no doubt in my mind. Who knows, he may be at this very racecourse.'

The air around us filled with gasps and tentative laughs, but Irani's face remained impassive. I had to hand it to him, he was certainly a cool one. But he was stupid with it. What he failed to realise was that the key to a plausible cover was not just equanimity, but the ability to behave naturally. With everyone around him reacting with the shock of titillation, his very lack of expression stood out like a beacon. It didn't necessarily mean he was guilty of Mukherjee's murder of course, but it suggested he was guilty of something.

I gave a tight smile. 'I'm joking, of course. While I *am* here on a case, tonight is my night off. I very much doubt, as Sherlock Holmes might say, that the killer is in our midst.'

Irani made a show of his disappointment. 'Can't you tell us any more?'

'Unfortunately not,' I said. 'I'm sure you understand; confidentiality and all that. But you can be certain I'm going to arrest the bastard soon, and when I do, he'll face the gallows.' I drank down my whisky. 'Excuse me, gentlemen, I seem to need a refill.'

I refreshed my glass and located Ooravis Colah, who was now chatting to several men, albeit with one eye still trained surreptitiously on Jehangir Panthaki who, as chance would have it, once again seemed to find himself at the centre of a rather female-heavy crowd.

She caught me watching, extricated herself and ambled over, a princess with a cocktail glass for a sceptre.

'Having a good time?'

I took a sip of whisky. 'Marvellous. You?'

'I've been to better parties. What about Irani? You think he's the man you're looking for?'

I let out a sigh. 'Who knows. I've shaken the tree. Let's see what falls out.'

She was only half listening, once more casting stray glances at Panthaki.

'May I give you a word of advice?' I said. 'Ignore him for an hour. Go and chat to some other men; it doesn't matter who. Men like your friend Mr Panthaki are used to women fawning. It's all very dull. What interests them is the thrill of the chase. Trust me, give him the cold shoulder for a while, he'll come running along soon enough.'

She looked at me and stifled a laugh. 'Make him jealous? You really are charmingly out of date, aren't you, Captain.'

I shook my head. 'It's not about making him jealous. It's about setting yourself apart from the crowd. It's about being different; being interesting. In my experience, men born into too much money are afflicted by a disease the rest of us can only aspire to.'

'And what would that be?'

'Ennui,' I said. 'Everything is handed to them, too early and too easily. Money, women, material possessions. When you've been given all the good things in life by the time you're twenty, where's the challenge? Where's the interest? They're haunted by boredom, you know. You need to be the challenge.'

Miss Colah bit her lip in contemplation. 'Talk to other men, you say?'

'Absolutely.'

'Well, let me start with your new friend Cyrus Irani.'

'That's not what I meant,' I stammered, but she was already sashaying off before I could stop her.

I sipped my whisky and tried not to stare as she joined the group of gentlemen around Irani. There was something about the man, something cold, a cruelty in the eyes, that worried me and suddenly I couldn't help but feel that Miss Colah was walking into terrible danger.

'Wonderful night,' said a voice behind me. I turned to find a pretty Englishwoman in a green dress. She tucked a stray strand of breeze-blown auburn hair behind one ear. 'The weather's mild for the time of year, wouldn't you say?'

Thank God for weather, the backbone of British small talk for at least a hundred years. Back on our sceptre'd and sodden isle, it acted as patron saint and saviour, sustaining our conversations, and here it was, exported to foreign climes and being put to sterling use.

I turned on a smile. 'Rather chilly for my tastes,' I said. 'I'm from Calcutta.'

It was odd how I'd fallen into calling that benighted city *home*.

'I thought I hadn't seen you around here before,' she said and held out a hand and I caught the scent of floral perfume and gin. 'Cecily Parsons.'

'A pleasure to meet you, Miss Parsons,' I said. 'Sam Wyndham.'

'*Mrs*,' she corrected me. 'Well, technically at least. Widowed.'

'I'm sorry.'

'Long time ago now. Back in the war.'

'I lost my wife around the same time,' I said.

I took out a pack of cigarettes, offered her one, which she accepted graciously.

'You haven't remarried?' she asked.

I shook my head.

'It doesn't get easier, does it? That gnawing emptiness. Time files down the edges, but that crater is still there.'

She might have had a skinful, but I couldn't fault her words. As they say, *in vino veritas*.

'And these dos are the worst.' She waved at the gathering with her glass. 'Everyone pitying you or thinking you're on the lookout for a new man.'

'So why did you come?'

'Work,' she sighed. 'I run a charity called the Sisters of Hope. We try to help girls who are sold into a life of prostitution. We live off donations, and this is where the money comes out to play. And you, Mr Wyndham? What brings you out tonight?'

I should have been guarded, told her nothing, but I have a weakness for alcohol and a woman with a sad story. There's probably some psychological explanation for it, and I'll probably never know what that is.

'The same,' I said. 'Work. I'm a de—'

'Yes, I know, a detective. I couldn't help overhearing you earlier. That must be jolly exciting.'

People always assumed that. Most of the time a copper's job oscillated between the mundane and the malevolent and any excitement was a fleeting, adrenaline-fuelled frenzy of action to save a life, too frequently one's own.

'It has its moments,' I said. Near the racecourse boundary, Ooravis Colah was smiling beatifically as Cyrus Irani and his cadres talked at her, while at a distance Jehangir Panthaki watched her furtively. I raised my glass to young love and took a sip. As I did, I noticed a man at the top of the clubhouse stairs, and almost choked on my whisky.

'Are you all right, Mr Wyndham?' asked Cecily Parsons.

Still coughing, I looked up. Walking down the steps was the unmistakable figure of Farid Gulmohamed. For a moment I stood dumbstruck. Was there an etiquette for meeting a man at a garden party whom you'd threatened to throw off a cliff the night before?

'Mrs Parsons, I'm afraid I'm going to have to go. Please don't think me rude. The truth is, talking to you has been the highlight of the night, but I need to leave.'

Cecily Parsons looked like she'd heard that line, or a variation of it, before, which was a pity because it was true. Nevertheless she smiled gamely and saluted me with her gin and tonic.

I glanced over at Ooravis Colah. She was still talking, but Irani had suddenly disappeared from the group. Quickly I scanned the assembly and spotted his hulking shoulders heading towards the far side of the clubhouse. I hurried over to Miss Colah.

'I need to go,' I said, guiding her away from the scrum of gentlemen.

'Is everything OK? Are you going after Irani? He just took off like a scalded cat.'

'I saw. You stay here. I'll make my way back to Malabar Hill.'

'One thing before you go,' she said. 'Irani.'

'What about him?'

'If's he's a Parsee, then I'm Cleopatra. What he knows about us and our customs, you could fit on the back of a postage stamp.'

FORTY-EIGHT

Surendranath Banerjee

The Gateway of India stood out like a tombstone against the ripples on the moonlit bay. Miss Colah's chauffeur drove on past, and a few yards later, turned in to the entrance to the Taj Hotel, the car falling in nicely beside the Rollses and Bentleys parked nearby.

A doorman, bearded and dressed in a stiff-fanned turban and pristine white uniform, strode promptly down the red carpet and opened my door. I gave him a nod, then walked into the hotel as though it were my second home.

The lobby was a definite step up from the Far Bengal. I skated across the marble to the front desk and approached a morning-suited concierge who offered me the sort of gracious welcome that a suit like mine was apt to receive. One of a series of clocks behind him, the one set to Bombay time, read half past eleven. Miss Colah had intimated that the party at the racecourse would not get properly into its stride until at least half past ten. I assumed Irani would stay for a good hour and a half, more likely two, and would require another thirty minutes to return to the hotel. I calculated I had the best part of an hour, maybe more, before he'd be back.

'You have a guest here by the name of Irani,' I said. 'I need his room number, please.'

The man was happy to oblige, furnishing me with the number of a suite on the second floor. I thanked him and headed for the inner atrium and to the grand staircase which led to the first floor before splitting and snaking off to both left and right.

I took the stairs at pace, bounding up to the first floor and then, instead of continuing to the second, I headed left, along the balconied corridor of the west wing until I found a door leading to another, smaller stairwell, this one utilised by the hotel staff. Removing my jacket and tie, I sprinted downwards, past the ground floor and to the basement. There I walked past the laundry, where the bedsheets from what I assumed were several hundred rooms were collected, past a deserted mess hall, and eventually found what I was looking for.

If the hotel's upper storeys were a palace, then the changing room for the staff was an army barracks, its walls lined with battered metal lockers in place of oil paintings and the chandeliers upstairs replaced by naked bulbs of dubious brightness. The scent of fresh flowers was also gone, obliterated by the pungent tang of male sweat. The room, though, was blessedly empty, which was not surprising given the lateness of the hour, but it still came as a relief.

There was no time to waste. I rattled a row of lockers till I found one containing the white jacket of a porter and, replacing it with my own own jacket and tie, removed it and slipped it on. From there I took the stairs back to the second floor and located the small supply pantry where were stored fresh linen, cleaning aids and, most importantly, the master keys which provided the chambermaids with access to all rooms on the floor.

Availing myself of one such key, I hurried back along the corridor until I found room 214, Irani's suite.

With my heart thumping in my chest, I knocked gently.

'Mr Irani?'

From inside came nothing but silence.

I knocked again for good measure, then slipped the key into the lock and turned it.

The room was shrouded in the pale grey light of the moon falling through a muslin screen to the balcony beyond. Closing the door softly behind me, I reached for the light switch, illuminating a marble-floored sitting room with the sort of solid furniture that was either fashioned *in situ* or broke the backs of a dozen men transporting it to its destination.

The room was spotless, the floor polished almost to the point of reflection, with not so much as a mote of dust on the coffee table or the teak desk in the corner. The bedroom was similarly pristine, the sheets on the four-poster bed turned down and tucked in with military precision, and in the attached bathroom the mosaic mirror and golden taps glittered like a votive offering at the shrine of Varuna, god of the oceans.

Back in the sitting room, I began my search, going through the desk drawers, lifting the cushions of the sofa, checking the gaps between the furniture and the floor, in a fruitless search for something, anything that might provide a clue as to what Irani's business might actually be. I found nothing, save for a layer of dust beneath the sofa which restored my faith in human nature. It seemed the chambermaids at the Taj were apt to cut the same corners as our manservant, Sandesh, back home.

The process took longer than I had anticipated, what with the need to return every cushion on the sofa and sheet of paper on the desk to its rightful position. It also proved fruitless. Only when I was satisfied there could be nothing hidden in the sitting room did I realise that I should have started in the bedroom. If there was something to find, it would surely be there, among Irani's personal possessions. I started with the wardrobes: floor-to-ceiling wardrobes, not the short, stand-alone almirahs that most hotels and houses had. Opening the first of them, I stopped dead. It was empty, save for two hangered shirts and a briefcase and suitcase resting in one corner. Gulmohamed had said that Irani had been residing at the Taj for several months, and yet it looked as if he had hardly bothered to unpack. I wondered if I'd stupidly been searching the wrong room, but I had checked the number on the door, and I doubted the concierge would have made the mistake of directing me to another guest's suite. This had to be Irani's room. I'd invested too much already for it not to be.

I pulled out the briefcase, an unblemished brown leather affair, what the British call a Gladstone bag, and tried the clasp but it was locked. I considered attempting to pick the lock, but time was short and my objective was to get in and out without Irani suspecting anything. Instead I turned my attention to the suitcase, laid it on the hard marble floor, pressed the button to release the catch and unsnapped the clasps. Opening it, I was hit by the camphorous scent of mothballs. I slipped my hands inside and gently felt for anything with shape and form, anything that might not be clothing, and eventually pulled out nothing more incriminating than a tin of talcum powder and a small bag that contained a shaving kit. Closing the case, I returned it to its nest in the wardrobe, then turned my attention to the bedside tables. Again they were empty, save for an alarm clock which informed me it had just struck midnight.

I moved on to the bed and began to struggle with the mattress, heaving up one corner and all but collapsing under its weight. Inch by inch, I ran my hands under it, searching the space between it and the bedframe, and finding nothing.

Releasing the mattress, I collapsed on the floor beside the bed, panting and wondering just what it was I had expected to find. Irani's room was clean, almost surgically so. Other than the shirts in the wardrobe and the dust under the sitting-room furniture, it was as though the room had been hermetically sealed. Out of instinct, I ran my hands along the floor under the bed frame behind me and made to stand. As I rose though, I noticed something odd. The fingers of one hand had come back coated with grey dust. Those of the other had come back clean. I raised both towards my face and stared at them, and then dropped down to the floor. In a frenzy I pulled the torch from my pocket, flicked it on and shone it under the bed. Sure enough, amid the thin field of dust was a track of clean marble running from the edge to the middle of the bed frame.

It could have been a coincidence, a channel cleared by a stray stroke of a cleaner's mop, but that seemed unlikely, given how far under the bed the channel ran. There was only one way to find out. I squeezed into the narrow space beneath the bed frame and aimed the torch at the underside of the bed frame. Then I saw it, taped to the bed was what looked like a folder. I slid forward and reached for it, carefully detaching the tapes that held it in place. It dropped to the floor with a slap, and with my heart racing, I dragged it out and placed it atop the bed.

It was a manila folder, no different to those I'd discovered at Irani's office, and I opened it to find forty or fifty sheets of paper. The first few were records of some sort, handwritten in blue ink, and looked like ledger entries in some sort of code. The rest appeared to be pamphlets, the type of flimsy flyers that were found pasted on walls and lamp posts in the poorer parts of towns. They were printed in a plethora of languages: Hindi definitely, possibly Maratha and Punjabi and several South Indian scripts. I rifled through them, and thanked the Fates when, towards the back, found one written in Bengali. It was a copy of the one that had been plastered all over the Muslim sections of town the day immediately after Mukherjee's murder, when the Hindus had begun their rampage.

I flicked back to the handwritten pages, hoping to make sense of the code when I heard a noise from the sitting room and froze. I wondered if I'd imagined it, but a split second later I heard it again, and this time it was unmistakable. A key was turning in the lock.

FORTY-NINE

Sam Wyndham

Irani was out of sight. I'd lost him as he'd turned the corner and by the time I reached the front of the clubhouse, he'd gone. It was only once my eyes became accustomed to the relative gloom that I spotted what I thought was his hulking back slipping through the dark and making for the main road.

It seemed he'd been no keener to bump into Gulmohamed than I had, which lent credence to the politician's statement that Irani had sent him to Mukherjee's house under false pretences. Then again, there was always the possibility that the two of them were somehow involved in this together and Irani, now aware that I was on to him, just didn't want to be seen in public with Gulmohamed. I only hoped Suren had been able to find something tangible at Irani's office – something that might point to who was responsible for the attacks on Mukherjee and Taggart and provide us with some idea as to why.

I had to hand it to him. For a big man, he moved pretty damn quickly. But I was no slouch myself, and trailed him out into the street. There he took a taxi from the rank on the corner and I, some thirty seconds later, took the next one.

I had a fair idea where he was heading, but decided to follow him, just in case he made for his office. The last thing I wanted was for him to show up while Suren was rifling through his papers.

I followed him south, through dark streets, empty of life save for the smiling faces of advertising hoardings and the odd stray dog dozing under a roadside tree. Eventually we reached Colaba and I breathed a sigh of relief as the taxi pulled to a stop outside the Taj.

Irani got out and made for the entrance and I was about to order my cabbie to drive on when something caught my eye. There, parked only feet away, was Ooravis Colah's Mercedes. Now there might have been more than one of that particular make and marque in Bombay, but this one was clearly Miss Colah's. I'd been in it only hours before and recognised not only the registration plate but also the chauffeur dozing in the front seat.

I paid the cab-wallah, jumped out and sprinted across the road to the car. The chauffeur woke with a start as I rapped on the side window.

'Sahib?'

'Where's Suren?'

The man wiped saliva from his chin.

'Suren,' I repeated. 'Where is he?'

'He go in hotel, sahib.'

I let out a curse. That boy was going to be the death of me, and the way things were going, of himself too. What the hell was he doing at the Taj? Of course I knew the answer, but that didn't stop me marvelling at his idiocy. It was dangerous enough breaking into Irani's office, but that was at least a calculated risk. Breaking into his room, at one of Bombay's biggest hotels, while the police were after you and your name was in every paper in the country, seemed suicidal. And that was before factoring in the element of the twenty-stone colossus who was even now making his way up to his bed.

There was nothing else for it. Against my better judgement, I sprinted towards the entrance and into the hotel lobby, in my haste all but slipping on the polished floor and breaking my neck.

Steadying myself against the back of a gilded sofa, I looked up, hoping to catch sight of Irani, but once again he'd disappeared. I skidded up to the deserted reception desk and rang the bell.

The night concierge, a thin Indian with the gaunt face and weary expression of the perpetually sleep-deprived, emerged from the back office.

'Cyrus Irani,' I gasped. 'What room's he in?'

The man stared at me, not quite sure of the correct reaction to the sight of a sweating sahib requesting a guest's room number at a quarter after midnight.

'May I ask your name, sir? I can send a boy up to Mr Irani's suite with a message.'

I took out my warrant card and slapped it on the desk in front of him. 'How about you just answer my question?'

He didn't even need to consult the guest register.

'Room 214, sir. Second floor,' he called out, but I was already sprinting for the stairs.

FIFTY

Surendranath Banerjee

I heard the key turn and the door to the sitting room open. A hurricane of thoughts swirled through my head and for the longest of moments I stood rooted to the spot. The trick was not to panic. If I was to have any hope of extricating myself, it would only be through keeping my head. I forced a deep breath, then turned to the file on the bed. Pocketing the handwritten ledger records and a few of the flyers, I pushed all the other papers back into the file. As I did so, I noticed that its inside flap was covered in a handwritten scrawl: the sort of notes one takes from a telephone conversation. I didn't have time to decipher it all, but in the middle, the words 'HAJI ALI, 12 NOON' stood out in capital letters. The note ended with a telephone number: Bom 2636.

From the adjoining room, I heard the scraping of a chair leg. I closed the file and hurriedly slipped it under the bed. The sound of footsteps tapped across the sitting room, growing louder. Quickly, I pulled at a corner of the bedsheets as inches away, the door opened.

'What the bloody hell?'

I turned and bowed low, remained with my head down and affected a heavy accent.

'Turn-down saarvice, *saahb*.'

'At this hour?'

'Two three staffs off sick, *saahb*. All very late.' I kept my eyes planted on his feet in mock supplication, but even his shadow was intimidating.

'Get out,' he commanded.

'*Hā, saahb*,' I said, touching my forehead, before skirting past him, through the sitting room and out into the corridor where, in my haste to escape, I collided with a man coming the other way.

'Suren? What the hell? Why are you dressed like a bellboy?'

'No time to explain,' I said. 'Just run.'

Quickly I led him along the corridor and back to the service stairs, reaching it just as we heard a door open behind us and Irani's voice shout for me to stop.

Not bloody likely, I thought as we ran through the door and down the stairs. Even with Sam in attendance, I didn't fancy tangling with a man as substantial as Irani. I had hoped to return to the staff changing room and recover my brand-new suit jacket, but alas there was no time for that now.

'Hurry,' I said. 'The car is parked out front.'

'I know it is,' said Sam vehemently, from two steps behind. 'I saw it. How d'you think I knew you were —'

He was interrupted by the sound of a door opening into the stairwell above and the crash of boots on the concrete steps.

'Never mind,' he said. 'Just go!'

FIFTY-ONE

Sam Wyndham

We burst through the doors and out into the night. For a moment, neither of us quite knew where we were.

'That way,' I said, and we ran in what I hoped was the direction of the front entrance. We were a couple of feet from the corner when I heard the door behind us fly open. Irani was gaining on us. At this rate he'd be on top of us before we made it to the car.

'Keep going,' I shouted. 'I've got an idea.'

Suren almost stopped in his tracks. 'What?'

'Just go,' I said. 'Get to the car and wait for me at the Gateway.'

For once he didn't argue. I continued with him till we'd turned the corner and then halted and turned.

I could hear Irani sprinting towards me.

Just as I thought he was nearing the corner, I steeled myself and stepped out into his path. By the time he saw me, it was too late to stop. He ploughed straight ahead, sending both of us sprawling.

Even though I'd braced for the collision, it still felt like being hit by an omnibus. The only consolation was that I'd managed to stop him. He raised a fist as I got to my feet and I prepared to block it, but at the last second he recognised me and stayed his hand. I was gambling that he hadn't caught sight of me outside his room, and that as far as he knew, he was chasing one solitary Indian masquerading as a hotel employee. It was gratifying, not least for the state of my face, that I was right.

I saw the confusion in his eyes.

'Wyndham?'

'That's right, Mr Irani.'

'What are you doing here?'

'I could ask you the same question,' I said, straightening my tie. 'You left the party in an awful hurry. Just as another gentleman walked in.' He peered over my shoulder into the darkness, no doubt looking for Suren. 'And now you're running around in the dark like a madman.'

The last sentence caught his attention and dragged his focus back to me.

'What?'

'Is Mr Gulmohamed an acquaintance of yours?' I asked.

Irani shook his head. Behind me, I heard a car start up. Suren would be gone in seconds.

'You followed me back here in the dead of night to ask me questions about some politician?'

'I didn't see any point in waiting,' I said.

He pulled himself up to his full height and shoved his chest in my face.

'I don't care who you are, I'm not answering any more of your questions.'

Pushing past me, he headed for the hotel's main entrance.

'You'll answer my questions soon enough,' I called out behind him, 'or I'll have you arrested.'

Irani didn't even bother to flinch. He just kept walking.

I made sure he'd entered the lobby before doubling back and heading to the Gateway. Ooravis Colah's car stood idling close by, with

Suren peering out from the back seat. I opened the door and got in next to him.

'Drive,' I said to the chauffeur.

Suren looked at me as though I were the risen Lord.

'You're not injured?'

The chauffeur revved the engine and eased the car forward.

'I'll live,' I said.

'What happened back there? What did you do?'

'What I always do,' I said. 'Put myself in harm's way to save your backside. Got a cigarette?'

He patted the pockets of his bellboy's coat and smiled, before pulling out a crumpled pack of Charminar.

'Apparently I do,' he said, offering me one.

I put the cigarette to my mouth. 'Where's *your* jacket?'

'Long story.'

He brought out a box of matches, struck one and held the flame to my cigarette. I took a drag, the harsh, unfiltered tobacco hitting the back of my throat with a punch.

'How did you know I would be here?'

'I didn't,' I said. 'I was just following Irani. It was only when we got to the Taj and I saw the car parked up that I realised you were probably inside doing something stupid. I told you to search his office – what the hell were you doing in his hotel room?'

'There was nothing in the office,' he said. 'And I mean nothing: no ledgers, no invoices, no bills of lading, merely a few inconsequential files. It felt suspicious. So I came here and thought I might search his rooms. You should have kept him at the party for longer.'

'I tried my best,' I said. 'He got spooked when Gulmohamed turned up.'

Suren's eyes widened. 'Gulmohamed was at the party?'

'He turned up pretty late.'

'Did he see you?'

'I ducked out before he got a chance, as did our friend Irani.'

'Interesting. That would seem to substantiate Gulmohamed's story.'

'Yes, but it's not conclusive proof of anything. They may be in cahoots and just didn't want to be seen together. Remember, Irani wasn't supposed to have been at the party. His invitation was a last-minute thing.'

'Did you manage to question him?'

I exhaled cigarette smoke and nodded. 'He knows something about Mukherjee's murder, I'm sure of that.'

'Might he have killed him?'

'It's possible. He's certainly big enough to have wrung Mukherjee's neck. Which begs the question, how did *you* get out of his room in one piece?'

Suren gave a laugh. 'I kept my head down, apologised and told him I was there to turn down the bed.'

'At midnight?'

He shrugged. 'Irani saw what he expected to see. A little Indian bellboy grovelling an apology. I was out of the room before he could figure any differently.'

'Well, I hope it was worth the risk.'

'Maybe.'

Now it was my turn to stare.

'You found something?'

'I don't know,' he said, pulling some scraps of paper from his pocket. 'Possibly. We will find out when we get to Miss Colah's. I cannot read in the dark.'

FIFTY-TWO

Sam Wyndham

Ooravis hadn't returned yet. Her bungalow was quiet, with only the orange glow of the portico light visible from the driveway. Inside, the manservant, bleary-eyed and still dressed in his morning suit, which I suppose was apt as it was, technically, morning, showed us through to the dining room before bringing coffee.

Suren took a chair, pulled out the papers he'd liberated from Irani's room and flattened them out. I left him to it and went to make a telephone call.

I asked for the number Dawson had given me and waited. It rang for almost a minute before someone answered.

'Hello?'

The voice was male, groggy from sleep and not the colonel's.

'I need to speak to Dawson,' I said.

'He's not here. If you leave a message, I can get him to telephone you back in the morning.'

I sighed. It was clear Section H didn't have their first XI manning the switchboards during the small hours.

'If it could wait till morning, I'd have called in the morning. I need to speak to him now.'

There was a pause as the man considered his options.

'And before you ask, I can't leave a number. Just tell him it's Wyndham.'

'Can you telephone again in five minutes?'

That seemed reasonable and I did as he asked, calling back exactly five minutes later. This time there was no delay.

'Captain Wyndham? Please hold ... Connecting you now.'

I heard static on the line and then Dawson's voice.

'What is it, Wyndham?'

'I met Cyrus Irani tonight. He knows more about Mukherjee's death than he could have gleaned from the papers.'

'You think he's involved?'

'It's possible. Have you managed to dig up anything on him?'

'I checked with Rangoon. There's no information on anyone by the name of Cyrus Irani. My source checked with the local Parsee community. No one seems to have heard of him.'

That was hardly good news, but if there was a silver lining, it confirmed our suspicions that Irani wasn't whom he claimed to be.

'And the army? Maybe he was stationed there?'

'That's where it gets interesting. Again, there's no record of an Irani, or any Parsee for that matter, stationed in Rangoon, but there was something that caught my attention.'

I found myself clenching the receiver tightly.

'While there were no Parsees, there was an Armenian. A chap by the name of Atchabahian, Sarkis Atchabahian. He hails from a family of traders who settled in Rangoon. Young Sarkis seems to have had rather a tough time of it. His father's business went bankrupt while he was young. Joined the army at sixteen, fought against the Turks during the war and was made a sergeant. After the Armistice he was shipped back to Burma, but wasn't demobbed. This is where it gets interesting. Turns out our man's got a screw loose. A medical report during the war highlighted a propensity towards psychopathy. Then in '22 he beat an Indian orderly to death. The matter was hushed up of course, but he was dishonourably discharged. Atchabahian ostensibly went into the

import-export business, much of which seems to have been smug-
gling, and by all accounts he was pretty lousy at it, scraping a
living and finding himself in and out of prison. Then at some
point last year, he pulls down the shutters and disappears. No one
there has the foggiest notion of where he went.'

I tried to join the dots. Was our man, Cyrus Irani, in fact this
chap, Atchabahian? It was possible. Armenian traders were to be
found in every outpost of the empire and their communities in this
part of Asia had existed for centuries. Calcutta in particular was
home to a good number of them. Armenia wasn't a million miles
from Persia, where the Parsees originated, and while an Armenian
might struggle to pass for an Englishman or an Indian, he could, at
least to the casual observer, pass himself off as a Parsee. The links
to the army and to trading, and his sudden disappearance from
Rangoon just before Irani turned up in Bombay, was also interesting. But it still made no sense.

'Irani's been living in a suite at the Taj Hotel for the past few
months,' I said. 'That takes quite a bit of cash and this man,
Atchabahian, doesn't sound like he'd have those sorts of resources.
I'm also wondering why an Armenian ex-sergeant from Burma
would suddenly up sticks, head to India under a false identity and
get himself involved in the murder of an Indian politician.'

'You're the detective,' said Dawson.

'I need you to check something else,' I said. 'Can you find out if
Gulmohamed had been in Rangoon shortly before Atchabahian
disappeared?'

I could hear Dawson thinking on the other end of the line.

'Call me in the morning at ten.'

I headed back to the dining room where Suren was waiting with
the papers spread out over the table. His expression suggested the
news wasn't good.

'Any luck with Dawson?' he asked.

'You first,' I said, pointing to the papers in front of him. He was staring at a flyer, printed in Bengali.

He shook his head. 'It's poison,' he said. 'The sort of inflammatory rubbish you see posted on walls in the rougher neighbourhoods. It calls on the Muslims to rise up, claim the inheritance of the Moguls, to fight back or be enslaved by the Hindus. It mentions the violence wrought on Muslims in recent days.'

'Does it mention Mukherjee by name?'

'No, but it alludes to him,' said Suren. 'Which means it must have been printed in the last few days.'

'So Irani picks up this flyer in Calcutta. As a souvenir of a murder he either commits or gets Gulmohamed to carry out? Some sort of sick memento?'

'I do not think so. I also found a host of others in the same folder, printed in a variety of languages, North Indian and South Indian, but none in English.'

I took his point. Flyers in those other languages wouldn't have been plastered around Calcutta, because not many people would have been able to read them. He reached for the flyer and peered at it, as though staring at it hard enough might unlock some clue.

'And Mukherjee's murder,' he continued, 'while significant back home, would not resonate in Madras or Bombay. He wasn't a national figure, certainly not in the way someone like Gulmohamed is.'

I gestured to the handwritten sheets. 'Any luck with those numbers?'

'Not really. I think they might be payments or receipts. The descriptions for most are beyond me, but there's one here that includes a series of numbers. I think it might be a bank account.' He passed the pages across the table and I stared at them gamely. It was useless of course. If Suren couldn't decipher them, I was hardly going to be able to, but it was important to try. He pointed out the series of six digits in among a jumble of letters.

'It's possible that the number itself has been encoded, but that I think is less likely.'

'Why?'

'Because there are only ten digits. When people invent codes, they generally use other symbols for numbers. Otherwise, transposing one digit for another can become confusing.'

If it was a payment to a bank account, that raised interesting possibilities. If Irani really was this penniless Armenian, Atchabahian, it might explain how he was now living it up at the Taj.

Gulmohamed had suggested that Irani was a benefactor to the cause of the Union of Islam, but that made no sense. Why would an Armenian Christian, masquerading as a Parsee, want to fund a Muslim political party? But what if the truth were the other way round? What if the source of Irani's new found wealth was in fact Gulmohamed? The politician had been reluctant to give up Irani's name when we'd questioned him. Indeed we had to all but throw him off a cliff before he gave it to us. He might have given us the name, but might still have lied about the specifics of their relationship. Maybe Gulmohamed had hired him to kill Mukherjee? If we could prove that link, I felt we'd be a step closer to proving Suren's innocence. It wasn't much, certainly not enough to stand up in a court of law, but it was a glimmer of hope, and that was better than nothing.'

I returned the sheet to him. 'Anything else?'

'There *was* something. Some notes, handwritten on the cover of a folder. I did not have time to read it all, what with Irani turning up, but there was a Bombay number, 2636, and also a name and a time: Haji Ali, twelve noon.'

'That mean anything to you?'

Suren shrugged. 'It's Muslim. That's all.'

'Right,' I said. 'Come on.'

'Where?'

'To the vestibule. We've more telephone calls to make.'

I called Dawson again, just to give him the numbers that Suren thought might be a bank account and asked him to look into it. Then I turned to Suren.

'Shall we telephone this Mr Haji Ali?'

'But it's half one in the morning.'

'Best time to telephone,' I said. 'If you want the truth, call some-one in the middle of the night. People are generally too sleep-addled to lie well.'

I asked Suren for the number again, then requested the operator to place the call and held my breath. I was prepared to wait for as long as it took for someone to answer, but after a minute or two, my hopes began to fade. A few minutes more and they'd failed com-pletely. I replaced the receiver.

'You could ask the telephone exchange?' said Suren.

'What?'

'You could call the telephone exchange, give them the number and request them to supply you with the name and address to whom it's listed. If they can give you a number for a name or an address, it stands to reason they might have a list going the other way with all the numbers listed sequentially.'

I looked at him with a new-found admiration. It wasn't a bad idea, certainly worth a pop, and anyway, we had nothing to lose.

I picked up the receiver and pressed once more for the operator. A female voice which seemed far too perky for the time of night answered.

'How may I connect you?'

'It's not a connection I need,' I said. 'What I'm after is a name and address for a phone number I already have.'

After explaining the urgency of the situation, and the fact that it was police business – *who else would make such a request at this time of night?* – she asked that I hang up, promising to call back as soon as she had the information.

'How long will it take?' I asked.

'It'll take as long as it takes,' she said.

In the end it took ten minutes.

'The number isn't registered to a person,' she said. 'It's registered to an organisation, the Union of Islam.'

Gulmohamed's organisation.

'You're sure?' I asked.

'Certain, sir.'

I thanked her, hung up and turned to Suren.

'You'll never guess who that number belongs to …'

We were back in the sitting room when the door opened and Ooravis Colah sauntered in, looking only slightly less glamorous than when we'd set off earlier in the evening. The smile on her face and the faint trace of gin that accompanied her suggested she'd had a pleasant evening.

'Hello, boys,' she said. 'I hope you've been enjoying yourselves.'

Suren sat her down and poured a coffee while I, against my better judgement, set about explaining what we'd learned. I'd rather not have included her in our deliberations, but she was quite insistent, and given that this was her house and that none of what we'd found out would have been possible without her active assistance, I reluctantly consented.

I explained to both of them what Dawson had told me about the man called Sarkis Atchabahian, the Armenian ex-soldier who'd disappeared from Rangoon around six months ago.

'He could definitely be Irani,' said Miss Colah. 'That man is no more a Parsee than you are.'

'You're sure?'

'Positive. Did you see the cut of his suit? He's got no style at all. If he's a Parsee, he's the worst dressed Parsee in the world.'

'That's it? Anything else?'

'Well, yes, actually. We could talk about his limited knowledge of our practices, or how he spent the whole time trying to avoid other Parsees. We're a clannish bunch, Captain, almost an endangered species, so when we meet others of our kind, we tend to club together like the cormorants at Lokhandwala Lake. There were at least a dozen of us there and, other than me, your man didn't speak to a single one. Mainly, though, it's the clothes.'

Suren ran through the facts.

'So this man, Atcha-, Atcha- —'

'Atchabahian,' I said.

'Atchabahian, arrives in Bombay, masquerading as Irani and gets involved with a Union of Islam plot to assassinate Mukherjee. Why?'

Having had the benefit of a call with Dawson, I felt myself inching towards an answer. I was still groping about in the dark, but now at least I knew which direction to grope in.

'Let's get some sleep,' I said. 'We'll figure it out in the morning.'

FIFTY-THREE

Surendranath Banerjee

Our fates, they say, are written the moment we are born, our destiny sealed by a combination of celestial chronology and terrestrial geography. I was born, in the ancestral home in Shyambazar, on the fifth day of the month of Agrahayan, in the year 1304, by the Bengali calendar, a Saturday, at precisely eleven minutes past seven in the morning . Those details, and the corresponding position of the heavenly bodies at the time, so we Hindus believe, set the course of my life as certainly as iron tracks do a railway engine. From an early age, time, date and place of birth are etched into a Brahmin's consciousness as if into granite, such is their importance. In the same way, the details of my death had also been written, marked on a tablet which I was not yet privy to. Still, I awoke that morning, burdened with the sense that the day would be a black one.

I had slept fitfully, my nightmares replete with visions of Irani, or Atchabahian, or whoever he was, dressed in military fatigues and charging towards me with bayonet fixed.

I rose before the sun, showered and, having dried myself, donned my sacred thread, the mark of the Brahmin, looping it over my head and one shoulder with a self-conscious solemnity that I had not felt in many a year.

I cannot quite describe my state of mind. Fear, agitation, all those emotions I expected, were curious in their absence. It is true my heart was heavy, yet my mind was curiously clear, as though freed from the shackles which daily bound it. It may sound strange, but the thought that my destiny was written and unchangeable was strangely liberating.

The dining room was empty. Miss Colah did not seem the type to rise early, and Sam, though his hours had improved since he'd achieved victory over the opium, still rarely surfaced before seven. I troubled the maid for nothing more than a glass of orange juice, took it out to the veranda and watched the sun climb over the bay, the same sun which would have risen and warmed Calcutta for more than an hour already. My thoughts strayed to my homeland. Shonār Bangla, we called it, Golden Bengal. It was always easier to appreciate that epithet with the benefit of distance and the rose-tinted yearning that blinded the wandering son to its blemishes.

I sat down and began going through Irani's papers, trying to work out the meaning of the columns of numbers. I do not know how long I had been at it, but the sun was high by the time the insolent creak of footsteps on floorboards fractured my introspection. I turned in the expectation of once more seeing the maid and instead found Sam standing in the doorway.

'Bad night?'

He had a way of sensing my mood. He said it was a Bengali characteristic, wearing one's heart on one's face.

'I do not see how we get through this time,' I said. 'Even if Gulmohamed and Irani are working together, even if they killed Mukherjee, I just cannot fathom how we could prove it. And if we cannot do that, well, I'm finished.'

'We've been in tight spots before,' he said. 'We come through them. It's what we do. The show goes on.'

'All shows come to an end eventually,' I said. 'Maybe this is simply my time?'

He walked over and placed a hand on my shoulder.

'Listen to me,' he said. 'We aren't leaving the stage, not now, and certainly not before belting out one final hurrah.'

FIFTY-FOUR

Sam Wyndham

We reconvened in the dining room, getting back to work only after we'd requested, received and polished off breakfast. Suren, bless him, was always maudlin on an empty stomach.

The maid cleared away the plates and he spread the papers pilfered from Irani's office over the dining table. The flyers he all but ignored, concentrating on the few pages of what we assumed were financial transactions.

'This would be easier if we knew the context.'

'We can guess,' I said. 'An Armenian soldier, in less than stable mental health, is kicked out of the army for murder. He's all but broke, gets involved in certain unsavoury activities and is in and out of prison. Then he disappears from Rangoon and turns up in Bombay as Irani, claiming to be a businessman, staying at a luxury hotel and splashing cash like it's going out of fashion. A man whose only real skill seems to be killing people suddenly finds himself in demand.'

Suren stared. 'What are you suggesting?'

'I've slept on it,' I said, 'and I'm convinced. A politician such as Gulmohamed likely has some shady friends in the underworld. Say one of his contacts mentions Atchabahian, a man with no money and no love of Hindus, sitting out in Rangoon. Gulmohamed gets in touch, brings him to Bombay, smartens him up and installs him at the Taj as Irani, and then pays him to do his dirty work.'

'Including murder?'

'*You* saw him with Gulmohamed on the day Mukherjee was murdered. Maybe they're planning to destabilise the other parties prior to the elections next month? They murder a prominent Hindu – but no one *too* important of course – knowing that the Shiva Sabha will react with riots and anti-Muslim violence, which in turn will solidify the Muslim vote behind them. When Gulmohamed told us he didn't kill Mukherjee, maybe he was simply telling the technical truth. He didn't kill him. He just got Irani to do it.'

I could see the cogs turning as Suren pondered the premise.

'If he's Armenian, what's he doing helping the Muslims? I thought there was no love lost between them after what the Turks did to them during the war.'

That was a fair point, and one which I hadn't considered. Yet I questioned its relevance.

'As far as we know, the man grew up in Burma. He might be Armenian by background, but I'm not certain that means a whole lot.'

Behind us the door creaked open. Miss Colah entered, draped in a blue silk robe.

'Good morning, gentlemen.' She sounded hoarse from the night before. 'You're up early.'

The maid approached and Ooravis rattled off an order for breakfast, then came to the table and pulled out a seat.

'Hard at work already, Suren?'

'Just trying to make sense of these papers.'

Ooravis gave the sheets the most cursory of glances, then turned to me.

'Well, Mr Detective? What do you plan to do now?'

It was a good question.

'Suren can keep working on these documents,' I said. 'Meanwhile I've got a suspect to track down.'

She arched an eyebrow.

'Really? Anyone I know?'

'I doubt it. Someone called Haji Ali. I think he works for the Union of Islam.'

Miss Colah looked at me and laughed.

'You're sure about that?'

'We found his name and a telephone number among Irani's papers,' I said. 'The number is registered to the headquarters of the Union of Islam.'

Colah shook her head. 'The number might be registered to the Union, but I doubt it's the number for someone called Haji Ali.'

'Why?' asked Suren.

'Because Haji Ali isn't a person, at least not any more. He's been dead for about five hundred years. These days he's a place. A mosque to be precise. Out on a causeway near Worli.'

Suren shrugged. 'Maybe that's where he and Gulmohamed meet?'

'Or met,' I said. 'We've no idea of a date.'

'It's today,' said Ooravis Colah.

We both looked at her.

'It stands to reason,' she continued. 'It's Friday. Gulmohamed will be going to Friday prayers at the mosque. The area around it is always packed at that time. If you want to meet someone in a crowd, that's where and when to do it.'

'You should have been a detective,' I said.

'Maybe,' she said, then gestured to Suren, 'though looking at the predicament Suren finds himself in, maybe being a detective while being Indian isn't such a good idea.'

I left Suren with his numbers and once more borrowed Miss Colah's car and chauffeur. The man seemed rather bemused by my request to go to Haji Ali, but any doubts he may have had, he kept to himself.

I wasn't sure exactly what I hoped to achieve, but if I could intercept Gulmohamed handing cash over to the man calling himself Irani, maybe that would be enough to arrest the pair of them. Granted, there was the fact that I had no proof of anything, but that was the great thing about our laws. If you had the merest suspicion that an Indian had committed a crime, you could simply arrest him and come up with a rationale later. I figured that once they were both in custody, it'd only be a matter of time before Suren deciphered Irani's coded notes or one of them cracked.

There was, of course, the small detail that I had absolutely no authority to arrest anyone in Bombay, but if Dawson was right and Gulmohamed wasn't a Section H operative, then I hoped a call to the spymaster in Calcutta would help smooth the way and provide me with the clout I needed. I should have called him already that morning, but in my haste to get to Haji Ali, it had slipped my mind.

The journey was slow, the car waylaid by a mass of thousands of Mohammedans all heading for the mosque. It was still far too early for Friday prayers, and I wondered what was going on. Maybe they did things differently in Bombay, but that felt unlikely. If there was one thing I'd found all religions to have in common, it was a certain dogmatic following of ritual. The precise timing of a service or the protocol of a liturgy were usually set in stone, generally by some priests many centuries after the god or prophet in question had washed his hands of us all and headed back to the heavens. That was the thing about religion. It was an open question as to how much of it was divine inspiration and how much was just bureaucratic packaging.

We carried on, inching forward, with the chauffeur making loud and liberal use of the horn with about as much effect as it would on a herd of water buffalo.

'What's the hold-up?' I asked.

The chauffeur shook his head. '*Mujhe nahin pata, sahib.*'

'Then ask someone,' I said.

He leaned out and shouted to one of the men streaming past. Like the others, he was dressed in white, complete with a small white cap on his head. The man gestured back with a shake of the head, that strange Indian gesture that after five years I was still unable to quite fathom.

The driver turned to me.

'Rally,' he said. 'Islam Union holding meeting at mosque today.'

A rally at Haji Ali. It felt like Gulmohamed was building up to something. With the elections only a few weeks away, today felt like it would be his call to arms. That Irani had made a note of it essentially sealed the connection between them. Gulmohamed probably wanted his fixer close at hand, maybe he had other people he needed killed.

FIFTY-FIVE

Surendranath Banerjee

Miss Colah had lost interest shortly after Sam had departed, leaving me to pore over the coded documents, so it came as a surprise when forty minutes later, she returned to the dining room looking for me.

'Telephone call for you.'

'Me?' I was on the run from the authorities. No one was supposed to know where I was, let alone have a telephone number for where to reach me.

'The caller asked for Captain Wyndham, but in his absence, he said you'd do.'

'Who?'

'He didn't give me his name. Maybe *you* should ask him.'

There was no point in refusing.

I followed her out to the hallway and to the telephone.

'Hello?' I ventured.

'Banerjee?' said a clipped, English voice. 'It's Dawson. Where's Wyndham?'

I breathed in relief.

'He's gone to try and catch Gulmohamed paying off Irani, or Atchabahian or whatever his name is. He thinks Atchabahian is working for Gulmohamed. If he can catch them in the act, he'll be able to arrest them.'

'Well, that's not going to happen,' he said.

I agreed.

'I told him it was naive.'

'I don't know about naive, but it's certainly foolish. Because Atchabahian isn't working for Gulmohamed.'

'What?'

'Wyndham asked me to check whether Gulmohamed had been in Rangoon prior to Atchabahian's disappearance. I couldn't find any record of that, but it turns out someone else was there. A man named MacRae. He used to work for Section H's Bombay station. He was dismissed about a month ago.'

'You mean he's working for *you*?'

'You think I'd be telling you any of this if he worked for me?'

'Why was MacRae dismissed?' I asked.

'I don't know, but rest assured, I'll find out.'

'I'll let Captain Wyndham know as soon as I can.'

'There's one other thing,' said Dawson. 'That bank account you wanted the details of. It's an account at Grindlay's, Calcutta branch, registered to the Shiva Sabha. The payment was made from an account registered in Bombay, to which Irani is the sole signatory.'

'Irani is paying cash to the Shiva Sabha? Why would he do that? Especially if he's responsible for Mukherjee's murder?'

Dawson paused. 'Join the dots, Sergeant. You're smart enough to work it out.'

My head spinning, I returned to the dining room. I needed to make sense of what Dawson had told me. Opening the door, I found Ooravis Colah idly flicking through the flyers I'd left on the table.

'So many languages,' she marvelled. 'Who can govern a country with so many?'

I stood beside her as she pointed out the different scripts: the South Indian languages with their neat and compact curls; the blocky, Aryan scripts of North India, and the sharp, angular letters of Bengali.

She picked one up and began to read out loud.

'Is that Gujarati?' I asked.

'Marathi,' she corrected. 'But it doesn't make sense.'

I looked at her. 'What does it say?'

'*Sons of Islam!*' she read, her brow furrowing as she translated the words. '*Rise up and avenge the slaughter of innocents. Avenge the death of Gulmohamed and the martyrs of Haji Ali.*'

For the longest of seconds, I stared dumbfounded at the flimsy paper. I turned my attention to the rows of numbers on the ledger pages I'd stolen. One of them had been a payment to the Shiva Sabha. Suddenly, in a moment of terrible clarity, the truth hit me.

'I need to get to Haji Ali,' I said. 'I need to find Sam.'

FIFTY-SIX

Sam Wyndham

There seems to be a tradition within Eastern religions for holy men to place their shrines and places of pilgrimage in as remote locations as possible. Buddhists and Hindus have a thing for setting monasteries high up in the Himalayas, and Jains, I've found, like to place their temples in locations which are generally a day or more's journey from the nearest road. For the most part, Muslims seem more sensible, but the tomb to Haji Ali and the mosque that bore his name managed the supreme feat of being within a city but still rather inaccessible.

The edifice was built on a small island which jutted out into a bay and was quite unlike any mosque I'd seen before. It seemed to rise straight out of the water, its thick white sea walls giving way to intricate Mogul architecture. At first it appeared to be completely cut off, but as we drew closer, a single causeway came into view, linking it to the mainland and packed with people.

Ordering the driver to park up and wait, I got out and, along with what seemed like many hundreds of the faithful, headed for the mouth of the causeway.

Raised a few feet above the water, the path from the mainland to the mosque ran for almost four hundred yards. Ordinarily it might have been a pleasant stroll, but today, with so many crossing, it was close to perilous. Men walked six abreast along the unfenced channel as the water lapped close to their sandals.

There was no way of skirting them unless you wanted a bath in the sea, and so I joined the procession as it slowly crossed over to the island. The causeway widened as it reached the islet, but even then things didn't improve much. The flat ground in front of the mosque's arched entrance was already filling up and at the far end, a stage, draped in Islamic green, had been erected and a number of men were rigging up a tannoy system.

I waded through the crowd and over to the stage, garnering curious glances as I went. Here on holy ground, or at least within ten feet of it, and as the only infidel in the vicinity, I was relieved to find that the crowd parted willingly to allow me to pass. Reaching the stage I collared one of the workers fiddling with the tannoy and asked him where I could find Gulmohamed. I didn't need to wait for a reply. Just then, the man himself appeared from a curtained-off area beside the stage.

He saw me and froze, his face a rictus of fear, yet he regained his composure commendably quickly. He was among friends here, probably a thousand of them, and I daresay could have had me torn limb from limb should he have chosen to.

Indeed, from his expression there was a chance he was actually considering it. I decided to seize the initiative before he came to a decision.

'I know about Atchabahian,' I said, walking over to him.

He made a good fist of feigning ignorance.

'Who?'

'Your friend, Irani. He's really an Armenian. I know you recruited him from Rangoon, brought him over to Bombay, set him up in the Taj with his new identity.'

He looked at me as though I'd taken leave of my senses.

'What are you talking about? Irani doesn't work for me, and I certainly don't know any Armenian chap.'

Close by, a few of his minders sensed the tension and began to move closer. I felt their eyes upon me.

'Don't play dumb,' I said. 'I know you paid him to kill Mukherjee.'

Gulmohamed broke into a laugh. '*I* pay Irani? I've never paid Irani for anything, except maybe a taxi. On the contrary, he was the one who donated a considerable sum to our party. And as for Mukherjee, I told you, I'd never even heard his name till the day after his murder. I didn't know he was in that house and I didn't even enter it. Now I suggest you leave before my friends here decide to help you swim back to the mainland.'

I tried one last roll of the dice.

'I know he's coming here to meet you here.'

Gulmohamed shook his head. 'I hardly think so.' He gestured towards the stage. 'I have a speech to give. You are more than welcome to stay and listen if you like, but I shall be delivering it in Urdu. I doubt either you or Irani would find it comprehensible.'

Before I could respond, he turned and headed back behind the curtain. I made to follow, but my path was barred by two rather large chaps whom I was sure Gulmohamed hadn't employed for their conversational skills.

I considered going through them, fists first, but that might not have been the smartest idea, given that I was standing outside a mosque, surrounded by a thousand men who saw me as an infidel. When it came to lynchings by a religious mob, we British had already set a fine precedent in the form of General Gordon in Khartoum. He'd had a couple of companies of soldiers and the divine counsel of the prophet Isaiah on his side and still hadn't done too well. I, by contrast, had only Suren sitting in a bungalow in Malabar Hill and a borrowed chauffeur in a car five hundred yards away.

The sensible course would have been to back away, but I hadn't finished with Gulmohamed. Discretion might be the better part of valour, but I'd never understood why. In the end I decided to steer a middle course, made to leave, then turned and rushed between them. It must have been a while since someone had last defied them quite so brazenly and my actions seemed to take them by surprise. I was several feet past them and flying when I felt a thick hand on my collar hauling me back. I was swivelled round and received a punch to the gut which knocked the wind out of me. I doubled over, fighting for breath, and before I knew it, was being frog-marched back out and away from the stage. For a moment I thought they might actually carry out Gulmohamed's threat and throw me into the sea, and maybe if I'd thrown a punch or two, they might just have done so. Fortunately they decided that marching me back down the causeway was a better course of action, and I had to agree with them. Despite the ever growing number of men heading in the other direction, they'd no trouble getting me to the far end. The sight of a sahib being manhandled by two gorillas caused the crowd to part like they were the Red Sea and I a reluctant Moses.

They deposited me back on the mainland with a rather unceremonious shove, then remained there to make sure I had no thoughts of trying to get across again. I decided, rather belatedly, to give discretion a try and retreated several paces into a lane to regroup and wait for the *goondahs* to head back to the mosque.

Leaning against a crumbling wall, I lit a cigarette and considered Gulmohamed's comments. If he was telling the truth, there *was* no meeting scheduled with the man who called himself Irani at midday. Yet I had a feeling that Irani was coming anyway. I checked my watch. Twenty minutes to noon. I'd find out soon enough.

Finishing my cigarette, I tracked back to the mouth of the causeway. Gulmohamed's heavies were still there, and a few minutes later, my worst fears were realised. Irani, dressed in a linen suit and carrying a brown leather briefcase, was approaching. He was a foot taller and wider than the other pilgrims and the two bodyguards gave him more than a passing glance but did nothing to stop him. With Gulmohamed's goons still there, attempting to follow Irani across the causeway would be a fool's errand. I had my revolver with me, but taking it out and threatening them with it would probably do more harm than good. Instead I stood there impotently, that is until I suddenly saw a familiar face in the crowd.

FIFTY-SEVEN

Surendranath Banerjee

I ran from Miss Colah's house and commandeered the gardener's bicycle. It was hardly the fastest mode of transport but as the British say, *beggars can't be choosers.*

I cycled out of the drive and down the lane. As luck would have it, most of the journey was downhill and I picked up a decent turn of speed on the descent towards Chowpatty beach. At the crossroads there I came across a taxi rank. Skidding to a halt, I thanked the gods, ditched the cycle and ran for the nearest cab.

It was only once I was settled in the back and the taxi was speeding towards Pedder Road that I had the chance to take stock. Irani was, in actuality, Atchabahian. He had been hired by Section H, or at least by a rogue Section H officer: MacRae. His purpose? Playing both sides against the middle, funnelling clandestine British cash to both hardline Hindus and extremist Muslims, in an attempt, I assumed, to sway votes away from the more moderate parties in the forthcoming elections, or worse, in an attempt to trigger violence and provide a pretext for cancelling them altogether.

Set against that objective, the rationale for the murder of Mukherjee became clear. Atchabahian had lured Gulmohamed to Budge Budge on the pretence of meeting a wealthy donor. He'd then strangled Mukherjee, hoping to pin the blame on

Gulmohamed and kill two birds with one stone. However, Gulmohamed had smelt a rat and fled the scene. I, on the other hand, had stumbled right in. I guessed Atchabahian had probably tipped off the local police in advance too, which explained why their officers had turned up on the scene so quickly.

Had his actions gone to plan, Mukherjee's murder and Gulmohamed's arrest would have been enough to light the touchpaper and set Hindus and Muslims across the whole of India at each other's throats. As it was, Mukherjee's death alone had led to Calcutta going up in flames, aided in no small part by the thousands of flyers which had been posted up overnight in both Hindu and Muslim areas, flyers which I now assumed Atchabahian had printed in advance and then distributed to extremists on both sides.

That the violence had failed to spread was probably due to Mukherjee's second-tier rank among the Hindu radicals and the fact that Gulmohamed had not been implicated. Atchabahian, though, was now out to rectify his mistake. If the flyer translated by Miss Colah was to be believed, what Atchabahian had failed to do in Calcutta, he would set right in Bombay. He would kill Gulmohamed at the mosque and stir the Muslims of the subcontinent to rise. And that would play right into the hands of our British overlords. What better way to show the outside world that Indians weren't fit to govern themselves. '*Look!*' the British papers and their Indian surrogates would gleefully crow. '*These people are at each other's throats. We must continue to rule India if only to save the natives from themselves.*'

It was a daring plan, and I had to remind myself that Atchabahian hadn't hatched it. He was merely the tool. The plan had been British, or at least dreamt up by a rogue British agent.

Even now, I had trouble accepting it. My father's words, uttered many times since I was a child, suddenly came to me.

'*Divide and rule. It has always been the British way. That is how they first enslaved us and that is how they even now keep us in our servitude. Yet should we blame them or ourselves? They only exploit our stupidity and prejudices.*'

It should not have come as a shock, and yet it did. The British were the people I worked for, whose institutions I upheld. It struck me that they were also the same people who were currently seeking my capture and trial for a crime I hadn't committed. Yet that was a matter for a different time. Right now I had to stop the chaos and carnage that would be triggered by the assassination of Farid Gulmohamed.

The car sped downhill until, in the distance, I saw the mosque appearing out of the sea like something from a dream. A dome and a single minaret floating serenely and gleaming white in the high sun.

I wondered where Sam was. With any luck he would have arrested Gulmohamed and taken him into custody. He would have done it for the wrong reasons but it might just save the politician's life. That, however, seemed unlikely. Even Sam would surely recognise the folly of a lone Englishman, without a uniform, attempting to effect the arrest of a senior Muslim politician outside a mosque.

Just as I was beginning to feel I might reach there in time, the taxi ground to a halt, its progress stopped by a wall of men clad in white.

'What is it?' I asked in pidgin Hindi.

'*Masjid mein ek baithak hai,*' said the driver, which I took to mean that some sort of gathering was being held at the mosque. And if the crowds in our path were anything to go by, it was going to be a damn large gathering.

The note in Irani's papers suddenly made sense. Haji Ali, twelve noon. What better place to assassinate the leader of a political party than in front of a thousand of his followers? I checked my watch. It was a quarter to twelve. I flung a rupee note at the driver and jumped out. From here it would be faster on foot. Throwing myself into the maelstrom, I began to push through the sea of bodies and fought my way forward towards the causeway.

From somewhere came the sound of commotion, voices raised in complaint. I turned to see the crowd ripple then part and there in front of me, as though spat out by the throng, stood Sam looking somewhat dishevelled.

'What are you doing here?' he said, limping over. 'Anyway it doesn't matter. I'm just glad to see you.'

'Likewise,' I said. 'What happened?'

'I tried to arrest Gulmohamed,' he winced, 'but that didn't go down too well. I was right, though. Irani is here. I just saw him walk down the causeway. They're in cahoots.'

'No,' I said. 'We were wrong. Atchabahian isn't here to meet Gulmohamed. He's come to kill him.'

The look of relief vanished from his face.

'What?'

'There's no time to explain,' I said, turning towards the path. 'We need to get after him.'

He put a hand to my shoulder and pulled me back. 'It's not that simple. I've already had a run-in with Gulmohamed's bodyguards.' He gestured towards two large men standing with arms folded at the entrance of the causeway. 'I tried to force Gulmohamed to talk to me. They didn't approve.'

That explained why he looked like he'd been in a fight. I sometimes wondered whether he had a death wish.

'I'll go alone, then,' I said.

'Wait,' he said. 'There's more than one way to skin a cat. Come on. This way.'

FIFTY-EIGHT

Sam Wyndham

With Suren in tow, I sprinted over the road to the quayside. There, close to the waterfront, a tugboat, its hull dented and funnel blackened with age, was pushing another vessel, towards the low sea wall.

As the smaller vessel approached, I held my breath and leapt, landing on the rickety wooden deck with all the poise of a sea cow, practically scaring the life out of a skinny fisherman who stood close by. He barely had time to regain his wits before Suren barrelled in beside me, shaking the deck's loose timbers.

Then we were off again, running the length of the vessel to the stern. From there, I clambered onto the tug's vulcanised bumper and hauled myself up and onto its deck. I helped Suren up, then ran for the wheelhouse.

The pilot came out, his face suggesting he was unsure whether we were pirates or just the officials of the Bombay Port Authority. I pulled out my warrant card and shoved it in his face.

'Police business. You need to take us to Haji Ali.'

He seemed confused, and Suren's attempt at explaining it to him in sub-par Hindustani didn't much help.

The man pointed towards the mosque. 'Haji Ali is there only. You can walk to it.'

Suren embarked on some exposition which I imagined covered exactly why that wasn't a practical option, but in the interests of time, I decided to speed things up and pulled out my revolver. The sight of the Webley curtailed further discussion, prompting the pilot to return to the wheelhouse and begin the process of turning his tugboat towards the mosque.

Within minutes we were chugging forward, closing the short distance to the island at, if not a high rate of knots, then at least at enough of a pace to feel like we were actually making progress. I kept the revolver trained on the hapless pilot, just to keep him focused on the task.

Ahead of us, the white walls of Haji Ali grew closer. Over the air came the metallic screeching of a tannoy being coaxed to life, and then the deep baritone of a voice.

'They're starting,' said Suren.

I checked my watch. Twelve noon on the dot. In five years in this godforsaken country, I couldn't recall another native event actually commencing at the advertised time.

Suren ordered the pilot to make for the spit of land in front of the mosque, where the stage had been set up and the faithful were gathered. The man shook his head.

'Not possible, sahib. Rocks. Boat cannot get close. But there is landing ghat on other side,' he ventured.

'Go round then!' Suren roared in relief. *'Jaldi!'*

The man put his foot down but other than an increase in the stench of diesel, not much seemed to happen. Gradually the vessel wallowed its way further out into the bay and around to the far side of the mosque. Over the tannoy came another screech, then the sound of a voice we both recognised.

'Gulmohamed,' said Suren. 'He's starting his speech.'

I looked to the pilot. 'Can't this bucket go any faster?'

He seemed to take my words as a personal insult.

'She is going already top speed, sahib. If you want faster, maybe next time you hijack Cutty Sark?' It was a brave statement, especially given I still had a gun pointed at him, but captains are often sensitive about their tubs.

Five minutes later, we rounded to the far side of the islet and the walls of Haji Ali gave way to an open space which doubled as a landing ghat. The vessel inched closer and then, when the water looked to be knee height, we jumped out and waded ashore.

The area looked deserted. I assumed all eyes were trained on the rally on the other side of the mosque. Suren and I scrambled up the steps, and in the shadow of its minaret, ran through the concourse towards the mosque's arched entrance and the rally beyond.

Gulmohamed's voice was louder now, his words clearly audible. The same went for the crowd's roars of approval. Skidding to a halt, I surveyed the scene. In front of us were a thousand men crammed into a space half the size of a football pitch, all focused on the figure on the green-draped stage. I scanned the faces looking for any sign of Irani.

Beside me, Suren gasped for breath. 'Where is he?'

'I can't see him.'

'Maybe he's making for the front of the crowd? He could get a clean shot from there.'

I was about to agree with him, but then stopped. If Irani was to shoot Gulmohamed here, in front of so many of his most ardent followers, he'd be signing his own death warrant. The crowd would rip him limb from limb before he managed to flee five paces. Whatever he was planning, it wasn't a pistol shot up at the stage.

'He's not going to shoot him from the front,' I said. I scanned the high windows and roof of the mosque buildings that looked onto the stage. 'He's planning a sniper shot from somewhere ...'

'No he's not,' said Suren.

I turned to him. His face was ashen.

'Miss Colah translated a flyer. It talked about avenging the *martyrs* of Haji Ali. Plural. I think he means to bomb the crowd.'

I thought back. When I'd seen him on the causeway, Irani *had* been carrying a briefcase. I'd assumed it was to pick up a payment from Gulmohamed. But if what Suren was saying was true, the case was far more deadly.

'We need to get these people out of here.'

With one hand close to my revolver, I plunged into the mass of men, pushing a path through them to the front. Any protest was drowned out by the sound of Gulmohamed's voice echoing from the tannoy. Still, by the time we reached several feet from the front, even he noticed our approach. His tone changed. I didn't understand the words, but the crowd's reaction was enough to tell me we were in trouble. Before I knew it, men were turning towards me, grasping at my shirt and arms. For a split second, before my view was blocked by half a dozen irate souls, I saw Irani in his linen suit, making towards the curtained-off area backstage.

I felt hands on me. Fingers pulling at my shoulders. Another second and I'd lose any chance of stopping him. With what felt like my last reserves of strength, I wrenched my arm free, reached for my revolver and fired into the air. The effect was instantaneous. Even as the sound of the shot reverberated off the walls, the hands that had sought to grab me fell away as though hit by an electric charge. Men fell to the floor in a fruitless search for cover. Only Irani kept running.

By now he'd reached the entrance to the backstage area. He was about to disappear behind the screens. Onstage, Gulmohamed's minders were running to his side.

Free of the crowd and with Suren beside me, I chased after Irani, but something felt wrong. It was several precious seconds before I realised what. I stopped in my tracks.

'The briefcase!'

Suren stared at me. 'What?'

'Irani came in with a briefcase. He's dropped it somewhere. We need to find it,' I said.

Suren swallowed hard. 'I'll find it. You go after Irani.'

'Nonsense,' I said. 'Irani can wait. We'll find it together.'

'These people will tear you apart if you stay here!'

I didn't like it, putting him in harm's way, and made to remonstrate, but he cut me short.

'There's no time to argue,' he said. 'Now go after him!'

He was right of course, but I couldn't let him go back into the crowd unarmed.

'Sergeant,' I shouted, and threw him my revolver. 'Be careful.'

FIFTY-NINE

Surendranath Banerjee

Instinctively I reached out and caught the revolver, its handle slick with sweat.

Around me, men were once more rising to their feet. Fortunately their attention had been on Sam, and to my surprise, I survived any real scrutiny. Maybe they were simply relieved not to have been shot, but no one appeared to realise I'd been an accomplice to the mad Englishman who'd just fired his pistol into the air.

I traced a path back to where I thought Irani had stood, but found nothing. Onstage someone was shouting. I looked up and saw Gulmohamed, flanked by his bodyguards and pointing at me. The crowd might have failed to notice me, but he certainly hadn't. It was then that I saw it. At the foot of the platform, wedged between two of the wooden struts which held up the stage and almost directly below where Gulmohamed now stood, was the brown leather Gladstone bag I had seen in Irani's hotel suite.

Without a thought, I began to run towards it. Gulmohamed must have thought I was coming for him, for a moment later one of his men leapt from the stage. There was but one thing for it. I lifted the revolver and pointed it squarely at his head.

The man froze.

'Police!' I said, then pointed behind him to the bag and shouted in Hindi. 'I don't want to hurt you, or your boss. I just need to get to that bag.'

He stood aside and I brushed past him. Reaching the case, I tried the clasp. It was locked, but this time I had no choice but to snap the flimsy mechanism. I threw it open and stumbled backwards. What was inside was unmistakable. Sticks of explosive and a few wires attached to a timing clock. I'd seen bombs before, but nothing like this, at least not outside of a training manual. The bombs used by our Calcutta anarchists were crude devices compared to this thing, just metal spheres with an explosive charge and a fuse sticking out of the end. Only once before had I seen a timed bomb, and even then, it had been an amateur affair which had failed to go off. This appeared to be something quite different. Either Irani had received professional instruction while in the army, or someone with a detailed knowledge of these things had given it to him. Whatever the explanation, the chances of my defusing it were negligible.

I turned to Gulmohamed's bodyguard who still stood with his hands in the air, beckoned him over and pointed to the bomb. 'Your *burra sahib* needs to tell the crowd to get as far back from the stage as possible, and then *you* need to get him out of here and into the mosque.'

The man quickly understood what was at stake. He clambered onto the stage, explained to Gulmohamed what he had seen and what I had told him. The politician stared down at me, then reached for the microphone and in a voice that hardly wavered, ordered his followers to get up and quickly make their way either into the mosque or back along the causeway.

It took agonising seconds for the people to react. If the device exploded now, tens, if not hundreds of men, myself and Gulmohamed included, would be killed. I'd no idea how long we had, but

I needed to speed things up. Once more I reached for the revolver, and as Sam had done earlier, I lifted it skyward and fired. It achieved the desired effect and a minute later I had succeeded in clearing an area of some twenty feet around the bomb.

From there, I risked a glance back at the stage to make sure Gulmohamed had also heeded my advice, but before I could focus, there was a flash and a sound like thunder rent the air. I felt myself hurled backwards, and the last thing I remember before blacking out is the platform collapsing amid a cloud of dust and debris.

SIXTY

Sam Wyndham

I heard the explosion, followed by the screams of men and boys. Irani had torn through the area backstage and I'd given chase, through an archway which led into the grounds of the mosque. He too turned at the sound of the explosion, and on seeing me, flashed a smile.

'Give up, Atchabahian!' I shouted. 'You're under arrest!' Empty words, of course. The man had a head start and a gun. If I were him, I'd have taken those odds. As if on cue, he raised his revolver and fired, the bullet exploding in the wall behind me in a shower of brick dust. I dived for cover, lifting my head in time to see him disappear round a corner.

Picking myself up I sprinted after him, out into the blistering sunshine of the same courtyard that Suren and I had run through after jumping from the tugboat. Irani, though, wasn't making for the sea. Instead he turned and made for the path to the archway at the front of the mosque, the one that had brought us out close to the rear of the crowd. By now, the area beyond the archway was a maelstrom of bodies, crushed together at the mouth of the causeway leading back to the mainland. Men were stampeding towards us. I stopped, horrified by the sight. The tide was rising, and with nowhere else to go, people trampled others in a fight to escape. Some jumped straight into the water. Irani disappeared into the torrent of bodies. I considered going after him but helping the wounded took priority.

I turned and fought my way back towards the stage and the stench of smoke and charnel. The scene was one of hellish devastation. The stage had collapsed into a pyre, its green coverings burning amid a skeleton of bamboo pillars.

In front lay bodies, prone and dust-smeared. A few souls began to move among the wreckage, shambling about in shock. I scanned the carnage for any sign of Suren, uttering a prayer to a god I didn't believe in that he'd been outside of the blast radius when the thing had gone off; that even now he was somewhere backstage, making sure Gulmohamed was safe.

Frantically I checked the faces of those who were left, hoping I wouldn't find the sergeant among them. There, closest to the stage, lay a body, face down in the dust. As I drew closer, my fears multiplied. The figure was Suren's height and build. Reaching him, I fell to my knees. The shirt matched his. Delicately I turned him over. His face and chest were bloody, but it was impossible to tell how badly he'd been hurt. A wave of guilt crashed over me. This was my fault. I should never have agreed to his plan. It should have been me lying there, not him. I reached for his wrist and, with a shaking hand, fumbled for a pulse. I closed my eyes. It was there.

Suren looked up. He took a few moments to focus, then seemed surprised to find me with his wrist in my hand.

'Are you OK?' I asked, placing his arm back on his chest.

'I think so.' He looked around. 'Gulmohamed?'

I hadn't given that much thought. I glanced over to the remains of the stage. There didn't seem to be bodies among the burning wreckage.

'I think he's OK.'

Suren wiped blood and dust from his face. I reached out a hand. 'Come on,' I said. 'Or do you plan on just lying there all day?'

He took it and I helped him to his feet.

'What of Irani?' he asked hopefully.

'He got away.'

'Then it's over,' said Suren. 'Without him, I can't prove my innocence.'

'That's not true,' I said. 'Taggart's still alive. Once he pulls through, he'll corroborate your story.' The words rang hollow, even to me.

From the mainland, the sound of wailing sirens grew louder.

'Come on,' I said. 'We should get out of here before the police arrive.'

SIXTY-ONE

Surendranath Banerjee

We stumbled back along the causeway, just as the first police vans and ambulances arrived on the scene. Constables and stretcher-bearers ran past as Sam and I blended into the crowd.

The car was waiting, the engine running. Miss Colah's driver, alerted by the explosion and the ongoing exodus across the causeway, had sensed the need for a quick getaway.

We drove south in silence, back towards the heart of the city, detouring via the Taj Hotel in the desperate hope that Irani might have returned there. It was futile of course, but the English have a phrase about a drowning man clutching at straws. We were informed that Irani had checked out the previous night, and I doubted the man would even exist by sundown. Atchabahian would simply discard the persona and disappear.

Back on Malabar Hill, Miss Colah's maid tended to my wounds while Sam attempted to contact Dawson. I tried to focus on the positive. We had saved Gulmohamed's life and hopefully averted the sort of bloodbath which had engulfed Calcutta after Mukherjee's murder. That was surely worth celebrating, whatever lay in store personally.

Ooravis Colah attempted to lighten the mood in the way only a woman of wealth and leisure can, but even her levity failed to rouse me from black despondency.

How had things come to this? Even now, with the facts becoming clear, I still struggled to comprehend. A plot by Section H to funnel money to extremists – both Hindu and Muslim – in an attempt to destabilise the consensus which Gandhi had built, in order to sway the elections. It had, if you believed Dawson, led to MacRae, a rogue agent setting in train a series of assassination plots to set Hindus and Muslims at each other's throats. And yet it was I who was the fugitive, *I* who would be put on trial for Mukherjee's murder. It would not be a fair trial of course. There was no such thing as a trial by jury, not for Indians, not under British law. I would be tried in camera, by a panel of British judges. None of the facts of Section H's involvement could be corroborated by hard evidence, and even if it could, I doubted it would be deemed admissible. The military would see to that; invoke articles of imperial security and that would be the end of it. Even if I somehow avoided the gallows, my life as it had been, and the promise it held for the future, was finished. There would be no family, no career, no honour. The more I considered it, the more I came to the conclusion that I had no choice.

The last week had felt as though the mountains of the Himalaya had rained down upon me, and now, with the avalanche finally having passed, I was emerging, bruised and bitter.

Yet these few days, I realised, were merely the end of a road I had been on for several years. No, not the end, but another junction. A definite decision to be taken between what was left and what was right. I felt a molten anger at the hypocrisy. The authorities I worked for and had served selflessly for more than five years were the same authorities who would now put me on trial for crimes which their own agents had committed.

Sam returned, grim-faced.

'They're putting out an alert for Atchabahian: all ports, all stations. There's a chance they'll catch him. In the meantime, Dawson says they're leaning on Gulmohamed to make a statement to his people calling for calm. It should be fairly straightforward. If he doesn't, the press might get to know where his funds have come from.'

He paused, waiting for me to speak, but I had nothing to say. The silence sat awkwardly between us.

'He's confident he can get the charges against you dropped. He says it might take a while, but once we're back in Calcutta and you turn yourself in, he can put in a quiet word to the right people, and if they catch Atchabahian in the meantime, well —'

'I'm not going back to Calcutta,' I said. 'I can't take that chance.'

Sam stared at me. 'You can't just stay in Bombay. They'll find you and arrest you. It's better we go home and you surrender voluntarily.'

'I'm not going to stay here and I've no intention of surrendering to anyone.'

I explained my plans to him.

'Well,' he said finally, 'maybe *Surrender-not* wasn't such a bad name after all.'

SIXTY-TWO

Sam Wyndham

The rain was falling, haemorrhaging from a dark sky. It had been thirty-six hours since the explosion at Haji Ali. We were back in Ooravis Colah's car, the driver impervious to the weather, gunning it along the deserted streets and crashing through pools of black water.

At Suren's insistence, we'd stopped en route at a small roadside shrine to Lord Ganesh, the elephant-headed Hindu god. That had come as a surprise as he was supposedly the god of good luck and we'd had precious little of that recently.

'He is also the god of auspicious beginnings,' Suren had replied.

The driver brought the car to a halt, near the dripping awning of a building, then ventured out to open the door for his mistress.

It was generous of Ooravis to come, especially given the filthy night, but she'd insisted on it, saying it'd be wrong not to. I lit a cigarette and gave her a few moments to say her goodbyes to Suren. There were no tears of course. She hadn't known either of us more than a few days, and while friendships are fast, emotional attachments take longer. Besides, she struck me as the kind of woman who was far too level-headed to contemplate tears.

Suren, for his part, was nodding appreciatively at some no doubt worldly advice the young woman was offering. I couldn't help but smile. When I'd first met him, he couldn't look at a woman without blushing. Now, here he was, chatting away to a Bombay millionairess like Rudolph bloody Valentino.

Ooravis hugged him, and gave him a few last words of wisdom. He thanked her, then watched as she got back in the car. These final steps would be taken by just him and me.

I checked my watch by the jaundiced light of a street lamp. Half past eight.

'Ready?' I asked.

He tipped the brim of his hat. 'Ready.'

I opened the black umbrella to raise it above his head, but Suren was already several paces away, crossing the road towards the heavy iron gate. I strove to keep up, reaching him as he stopped in front of a small wooden box of a sentry post.

The guard inside looked like he'd picked the short straw. His uniform hung off his frame, as though it belonged to a larger, luckier man who was sheltering somewhere else. He was seated awkwardly, trying to avoid the persistent drip, drip of water leaking in through the tin roof of his box.

I showed him my warrant card.

'Where's the customs office, sonny? Police business.'

'First on the left,' he said, giving a vague nod in what I presumed was its general direction.

We walked the hundred yards or so as the sky wept and the rain fell hard on the cracked concrete of the dockside forecourt. The SS *Durban* wasn't due to leave port for another forty minutes, but there were still formalities to be gone through.

The customs office was little more than a dilapidated wooden shed set between two other wooden sheds which were larger but just as decrepit. The door hung half open. I guessed the wood was so warped that it no longer shut properly without the aid of brute force or a padlock and chain. I pushed it open the rest of the way and let Suren enter.

At the far end, behind a desk and illuminated by a watery halo from a naked bulb above, sat a customs official poring over a ledger. Another man, a sailor judging by his clothes, sat lounging close by.

Beside me I felt Suren hesitate. The customs official, a brawny chap with a paper-white complexion that had no business being in the tropics, looked up.

I turned to Suren. 'You can still change your mind.'

But he shook his head and walked forward.

'Name?'

'Nihar Dey.'

'Papers.'

Suren reached into his coat and pulled out the passport Dawson had given him and handed it to the official.

The man examined it with disinterest, flipping through the pages.

'Destination?'

'Southampton.'

That might have been the SS *Durban*'s destination, but it wasn't Suren's. He planned to leave the vessel at Genoa or Marseilles and travel to Paris or Berlin. There were émigré communities in both cities, Indian political refugees who'd received sanctuary from both Britain's erstwhile enemy and its ally. Suren said he'd been told the welcome was warmer in Germany, but the food was better in France.

Satisfied, the official handed the passport back.

'And you, sir?' he said, turning to me.

'I'm not travelling.'

'Fair enough. You'll find the *Durban* at pier C.'

Back outside, the rain was still falling, but the sojourn to the pier was blessedly short. Above us the SS *Durban* sat silhouetted against the lights on the hills beyond. The vessel was a merchantman with a few berths for the odd traveller. Ooravis's friend Mr Panthaki had organised it, and it felt safer than a passenger liner. Suren had once complained to me that merchant vessels like the *Durban* carried away the wealth of India in their holds. Tonight the sentiment felt apt.

We stopped at the foot of the gangway.

'My father believes that starting an endeavour during the rain is auspicious,' he said.

'Well, between him and the Lord Ganesh, I'd say you're pretty well covered for auspicious beginnings.'

He gave a short, bitter laugh. 'I hope so.'

'Just make sure you go on in the same fashion.'

A sailor passed, shooting us a curious look as he ascended the gangplank.

'I'll send you a telegram when I get to Europe,' he said.

'Bugger that,' I said. 'I'll expect a postcard from the Suez Canal long before. A picture of something tasteful like the Pyramids, or failing that, a camel.'

We made small talk for a few minutes; inane conversation, instantly forgotten, instead of so much that needed to be said. I thought back to the last time I'd seen my father. Then, too, we'd parted with few words of any consequence. More than once I'd wished I'd made more of that last opportunity, and yet here I was, doing the same thing. The world changes, the Englishman remains constant. Like a dinosaur.

There came a blast from the ship's horn.

'I should get aboard,' he said.

I nodded and he turned towards the gangway.

'I'll sort this out, Suren,' I said. 'I'll find Atchabahian, get the charges dropped and an apology to boot. I expect you back before Christmas.'

I doubted he believed me, but he was good enough to smile.

I held out my hand. He took it and shook it.

'Look after yourself, Sergeant,' I said.

I saw him choke back the emotions; the sensibilities with which his people are cursed.

'Yes, sir.'

He released his grip and headed up the walkway. At the top, he turned, gave a final, stiff salute, then disappeared from sight.

I lowered the umbrella and felt in my pocket for the packet of Capstans. My fingers brushed against the envelope Suren had entrusted to me, within it the letter he'd written to his parents, explaining his actions and which I'd promised to deliver. I fished out the last cigarette and lit it with a match and flame carefully cupped against the rain. I wish I could say what thoughts went through my head during those last minutes, but in truth there was nothing. The war had taught me to cauterise any feelings of loss. Too many friends had been taken away for me to harbour such things.

In the end, I smoked only half, flicking the rest into the coal-black water and taking one last look at the vessel before turning and slowly retracing my steps along the quayside, out past the gate and back to Miss Colah's car.

SIXTY-THREE

Sam Wyndham

I took the slow train back to Calcutta. Colonel Dawson had offered a military flight, but I was in no great hurry. Besides, he still didn't know about Suren's little disappearing act, facilitated by the passport which he himself had provided. And though I doubted the spymaster would pass that information on to the authorities which might interdict Suren's flight, I saw no reason to tempt fate.

And so it was a full two days later that I arrived back at Howrah station, to be met with the usual crowd of a million souls, among them, the familiar face and pipe of the colonel.

He saw me as I descended, his face lighting up in recognition and I daresay the expectation of seeing Suren behind me, but that quickly changed to consternation when he realised the sergeant was missing. For once it seemed, this was a situation he hadn't anticipated, and that made me happy.

'Where is he?'

'Good to see you too,' I said. 'As for Suren, he sends his regards but he won't be returning to Calcutta just yet.'

'I can't protect him if I don't know where he is.'

'How's Taggart?'

'Stable. The doctors think he'll recover, they just won't say when.'

'I don't think we'll be seeing Suren before Taggart's back on his feet and the charges against him are dropped. Unless you can convince his stand-in, Halifax, to drop them?'

'That's not going to happen. Halifax seems to have taken your friend's escape as a personal affront. He'd like to see the sergeant strung up, ideally with you next to him.'

'That bad?'

Dawson nodded. 'Word is he's after your blood. Charges of aiding and abetting. You might want to prepare for a grilling.'

I'd been expecting as much. 'Any news on Atchabahian?'

'Nothing yet. We pulled MacRae in for questioning, and he admitted recruiting Atchabahian and giving him the Irani cover, but he claims it was only for the purpose of funnelling money to certain political parties. He says he hasn't seen or heard from him since before the attack on Mukherjee.'

'And you believe him?'

'I didn't say that.'

'Good,' I said, 'because Suren said that bomb at Haji Ali looked like something built by professionals rather than ordered on room service at the Taj Hotel.'

'The point is, we have MacRae under surveillance. If he makes contact with Atchabahian, we'll know about it.'

'And then? I doubt your superiors in Delhi would want Section H's activities brought under the microscope. Atchabahian would be an embarrassment.'

'True,' he said. 'But let's cross that bridge when we come to it.'

Dawson had been right of course. No sooner had I reported back to Lal Bazar than I was called in by Halifax and his coterie, hauled over the coals and then placed on suspension under charge of assisting a fugitive.

I explained everything to them: how Atchabahian, a rogue agent of Section H, had murdered Mukherjee in an attempt to frame Gulmohamed and propel the whole country into a religious bloodbath. But that truth was rather too unpalatable to accept, especially when the military denied every scintilla of it.

There was also the small matter of the attack on Taggart which Suren had taken advantage of to effect his escape. I told them I suspected Uddam Singh had been behind that, hoping to kill Suren and me rather than the commissioner. But I had no proof to back up that assertion, and no one cared to believe that the city's British police chief could have been the victim of dumb luck rather than a meticulously planned attack.

Speaking of Singh, he'd been as good as his word and reined in his hoodlums. Maybe it was a case of honour among thieves, or just that the cash funnelled by Atchabahian to hardliners had dried up and religious violence was no longer as profitable as the good old-fashioned rackets of drugs and prostitution. Either way, I wasn't complaining. I'd even upheld my side of the bargain, or at least part of it, and made sure that his son Vinay had been released from prison.

I'd spent the next fortnight quietly stewing and rattling around in the flat in Premchand Boral Street which now seemed a tad too large. I'd visited Suren's parents in Shyambazar and delivered his letter. His mother had left the room in tears, but his father had reacted with a curious pride, which wasn't entirely surprising. In certain circles, being a fugitive from British justice was a badge of honour; certainly more so than being an instrument of that justice.

I had another letter to deliver, this one sealed in an ornate envelope and enclosed with a twenty-rupee note. It entailed a trip down to Metiabruz, to a large house beside the river and a girl called Ayisha.

Suren had told me the tale of his meetings with Gulmo-hamed's niece, together with stories of her skill on the santoor. What he'd neglected to mention, however, was that she was rather beautiful, which was odd because the boy was apt to bandy about that particular term, applying it liberally to many ladies who scarcely deserved it. But now, with this girl to whom the appellation most definitely applied, he'd singularly failed to mention it.

She was of course surprised to see me.

'I've a letter for you, Miss Gulmohamed,' I said, 'from a mutual acquaintance.'

She took the envelope and opened it, tearing the seal with one elegant finger. She read the contents quickly, sating her initial curiosity, then once again, more slowly this time, coming to terms with its content.

She looked up. 'Where has he gone?'

'Europe,' I said. 'I can't say more than that,' and to be fair, that seemed to satisfy her.

'Well, thank you for delivering it, Mr …?'

'Wyndham,' I said. 'I'm a friend of Suren's.'

'Thank you, Mr Wyndham.'

There was no reason for me to linger, but something within me stirred. I felt I should put in a word on Suren's behalf.

'I take it you're aware of the attack on your uncle's rally at Haji Ali Mosque in Bombay. Well, it was Suren who saved your uncle's life that day.'

That caught her interest.

'Honestly?'

'And a lot of other people's lives too. He's a hero.'

Suren wouldn't have thanked me for using the word, but he wasn't here and I thought it might go down well with the girl. It certainly had an impact, though not quite in the way I'd expected.

'A hero? And yet in his letter he says he has been forced to leave the country. It seems an odd way to treat a hero.'

How was I supposed to answer? I should have agreed with her. Suren had played his part in averting a bloody civil war. He should have been feted for that. Instead he'd hounded out of the country. Yet what did it say about me that my first reaction was not to support my friend but to obfuscate, to utter an ill-defined, insincere defence of the system that had banished him?

Exhaustion – or was it self-loathing? – washed over me. I was tired of always being on the back foot, always defending the indefensible. Placing oneself in a position of semi-permanent hypocrisy, that's what it meant to be an Englishman in India, and I certainly wasn't the only one who felt that way. God knows there were enough embittered, broken colonial men and women of good conscience, driven to drink and ruin by the irreconcilable absurdity at the heart of it all: the claim that we were here for the betterment of this land, when all the time we merely sucked it dry.

We never spoke of it of course. That would be bad form, enough to make one an outcast. Instead we maintained the fiction of the wonderful munificence of the Pax Brittanica, claiming to be on the side of the angels while doing the work of the devil.

In the end, I said nothing, merely bade her good day and assured her that Suren would return soon enough.

If there was a silver lining to those days, it was that I was able to spend a little time with Miss Grant. I'd been ordered not to leave town, and I might have obeyed had they not provoked me by placing a watchman across the road from the flat. That was hardly a challenge I could ignore, and so I set myself the objective of finding ever more creative ways of giving my minder the slip and getting as far out of Calcutta as possible before returning by midnight and making sure my surveillance watched me enter the front door.

On a whim, I organised a picnic out to Barasat some forty miles south of the city, by which I mean I came up with the idea. It was Annie who supplied the car and the food and the *bagan-bari*, the bungalow out in the countryside where we ate it.

We sat outside, on a tartan rug thrown on the grass and a wicker hamper between us. Around us, the flowers of Bengal – marigold and jasmine, bougainvillea and hibiscus, and a dozen others I couldn't name – blossomed in a haze of colour. In the palms nested green parrots, ever-watchful for the langur monkeys that foraged below.

It was a moment of peace, a brief hiatus between storm fronts, but I was grateful for it. I watched as Annie sipped from a glass of freshly squeezed *mosambi* juice, the green husks of the fruit arranged in a neat, sunlit pile on the grass beside her. Sitting there, with her, it was almost possible to forget my troubles; almost, but not quite. They still circled my thoughts like vultures. Most revolved around Suren, and Annie seemed to sense that.

'Are you going to tell me where he's gone?'

'Europe,' I said. 'France, to start with. There's a group of Indian émigrés holed up in Paris. He said he'd make contact with them and take things from there.'

'Paris?' Annie's eyes lit up. 'I bet he'll love it.'

'Trust me, he'll hate it,' I said. 'He can't speak the language, he's got no palate for wine, and where's he going to find a bloody hilsa fish in France?'

Annie couldn't help but laugh. 'He'll get used to the food and he'll learn to drink wine. The only reason he hasn't already is because you spoiled him with whisky.'

'I *educated* him.'

'Of course you did.' She took another sip. 'He's going to be fine. It's *you* I'm more concerned about.'

Well, that was clearly nonsense, but I didn't wish to dwell on the matter.

'I wonder where he is now,' I said, as a cloud passed in front of the sun.

She looked up. 'You've not heard from him?'

'No. And I don't expect to, not for a while yet. The last thing we need is for him to break cover and get himself arrested on the high seas.'

'And then?'

'What?'

'When is he going to be able to come home?'

I shrugged. 'I don't know. Not until Taggart recovers, or we catch the bastard who actually killed Mukherjee. I doubt we'll ever catch him though.'

'And you, Sam?'

'What about me?'

'Oh, come now,' she said incredulously. 'You've been at a loose end for ages now. Have you thought about leaving the force?'

'And do what?'

'Anything you wanted to! There must be a thousand other careers you could follow.'

The thought was seductive, at least for a few seconds before it hit the rocks of practicality.

'Such as?' I said. 'I'm not cut out for anything else.'

'Well, maybe take some time to think about it,' she said. 'Suspension from duty has worked wonders on you. Imagine what it'd be like if they actually sacked you. You'd be wonderful!'

I raised my glass to her. 'I thought I already was.'

Suitably buoyed, I moved on to planning a longer trip, one to Tagore's university in the woods at Shantiniketan. I'd heard it was pleasant out there, and along with almost every non-white in the city, Annie was mad about the man's poetry. I, for my part, found his work rather sentimental, which Suren had once put down to the fact that I was reading it wrongly.

Of the sergeant there'd still been no word and no postcard from the Pyramids.

Rather than worry, I focused on planning the perfect trip for Annie. Shorn of other responsibilities, I found myself investing all my energies into this one endeavour.

I'd planned the Shantiniketan trip down to a tee, but the night before we were scheduled to leave, I received a call from Dawson.

'They've found him.'

My stomach turned. 'Who? Suren?'

'No, Atchabahian. He slipped aboard a vessel called the *Rajputana* last night, bound for Rangoon. Booked in under the name of LeClerc, an alias, but like Irani it's one that Section H created. It's definitely him.'

'Your colleagues have arrested him?'

'The ship left port before they got a chance. And just as well too.'

My head spun. 'You want him to get away?'

'No,' said Dawson. 'It's just that if you're keen on exonerating the young Sergeant Banerjee, it would be far better if *you* were the one to make the arrest.'

'I'm suspended, remember,' I said. 'Right now, I don't have the power to arrest anyone.'

I heard the disappointment in his voice. 'Don't be obtuse, Wyndham,' he said. 'I know that, and you know that, but Atchabahian doesn't. Do you have a uniform?'

'Just my police dress whites.'

'That'll have to do,' he said. 'Put 'em on. I'm sending a car for you.'

An hour later I was at Annie's door, apologising once again.

'It's for Suren,' I said. 'If I can catch this bastard Atchabahian, then there's a chance I can get him to confess. That would put Suren in the clear.'

'Do what you have to do, Sam,' she said. 'Shantiniketan can wait.'

I thanked her and readied to go.

'And, Sam,' she said.

I turned back to her and was startled to receive a kiss.

'Come back safe.'

And so, as a red sun rose the next morning, I found myself not on the way to Shantiniketan with Annie, but staring out over the mist-covered stillness of the Bay of Bengal from the shore of a speck of a settlement called Frasergunj. The place felt like the end of the world, just mud and mangrove and the mingling of fresh and salt water as far as the horizon.

A grey military launch was waiting at the jetty. I climbed aboard and soon we were skimming thorough the olive-green waters, heading out to sea and a rendezvous with the SS *Rajputana*, whose captain had been ordered to discreetly alter his course to the north.

It was over an hour before the black outline of the vessel appeared on the horizon and I felt a twinge of anticipation. The distance closed agonisingly slowly and it seemed that we might never reach her, but gradually her silhouette grew and finally we drew close and ordered her to heave to.

In my white dress uniform, I stood on the deck like a lighthouse on a shoreline, feeling like Nelson waiting to get shot on the deck of the *Victory*. I just hoped Atchabahian was a late riser.

I led a party of three soldiers up a rope ladder and onto the deck of the *Rajputana*, where a petty officer stood waiting.

'You have a passenger travelling under the name of LeClerc,' I said. 'He's a fugitive wanted by the Imperial Police.' I didn't mention the fact that I didn't possess an arrest warrant, nor that the only member of the Imperial Police he was wanted by was me. Fortunately, the uniform and the three armed men behind me were corroboration enough and the sailor led us first to the bridge and then on the captain's instructions to a cabin near the stern.

I knocked, waited a gracious fraction of a second and then ordered the officers to force the door. Inside, an unmistakable fig-ure jumped from his bed and made for a revolver that sat on a desk nearby.

'Leave it!' I shouted as two officers pointed their rifles at him.

The man froze, then slowly raised his hands.

'It's good to see you again, Mr Atchabahian,' I said. 'You're under arrest.'

SIXTY-FOUR

Sam Wyndham

Three hours later, I had Atchabahian in the back of a car, heading towards Calcutta.

Of course I'd had no real authority to arrest him, other than that which stemmed from the rifle barrels of the two soldiers behind me, and fortunately that had proved more than enough to detain him, but it left open the question of what I was to do with him.

That's why, as night descended, we drove not to Lal Bazar or any other police station, but to the hulking stone mass of Fort William, the military's command post in Calcutta, and home to Dawson's Section H.

That came as a shock to the Armenian. For most of the journey he'd been silent, possibly in the belief that his erstwhile military backers might still bail him out, but the sight of the military garrison did more to unsettle him than any of my threats had done during the journey.

Dawson was waiting beside a nondescript door which led to a series of dank underground cells. I knew because I'd once been a guest in one myself.

'He give you any trouble?'

'None.'

'Tell you anything?'

'Not yet, but the real work starts tomorrow.'

'It can start tonight if you want. I can have one of my chaps soften him up a little.'

I stared at Dawson. It went against everything I stood for. Yet Atchabahian had cost me my friend and possibly my career, and besides, what was the point in standing on principle when the entire edifice around you was rotten?

'Do what you have to,' I said.

I slept soundly that night. They say *the sleep of the just* is reserved for those with a clear conscience, but the truth is one could sleep quite as well by having no conscience at all. We always like others to see the best in us, and my conscience I realised, or what little remained of it after the war, had in recent years been invigorated by the desire to act as an example to Suren of what a good policeman should be. One could argue that my opium addiction had made me a less than sterling role model, but no one is perfect. Now, with Suren gone, I felt free to let my worst impulses reign, and that's why, when I showed up at the underground cell at Fort William the next morning, I was glad to see that Atchabahian's face bore scars similar to those which had been inflicted upon Suren at Budge Budge thana all those weeks before.

He'd been shackled and dragged from his cell into a small ante-room furnished with a table, two chairs and low-hanging bulb

I took a seat.

'Feeling more talkative?'

He looked at me through the slit of one eye.

'I want to see a solicitor,' he lisped through cracked lips and the odd broken tooth.

'And I want snow for Christmas,' I said, 'but neither's going to happen while we're sitting here in Calcutta. Shall we start at the beginning? Why did you kill Prashant Mukherjee?'

He hadn't answered. And it was the same with all my questions that day, and the next. It was on the third morning that he had a change of heart.

There was something in him that had changed. Or possibly snapped.

'Shall we try again?' I asked. 'Who ordered you to kill Prashant Mukherjee?'

'You must already know that.'

'Humour me.'

'You did.'

'Me?'

'You and your friends, at any rate.' He pointed to the guards that flanked the door behind me. 'Or men just like you. British officers in Bombay. You should be treating me like a hero.' He laughed bitterly. 'Instead you lock me up in the Ritz Calcutta. Bloody hypocrites.'

'So you were working for Section H?'

'I don't know who that is, but I was working for the military.'

'Who recruited you?'

'Some chap called MacRae. He came out to Rangoon, paid off my debts, took me to Bombay and set me up in the Taj.'

'As Irani?'

'That's right.'

'Why?'

'To funnel cash to the religious crazies. I was to pose as a ben-efactor, someone with money keen to donate to their cause. And if I was to ingratiate myself with both Hindus and Muslims, I could be neither myself. And I couldn't be a Christian either, for obvious reasons, so MacRae decided I had to be a Parsee.'

'You funnelled cash to the Union of Islam *and* the Shiva Sabha?'

Atchabahian nodded. 'Others too. Fringe parties, gangsters.'

'You passed money to gangsters?'

He wiped a dab of saliva from the corner of his mouth. 'MacRae wanted to raise tensions, get the rival Hindu and Muslim gangs killing each other, so that come the elections, people would vote with their own kind rather than for Gandhi's mob.'

'Why start with Calcutta? Why not Bombay or Delhi?'

He gave a smile. 'I don't know. It was MacRae's decision. Maybe he just found the right sort of useful idiots here.'

'Who'd you pass funds to in the city?'

'Both sides. Muslim gangs and Hindu hardliners.'

'And Mukherjee? Why'd you kill him?'

'Because the gang violence wasn't working. We expected the Muslim gangs to target more ordinary Hindus, but the bastards just took the money, said *thank you very much*, and then continued with their own underworld vendettas. That's when MacRae decided to change tack. He thought a political assassination would work where the gang violence had failed. And he was right. Killing Mukherjee and pinning the blame on Gulmohamed was a good plan. I'd already befriended Gulmohamed in Bombay. Hell, we'd even siphoned the best part of a million rupees to his Union of Islam. I convinced him to come to Calcutta. Told him a potential benefactor wanted to meet him.'

'And Mukherjee?' I asked. 'Why'd you choose him?'

'Let's just say he was chosen for me.'

'So you turned up in advance, wrong Mukherjee's neck and hoped to pin it on Gulmohamed?'

Atchabahian had a far-away look in his eyes. 'Imagine if we'd managed it,' he marvelled. 'The bastards would even now be slitting each other's throats across the length and breadth of the country.'

'But it went wrong.'

That brought him back to earth. 'Some local fellow came sniffing about, and by the time I'd dealt with him, there was no sign of Gulmohamed.'

I thought back to Suren. It seemed he'd blundered into Atchaba-hian, taken a beating, and by doing so had accidentally saved the country from destroying itself.

'What was in it for you?' I asked.

The question seemed to surprise him.

'You're an Armenian living in Burma. India isn't your fight. Why'd you get involved?'

'You mean other than the money?'

'There was nothing more to it?'

'Actually, there was. I'm a citizen of the Empire. I fought for it and I wish to see it preserved. And it was the right thing to do.'

'The *right* thing? You tried to set this country ablaze. It could have descended into a hell of communal violence.'

Atchabahian shook his head. 'Don't you understand? That's all these people are capable of. Hatred of one another is their natural state, and the empire is cemented upon that hate. Learn your his-tory, Wyndham. Your own General Clive, the one you call Clive of India, British India is built upon his defeat of the Muslims at the Battle of Plassey. And who paid for his army? It wasn't your king in London, or the shareholders of the East India Company. It was the Hindu merchants of Bengal! And when he'd thrown off the yoke of the Muslims, those Hindus of this very city feted him as the weapon of their goddess Durga! They were too short-sighted to see consequences of their actions then and it's no different today.'

'You're no Clive of India,' I said.

'No? I did the same thing. I played Hindu against Muslim and strengthened the British Empire.'

'Nonsense.'

'You shouldn't feel bad about it, Wyndham. The British pres-ence in this country has been for the best, and mark my words, if they do one day kick you out, you can rest assured they'll be back to killing each other before the Union Jack reaches the foot of the flagpole. It's in their nature.'

I said nothing. The man was mad, and it is disconcerting to interrogate a madman, especially when deep down, part of you suspected his madness might contain a germ of truth.

'You want to know what the most ridiculous part is?' he continued, warming to his theme. 'They're basically *all* just the same people! Hindu, Muslim, Muslim, Hindu. They're so preoccupied with hating each other that they don't realise that to the rest of us they're all just the same bunch of little brown-skinned savages. If you British do leave, someone else will just teach them the same lesson. Maybe next time it will be the Russians, or the French, or maybe even the Chinese. It doesn't matter who it is, they're too stupid to learn. What does the Bible say? *A kingdom divided against itself is brought to desolation, and a house divided will surely fall.* You would think their holy books would have taught them something similar, but apparently not.'

'I'm not interested in a political history lesson,' I said.

'No?' He smiled. 'Maybe you've become too Indian for your own good.'

I took a break between interrogations, leaving Fort William and driving north, to an office building not far from the town hall. Atchabahian's words had got me thinking, and now I needed to have a chat with someone. The exterior bore a fresh coat of paint, but the walls were stained with gobbets of red betel spit and the stairwell still stank of piss.

The room I sought was on the second floor, halfway down a corridor, and belonged to a newly elected council official who was seated behind a battered desk. He seemed surprised to see me and took a moment to place my face.

'Dr Nagpaul,' I said. 'You may remember me from Prashant Mukherjee's funeral. Captain Wyndham.'

The light of recognition dawned on his face and was followed by the scalpel edge of a smile and a half-dozen questions.

'Of course, Captain. Take a seat. How may I help you? Is this about Prashant's murder? You have arrested someone?'

I remained standing. 'Not exactly, but it is Mukherjee I'm here about.'

His eyes betrayed no sign that he knew what was coming.

'You see, a couple of questions keep bothering me. Why would anyone want to murder Mukherjee, and why do it down in Budge Budge?'

Nagpaul's forehead creased.

'I'm not sure I follow.'

'Why Mukherjee? If, as you told me the last time we met, that this was clearly the work of Muslims attempting to instigate a religious conflict, then why Mukherjee? He was just a theologian, a man all but unknown outside of Calcutta and with little real clout even within it. Why not go for someone more important? Someone, say, like yourself?'

'Maybe because my security is tighter?' he volunteered.

'I doubt it,' I said. 'I've just walked into your office and I wasn't even challenged by your flunkeys in the corridor.'

Nagpaul conceded the point with a smile. 'But you are a white man. They would be more diligent with an Indian.'

'Really? I've had dealings with other Indian political leaders – like Subhash Bose and Farid Gulmohamed – and I'll tell you something, I couldn't get within twenty feet of them without being questioned by at least three men.' There was of course the small matter of Suren and me kidnapping Gulmohamed outside of Victoria station in Bombay, but I didn't think it merited mention to Nagpaul. 'I think the reason I breezed in here so easily is that your security men are used to letting non-Indians into your presence.'

For the first time I saw a spark of something, a twitch of the cheek, a flash, gone in an instant.

'But we'll come on to that. Let's stick to Mukherjee for now. Why lure him down to Budge Budge?'

He decided to humour me, making a point of appearing helpful. 'I would imagine it easier to kill him somewhere away from his home.'

'Certainly,' I said, 'away from his family and his servants, but I meant why lure him to Budge Budge specifically?'

Nagpaul expressed ignorance with a shrug.

'And then,' I continued, 'I remembered something which Mukherjee's widow, Kamala, said that night at the cremation grounds. She said that her husband hadn't been down to Budge Budge in a long while, not since he stopped teaching. I didn't dwell on it, but later, I put it together with something else she said. She mentioned that you and he had fallen out, and that you'd cut off his stipend and put a stop to his religious lectures for the Shiva Sabha rank and file. Those lectures he gave, to your party cadres, they wouldn't happen to have been the lectures he used to give in Budge Budge by any chance? Maybe even at the house in which he was found murdered?'

The good doctor said nothing, but I noticed the twitch in the cheek once more.

'If I were to check, Dr Nagpaul, would I find that your party has paid to use that house in the past? Could it even be owned by a sympathiser or a party member?'

Nagpaul shook his head. 'I have no—'

'Here's what I think happened,' I said. 'I think Mukherjee disapproved of the direction in which you were taking the Shiva Sabha. The two of you fell out and you expelled him from the party, stopped his lectures and cut off his financial lifeline in an attempt to silence him. Despite that, he continued to speak out, if not for tolerance, then at least for moderation. That didn't chime with the kind of robust Hinduism you wanted to champion. Then, with the elections approaching, you were contacted by a man who called himself Irani. He probably told you that he had some rich contacts, maybe industrialists who believed in your cause and wanted to provide your party with funds while remaining anonymous. You probably met with Irani several times. Maybe that's why your men outside didn't react to the sight of a non-Indian walking through your door just now. Maybe they'd seen Irani or others like him come to meet you before?

'At some point, you and Irani decided to escalate matters. I don't know who came up with the plan, maybe it was Irani, whispering in your ear, suggesting that the best way to win votes was to stage a murder and pin the blame on a prominent Muslim. I'm guessing you suggested Mukherjee as the sacrifice and he came up with Gulmohamed as the scapegoat. Seen in that light, Mukherjee was an inspired choice. By murdering him, you'd not only be ridding yourself of a thorn in your side, you'd make him a martyr to Hindus everywhere. In death he'd be the champion of your cause that he would never agree to be in life.

'I think Mukherjee went to Budge Budge believing he was going to meet *you*, maybe on the pretext of a rapprochement. Maybe you told him you'd come around to his point of view, or promised him a return to his teaching role – you knew he could do with the money. Whatever the story you spun, *you* lured him there and Irani killed him.'

Nagpaul sighed. Slowly he stood up and walked over to the window. He looked down into the street, then turned to me.

'Where are the others?'

I'd no idea who he meant. 'What others?'

'Your reinforcements? The police officers, the car or the van – whatever you need to arrest me and take me from this place.'

I said nothing.

'There are none, are there?'

He walked over, stopping inches from my face.

'What are you going to do – drag me to prison by yourself? I am an elected representative of the municipal government. You'd be stopped before you reached the stairwell. Your story is a fantasy, and given the lack of constables at your back, I believe it is one that has failed even to convince your superiors at Lal Bazar. That being the case, I shall not dignify it with a response. If you wish to arrest me, please, be my guest. And if not, I would request you to kindly leave my office.'

For a moment I was tempted to punch his teeth in. In other circumstances, I might even have done it and taken my chances with an inquiry, but I was on thin ice as it was.

'I'll go,' I said, 'but before I do, you should know something. The cash that Irani funnelled to you, from his rich friends. It didn't come from any staunch Hindu industrialists. It came from us. Or rather it came from a branch of military intelligence.'

The colour drained from his face. 'That's not … that is a lie …'

'I assure you, it's not. I've seen the proof. How do you think your followers would react if they found out you were taking money from the British, that you were nothing more than an imperialist stooge?'

He fell silent and I took it as my cue to leave. I'd reached the door when he finally spoke.

'Your days in this country are numbered. Make no mistake of that. The writing is on the wall and everyone sees it. When you British do finally tuck your tail between your legs and set sail, we shall still be left with the threat of the Muslims. Rest assured, we will be ready for it.'

I recalled Atchabahian's words from earlier in the day, of Indians so preoccupied with hating each other that they failed to see the world beyond. I shook my head, walked out of the door and left Nagpaul to his madness.

Atchabahian's interrogation lasted a few days more. Dawson wanted to wring the man dry, extract every last drop of information he had till the pips squeaked. He'd offered him immunity, and the Armenian had sung like a canary. It was of little use to me. Suren had been right. Atchabahian would never see the inside of a courtroom. The military wouldn't allow it. But knowledge, as they say, is power, and Dawson could use what he'd gleaned to further his own cause against his rivals within Section H, be they in Bombay or Delhi or anywhere else.

He offered me one sop, however: the chance to drive Atchabahian to the airfield at Dum Dum where a plane stood waiting to take him to Rangoon.

It was late when we set off. The car was Annie's and the chauffeur was my man, Shiva. If it seemed unusual, Atchabahian didn't notice. We headed north, through streets still bearing some of the scars of the violence of the previous month. A hollowed-out building here, a boarded-up shop there. The sight still pained me, but Atchabahian was oblivious to it all. This wasn't his city. It was mine. I knew the buildings, I knew the streets. And I knew the alleys.

He had no idea. Not even an inkling until the car stopped.

'Where are we?' he asked.

'North Calcutta,' I said.

'Why are we stopping?'

I gave the order and Shiva flashed the headlights on and off.

'This here is Gola-katta Gullee,' I said. 'There's someone here who'd like to meet you.'

The door of the shebeen opened and the bullet-headed frame of Uddam Singh walked down the step, flanked by his son, Vinay, and two toughs. As he stepped over the drain, I pushed open the door and got out of the car. Shiva too left his seat, pulled a revolver and opened Atchabahian's door.

'Out,' he growled.

Uddam Singh walked over and inspected Atchabahian. 'Is this the man?'

'This is him.' I said.

I'd promised Singh I'd bring him the man who'd killed his son. I'd probably never find the man who'd actually stuck the blade in his chest – he might even be dead already, just another victim of the violence that had torn the city apart – but I could give him the man who'd provided the cash and ordered the turf war.

Singh sniffed like a man examining substandard merchandise. He turned to his men.

'Bring him.'

The toughs walked round and grabbed Atchabahian's arms. The Armenian began to struggle. 'What is this?' he cried, but a couple of punches to the gut soon shut him up.

'Our business is complete?' asked Singh.

'Yes,' I said.

'Then I see no reason for you to remain.'

I nodded, then turned and headed back to the car.

Shiva cranked up the car and as the engine exploded to life, I thought I heard a scream from somewhere in the dark.

'Where to, sir?' asked the driver.

'Lal Bazar,' I said.

It was the day Lord Taggart regained consciousness.

SIXTY-FIVE

Surendranath Banerjee

I received a transcript of the radio transmission mere hours before the dockside cranes of Marseilles came into view. A few terse lines which signified a future restored.

TAGGART AWAKE. CHARGES DROPPED.
TIME TO COME HOME.
SAM.

I held the note in my hand and stared out at a sea the colour of topaz. I gripped the railing tight and breathed, long, slow breaths, and gave thanks to the gods. They had delivered me. I went to my cabin, quickly penned a reply and took it to the wireless operator. Then I returned and packed the last of my things.

The day was grey and the seagulls called out in complaint against the rain. I pulled my overcoat tight, grabbed my case and descended the gangplank onto the soil of France. Taggart's return had vindicated me. In the eyes of the British, I was exonerated. That though did not mean that all was forgiven; at least not from *my* side. I had worked these past years for a system which I now realised was built to keep my people in subjugation, regardless of morality, regardless of the cost. It was a system I would no longer work for.

I would go home.

But not just yet.

Acknowledgements

The Shadows of Men marks the fifth outing for Sam and Suren and comes five years after the first publication of *A Rising Man*. Back then I had no idea that so many people would take those two to their hearts and in the process change my life. So it's only right that I acknowledge the debt of gratitude I owe to each and every one of you who've read and enjoyed the series. Thank you for your time and your support.

Thank you too, to all the booksellers and bloggers and reviewers who've recommended the series to readers. In the midst of so much despair over the last eighteen months, good fiction has been a source of comfort, and we writers are honoured by your dedication and love for books.

I'm indebted once more to the team at Harvill Secker/Vintage: to my editor, Jade Chandler and to Dredheza Maloku; to Anna Redman Aylward, Bethan Jones and Isobel Turton for all the wonderful publicity they garner; to Sophie Painter and Helia Daryani for the online marketing; to Jane Kirby, Lucy Beresford-Knox and the team, who take the books to the wider world; to Liz Foley, Hannah Telfer, Rachel Cugnoni, Faye Brewster, Tom Drake-Lee and the wider team at Vintage for all their support and for signing off on my advances.

A special mention too, for Richard Cable. Thank you, sir, for backing me as a writer and for all your support over the years. We need to have that drink soon.

Thank you also to Alexa Murray, Alishia Strydom and all the team at PrimePixels who have pulled me, Sam and Suren, kicking and screaming, into the age of social media.

This list would not be complete without mention of Honor Spreckley and the whole team at Rogers, Coleridge and White who do such a great job of carrying my agent, Sam Copeland, and making him look good.

Thanks of course, to those good friends who let me borrow their names without worrying too much about what I'd do to them: to Farid Gulmohamed, my friend and mentor for over twenty years; to the wonderful Ooravis Panthaki-Colah, and the charming Jehangir Panthaki. I expect you all to pull strings and sell many millions of copies in India. And thank you to my old pal, Mark MacRae. Maybe we'll get to see you in the flesh in another book?

Thanks too to the Red Hot Chilli Writers, Vaseem Khan, Ayisha Malik, Alex Caan, AA Dhand and Imran Mahmood: thanks for the support and all the *bakwaas*. Ladoos all round.

And finally of course, thank you to my wife, Sonal, without whom the world wouldn't make sense. Fourteen hundred years now, but who's counting?

Abir Mukherjee is the bestselling author of the award-winning Wyndham & Banerjee series of crime novels set in Raj-era India. He is a two-time winner of the CWA Historical Dagger and has won the Wilbur Smith Award for Adventure Writing. His books have also been shortlisted for the CWA Gold Dagger and the HWA Gold Crown. His novels, *A Rising Man* and *Smoke and Ashes* were both selected as Waterstones Thriller of the Month. *Smoke and Ashes* was also chosen as one of *The Times'* Best Crime and Thriller novels since 1945. Abir grew up in Scotland and now lives in Surrey with his wife and two sons.